The MATRIARCH

Books by
Charles MacKinnon

Castlemore
Mereford Tapestry
The Matriarch

The
MATRIARCH

a novel by
Charles MacKinnon

FREDERICK MULLER LIMITED

First published in Great Britain in 1976 by
Frederick Muller Ltd., London NW2 6LE

ISBN: 0 584 31071 4
Printed and bound by A. Wheaton & Co., Exeter-

FOR
ROSEMARY MACOMBER
without whom . . . nothing

ACKNOWLEDGMENT

The author wishes to acknowledge the considerable help given to him by T. W. Service, Esq., of James Robertson & Sons Ltd., by appointment Marmalade Makers to Her Majesty the Queen.

Come, my friends,
'Tis not too late to seek a newer world . . .
for my purpose holds to sail beyond the sunset,
and the paths of all the western stars, until I die.

Alfred, Lord Tennyson,
"Ulysses"

The MATRON

1854–1879

*Every man who is high up likes to feel that he
has done it all himself; and the wife smiles,
and lets it go at that. It's our only joke.
Every woman knows that.*

Sir James M. Barrie,
What Every Woman Knows

ONE

WEDNESDAY, October 25, 1854. Far off, in the Crimean Peninsula, men had already died in what became known as the Battle of Balaklava. This day would witness two great military clashes—the Thin Red Line of the Highlanders and the lunatic Charge of the Light Brigade.

In St. Andrews, on the exposed east coast of Scotland, it was a dull, wet, threatening morning. The rain came down in steady streams, flooding the gutters, dripping from sodden foliage, relentless and daunting. Upstairs in St. John's Rectory, twenty-year-old Barbara Darling lay in difficult childbirth. She looked pitifully small and doll-like in the great double bed, and she moaned and groaned as perspiration beaded her forehead and upper lip. Dr. David Gardiner frowned at his patient, ignoring the midwife who hovered by his side. He did not like the look of things at all. He took out a gold hunter, opened it and looked at the time, pursing his lips under his heavy brown moustache. He turned to the midwife.

"A little longer yet. I'll have a word with Mr. Darling. Call me if you need me."

"Yes, sir."

He went out of the room, a man trapped in his ignorance. He could bleed a patient, order simple remedies, bandage a wound and deliver a child. He had even assisted in the cruel surgery of the day. His ignorance of medicine was vast, but he was nonetheless a good doctor, the best in the town.

In the library-cum-study, where he was wont to compose his strangely tender and moving sermons, the Reverend Lawrence Darling, M.A., rector of St. John's, paced by the window, part hypnotized by the rain. He was thirty-two, twelve years older than his bride of one year, and he loved the delicately fashioned, vivacious daughter of the late Bishop of Moray. As he heard the rattle of the door handle, he turned and looked hopefully at Dr. Gardiner.

"Any news?" he asked anxiously.

"None. It will be a little time yet. Lawrence, I'm worried."

"Something is wrong?"

"It's not so much that, although she is having a harder time of it than some. It's her heart."

"Her heart?"

"Does she have a heart condition? Were there any severe childhood illnesses?"

"Nothing that I've ever heard of."

"It wouldn't be so bad if she were . . . well, if it were a simple birth." Dr. Gardiner did not wish to discuss the physique and childbearing qualities of the rector's wife. "You know how it is. With some women it is easier than with others."

"Yes, yes," Lawrence Darling said impatiently. Enough of his little flock died in childbirth for him to be aware of these differences.

"With the trouble she is having, and a possible heart condition, I'm concerned about the effect the strain may have on her."

"Is she in danger?" the rector asked, subdued.

David Gardiner thought again of the slim-hipped, narrow-built woman and the bouncing baby she was trying to deliver, and his lips tightened.

"It's possible. I'll be glad when it's over."

Lawrence Darling was no coward, but now he turned white and his hand went out to grip the back of a chair for support.

"She may die?" It was scarcely a question.

"Let's hope it won't come to that, but she is going to be ill for some time. You'll need a wet nurse for the baby. I can arrange that for you."

"Thank you. I'd be grateful." There was some slight relief in talking about the baby.

Upstairs a tired heart fluttered frantically in its cage, like a trapped bird, and Barbara Darling let out a small scream. The midwife scowled as she wrestled with the problem. She did not hold out much hope for this patient; she had seen the approach of death too often. She decided to call the doctor quickly. He should be here with his patient. If anyone could save the woman in the bed, it was Dr. Gardiner.

When he responded to her call, the doctor was shocked at his patient's appearance as she writhed in pain, eyes wild and staring, features pinched, skin yellowish and waxy, lips blue. He hardly recognized her. This creature with the matted hair and dribbling mouth bore no resemblance to the lovely Mrs. Darling at whose table he had frequently dined.

He had little time to philosophize. It was the moment of birth. The child began to emerge from the womb and his attention was focused on the baby. As it came free, Barbara Sharpe who was now Barbara Darling gave a little sigh and the heart that had fluttered vainly became still.

David Gardiner felt his patient's pulse and tried to detect a heartbeat, but he knew it was a vain gesture. He pulled up the bedclothes to cover her face and turned to the midwife who had knotted the cord and was cleaning the baby, now screaming its first screams.

"A girl," the woman remarked, and Dr. Gardiner sighed.

Several moments later he went back down to the library.

"Well?" Lawrence asked eagerly, for he had heard the sounds from upstairs.

"It's a girl. A fine girl."

"What about Barbara? Will she be all right?"

David Gardiner closed the door. Now he came and put a hand on his friend's arm.

"Brace yourself, Lawrence."

"She's dead?" The words were a whisper.

"I could do nothing to save her. Nothing. It was the heart, I'm certain."

Lawrence stood openmouthed for a second and then turned again to stare out of the window at the rain. For a moment it seemed the world had come to an end.

"I beg your pardon?" He was vaguely aware that Dr. Gardiner had spoken.

"Let me get you a brandy. I asked, what will you do about the baby? You've got a sister, haven't you?"

Lawrence Darling was silent while the doctor found the decanter and poured brandy into a glass and brought it to him. In those moments his mind quickly weighed up the situation. He did indeed have a sister, older than himself by some four years. She lived in Bristol with her dissolute merchant husband, and Lawrence had approved of her marriage no more than his late father had.

No, he could not send his child to Nancy to be cared for —that would never do. Besides they did not even correspond nowadays. There were his wife's relatives, but they were almost equally unsatisfactory and none was in Scotland. In a fleeting instant he made up his mind. He would rear his child himself. He would not permit her to be taken from his side. She was all he had to remind him of Barbara.

"I shall keep her," he replied calmly, absently taking the brandy and putting it down untouched.

"Will you be able to manage alone?" the doctor asked, raising his eyebrows.

"I expect so. I intend to. You said something about a wet nurse."

"That's only to nurse the child. There must be a woman to look after her. That means finding a nanny."

"How does one do that?"

"I should ask Mrs. Carstang if I were you," the doctor advised, referring to one of Lawrence's faithful flock. "She's the best person."

"Ah, yes, of course. I shall be seeing her soon."

"You'll manage all right," Dr. Gardiner said reassuringly, recalling that Lawrence Darling did not have the rigid calls on his time that men in other occupations did.

"With help, yes. Now I must go up to see her."

They went upstairs together. As they entered the bedroom, Lawrence ignored the midwife and the child and went straight to the bed. He turned back the sheet and gazed at his wife's face, biting his lip as he did so. He had seen death many times, but this was the first time it had struck so hard.

So young, he thought miserably—so young and full of life and laughter. He leaned forward and kissed the cold lips and pulled the sheet up again. Only then did he turn to his daughter. He was dismayed to see a child red-faced, gnarled, incredibly ugly.

"Isn't she beautiful?" the midwife remarked. "She'll be just like her mother."

Lawrence gave her a quick, suspicious glance, but she seemed serious.

"Do you think so?"

"Oh, yes," she answered confidently.

His shoulders drooped and he turned to the doctor. "Can you arrange things please, David? The wet nurse and whatever?"

He wandered out of the room, not hearing his friend's agreement, wrapped in absorbing thought. This was to have been a morning of such joy and happiness. He and Barbara had looked forward so much to the baby's birth. His mouth tightened a little as his emotions surged. He must not give way to grief. He was an ordained priest, a man of God. God's will would be done, and he of all men must not question it, not ever. He entered the study and stood stock-still, unable to move, blinded by a mist of tears. He was scarcely aware of a hand on his arm, guiding him to his favorite chair. Then the mist cleared and he saw the doctor's concerned face.

"Come along, Lawrence. Drink this brandy. That's doctor's orders."

He seemed to stiffen. "No, thank you. I'll have tea instead, please. Then I must see to the funeral arrangements and write a few letters."

Thank goodness, he was thinking quietly, there would be few relatives at the funeral. Barbara's death was a private thing. She had been his and the loss would be his.

Dr. Gardiner swallowed the brandy himself and felt the better for it.

"What will you call her?" he asked curiously. "Will you give her her mother's name?"

"No. We had already chosen names. If it was a girl she was to be named Janet, after Barbara's grandmother. It is not a name I admire greatly, but it was Barbara's special wish, and I shall see that it is carried out."

Dr. Gardiner gripped his arm and gave it a friendly squeeze. "I have a few things to attend to, and I must get on with them. I'll be back quite soon, Lawrence. Count on me for anything."

Lawrence looked up and smiled, grateful for the other's confident manner.

"Thank you, you are a good friend."

"You will find St. Andrews is full of good friends," the doctor promised, knowing how popular the mild-mannered, gentle rector was with everyone.

"Thank you, thank you."

When the doctor had gone, he walked over to his desk and picked up his prayer book, but did not open it. Instead he went down on his knees, beside the desk, the book in one hand, his head bowed.

"I don't know why you have done this," he said to his God, and he was without bitterness, filled only with sadness mingled with wonderment. "There must be a reason. I shall bring her up to be like her mother. That's what you want, isn't it? You must love her mother very much to take her back so soon. Yes, I know what you want. You are testing me. I don't know why, but I shall keep my daughter and I shall rear her in your name, and I will teach her to be exactly like her mother. Perhaps one day you will reveal your intentions."

He bit back a sudden sob, dismayed by his weakness. "Show me how to be strong," he said quietly. "People will be watching me. Let me show them that I rejoice in you, even at this time . . . no," he added quickly, "*especially* at this time."

He remained in bowed silence for several minutes, seeking that peace of mind which, he was wont to assure his parishioners, was the invariable reward of those who loved and trusted in God.

At last he finished his quiet communion and went off in search of tea. A little later he went out, for there were many things to arrange, people to see. That evening, after an early dinner at the doctor's house, he sat down to write a brief note to his sister in Bristol and a longer one to Barbara's aunt in Cheltenham.

TWO

IN a stern age, Lawrence Darling was preoccupied with God's love for men, and his God was a friendly, familiar, everyday person. He preached mainly from the New Testament, with a strong preference for the Gospels, especially the second and third; and when he did touch on Old Testament topics, he avoided the retributive texts that were fashionable in Scotland. Had he been a Presbyterian he might well have been thought of as impious, even heretical. In the more liberal atmosphere of the Episcopal Church he was regarded merely as an eccentric. No one could seriously take issue with him, for he was full of the love that he implicitly believed was but a pale reflection of God's.

Rather to his surprise, the midwife's prediction came true. Janet grew to resemble her mother after all. She had the same white-gold hair, the same vivid blue eyes, the same fine features. After a year or so, the tenuous links of family were quietly dropped, and Lawrence preferred it so. He could never quite understand why some people assumed that he must need help, and female help at that. He ministered to many—could he not then look after this little one? Of course he could.

By the time Janet was six he had solved one problem in his customary fashion. Her education was now important, and he considered engaging a tutor. Finally he decided that his own qualifications were better than those of most,

and that he himself best knew how to rear his own child.
Accordingly he spent three hours every morning with her.
If he had to go out in the afternoon, he often took Janet
with him. When he visited his parishioners, many a sickbed
was lightened by the girl's radiance. Apart from death-
beds and funerals, he took her almost everywhere, and
people soon got used to it. Indeed they came to like it, for
Janet was a happy child. She lived in a world where nothing ever went wrong, and her temperament was naturally
sunny and cheerful. She grew tall and straight, her hair
was more lustrous, and her burgeoning figure was nicely
outlined by the crinoline styles that could be so flattering.

By the end of 1869 she was a girl no longer, but a
woman full grown. That Christmas she put her hair up, a
little earlier than most girls, and she took her mother's
place at her father's side when an uncle and aunt of whom
she had never heard came unexpectedly from England to
visit them.

Lawrence was proud of her. The most noticeable thing
about her was, and was always to remain, her smile.
Sometimes, watching her in a happy mood, he had the
feeling that God must have created her in a moment of
rare exuberance. The very joy of God seemed to shine in
her eyes when she smiled, and he had the peculiar sensation that she never walked alone, but that the Almighty
was always with her in some special way.

It did not cross his mind that she was unprepared for the
realities of life. He saw her as a happy, secure, outwardly mature, very gracious young woman, older than
her years, and he congratulated himself on a good job
well done. Her education had been thorough, and she was
not only proficient at geography, history, mathematics,
Latin, and Greek, but she danced well, played the piano
competently, and was, he was assured, an excellent needle-
woman.

The other side of the coin, of course, was that she had
never had a mother, brother, or sister, and had had very
little contact with people her own age. Her life was

wrapped up in one unusual man, a gentle clergyman whose view of his faith was euphoric, and who shielded her from any direct contact with experiences that might cast doubts upon the all-wise benevolence which, he taught her, ruled the universe.

Even Lawrence Darling, however, realized that growing up must bring changes.

"What are we going to do about you?" he asked lightly, one day in the late spring of 1870.

"What do you mean, Papa?"

"It's an unnatural life for you, taking your mother's place when you are so young. You ought to get out and about more, and meet other people."

"But I do," she protested.

"I meant young people of your own age. Young men," he added.

"Young men bore me so. They have no conversation."

"I still think you should have friends of your own age."

She was silent and thoughtful. She was really a little afraid of people her own age, but she did not know how to tell him, for it sounded silly. It would have surprised her to learn that the reverse was also true, and that the contemporaries she sometimes met in the homes of her father's friends felt awkward in her company.

"Leave it to me," he suggested. "I'll think of something."

He had no idea what he would think of. By now she went out with him less often, although she enjoyed accompanying him on his calls. She spent more time in the rectory. She also belonged to a sewing group which made things for distressed gentlewomen, and moreover was treasurer of the missionary fund. She herself felt that she led a full, active, and enjoyable life.

Luckily Lawrence Darling did not abandon an idea lightly once it took root in his mind. He had decided that she should have a more social life, therefore she would. He began quietly to canvass among his friends and parishioners, not a few of whom felt just a little bit sorry for Janet.

As a result, in June of that year Janet was invited to a

croquet party at Whinbriggs House, just outside the town. Whinbriggs belonged to the Cruickshank family who were wealthy and sociable. Like some others, they had avoided inviting Janet out because they feared a snub. Lawrence's devotion to his daughter was, after all, a byword. At the first hint from him, however, that he wished to launch his daughter in local society, invitations quickly arrived. Janet began to discover a strange and bewildering world of people her own age, a world of which she had been almost totally ignorant. It was a stimulating experience and she looked forward to the visit to Whinbriggs.

She played croquet well, because Lawrence was almost a master of the game, and since nobody had ever told her about being ladylike she played to win. One or two young women did not much appreciate this, but most young men did, and the word quickly went around that Janet Darling was a good sort, not like some, and not at all stuffy. This was high praise indeed, and at the end of June she was invited again to Whinbriggs, to her first dance. It was the eighteenth birthday of Margaret Cruickshank, a vivacious girl who secretly admired Janet's composure.

Lawrence saw that she was properly dressed in a narrow-waisted, low-cut, white evening gown. She wore her mother's jewelry, and her hair was fashioned into an enormous chignon of plaits. She was so lovely that it wrenched his heart to see her leave for the dance. She was the immediate sensation of the evening. The good sort had been transformed into a charmer, and young men, two years or more older than she, felt their callowness as they had never felt it before.

One young man, however, was unabashed by the vision of loveliness. He was a stranger to her, and when he was introduced to her, he looked boldly into her eyes, and for the first time for many years she blushed. His name was Andrew Cunninghame and he lived in Dundee. He was a house guest, twenty-one years old, almost twenty-two, which made him six years older than she was, and his self-confidence was noticeable.

"Why haven't we met before, Miss Darling?" he asked, steering her to one side away from possible interruption.

"I . . . I . . . that is . . ."

"Do you live in St. Andrews?"

"Yes."

"Ah, and I live in Dundee. That explains it. Allow me to fetch you a cordial."

He produced drinks and they sat down together in a far corner.

"Do I know your father?" he asked, and she thought what a strange question it was.

"Probably not. He is the rector of St. John's."

"I see. No, I have never met him—or his beautiful daughter. I did not know till now that Dundee is a prison."

"I'm sure it is no such thing," she contradicted, suspicious of his flattery.

"But it is. It has kept us apart. May I call on you tomorrow?"

"I . . . I . . . I don't know." Again she stammered. No man had ever before asked if he might call on her.

"I'm an Episcopalian, too," he smiled. "Perhaps there is something I could do for your father."

"Do for Papa?" She stared blankly.

"I meant for his church, of course. I did not presume to mean him personally. You must not think me rude, but perhaps you have some charity?"

"We have the missionary fund," she said eagerly. "I'm the treasurer."

"Now that is what I call a perfect arrangement. You are the very person I wish to meet."

"Why?" He was too quick for her.

"Because," he smiled, "I wish to donate two hundred guineas to your fund."

"Two *hundred!*" Her face was a study.

"Guineas."

"Did you really say two hundred?" she asked.

"Certainly. You seem surprised."

"We don't collect that much in a year. Or in two years," she added truthfully.

"Yes, well, of course there is much more industry in Dundee and therefore more prosperity. St. Andrews is more of a cultural center, isn't it? I shall call in the morning, without fail, to see you, not your father."

"Thank you," she said breathlessly.

"At the rectory, I take it?" he asked.

"Yes."

"Now." He became brisk. "Someone is sure to interrupt us at any moment, but I claim the last four dances, Miss Darling. The last four. You'll remember?"

She nodded, her head spinning, and a few moments later they became separated. Soon afterward she found herself beside Mrs. Cruickshank, her hostess.

"Well, Janet, you've certainly made a conquest," the older woman said pleasantly. "Andrew Cunninghame, of all people."

"Who is he?" she asked.

"You don't know?"

"I've never heard of him."

"Oh, my dear! Rowan's Marmalades and Jams. In Dundee. His father died a year ago and *he* is now the head of the company. He is a very rich young man, and important too. There's many a cap set at him."

Janet nodded dumbly. She knew of Rowan's, of course. Like most larders in the country, that in the rectory was no stranger to the jars of marmalade and jam. But if he was so rich and important, why had he singled her out for attention?

Between the first and second of their four dances together he craftily broached the subject of her age.

"I wish you had been at my twenty-first birthday party," he told her. "We could have danced all night. Perhaps I can come to yours, one day soon?"

"Not for a very long time," she laughed. "I'm only fifteen."

"Surely not, Miss Darling." He was visibly shaken.

"Believe me, Mr. Cunninghame, I am quite positive of it." She gave him a mischievous smile which made him feel quite weak at the knees.

"I can hardly believe it. Your hair . . ."

"I put it up last Christmas, shortly after my birthday. I shan't be sixteen till October. I have no mother you see," she explained, "so I run the house for my father now."

"Good gracious. You look like eighteen. Never mind," he added absently. "You soon will be."

"I beg your pardon?"

"I am sorry. I was thinking out loud." He gave her an encouraging smile. "I do believe the next dance is about to begin. Shall we, Miss Darling?"

"Oh, yes," she said happily.

THREE

JANET said nothing to her father about Andrew Cunninghame, mainly because she could not bring herself to believe that he really would call next morning, far less that he would bring a two-hundred-guinea donation to the missionary fund. Nevertheless he arrived promptly at ten thirty, taking Lawrence by surprise.

Andrew looked a little younger this morning than he had done last night, despite the thick brown hair and silky moustache. He was smartly and expensively dressed, and he introduced himself easily to the rector.

"Perhaps you would excuse us, Janet?" Lawrence suggested, still not properly realizing what was afoot.

"If you will permit, sir, I wished to see Miss Darling as well as yourself. Indeed, particularly Miss Darling. As I mentioned, we met last night at the Whinbriggs House dance."

"Yes." Lawrence was puzzled.

"I promised Miss Darling a contribution to your missionary fund, of which she told me she is treasurer."

"Indeed she is. This is most kind of you, Mr. Cunninghame. Janet, my dear, you had no business to solicit donations at a social function like that."

"I assure you she did nothing of the sort," Andrew smiled. "I offered. I have my check with me, Miss Darling."

He took out an elegant pocketbook, extracted the check

and handed it to her. She received it gingerly and stared wide-eyed at the amount. It was as he had said. Silently she handed it over to her father, whose eyebrows shot up in amazement.

"Good gracious. This is *most* handsome of you, Mr. Cunninghame. Tell me, are you one of the Cunninghames of Rowan's?"

"Indeed. Since my father's death I am the head of the company."

"I had heard of that sad event. I am sorry."

"It was cancer. A merciful release."

"Quite, quite. I really don't know what to say." Lawrence was still bewildered. There was something here that he did not yet understand.

Andrew removed the check from his nerveless fingers and handed it back to Janet.

"Perhaps the treasurer should have it?" he suggested lightly.

"Oh, yes, yes. Janet, my dear, could you order some tea, please? You will take tea with us, Mr. Cunninghame? Or sherry, perhaps?"

"Tea please, but I wondered if I might have a few words with you, alone, sir, beforehand."

"I'll see to the tea," Janet said, rising. "It will take some ten minutes." She went out wonderingly. What did he want with her father? Another check? Surely not.

Inside the room, Andrew drew his chair closer to the rector's desk.

"Mr. Darling, I do not believe in beating about the bush."

"No?" Lawrence cocked his head expectantly.

"I met Miss Darling last night. I have fallen completely and deeply in love with her."

Lawrence swallowed hard.

"I discovered her age," Andrew continued. "She herself told me that she is not quite sixteen, so I realize that my declaration must sound premature to you."

"It does a bit," Lawrence agreed.

"However, sir, I would like your permission to see your daughter occasionally—to visit you and perhaps to have you visit my mother and me in Dundee. I would like to say, though, that I intend to offer for Miss Darling on her eighteenth birthday."

"You think eighteen is old enough, do you?" Lawrence asked, impressed both by the young man's sincerity and his air of authority.

"My own mother was married at that age."

Lawrence grew thoughtful. Barbara had been only twenty when she died in childbirth. Good heavens, he thought, only a few years older than Janet. Janet is almost a woman. Why, in five years, I may be a grandfather!

"I appreciate your speaking so frankly," he answered cautiously. "Of course I have no objection to your seeing Janet, as long as the proprieties are observed."

"You have my word on that."

"I don't doubt it, Mr. Cunninghame. Tell me, does Janet know anything of this?"

"No."

"Then may I suggest you proceed with caution? She *is* still fifteen, even if her appearance and manner suggest someone older."

"I certainly would not speak of marriage to her, sir. At least, I don't think so."

"I don't want to tie you down," Lawrence said, "but if you present her with a cut-and-dried plan of campaign, such as you have revealed to me, you may frighten her."

"Oh, I wouldn't want to do that."

"Well, there is nothing more to say, is there? It is really up to Janet and, as you began by reminding me, she is only fifteen."

"And a half."

"And a half," Lawrence agreed gravely. "You have not told me your age."

"I am twenty-one, sir. I think I need not discuss my prospects. I am the sole owner of Rowan's, and in addition my father left me half his private fortune. I will receive the balance, plus Aberneist House, on my mother's death."

"I wouldn't dream of questioning your financial position, Mr. Cunninghame. Rowan's is a household name in Scotland."

"Our products sell well south of the border, too, I am happy to tell you."

"Really? That must be very satisfactory." He paused. "That check you gave to Janet . . ."

"Was not a bribe." Andrew Cunninghame smiled. "It was an impulse, if you like. After all, not many charities are blessed with such a treasurer. But it was not a clumsy attempt to buy approval. After all, in my circumstances . . ."

"I understand. Well, that seems to be that. Would you mind opening the door and seeing if Janet is waiting in the hall? I imagine tea must be ready by now."

Andrew decided that he liked this prospective father-in-law, with the oddly ageless face, the gentle manner, and the graying hair. He went into the hall, found Janet, and returned with her, and the tea followed. They discussed the Suez Canal, which had opened the previous year, and the Franco-Prussian War, which was raging, and then quite naturally talk turned to the local topic, the bill before Parliament for the North British Railway to build a bridge across the River Tay.

"I'm rather inclined to agree with the Seer of Gourdie," Lawrence smiled. He was referring to one Patrick Matthew of Gourdiehill, an old man who had been prophesying all sorts of dire consequences that would attend such a rash venture. "It does seem to me to be overambitious."

"I am certain, Mr. Darling, that the bill will receive the royal assent very soon. I for one welcome the project. It will give us in Dundee a shortcut to the markets of the south, and so to the rest of the world."

"But a bridge of such length . . ."

"Thomas Bouch is a fine engineer," Andrew pointed out. "If he says it can be done, it can be done."

"I agree he has a reputation as an able man. Perhaps I am growing old. Such a scheme seems fantastic to me."

"I'd like to see it," Janet remarked. She had been an interested audience. "Just imagine what it would look like, Papa."

"It will be the longest bridge in the world," Andrew laughed. "It must come. Bouch has been offering to build it for years."

"If you say it must come, I have no doubt you are right," Lawrence smiled gently. "You are a man of business affairs, much better informed than I am, and much younger. Of course it won't help us here in St. Andrews, you know. What *we* need is another one over the Forth, to link us with Edinburgh."

"Believe me, Mr. Darling, you will have both bridges before another twenty years have gone—long before, I hope."

"I may not have twenty years to live," Lawrence chuckled.

He was sorry when Andrew Cunninghame took his leave. Janet accompanied their visitor to the front door where he stopped and smiled down at her.

"Miss Darling, may I call you Janet?"

"If you wish."

"My name is Andrew."

"I know."

"Janet, I should like to see you again soon. I have to return to Dundee, but may I call again?"

"I am sure Papa will always be pleased to see you."

"Not your father; *you*."

"That is hardly polite, Mr. Cunninghame . . . Andrew."

"Your father understands."

"Understands what?" she asked, her blue eyes wide.

"That I love you. I know you are too young to consider me seriously, but I must see you."

"Must? You have told my father this?"

"Yes."

"What did he say?" she asked.

"In effect that it would be up to you."

"Oh." She flushed and looked away, and he wondered if he had overplayed his hand. She was so lovely that he had to fight to stop himself reaching out to touch her.

"May I call again, Janet?" he asked softly.

"Yes." She smiled, bright-eyed. "If you wish."

"Has no one ever said they love you, before?"

"Certainly not."

"I'm glad. That gives me a start." He took her hand and kissed it impulsively, and rushed to his carriage, leaving her speechless and prey to a welter of conflicting emotions. When he had gone from sight, she returned to the study and confronted her father.

"He says he loves me. He says you know."

"He doesn't waste time, does he?" Lawrence remarked. "He did ask if he had my permission to call on you, and I said it was up to you, my dear. I know he believes he is in love with you, but he is sensible to realize that you are too young to take that seriously."

"He *believes?*" she asked.

Lawrence came and put an arm around her shoulders and hugged her. "Yes, my dear. This is your first experience of this sort, and I am quite sure the young man is honorable and decent, and that he means what he says. However, he too is young and he only met you for the first time yesterday. You must learn to let people prove their words, and not to take them at face value. I don't say he'll change his mind; I merely say that it is much too soon to judge. By all means encourage him to call if you find him agreeable. He seems very nice."

"He is. Oh, yes, he is."

Her patent enthusiasm troubled him a little.

"There are other young men, Janet. Take my advice and do not turn your back on them. You will have other suitors. When the time comes for you to marry, and it won't be for a few years yet, be sure you know your own mind."

"Suitors, Papa?" She laughed gaily. "I'm not considering marriage, Papa. But it is nice to have a young man in love with one, especially someone so rich and important. I think he is handsome. Did you really like him?"

"Very much," Lawrence answered honestly.

"I told him that he could come back. It is all very exciting, isn't it?"

Andrew did not leave her long in suspense, for the following day a hamper arrived by special delivery, containing a selection of Rowan's marmalades and jams, all beautifully packed. It was addressed to Janet, and with it was a note.

"You will be able to think of me at breakfast and tea," Andrew wrote. "I shall come to St. Andrews before the hamper needs replenishing. I am sorry I can't come right away, but I have to make a business trip. I will write soon."

Janet's comment to her father was, "He's very practical, isn't he, Papa?"

"I never doubted it. You know, sometimes you look very like your mother."

She forgot the hamper for the moment. "Do I? I'm glad. I wish I had known her."

"So do I, my dear. She wasn't as pretty as you. No," he corrected, "that's not the word I want. Radiant, that's it. You have a radiance that is most unusual. I've never seen it in anyone else. Otherwise you are very like her."

She abandoned the attempt to continue the conversation, and turned to admiring the hamper and its contents again, and to rereading the first letter she had ever received from a young man.

In July 1870 the Tay Bridge Bill went through Parliament, as Andrew had forecast, and at the end of the month he called on Janet. Thereafter he called regularly every few weeks, his visits always prefaced by a letter. He spent the night at the rectory on her birthday, and that year for the first time she spent Christmas away from home at Aberneist House, near Dundee, the guest of Andrew and his mother. Lawrence insisted that she accept the situation even though his own duties kept him in his parish at Christmas.

Aberneist House overawed Janet when she first saw it. It was an enormous stone house standing in extensive grounds, with endless huge rooms, or so it seemed to her after the modest comfort of the rectory. It had been built by Andrew's grandfather, who had founded the family business by discovering a strange little man called Rowan and harnessing his obvious talent for concocting jams and marmalades. There were no Rowans in the business now, and Andrew was that rarity among his social class, an only child.

Mrs. Cunninghame was a forbidding dame who inspected Janet suspiciously, but who soon fell under the girl's spell. She was naturally suspicious of any girl in whom Andrew showed the least interest, but she could not stay suspicious long where Janet was concerned.

There were other guests of course, and Janet felt out of place among them. They were louder, jollier, and, she thought guiltily, more vulgar than her father's friends; but they were friendly, and she automatically responded to friendliness. Soon the strangeness of it all wore off.

Early on Christmas Eve, Andrew took her around the house, watching her reaction to its thirty-eight rooms, plus attics and servants' quarters.

"It's so big for just two people," she exclaimed, bewildered.

"Yes. I think my grandfather expected the Cunninghames to have large families, but it wasn't so. It's up to me now," he added with a little laugh. "I like the house. Don't you?"

"Oh, yes, it's beautiful," she agreed. "I've never seen so many nice things all in one place before. It must be wonderful in summer."

"It is. You and your father must come for a few days next summer. Does he ever take a holiday?"

"No," she laughed. "I don't think he feels he needs one. He loves his work."

"I wish I had employees like that," Andrew grinned. He turned and took her hands in his and became serious. "I still love you. I haven't had a chance to say so recently."

"I thought you'd forgotten." She could not resist teasing him.

"Never! Do you like me?"

"A little."

"Only a little?" His face fell.

"That is all I can admit to at my age," she teased.

There was a sudden frown and a look of impatience that startled her, and then they were wiped out and he became bland.

"You like to torment me, but I don't mind. I can wait."

Inexplicably she shivered.

"Is something wrong?" he asked, taking her arm.

"No, I just shivered. We'd better go back."

"I don't want to share you with the others. I've always had my own way, you know."

"A spoiled child?" she suggested.

"Completely spoiled. What do you think of Mama?"

"I like her."

"She likes you. She told me so."

"Did she really?" Janet wondered why.

"Yes."

"I'm glad about that," she said. "Come along, Andrew. Escort me."

She was very happy. She knew she was on show, and that apparently she had passed the test, whatever it was. This was flattering knowledge. He was tall, erect, good-looking, manly, and decisive, and much more important a person than she had realized at first. Furthermore, he was plainly devoted to her. As they walked along the corridor together, she knew then that one day they would marry.

He would not change, and neither would she. She made up her mind to stop teasing him. It wasn't nice, and she sensed that he hated it. When they reached the door leading into the hall, she surprised him by standing on tiptoe and kissing him lightly on the mouth. She was gone through the door before he recovered from his surprise.

Nonetheless they behaved with rigid propriety and the closest they came to sexual awareness was when he occasionally squeezed her hand. Any two chimpanzees would have thought them totally mad and unnatural, but then chimpanzees were hardly the backbone of mid-Victorian Scotland.

The following year, 1871, was the year of the Paris Riots, the year in which trades unions became legal in Britain— legal and almost totally unacceptable to most people. It was the year in which Janet and Andrew stood together on the south bank of the River Tay, at Wormit, on Saturday, July 22, watching the laying of the foundation stone of the wonder bridge.

It was a bright, breezy day, and Janet, looking across the mile-wide river mouth, frowned.

"I don't believe it, Andrew," she said. "It can't be possible to bridge the river here."

"Wait till you see it," he told her confidently. "That's Bouch over there, the man who is going to build it."

"He looks so ordinary."

Andrew laughed. "What did you expect?"

"I don't know. Not an ordinary sort of man like that! How strange. I must be a silly woman after all. I just don't understand these things."

"There's nothing silly about you, Janet. Nothing."

"You always say nice things," she replied, smiling. "Thank you."

It was now more than a year since they had first met, and by now all of St. Andrews knew that Andrew Cunninghame called regularly at the rectory, and that Janet Darling, sometimes with her father and sometimes without, occasionally made the journey to Dundee. Everyone thought it most satisfactory.

Andrew was patient, and if his patience was anything of a strain, he never showed it. Instead he talked a lot about Samuel Smiles, a paragon of Victorian virtue who was a hero to Andrew, and about the wonder bridge, and most of all about Rowan's marmalades and jams, and his plans to market them in the farthest corners of the earth before he died.

In 1872 he was like a schoolboy when he burst into the rectory one day and told them, excitement in every word, that he had received the royal warrant, that he was now by appointment Marmalade Maker to Her Majesty the Queen, and that he had been asked to send a supply of marmalades and jams to Balmoral.

He had brought rough designs for his new labels, to show them, with the royal arms prominently displayed.

"How splendid, Andrew," Janet exclaimed in delight.

"I know." He was grinning from ear to ear. "I thought you'd be pleased. Oh, if only my grandfather and father had lived to see this. Shall we walk in the garden?"

She nodded and took his arm. They strolled in the warm sunshine to the shelter of some rhododendrons where he stopped and faced her.

"Janet, there is something I must say."

"Yes?" Her heart beat a little louder.

"We have known one another for two years now. I've loved you all that time and I have never so much as looked at another woman."

"I know that, Andrew."

"Do you remember that first time we met, two years ago, at Whinbriggs?"

"I shall never forget it."

"When I saw your father alone, next morning, I told him that on your eighteenth birthday I would ask him for your hand. It's only a few months away now, Janet." His eyes bored into hers and she felt weak. "I still mean it. I am going to ask him on your birthday. I know what he will say."

"What?" she asked faintly.

"He won't refuse me. He will say it is up to you."

"Oh."

"And I will come to you, and I will tell you what he

said, and I will ask you to marry me. What will you say, Janet? Darling Janet."

"I'm still a girl. Ask me when I'm eighteen."

The words were scarcely out of her mouth when his hand gripped her arm like a vise. "Janet, don't play with me. After two years you must know."

"Let me go," she cried.

"I'm sorry." He dropped her arm. "I do apologize, only can't you see I'm serious?"

"Yes, and I'm sorry, too, Andrew. I didn't mean to tease you."

"Can't you tell me now whether or not you love me? I've waited a long time."

She colored, finding it difficult to say the words directly. "When you ask me," she replied, averting her eyes with embarrassment, "I shall accept you. At once. Without teasing."

He pulled her to him and his face was transformed.

"You're wonderful. Do you really mean it? Honestly?"

"Silly question," she chided. "Would I have said it otherwise?"

"Janet, could we get engaged on your birthday, and married soon afterward? Married before Christmas?"

"I suppose so. It seems hurried."

"I don't want to spend another minute without you, once it is all settled. We'll get the ring in advance and we can announce the engagement on your eighteenth birthday, on October 25. Yes?"

"All right." She laughed happily. "If that is what you want."

"Oh, God, how I want it, darling."

"That's funny," she said dreamily.

"What is?" There was a faint edge to his voice but she did not notice it.

"A little time ago you said 'darling Janet,' but I'm really Janet Darling."

"Not for long. Janet Cunninghame soon, but always 'darling.'"

She thought it a pretty remark and tucked her arm through his happily. She had known for a long time that this would happen, but now that it had, she glowed. He was so strong, and at the same time so uncertain and even afraid. Were all men such a mixture of weakness and strength?

"What are you thinking?" he asked.

She turned the full force of her smile on him, robbing him of his breath. "I was thinking how lucky I am, Andrew."

He squared his shoulders and took a deep breath. The royal warrant, the most beautiful bride in all Scotland— there was nothing he could not accomplish, nothing in this world.

FOUR

THEY were married in St. John's Church on Saturday, December 14, 1872. Lawrence married them, and Dr. Gardiner, now in his late fifties, gave the bride away. The best man was Hugh Stirling, a dandified man some eight years older than Andrew and related to John Stirling of Kippendavie, the chairman of the North British Railway and the driving force behind the Tay Bridge project.

As chance would have it, Lawrence Darling himself was the only relative of either bride or groom at the wedding. Andrew's mother had taken to her bed some months previously and was fast wasting away with tuberculosis, and the Darling and Sharpe relatives were either dead or lost sight of. The church, however, was crowded. The popularity of Lawrence and Janet had brought out almost the entire congregation, and Andrew had business and social connections with all the finest and wealthiest families in Dundee. If there was no family, there were lots of friends.

As Janet stood before the altar, looking up at her father, scarcely heeding or indeed hearing the words of the service, she felt as though her heart would burst. Lawrence, too, was much moved. She looked strangely young and defenseless, and he had an irrational impulse to throw down the prayer book and refuse to continue with the ceremony. He could not think what had got into him, but it took an effort to keep his voice steady.

Janet was, quite simply, happy. Where she had had a beloved father, she now had a beloved father plus a beloved husband. She was the most fortunate of women. Her good luck had been doubled at a stroke.

When Andrew slipped the ring on her finger, she looked at him for the first time, and her eyes were misty. Somehow she managed to get through the wedding lunch and the reception, as though in a dream, until it was time to leave. Then for the first time she felt panic. She turned to Andrew and whispered agitatedly, "Can't we stay here just tonight, Andrew? Please!"

"Of course not, my love." He was brisk, even businesslike. "We must go to our own home now. My mother is looking forward so much to your arrival."

"But Papa . . ."

"My dear, you are no longer your father's, you are mine. Your place is at my side. Now, we mustn't waste any more time."

You are no longer your father's, you are mine. The words reverberated through her mind, endlessly, like some childish jingle but infinitely more sinister. When she was ready, she slipped down the back stairs to where Andrew waited with Hugh Stirling and Lawrence. Their luggage had been carried out to the carriage and pair that waited to whisk them off to Leuchars, where they would take the train to Tayport, then across the river by ferry to Broughty Ferry, where they would be met by Andrew's own carriage.

Janet gripped her father's arm tightly as they hurried to the side door, and Lawrence, guessing at her feelings, bit his lip. It was a bad moment for him, too, but what could he do? All women came to this in the end. It was the way of life, God's way. He said good-bye brusquely to mask his emotions, kissed her in a somewhat perfunctory way, clasped his son-in-law's hand silently, and then stood beside Hugh Stirling and waved as they set off with a clatter of hooves.

In the carriage, Janet kept her head averted. Her fear

confused her. This was her wedding day, to which she had looked forward so eagerly. It was cold, wet, and windy, and she was miserable. Normally she did not care about weather, but today could not the sun have shone a little, and the rain have stayed away? She felt Andrew groping for her hand.

"Together at last," he said contentedly. "I thought we would never get away from it all. I wonder who invented wedding ceremonies. I'd far rather have left straight from the church."

"Yes." Her voice was muffled and he leaned over, put a finger under her chin, and turned her face to his.

"What's this? Glum today of all days?"

"I'm . . . a little overcome, that's all."

"Of course." She was a woman, a weaker vessel. He was prepared to make allowances.

"You'll feel better when we get home," he said solicitously. "We'll have dinner alone, just the two of us. I know it sounds cruel, but just for tonight I'm rather glad my mother can't come down for meals anymore. I want you all to myself."

Home, she thought. Doesn't he realize that I've just *left* home? She straightened her back and shoulders and raised her head. She was Lawrence Darling's daughter. She would not show weakness.

"How nice." Her voice was as false as the words she uttered, but he did not notice. Instead he felt mightily relieved.

"Come, my love." No one could see, so he pulled her closer and kissed her.

Immediately she stiffened. How could he, at a time like this? It was indecent. After a moment he broke away, sensing her displeasure, not understanding it. They remained silent until they reached the little station at Leuchars where the train awaited their arrival. The bridegroom, after all, had been attended at his wedding by a relative of the railroad's chairman. The train had its place in the scheme of things. They clambered into the reserved

first-class carriage, and a few moments later they were off
again.

"They waited for us, you see," Andrew pointed, making
sure she knew how important they were. He was quite
sure a train had never waited for her before.

"That was nice of them."

He suppressed a smile. Nice? Men would have lost their
jobs if the train had not waited! That was the whole point
in being a Cunninghame. What a ninny she was in some
ways. He rather liked her for it. She was innocent. He
stretched his legs in luxurious satisfaction. He really did
love her. She was the one person in his life he had ever
loved. He was fond of his mother, of course, and he had
admired his father greatly, but they had never been able
to stir him like this. Nor had there been any other women.
He had kept himself pure for his bride. Janet was really
getting quite a bargain. So of course was he, and he admitted it to himself. She was so incredibly lovely. He wished
she would smile—she would soon, he was confident of
that.

The ferry was a graceful, light vessel with paddles and
slender masts. By Tay standards the river was almost calm,
which is to say there was not actually a gale or storm.
The ferry responded to every motion of the water's surface and soon Janet felt sick. She turned white and was
silent. She was relieved when they got into Andrew's carriage at Broughty Ferry. She sank back into the cushions
gratefully, forgetting that this was the last stage of her
separation from home.

And so to the great gray house, lamps already lit and
casting pools of comforting light. She had a vague impression of saying something banal to the yellow-faced woman
in the big bed, and then a closing door, another big bed
and Andrew grinning at her. She swallowed hard as he
took her in his arms.

"Our own bedroom. Our bed," he said playfully, kissing
her cheek. His moustache felt bristly this evening. "Early
dinner tonight, and early bed, eh?"

She did not respond to his jocularity. She was rigid in his arms, trying not to think of the ordeal ahead.

Janet went through the remainder of the evening chilled and miserable. She hoped the meal would be delayed, but it was on time, beautifully cooked and utterly tasteless. Andrew was a rarity in many ways, among them being the fact that he did not smoke and rarely drank, so there was no lingering after dinner. He was also a virgin and tonight would see the end of that. Before she could gather her wits they were walking up the grand staircase together, to the big bedroom and the bed that waited relentlessly.

Fortunately there was the privacy of her dressing room. She took her time over undressing and putting on her new and voluminous nightgown. Then she sat, endlessly brushing her wonderful head of thick, glossy, golden hair until Andrew, growing tired, came in without knocking.

She jumped.

"You didn't knock," she accused, turning crimson.

"Knock? My dear, I'm your husband. Your bridegroom, in fact. What has been keeping you? Come along now."

"Be gentle," she whispered.

She was unaware that he was worse than ignorant, for somewhere along the line he had collected only a few snippets of misinformation from some of his more normal friends. These included the fact that girls always squealed the first time, and that the more they bled, the better they were enjoying it. It would have been infinitely better for both of them if he had sewn his wild oats, as his friends had, and visited Peg's or Boozie Mary's.

He propelled her toward the door and then to the bed where he gathered her close and kissed her. She closed her eyes and prayed. He released her, and when she opened her eyes a moment later, she saw him pulling off his nightgown. She stared at his nakedness, aghast.

"*Andrew!* What are you doing?"

"Getting undressed of course. Go on, off with your nighty, there's a good girl."

"Me? Undress?"

Did he really think she was going to show him her naked body, she wondered?

"Yes." He stood rather ridiculously, his nightgown trailing from his hand, while she turned away from him. Then he grew angry, frowned, and threw away the garment. He seized her, and before she could stop him he had drawn her own nightgown over her head. She squealed and struggled, and he grinned delightedly as he got it off and pulled her to him so that their bodies touched in their nakedness.

As her arms came free she struck at him wildly, one blow landing painfully on the end of his nose. He recoiled before her fury. Nothing had led him to expect this sort of reaction.

"What the devil," he growled menacingly. "I'm your husband. Don't play tease with me now, Janet."

"You have no right to behave like, like, like a s . . . s . . . savage," she stammered.

"Dammit, this is what people do," he swore.

"What sort of people?" she asked, picking up her nightgown and holding it between them. He had been staring at her body, and not just her body, but at some *parts* of it. She wished he would cover himself.

"Married people," he answered grimly.

Lower lip thrust out, he advanced on her, this time determined not to be opposed any further. Modesty was one thing, but slapping and punching one's husband was *not* a wifely privilege, by God. He tore the nightgown out of her hands and pushed her so that she fell back across the bed.

With a grunt of triumph he fell on top of her and thrust himself between her legs.

She did not fight against him again, but for two days she would hardly speak to him, and avoided him as much as possible. Gradually nature came to her assistance. The shock wore off, the memory of that first awful experience faded, and she was able to endure him with fortitude. By accident she made an important discovery. If she professed to feeling unwell, he would leave her alone. Indeed he was greatly concerned about her health, and tried hard to be tender and loving. Those days, when she knew there would be no ordeal in bed, were almost happy. She became plagued by a nebulous, often recurring, malaise and Andrew realized what she was up to. He said nothing at the time, but early in January Lawrence took a few week-days off to come to visit them. He was distressed by Janet's drawn look, but before he could ask her about it, Andrew took him off to his study where he wasted no time beating about the bush.

Janet had not had her wifely duties explained to her. She was feigning sickness in order to avoid them. Lawrence must speak to her. Couldn't he speak to her himself? No, of course not. She would not accept it from him. Lawrence sighed and reluctantly agreed, for Cunninghame was within his rights.

While Andrew was fetching Janet, Lawrence wondered what on earth to say. He and Barbara, by sheer good fortune, had found nothing distasteful about the act of love. Their love for one another had enabled them to face their bridal night with gentle understanding. Lawrence actually found the method of obtaining children quite pleasant, although he hardly admitted it to himself. He had no idea if Barbara had felt the same. What could he say to Janet?

Face to face with his daughter, he coughed and fidgeted.

"Andrew has been speaking to me about you," he began nervously.

"Yes?" Her voice was strained but terribly controlled.

"Yes. Janet, he is your husband, you know. I mean, you do want to have children, don't you?"

"I don't know. I'm not sure anymore."

"You must want them! That's what marriage is for. Didn't you listen to the service?"

"I know the words," she replied dully. "He's . . . I can't tell you."

"He's what?"

"He takes his nightgown off and forces me to do the same."

"Is that all?" Lawrence was surprised. He had half expected some tale of brutality.

"*All?*" She stared at her father, horror-stricken. He, too? This kind, good, Godly man—had he displayed himself naked before her mother? Her mind shied away from the idea. "All?" she repeated.

"Look here, Janet, my dear, you have your duty as a wife. All your life you have done your duty and done it nobly. No father ever had a more dutiful daughter. Now your duty is to your husband, and it is a different duty. You must have children. You must stop pretending you are ill."

"But I *am* ill," she protested with some slight truth. She was still scarlet with embarrassment. "The sight of him like that makes me feel ill."

"I see. Well, I'll have a word with Andrew, but you must not deny him his rights. You must be an obedient and dutiful wife. Oh, my child!" He came and hugged her tightly. "You are grown up, now, Janet, my dear. This happens to us all. It is the will of God. If he had wanted us to have children in some other way, could he not have arranged it? In his wisdom, he made us as we are."

This argument silenced her. Could it be right, she wondered miserably? Was it God's idea that you had to do those shameful things to have a child? It must be, and if so Andrew was not to blame. With desperate longing she wished she were back in the safety and protection of the rectory, unmarried. It was too late now.

She was not present during the stilted conversation in which Lawrence Darling conveyed to Andrew Cunninghame the news that his wife would be dutifully cooperative in the future if only he could be more modest in his demands. Andrew's first impulse was to argue, for having seen Janet's body, he quite naturally wanted to see it again, as often as possible, and he considered it a right.

Common sense, however, prevailed. His wife was a lady, after all, daughter of a clergyman, granddaughter of a bishop. Provided he got his way with her, did it really matter very much? So he agreed quickly and changed the subject as rapidly as he could.

Thereafter life began to assume an even tenor between them. The compromise miraculously worked. He was an unsatisfactory, animal-like lover. In bed he took her quickly, and, when he had reached his climax, he rolled off and turned on his side to fall asleep almost at once. She assumed that that was how it was meant to be, and indeed was always rather glad when he grunted his good night. It puzzled her that he got any pleasure out of it, but recalling her father's words, she knew that God, being wise, had made sure that *one* of them must have the impulse to indulge in these goings-on.

She began to hope that soon she would become pregnant. No child came, however, and except when it was physically impossible, they continued their determined, relentless, joyless mating for the glory of God and the increase of the human species, which was undoubtedly God's greatest handiwork.

Next time she saw her father she was able to assure him calmly that she was happy and that all was well with her marriage; and he, poor man, was relieved and content to drop an uncomfortable subject. He missed her very much, and he was sad to note how rarely she smiled nowadays. That wonderful smile of hers had lightened his life. He kept reminding himself that she was a mature woman now, and he threw himself into his religious duties with increased fervor.

Gradually Janet came to feel at home in Aberneist House. The servants were well-trained and respectful, obedient in everything. They were also very good servants and spared her much work and worry. Her duties as mistress of the house were minimal. She quickly found congenial work in spending long hours with the dying woman upstairs. Her awe of Marjorie Cunninghame had quickly turned to something approaching love, and Marjorie was, nowadays, the only person who saw Janet's smile.

They spent hours together during which Janet would either read, or talk. At first she read passages from the Bible, but soon she began to read the daily newspaper, *The Dundee Advertiser*, and then *The Lady's Newspaper* to which she had taken out a subscription. The latter cost 6d a copy and was regarded by Andrew as a ridiculous luxury. Finally she began to read aloud Scott's Waverley novels. Marjorie particularly enjoyed this, because her father had known Scott.

As she grew weaker and more listless and helpless, Janet fed and nursed her. Andrew admired her devotion to his mother and treated her with new respect. One afternoon when they were discussing the local news and gossip, Marjorie asked the girl at her bedside, "Are you happy here, my dear?"

"Oh, yes, Mama." She meant what she said. So far as she knew, she was indeed happy.

"You have such a lovely smile. It makes me feel better."

This produced one of Janet's sunniest ones. "But you are getting better. Soon we will be able to go out into the garden together for a little time each day."

"That will be lovely," Marjorie lied. She knew that she was dying, although nobody in fact had said so. She had seen enough of consumption in others. She would never leave this bed. This knowledge held few terrors for her.

"Andrew never tires of singing your praises," she said.

"I can't think why. The house looks after itself, and Andrew is away from home all day long."

This was true. Andrew Cunninghame, like any well-trained, ambitious young magnate, started work early and stopped late. He left home every morning before eight o'clock and returned in the evenings well after six. He did not come home to lunch. He worked on Saturdays. He made occasional trips to England, and more frequent ones to Glasgow and Edinburgh, acting as ambassador for his own products.

He had recently met a remarkable young man called Thomas Johnstone Lipton, who was two years younger than himself, but who had spent five years in the United States and who was busy creating a most remarkable grocery empire. Lipton at that time was interested in selling Rowan's marmalades and jams.

Andrew admired the younger man's dynamism, although Lipton's immense vision frightened him. He was considering visiting the United States himself, but the project kept being shelved as he concentrated more and more on improving his home sales. He was doing particularly well in London, now that he had the royal warrant and advertisements for Rowan's Royal Marmalade and Rowan's jams began to appear on London's horse-drawn buses and trams. Where Lipton was interested in finding mass markets, Andrew sought to supply the carriage trade, although he was glad enough of Lipton's business.

"You spend so much of your time with me," Marjorie remarked, patting Janet's hand. "You should have friends of your own. You have hardly any social life."

"That's all right," Janet reassured her. She and Andrew had agreed that while Marjorie lingered, which could not be for very long as the disease was rampant in her, they would entertain as little as possible. In any case Janet did not feel the need for friends.

"When Andrew's father was alive, we entertained all the time. I thought that when Andrew married, the house would come alive again. The servants like it, you know. They can take pride in a house in which there is always something going on."

"Andrew and I are perfectly happy as we are," Janet answered placidly. "Now, where were we reading?"

FIVE

BY the autumn of 1873 work on the new bridge was well under way. People had become accustomed to the glare from the foundry at Wormit, on the south bank of the Tay, where the girders for the wonder bridge were being cast on the spot.

Andrew had become friendly with and greatly under the influence of the energetic, tireless John Stirling of Kippendavie, who now in his early sixties continued to fight the enemy combine, the Caledonian Railway, and to promote the bridge which was taking much longer to build than had been forecast.

One September day Andrew arrived alone and unheralded at the rectory in St. Andrews, taking Lawrence by surprise. When they were settled down with tea and biscuits in the study, Lawrence looked inquiringly at his visitor.

"I've never asked you about money, sir," Andrew began respectfully, "but I feel it my duty to let you know that I can help you with a particularly good investment."

"Can you? That's very kind of you. I have a few thousand pounds on deposit, and some shares in shipping which are doing well. Not a lot," he added cautiously with a Scottish reluctance to reveal the extent of his wealth.

"Shipping?" Andrew shook his head as he uttered the word. "Your shares may presently be doing well, sir, but consider the risks. Ships may be lost; *are* lost. Entire cargoes are lost with them. The seas are untamed."

"What would you suggest?" asked Lawrence.

"I think you have heard me mention Mr. Stirling of Kippendavie more than once."

"Yes, of course," Lawrence chuckled.

"Mr. Stirling is the chairman of the North British Railway. I have been persuaded by him to invest in his company. As you know, sir, it is backing the Tay Bridge undertaking. The profits will be very satisfactory, and they will be sure. Railway engines do not sink in storms. Think of it—when the Tay Bridge is built, and then when the Forth is bridged, Dundee will have direct and cheap railway communication with the markets of the south. This will put an end to the Caledonian, indeed to all rival railways. And it is absolutely safe."

Lawrence Darling considered his son-in-law with some perplexity.

"Does it not all depend on the bridge?" he asked.

"Ah," Andrew laughed confidently, "you've been listening to some of the old wives' tales, I can see. We shall indeed have the longest bridge in the world, here in Scotland, linking Dundee with Fife. Of course there are those who have been casting doubts on the enterprise for many years now. There are always men who jeer at progress. I can assure you that this bridge will be the most magnificent feat of engineering the world has seen. Is Fife to remain virtually an island forever, do you think? Progress will come. We live in an age of progress. The North British Railway has allied itself with progress. It is a marvelous opportunity, sir."

Lawrence Darling knew what was meant by calling Fife an island. From time to time it was necessary for him to make short visits to Edinburgh—mercifully not often, for, although the journey was less than fifty miles, it took between three and four hours to make it. Nor was time the only factor. The journey was one of acute discomfort and, sometimes, misery. From Dundee it was infinitely worse, beginning with the train journey to Broughty Ferry. This was followed by the ferry crossing of the Tay, a bad business at best and downright frightening in winter. The next stage was another railway journey from Tayport, on the south bank of the Tay, to Burntisland on the north bank of the Firth of Forth. There was a second unpleasant ferry crossing to Granton on the south side, and finally the last stage of the journey was by train again from Granton to Waverley Station in Edinburgh.

It was one of the most unpleasant journeys devised by man, and Lawrence Darling did not doubt that someone would do something about it eventually, particularly when a man like Stirling of Kippendavie had decided to take an interest in it.

But to bridge the tempestuous Tay? Like most men of his calling, he was a mine of local folklore, interested in the district in which he lived and in its history. He knew the Tay's long record of violent weather, and he remembered uneasily the great gale of 1859. Dimly he felt that a bridge across the Tay would be subjected to so much strain that it might have to be reinforced or rebuilt at intervals, which would surely be costly.

All these considerations passed through his mind in a second or two, while he sat with pursed lips. Was he an engineer, a man of science, he asked himself? He was not. Was he a businessman, a man of affairs? No, he was not even that. But his son-in-law was, known among some of his older friends as "the young magnate." And Stirling of Kippendavie was a household name, standing for orderly progress. The North British had engineers and scientists to advise it, and Parliament had approved the undertaking. His own doubts were obviously those of the uninformed.

"I must think about it," he said at length.

"Do more, sir," Andrew urged. "Act. Five thousand pounds could be made to yield a handsome competence. Ten would be better."

"Ten thousand pounds?" This was almost to a penny

what Lawrence Darling was worth. "I don't think I could invest so much in a single venture."

"I'll guarantee your money," Andrew offered handsomely.

"I don't understand."

Andrew, who was genuinely trying to do his wife's father a good turn, to show gratitude for the older man's friendship, explained.

"Obviously a lot of my own money is tied up in Rowan's. I think you know I am considered a substantial man."

"Yes indeed."

"What I am saying is this. The bridge is costing a lot, and the N.B. are inviting fresh investment. If you can spare ten thousand, I can place it for you. If anything goes wrong, you have my word that I will reimburse you personally."

"That's handsome of you!" Lawrence exclaimed.

"My mother is dying, sir. You and Janet are all the family I have. Why at ten percent, your ten thousand could yield you a safe thousand pounds a year."

Lawrence was dazzled. "I don't know what to say," he stammered.

"I've put up forty thousand myself. I could have raised a great deal more, but I promised myself when my father died that I would never pledge nor part with any part of Rowan's. It's a question of principle. If I had had more ready money, I would have invested more. That is how confident I am. Railways are the coming thing, sir, and the North British is the most coming of all," he added with a grin.

"Very well. You've persuaded me. If you are prepared to guarantee my money, then obviously you are very well informed. I trust your judgment, Andrew. I can let you have half the money right away. It will take a week or two to free the balance."

"That's all right. I'll arrange everything at once, and you can let me have the cash at your convenience. You won't regret it, I promise you."

They drank more tea, and Lawrence asked hesitantly, for he did not wish to appear overinquisitive, "How are things with Janet nowadays? I hope you are both happy."

"Oh, indeed," Andrew replied truthfully, for he was fully satisfied with his life. "Janet is a wonderful wife. My mother adores her, and you know, sir, Janet really does devote herself to Mama. It is touching to see it. My mother can't linger much longer, I'm afraid. Later on, when we are out of mourning, I shall launch Janet in society. She will make a tremendous impression."

"I'm glad. That other business . . ." He coughed delicately. "There's been no further trouble?"

"None whatever." Andrew experienced a momentary awkwardness.

"I only asked because you have been married for the best part of a year now. I wondered if you would soon be expecting a happy event."

"Not yet." Andrew's face clouded. He desperately wanted a son. "But we are aiming in that direction," he explained, thus showing that all was well and that the nonarrival of an heir was due purely to malignant fate and nothing else.

Lawrence nodded. He felt that they had exhausted the subject, and once again admired his son-in-law's willingness to discuss what were really private and personal affairs.

It was early in 1874 that Janet realized that she might have conceived at last. She sent for their family doctor, one morning after Andrew had left the house, and shortly afterward that worthy man was able to assure her that her guess was fairly certainly correct, and that by the middle of the year a happy event could be expected. When the doctor had gone, she went upstairs to where the dying woman lay in bed. Marjorie gave her a wan smile.

"You will never guess my news, Mama," Janet said, sitting down beside the bed and taking Marjorie's hand.

"I think I can, but I would prefer you to tell me."

"Dr. Neish has been to see me. Mama, I shall have a baby in June."

"I thought so."

"How?" Janet demanded, baffled.

"Oh, a certain bloom on your cheeks. One can sometimes tell. Say rather that I am not completely surprised."

"Andrew will be so pleased," Janet went on. "He has never said anything, but I know he's been waiting for this."

"Yes, he'll be pleased," Andrew's mother agreed. "Especially if it is a boy."

"It must be a boy," Janet exclaimed. "It must."

"You'll have to take what you are given," Marjorie warned her with an attempt at humor. "Whatever it is, I'm sure you'll be happy. You'll make a good mother, Janet."

Janet blushed. "I can't think why you say so."

"Because of the way you treat me. If you can love an invalid so much, how much more will you love your own children?"

"I wish you wouldn't talk like that," Janet said quietly. "I do so little for you."

She was sincere. She wished with all her heart that she could do much more than just talk and read, that she could halt the march of the dread disease that was destroying Andrew's mother, a disease in the face of which the doctors were helpless.

"You do more than you think. I shall have a little rest now. Thank you for coming to tell me. Don't tell Andrew that I know. Men are funny sometimes. He will want to be the first to know, and then he will want to tell me, so we'll pretend, shall we?"

"If you say so." Janet gave one of her sunny smiles that lightened the room. "Men are terrible children."

"They're terrible, anyway," Marjorie agreed, her heart suddenly full. Then there came a lancing pain.

Janet leaned over her anxiously. "Can I fetch you something?" she asked.

Marjorie shook her head silently and closed her eyes. Tiredness took over. After a few moments, Janet tiptoed out of the room, her happiness gone. She went downstairs to the drawing room and took up her embroidery. A short time later she was interrupted by White, the butler.

"There is a woman at the door, madam," White said respectfully. "One of the poorer class. She has asked to speak with you."

"Then show her in, please. Who is she, do you know?"

"A Mrs. Robertson. She seems very agitated and says it is important."

"All right, thank you, White. Bring her in and have some tea sent in please."

She waited expectantly till White showed in a woman, poorly dressed as he had said, but with an oddly proud look about her. The woman advanced nervously. Janet tried to guess her age, but it was difficult, for although she had a youthful figure, her face was heavily lined and she had that unhealthy look Janet saw so often among the poor.

"Mrs. Robertson? Sit down, please. I am Mrs. Cunninghame."

"Yes I know, ma'am. Thank you." Mrs. Robertson sat and fidgeted with the fringe of her cheap shawl.

"Tell me, please, how I can help you?" Janet invited with a reassuring smile.

"It's Davie, ma'am. My youngest boy. He works for Mr. Cunninghame."

"Yes?"

"Mr. Cunninghame was very good to him. He made him tea boy, which is much better than being in the factory. He brings Mr. Cunninghame his tea in the office and runs messages for him. Davie is not strong, you know, but he's bright and Mr. Cunninghame gave him a job where his health wouldn't matter. I'm very grateful to Mr. Cunninghame."

"I see." Janet did not see at all. She had no idea where all this was leading.

"I'm a widow, and there are five others, but we manage all right."

"I'm certain you do." Janet recognized the proud, independent tone of voice. Mrs. Robertson's sort would always "manage all right" whatever the cost. Six children, though, and that slim figure. It was remarkable.

"I've a daughter a year younger than Davie. She's eleven. She has consumption, ma'am. I think Davie has it too, but it's not bad in him. The doctor and the medicines, they're expensive, and she's supposed to have nice things to eat."

"Of course. You'd like me to help, is that it?"

"Not with Janet! I can manage." The words were proud again.

"Did you say Janet? That's my name, too, you know. Mrs. Robertson, just why have you come to see me? Why are you telling me all this if you can manage?"

"It's Davie. He loves his wee sister. He dotes on her, and I think he knows she's dying. He's always doing things for her. Two days ago he brought home some nice chicken broth. He told me he had been saving up. He lied, ma'am. He stole the money. He stole one and threepence from Mr. Cunninghame, from something they call petty cash. It's money they keep in a drawer. I don't understand, but he stole it."

"Do you mean that my husband dismissed your little boy for taking one and three to buy things for his dying sister?"

"It's not that. That would have been all right. It would have taught Davie a lesson, and Mr. Cunninghame so kind to him and all."

"Then what?" Janet asked, totally baffled.

"He sent for the police. They've taken Davie away. They'll send him to a house of correction. You know what that means, ma'am, and he's not strong. He'll die." Mrs. Robertson's composure broke.

Janet was thunderstruck.

"I'm sure there is some mistake. My husband would never hand over a child of twelve to the police."

"He did."

"You mean, Mr. Cunninghame *himself* did this?"

"Yes, ma'am. He said he's a thief and must be punished by the law."

"Said to whom?" Janet demanded.

"To me. I went to his office to see him. It's not that I want any special consideration for Davie, but he's not strong." Her voice became a wail. "If they send him away it will be the death of him. I offered back the one and three but he wouldn't take it."

Janet was on her feet at once, her arm around the other woman's shoulder. At that moment the tea belatedly arrived. Janet signaled to the maid to put it down and go away. While Mrs. Robertson wiped her eyes and blew her nose, Janet poured.

"Drink this," she said firmly. "It will do you good. Now you must stop worrying. I shall speak to my husband tonight. I am certain he has not considered the whole case properly, but I have. When I explain it to him, he will see that Davie is released first thing tomorrow morning. What is more, he will get a second chance in the office. Just leave it all to me."

"Oh he'll never get his job back. I wouldn't expect it."

"He *will*," Janet said stubbornly. "You have my word."

The woman blinked away a tear and stared in surprise. This young girl, for she looked scarcely older than a girl, meant what she said. Mrs. Robertson compared Janet with Andrew, whom she had met for the first time yesterday, and wondered how such a pretty slip of a thing could wield power over the stubborn owner of Rowan's. She smiled, reassured.

"I wasn't expecting that. Just to get Davie back home. And to repay this."

She put two sixpences and three pennies on the table and Janet picked it up slowly, her mind working quickly.

"Davie will be back home. However I wish to see him. You must bring him here on Sunday after church. What he did was wrong, and I am sure he knows that, but I think he must love his sister very much. He has never done wrong before, has he?" she added hastily.

"No, never. He's a *good* boy."

"Fine. That's settled." She picked up her reticule from a nearby table and opened it. She took out a sovereign and held it out.

"I'm taking the one and three for a reason, but I want you to take this and to spend it on the other Janet. Please. I want you to take it," she urged as Mrs. Robertson drew back.

"I didn't come for money, ma'am. It's too much."

"I know you didn't." Janet smiled a tender, sympathetic smile. "Please believe me. I know you wouldn't think of it. This is my idea. Tell me, what do you do for money?"

"I take in washing, and I go out and do floors in the mornings. Then there's Davie's three and six a week, and two of my other boys have jobs. We manage just fine."

There she was, "managing" again. Janet chuckled and put the coin in Mrs. Robertson's hand, gave her more tea, and saw her to the front door. She spent the remainder of the day in a fever of impatience. Once she had made up her mind about anything, she longed to sweep into instant action. The case of Davie Robertson particularly moved her, because it was one of those situations where justice was less than fair. She was eagerly looking forward to explaining it all to Andrew. It would be a wonderful chance for Andrew to show what a good employer he was.

He returned later than usual, and was taken aback when Janet insisted that they have a talk before dinner. He poured himself a whisky and took it into the drawing room.

"What's all the excitement about?" he asked indulgently, thinking how alive and vital she looked.

"Two things. First, I had a visit today from Mrs. Robertson."

"Robertson? Do we know some Robertsons?"

"You met her yesterday at your office. Davie Robertson's mother."

He choked on his whisky. "That woman. What did *she* want here?" he asked indignantly.

"Oh, Andrew, listen, my dear. Let me explain."

She forced him to remain silent while she trotted out the full story, all except the bit about the sovereign. Then she came and stood beside him and smiled up into his scowling face.

"There you are. I promised you'd have him released in the morning and give him back his job. I knew once you heard all the circumstances . . ."

"How dare you, Janet! You had no business saying I'd interfere with the law."

She stepped back, eyes wide.

"What did you expect me to do?" she asked. "Connive at the murder of a consumptive child? He's not strong. You gave him a light job for that very reason. You can't just hand him over to the authorities!"

"He stole. He's a little thief. I gave him a good job and paid him well, and look at how he repaid me."

"Oh, fiddlesticks," she snapped, her eyes sparking and her face flushed. "He took one and threepence to buy little luxuries for a dying sister. How dare you call him a thief? Besides he's returned the money. I have it."

"He's a thief. I'll have nothing to do with him."

"*Andrew!* He's a child of twelve."

"He's an ungrateful little wretch who can't be trusted."

She sat down and stared at him closely, as if trying to recognize a stranger.

"I believe you mean it," she said softly.

He mistook her tone. "I do." He was arrogant now. "Kindly do not interfere in my business affairs again. Davie Robertson was my employee. He stole petty cash and the police were sent for. It happens all the time with the lower classes. I've dealt with it in the usual way, and there's an end to it. You stick to running the house, Janet dear, and I'll run Rowan's."

"What about my promises to his mother?"

"She had no business coming here. I'll see she doesn't trouble you again."

Suddenly Janet began to experience a new sensation. She

felt that she was suffocating, and her hands began to tremble. She had an overpowering desire to do something violent, anything. Instead she stood up, and Andrew instinctively flinched from the fury in her eyes and the expression on her face. Her words were tightly controlled.

"I gave my word. You will honor it. You will see that that child is released first thing tomorrow morning, first thing before you do anything else, do you hear? You will give him a day off to recover and you will give him back his job and you will deduct nothing from his wages. You will not punish him in any way, not even by a look. He is coming to this house on Sunday after church, with his mother. You will receive them with me. You will do all this because I am telling you."

"I'll do nothing of the sort," he stammered, still shaken. "You've taken leave of your senses."

"Oh, no, I haven't. I've just come to them. I know now the sort of man I married. Very well. You force me into a corner. I told you there were two things to discuss. If you do not do exactly as I have asked, about Davie Robertson, your child will never be born."

"What are you talking about?"

"Dr. Neish came to see me this morning and to confirm my suspicions. I am carrying your child."

"Darling. At last." He moved toward her, his face lit up, but she backed off.

"Listen carefully, Andrew. A life for a life. Davie Robertson for your son."

"I don't understand."

"There are ways of getting rid of a baby," she flung at him.

"You're mad."

"Oh, no, I'm not. Now you will give me your word. If you do not, I will leave for my father's home tomorrow and you will never see me or the child. There will be no child."

"God, you're serious."

"Never more so, Andrew. I know you now, and I pity

anyone who crosses you, but I will not let you do this to a child who only wanted to help a dying sister."

"Oh, damn the boy!" he exclaimed.

"Don't you dare to swear in my drawing room," she shouted, losing the temper she never suspected she possessed. "Don't you *dare*. You're a brute, an oaf, a cruel, wicked monster. Would you like me to tell your mother the whole story—before I leave?"

He flung up his arms helplessly. He didn't really believe she would get rid of her baby, but he knew with certainty she would tell Marjorie if she thought it would help. And she was so kind to Marjorie, too. Curse the boy, he thought hopelessly. This should have been an evening of pure joy.

"I don't know what to say," he muttered.

"Say nothing. Just do as you are told. I shan't try to interfere in your business again. Just make sure I don't know what is going on. I don't want to know. *Except* that I shall watch Davie Robertson's progress from now on. One cross word from you, Andrew, and I'll make you pay. I promise."

"All right, all right." He stared at the empty whisky glass in his hand and wondered when he had drunk its contents. "Shall we dine?"

"I have your word?" she insisted.

"Yes, you have my word, Janet, on one condition." He was calm now.

"What condition?"

"Everything which has passed in this room tonight is a secret. You will never mention it to a soul. In return I will do as you want with Davie."

She felt drained of all energy and emotion. She had won. She gave him a small smile.

"Then let us go in to dinner," she agreed. "Afterward, you must tell Mama about the baby. It will make her so happy."

"Er, yes." The change in her bewildered him. He felt that he was with a stranger, and it did not occur to him at all that she felt exactly the same. Where had happy, compliant, mild-mannered Janet gone? he wondered. What sort of woman was this who had taken her place?

She did not have to ask herself what sort of man he was. She had already decided. That evening at bedtime she showed her teeth again, this time without making a scene.

"Oh, Andrew, I meant to tell you that I've asked for a bed to be made up for you in the blue bedroom, and had your things moved into it."

"Why?" He was openmouthed, blinking at this bolt from the blue.

"Surely you know!" Her smile was gentle. "In my condition, my dear, I must have a separate bedroom."

"Oh. I hadn't thought of that."

"You are such a ninny in some things, Andrew."

"I'm afraid so. I shall feel very lonely without you."

"Just remember that it is for your son," she reminded, and let him kiss her. Privately she was determined that he would stay in the blue bedroom forevermore, but she was far too clever to cross that particular bridge prematurely. Instead she gave him another little smile.

"Good night, dear," she said sweetly.

SIX

ANDREW was not best pleased when the Robertsons, mother and son, appeared on the front doorstep on Sunday, after church, before lunch. However he was polite enough. Janet's attention was focused on the cause of all the pother, a thin, pale-faced boy with big intelligent eyes and soft dark hair, who fiddled with his cap while he stared at her, awestruck. She gave him her friendliest smile before turning to his mother.

"How nice of you to come, Mrs. Robertson. This is Davie?"

"Yes, ma'am. Davie, say how do you do to Mrs. Cunninghame."

"How do you do, ma'am," he said in a voice hardly above a whisper.

Janet sat down. "Come here, Davie," she said, and he moved reluctantly toward her. She was friendly, inspiring his confidence.

"Is everything all right now, Davie?" she asked.

"Yes, ma'am."

"They didn't treat you badly, did they, when they took you away?"

"No." It was a whisper, and she did not miss the flicker in his eyes, and she felt an unreasoning anger toward authority and all who wielded it.

"Anyway, it's all over. Do you like working in Mr. Cunninghame's office?"

"Oh, yes." He turned and looked shyly at Andrew, and Janet was astonished to see the admiration in the child's eyes. "Oh, *yes,* ma'am."

"He's very proud of his job, aren't you, Davie?" Mrs. Robertson urged.

"Yes." He spoke more firmly now.

"And he's never going to do anything wrong again, Mr. Cunninghame. Are you, Davie?"

"No, sir," Davie said, still looking up at Andrew.

"That's all right, Davie," Andrew said gruffly. "I know why you did it. We'll forget all about it."

"How is Janet?" Janet asked Davie.

He did not know how to reply and turned instinctively to his mother.

"She's keeping up her strength, ma'am," Mrs. Robertson said.

"Good. I got some things for her, which you can take home. Just a few little treats to brighten her up."

While Mrs. Robertson protested, she rang for the maid and had the basket sent in and then stood up to usher them out. As she did so, she saw Davie staring hard at her.

"Is something wrong, Davie?" she asked the boy gently.

"No, ma'am. It's your hair. It's like real gold."

"Why thank you," she laughed. "Thank you very much, Davie. Mrs. Robertson, I would like to come to see you one afternoon during the week, if that is all right."

"Yes, ma'am, but it's not much to visit."

"Don't worry about that. I'll come about four o'clock on Thursday if I may. I want to see my namesake."

"You're very kind."

They left, overwhelmed, and Janet turned to Andrew.

"Thank you, Andrew," she said, her voice friendly. "You keep your word handsomely."

"Well at least the little beggar is grateful and I got my money back, so perhaps there's no harm done this time."

She knew that coming from him this was almost an

apology. She wondered if it would ever occur to him that Davie Robertson's mother had exacted a terrible revenge on Andrew. Probably not, for he was not given to deep thought except where Rowan's was concerned. Yet it was because of Mrs. Robertson's visit that she, Janet, had discovered steel in her character, and because of it that she had come to appreciate the cold, hard streak in her husband. Things could never be quite the same again between them. And the strange thing was that neither of them would ever know if Janet would have carried out her threat. It was enough that she made it.

From that day on she was friendly toward him in a way she had not been before. It was perhaps something of a cool friendship, but it was real enough, and she appreciated the way in which he was keeping his word in the matter of Davie. He treated the boy kindly and raised no objection when Janet began to visit the Robertson household to take food and medicine for the sick girl. Instead he concentrated on his work, and in moments of lonely relaxation dreamed of the son who was to be born.

One fine summer night in the middle of June, Martin Cunninghame was safely delivered, and Andrew opened a bottle of champagne and drank it all, and followed it with another—an unusual piece of behavior in a man who never drank more than three whiskies in a night.

In another upstairs room, Marjorie Cunninghame heard the news, too, and gave thanks to God for sparing her so long. By morning the spirit had left her tortured body to find its peace, and there was a little smile on her lifeless face. They buried her three days later, and probably Janet mourned her more than Andrew did, because he had long accepted the fact of her impending death, and saw far less of her than Janet did.

Janet, observing Andrew on the day of the funeral, pondered on the hard, unfeeling streak in his character, something she had not suspected before she married him. Seeing him beside her father on that sad day, she wondered why she had ever given up the warm happiness of the rectory for marriage to Andrew, the young magnate. On one point she was firm. There would be no nanny for Martin Cunninghame. She did not intend to trust her son with another woman. Instead she engaged a nursemaid to help her rear her own son. Andrew did not really approve of this. He felt that in his position they ought to have a nanny. He gave way, however, with a proviso.

"While he is still a child, we will do things your way, but his education will be my department. He is not going to be tied to apron strings until he is a grown man. He will go to school and university."

"*School?* Surely we can afford a tutor."

"We can, but we won't. He will go to school and learn to fend for himself. I will choose a good school for him."

Janet bit her lip. Nothing that she knew encouraged her to have any faith in the educational system of the time, and there was a great deal of brutality at boys' schools.

"Say no more, Janet," he commanded. "At twelve he will go to school. Till then he is yours and he can have a tutor till then if you wish. He has got to grow up to be a man, because one day Rowan's will be his. I don't want a namby-pamby son."

She remained silent. Twelve years, after all, was a long time. She would not think about it.

Some eight weeks later she was surprised when her bedroom door opened at bedtime, and Andrew walked in in a dressing gown. She was brushing her hair before the mirror.

"Andrew? I didn't hear you knock."

"I didn't knock. Do I have to? I am your husband."

"It would be a politeness."

"There's been enough politeness. When is this ridiculous business of separate bedrooms going to end? It's been more than two months now."

She felt panic rising in her breast. "I . . . um . . . as a matter of fact, I'm not feeling too well. I was thinking of sending for Dr. Neish."

"I see." He scowled. "Then please do so soon, because if

you don't, I shall. If there is anything wrong with you, I wish to know about it. If not . . ." He let the sentence hang in midair.

"Yes, dear," she said meekly and let him kiss her cheek. When he had gone, she thought furiously of how to handle the situation.

By this time she and Dr. Neish were good personal friends. She had had him examine the entire Robertson family at her expense. His report was encouraging. Janet Robertson, of course, was dying, and he did not propose to move her, arguing that there was limited time and she was happier among her family. But the rest were tough and hardy. Mrs. Robertson suffered from nothing worse than hard work and tiredness, and Davie, far from being consumptive as his mother had suspected, only needed building up.

"It's a terribly hard life for people like that, Mrs. Cunninghame," he told her. "They live close to the borderline, only a step away from destitution. Not all children are born with equal strength. The weakest die, and the strongest flourish. In between you get youngsters like Davie who needs nothing more than a better diet, perhaps more rest, and a holiday by the sea now and then."

"I want you to attend the family at my expense, Dr. Neish. Spare no expense to make things easier for Janet, and to build up Davie. I'll see he gets holidays."

Dr. Neish had no idea why Janet should interest herself in this insignificant family, one of thousands in like distress, but he admired her for it. He was also glad to have patients whose bills would be paid promptly and in full. He was a kind man and often waived his charges. Not all his patients lived in fine big houses like Aberneist.

When Janet sent for him, he responded promptly and discovered her the picture of health, dispensing tea and biscuits.

"Is something wrong with Martin?" he asked, jumping to the obvious conclusion.

"No, it isn't that at all. Dr. Neish, I need your help."

"You know you can count on me for anything," he assured her, and she gave him a smile that made him wish he were twenty years younger. "What can I do?" he asked.

"It's my husband. I have endured a lot to give him a son." She blushed becomingly and dropped her eyes. "Now Andrew wishes . . . he wants . . . that is to say, Dr. Neish, he thinks we should share a bedroom again."

"That should be all right, my dear," he said in a fatherly tone. "You need have no fears after what? Two and a half months, something like that?"

"You don't understand. I think I should die if that happened again."

Dr. Neish concealed his agitation. Here was a healthy, attractive, strong girl, well-endowed by nature to have more children. It was ridiculous that she should try to keep her husband at arm's length.

"I don't know how to explain," Janet said quietly, looking him in the eye. "The mere idea of it makes me feel physically ill. Doctor, I've been married for almost two years. It isn't that I haven't tried. I have. I've done my duty. We have a son now. If you could only speak to Andrew, persuade him that during the birth something happened, that it is out of the question for me to share my bed or have more children. . . ."

He put his hand over his mouth and thought rapidly. In one sense, the relationship between husband and wife was none of his affair. It was a private thing. But his patient was upset, and that *did* concern him. Also Janet had struck a responsive chord when she said she had tried. Briefly he wondered what it was about Andrew Cunninghame that repulsed his wife, that made a normal relationship apparently impossible.

"Please, Doctor."

There was no avoiding the appeal in her eyes and voice. He made up his mind quickly. Later he could argue the ethics of it with himself until his conscience was still.

"I could have a word with him, of course. I only hope

he doesn't ask any awkward questions. There is nothing physically wrong with you."

"Andrew would not know what to ask, and in any case he would believe you implicitly. The vaguer you are, the better."

"Very well." He knew he could baffle Andrew with jargon anytime he felt like it. "I hope you know what you are doing. If you were to change your mind, it would look very odd."

"I shan't change my mind," she said firmly. "If I have to submit to him again, I shall leave him and return to my father. I'd do anything rather than submit."

"Then for your peace of mind I will help you. You may safely leave it all to me."

"Thank you, Doctor."

"You are feeling well, aren't you?" he asked.

"I have never felt better, apart from this one thing which was worrying me. Martin, too, grows bigger and stronger every day. He's a lovely baby." Her expression was radiant as she mentioned the baby, and Dr. Neish shook his head imperceptibly. Sometimes he felt he should have been a vet. People were the very devil to understand.

They had more tea, discussed the Robertsons for ten minutes, and he left to continue his morning rounds. It had all been very easy, Janet thought, with a little twinge of conscience. The feeling soon passed. The animal act was degrading and disgusting, and it was ridiculous to expect her to continue with it any longer.

There was one more hurdle to cross, and it concerned Davie Robertson. She waited till after lunch, one gray November Sunday. Martin was upstairs asleep and she and Andrew sat together by a roaring fire, quietly reading.

"Andrew, I wish to talk to you about Davie Robertson."

"Yes?" he asked cautiously.

"I want to take him away from the office for a while."

"What for?" he asked, surprised by this unexpected request.

"I want to send him to my father in St. Andrews, for

tutoring. I believe that he is intelligent and I know that he needs rest. I think a few years with my father will make a tremendous difference. When it is over and he comes back to you, think how much more useful he will be with a good education and good health. Perhaps he could go to university first."

"Good gracious me," Andrew exclaimed. "Is there no limit to your ambition for this brat?"

"I wish you wouldn't call him that."

"I'm sorry, but I have never forgotten that he once stole from me."

"And paid you back."

"Maybe, but he did not pay the penalty of the law. He is a lucky young scoundrel and I've treated him well. Anyway, why consult me? If your father will take him in, that is hardly my business."

"I was thinking of his employment later on."

"I can't promise him a place in Rowan's," Andrew said quickly. "That's out of the question. I can't see that far ahead. Besides, I thought his mother needed his wages."

"I will make good the loss."

"You must be a rich woman," Andrew said huffily.

Janet thought of the legacy of five hundred pounds that had been left to her, years earlier. It was hardly riches, but it was more than enough for her present purpose.

"I have a very little of my own, and I have no use for it."

"If you would give it to me, I'd soon find a use for it."

"I prefer to spend it my own way."

"Please yourself," he shrugged. "Let's not argue about your little bit. Just don't expect me to provide a job for life for young Master Robertson. If he resigns in order to live with your father, he must take his chances. I shall insist on a week's notice."

"You would, wouldn't you?" she said bitterly.

He was genuinely hurt. "Why not?" he complained. "Is there to be no discipline in that boy's life? Are all the rules governing human conduct to be suspended for him, just because he stole from me? I don't know where you get your radical ideas from, I honestly don't. Not from your father. He's a gentleman."

"And I'm no lady?" she asked, with a faint smile.

"I didn't say that," he apologized. "Of course you are, but you show an unladylike interest in that family."

"I do little enough for them. The girl is dying. I thought that at least would touch you."

He flushed at the implication behind the words, remembering his mother and how Janet had cared for her.

"I help them little enough, Andrew," she continued. "There is very little money in that house. How would you like to try to live on what you pay Davie? Have you ever considered that?"

"No. Nor do I know how I would live if I were a heathen cannibal. Now please, Janet, I do not want to get into a discussion about the Robertsons' finances. They are in the station to which God has called them."

"Yes," she said thoughtfully, "I often hear that said. I wonder if it is true."

"Do you doubt God?" he asked dryly.

"No, but I doubt man, and the phrase is his."

"Does your father know you are a blasphemer?"

"Oh, one can't talk to you," she said impatiently. "It's hopeless."

"You are a strange woman," he countered. "I wish I understood you. Let's not quarrel, please. Do as you wish about Davie but don't ask me to give pledges for the future."

"Very well. I daresay I can find him employment elsewhere when the time comes. You are a fool, Andrew. Do you realize that?"

"Teaching me business now?" he asked patiently.

"It would cost you nothing to do the decent thing," she pointed out, "and in return you'd earn his undying gratitude. You would have an intelligent, devoted employee who would lay down his life for you. I'd call that a good investment. You're always talking of investments. Do you know that that whole family think you are the reincarnation of the Good Samaritan?"

"What on earth are you talking about?" he demanded.

"You gave Davie back his job. You called off the police. You saved him from a house of correction. Even the little bits of money I give them and the things I buy, they assume come with your knowledge and approval. I've never told them I had to blackmail you into doing the right thing by Davie. I've never told them that the few shillings I spend are my own, that they don't come from you. *They think you're next to God,*" she flashed angrily. "Yet you'd throw it away. It means nothing to you. That's why I say you are a fool."

"I didn't know." Indeed he had never given the situation any thought. Davie had been lucky and was appropriately grateful and that was that.

"The world is full of things you don't know, and don't want to know. Stick to business, Andrew, but you know, you aren't really infallible in business either. Otherwise you'd offer to pay for Davie's education and take an interest in him. You'd make sure he came back to Rowan's later on. Well, you've had your chance. We can manage without you. If only they knew what you are *really* like!"

He felt his gorge rising. Women were so stupid and he was tolerant to the point of weakness. If he was going to start educating one child in the factory, then where would it all stop? He couldn't play favorites, particularly when everyone knew the boy had been taken off by the police for stealing stamp money.

How could she reproach him so unjustly? There seemed to be no point of contact between them sometimes—and she looked so pretty when she was indignant. Not pretty, beautiful. He longed to gather her into his arms, to cuddle her close, to kiss that lovely soft mouth—but for a long time their kisses had been chaste pecks.

He let out a heavy sigh and turned to the whisky decanter. He drank a little more than usual these days. Not a lot, because he was abstemious, but sometimes drink was a real comfort to him. As he poured ne heard a sound and turned.

She had gone.

On Monday, October 25, 1875, Aberneist House was ablaze with lights, and a stream of carriages moved up to the front doors. The Cunninghames were giving a dinner party to celebrate Janet's twenty-first birthday. White the butler and Shaw the footman were at the door, taking capes and furs, and in the big anteroom Janet and Andrew were receiving their guests. It was a select, rather than a large, party. Most of the guests were wealthy, influential, and above all useful to have on one's side. There were thirty of them altogether.

The last to arrive was a young man, scarcely older than Janet herself. He handed his cape, gloves, hat, and cane to White and hurried in.

"I hope I'm not late, Mr. Cunninghame," he apologized to Andrew, and Janet wondered who he was. She had never seen him before.

"Not at all, MacRae," Andrew said graciously. "My dear, let me present Mr. Torquil MacRae. He is said to be Scotland's most promising young artist. He is also one of your birthday presents."

"One of my . . .?" She looked puzzled and Andrew smirked.

"You'll understand later," he promised. "I'll tell you at table. It's a surprise."

Janet held out her hand, and MacRae raised it to his lips, smiling at her. He had dark, luxurious hair, was clean shaven, and his eyes were a greeny blue below strong brows. His mouth was wide with a humorous quirk at the corners.

"Mrs. Cunninghame, this is a surprise as well as an honor."

"Then we are both surprised," she smiled. "I had no idea we had invited an artist to dinner."

"And I had no idea that my hostess would look like an angel."

Andrew scowled and MacRae, seeing it, added politely, "I speak as an artist, of course." He was unabashed, however, and his eyes held hers.

Janet laughed delightedly and took his arm.

"Come, Mr. MacRae, let me show you where the punch is."

Andrew walked beside them, nettled and trying to look unconcerned. His unease soon evaporated, for Janet was in great demand and had little time for the disconcerting young artist. During dinner he was so far down the table that she could hardly see him.

It was during a lull between courses that Andrew said to Sir Ezekiel Gabnash, Dundee's wealthiest and most influential citizen, who was opposite him, "I expect you are surprised to find an artist among us tonight, Sir Ezekiel?"

"MacRae, d'ye mean?" The elderly man looked down the table to Torquil with scant approval. "Didn't know you were interested in art."

"Ah, but that is part of Janet's birthday surprise." He turned to her. "Mr. MacRae is going to paint your portrait, my dear, full length, life size. That is part of your birthday present, as I said. They say he is the best portrait painter in Scotland, even though he is so young. Cost me enough anyway," he added with a grin. "Your portrait will hang in this room, dressed exactly as you are now."

"And very pretty, too," Sir Ezekiel said gruffly. "Good idea, Andrew."

Andrew basked in the approval, and the word was passed up and down the table. Janet tried to get a glimpse of Torquil, but he was scarcely visible. She fingered the diamond necklace Andrew had given her that morning, and bit her lip. She had misjudged him. One should never judge people, she thought. They were too full of surprises. Who on earth would have thought that the prosaic, inartistic, coldly calculating Andrew would have had such an idea?

There was some awkward talk about art for a time and then the subject was dropped. After the meal they toasted her, and Torquil, leaning forward to get a proper view of his latest subject, saw her sunniest smile and knew that he could never do her justice. No artist could. There was a quality of serenity, of light about her that was more than mere loveliness. No, this was one portrait with which he could never be satisfied, but even so he was eager to get on with it.

Later she managed to get him alone in a corner where he had been examining an indifferent print on the wall.

"Mr. MacRae," she said nicely, "I owe you an apology. I am afraid I have been so wrapped up in domestic affairs since my marriage that I did not know of your importance."

"I'm not important at all," he laughed. "I just charge a lot."

"Everyone assures me you are the most brilliant artist in Scotland."

"That's because they know nothing of art. Besides Scotland is not rich in portrait painters. I try. We all do, we artists. I've been lucky, very lucky. There are others just as good who are much less fortunate. However this time I shall be inspired by more loveliness than I have ever seen at once in my life."

"I'm married. You shouldn't speak like that."

"Why not? Did you cease to be a raving beauty when you married into dull, drab Rowan's Jams and Marmalades, the best in Scotland?"

"I was always taught that it is impolite to make personal observations."

He laughed delightedly.

"Perhaps so in ordinary life, but I am going to paint your portrait and nothing could be more personal than that. This is one painting that will be greatly admired, that may even make me famous, and that will leave me permanently dissatisfied."

"How dissatisfied?" she asked, sidetracked for the moment.

"Because I can never do you justice. The most unforgettable woman in the world. It is not possible."

"One is almost tempted to think you have been drinking too much," she rebuked.

"Not a bit of it," he smiled. "I do homage where I must. You should see some of the freaks I have agreed to paint. But you will make up for all of that. Do you know what?"

"No."

"Taking money for this is the crime of the century. And now your husband is eyeing me with disapproval. I don't think he trusts artists. Quite right, too."

He kissed her hand, leaving her quite speechless.

SEVEN

IT took Torquil MacRae a mere four weeks to paint her portrait, for he was a fast and inspired artist. During that time she came to know him very well, and to like him. He was full of surprises, and before the first week was out she guessed that he was in love with her, and before the end of the second he had said so.

He was talking idly about beauty.

"You know," he said over his shoulder, "beauty takes so many forms, when one stops to think about it, but the greatest beauty of all is unseen and unspoken."

"What is that?" she asked, interested.

"It's the relationship between a man and a woman who truly love one another. It is without any doubt the most beautiful thing in the world, but unfortunately it is as rare as it is beautiful."

"Are you implying that married people do not love one another really and truly?" she asked, frowning.

"Are you saying they do?" he countered. "Do you love your husband? Don't answer. You're bound to reply that you do. Instead of answering, ask yourself the question quietly and reply to yourself quietly. *I* know the answer."

"How can you possibly?" she retorted, flushing.

"Because love is an understanding that transforms one's entire life. It may come in a flash, or it may take time to grow and mature, but love *is* understanding. How on earth can a clod like Andrew Cunninghame understand someone like you? And as he patently does not, how can *you* love *him?*"

"You seem to imagine you are omniscient, Mr. MacRae." Her voice was cutting.

"No. I love you though, and for that I don't need to be omniscient."

"This conversation will end right here," she ordered.

"Quite right," he agreed with a light laugh, standing back to look at the canvas. "It's awfully bad manners, and I should be horsewhipped, or perhaps drowned in marmalade." He turned to face her, grinning boyishly. "I don't really mean to be cheeky, you know. It's just the light-headed effect you have on me."

She dropped her eyes before his. It was very flattering even if it was all wrong and violated every tenet of social behavior.

"Where did you grow up?" she asked, changing the subject.

"I was born and raised in Glasgow. My father was a chandler who lived in a very solid and respectable house in Pollokshields. I went to school where they didn't know the difference between a paintbrush and a broom."

"What school?" Ever since Andrew had said Martin must go to school, she had been interested in hearing about these institutions.

"I went to Hutchesons' till I was twelve. My father was one of the patrons. Then I was sent to the Grammar School, but I didn't stay there for long. Three years only, for by then I knew I had to paint. My father never understood me, but I was the only son and he indulged me, hoping I'd come to my senses soon and go into the business."

"He is dead?"

"Two years ago, before I began to make a name for myself. Pity he didn't live to see it. I shall make more this year than he ever made in a year. He didn't understand me and he certainly didn't understand painting, but he understood money."

"You don't speak about him with respect."

"Why should I? Artists deal in the truth. He was a rather ignorant merchant who prospered and grew fat, and died of overeating."

"That isn't nice."

"It wasn't," he agreed, deliberately misunderstanding her. "Anyway, his labors weren't in vain, for I now have an income from the business that I own jointly with my married sister, and the world of art in Scotland will benefit because Torquil MacRae is independent. That makes for better art. So, you see, my father turned out to be a patron of the arts in spite of himself."

"What do you charge?" she asked, curious about this aspect of his work.

"Never less than two hundred guineas now. I don't think I'd better tell you what your husband's birthday present is costing, except that it is the highest fee I've ever charged."

Janet frowned. Andrew was not the man to pay over the odds for anything. It would be more in his nature to try to beat down Torquil MacRae's price.

"How did you persuade my husband to pay so much?" she inquired.

"My patron recommended me as a budding genius, which I think he honestly believes I am, bless him. I gave Mr. Cunninghame the impression that I was doing him a favor by painting you at all. Of course, I hadn't seen you then," he added with another grin.

"And who is this wonderful patron, who apparently knows my husband?"

"Stirling of Kippendavie."

"Mr. Stirling?" She blinked her disbelief.

"None other. A man of many parts. So, when young Mr. Cunninghame came to me with his pocketbook bulging, and showed me in two words that he knew nothing of art and that he was merely 'buying a picture' as a present, I decided to act the genius. After all," he explained with a twinkle, "Mr. Stirling may prove to be right about me, in which case you will have a bargain. Future generations will envy your family."

"You are not modest."

"What's the virtue in modesty?" he demanded. "Between ourselves, and this is strictly a lover's confidence, I paint portraits only so that I can earn time off to take my canvas, easel, brushes, and paints off to the coast to paint sea and shore, which is what I really enjoy."

"In other words, I am just your bread and butter," she remarked, smiling at him.

"Say rather marmalade and jam," he joked. "Thanks to this commission I can do a number of things next year. Also, once your price goes up, you keep it up. That's the way of life."

"I didn't realize there was so much money in painting."

"There isn't. Artists are poor. They are poor because nobody cares about art. They want pretty pictures at cut rates." He spoke with quiet emphasis. "I was lucky, but my luck won't last you know. I'll go out of fashion one day and be glad for my share of my father's business. Believe me, I save hard. One day I may need the money."

His talk fascinated her, and she envied his independence. His talk of love embarrassed her, and she was relieved when he did not pursue the subject after that conversation. Shortly before the portrait was complete, at her last sitting, she asked about his sister.

"Her name is Morag, she is four years older than I am, and she is married to an unpleasant character."

"What about your mother?"

"I think I told you; she lives with them. Last I heard, she was virtually locked away in an upstairs room. She drinks, poor old dear—has done so since my father died—and that's the sort of thing you don't want people to know about if you live in a big house in Pollokshields." He spoke mockingly. "I haven't seen anything of them since my father's funeral. They send me my share of the profits and they prefer my absence to my presence. The less said about them, the better."

Janet, brought up by a loving father, surrounded by friends from solid family backgrounds, was both horrified and strangely obsessed by this tale of unnatural relationships.

He changed the subject.

"I'll be able to finish this in a couple of days, without you. If you want a last look before I put the final touch to it, come and see."

She stood beside him and examined the portrait critically.

"It's flattering," she remarked at last.

"I can't let that pass," he told her. "Not flattering. I tried to capture something, and I have partially succeeded. It does you less than justice, believe me."

"I don't go around looking like that," she objected.

"Indeed, no, but sometimes you look almost exactly like that. That's what you're like *inside*."

"I beg your pardon?"

"I'm not just painting an outward likeness. All of us have two appearances. One is the usual face we present to the world, and the other is the face we present when our guard is down. That is when we accidentally let people see what we are like inside. Sometimes when you smile . . . it's not something a man forgets. On those occasions I can see right into your soul, when I know what the real Janet Darling is like."

"I don't understand a word you are saying."

"I think you do. It may be a new idea to you, but I think you understand it." He went off at a tangent, talking to himself. "There's still something all wrong about it. I must go to Paris. I can afford it now. There's a new school there. Perhaps they have what I want."

This time he really had lost her, so she asked.

"Will you paint a portrait of Andrew, too?"

"What? Oh, no, he hasn't asked me. I'm not sure I'd want to. He has been very generous with his money, and I wouldn't like to do him a bad turn."

"What bad turn?"

"I'd have to give him moneybags for eyes and a block of ice for a heart. Seriously, if I painted him it would be a wooden, lifeless image. People who didn't know might say it was excellent, but any artist would look at it and wonder why I didn't paint the real man."

"You love to speak in riddles, and I think you are very rude about my husband."

"Disrespectful, perhaps, but truthful, I hope. I could never paint the real man, only a likeness, and after painting you I'd rather not do that. As I said, it was a good commission. You see, I am grateful to your husband. It's a pity you married the wrong man."

"I had hoped you'd given up that nonsense."

"I don't muzzle easily." He sighed pleasantly. "Well, I can only hope that when your portrait is framed and hung, that you will approve of it, and that you will sometimes remember a man who really does understand and love you. You know what they say in the Highlands."

"No, what?" He had a trick of cutting short the tart rejoinders she intended to make by asking questions that sidetracked her.

"They say 'I place my hands beneath your feet.' I've always rather liked that. My hands are beneath your feet, Janet Cunninghame. Oh, damn the pity of it all!" he exploded in sudden anger. "I wish I'd never come to this accursed house. I've a good mind to take the canvas home and refuse the fee."

"You can't do that!"

"Like hell I can't."

"Don't swear at me." She had never been able to stand swearing. It was one of the few things that aroused anger in her.

"I'm not swearing at *you*, you darling girl. I'm swearing at cruel life, and when I get back to my studio I'll have a real swear, a proper man's one. Yes, I've a good mind to call this whole thing off."

"Please don't."

His temper subsided. "If you say so," he replied, once more mild and bantering. "I'd stand up to your husband and enjoy it, but I can't stand up to you. If you want the paltry thing, you shall have it. It's for you, not for him."

He turned and strode out of the room, leaving her a little dazed and unsure of her own feelings.

During the next few days Janet was fully absorbed with the Robertsons. Janet Robertson was on the very brink of death, and so Janet went to St. Andrews and brought Davie back home with her. She and Davie sat beside the dying girl all one long night, and early in the morning the child slipped away, silently, with no final words. Janet helped with the funeral arrangements and arranged to pay the costs. She returned home exhausted and lay down to rest.

When she went downstairs in the evening, she was not surprised to see Andrew by the fire, having his usual after-work whisky.

"Good evening, dear," she said dully. "I was resting. Janet Robertson died last night."

"I know. I heard. I'm sorry, Janet."

"We knew it was coming," she sighed. "Yet even so, it is still a blow when it happens. Poor child. She never had a chance. If only I'd known them years ago, she could have been sent away somewhere. Sorry, Andrew. What sort of day have you had?"

He pursed his lips thoughtfully. "I don't know. I have to ask you something. Is there anything going on between you and that MacRae fellow?"

"Going on? How dare you, Andrew? Of course not. I find his conversation most unusual, but I've only ever met him when I was sitting for him here in this house full of servants. Why do you ask such a question?"

"I'm sorry," he apologized hastily. "Naturally, I don't suspect *you* of anything. It is simply that something extraordinary has happened. It made me wonder."

"What?" she demanded.

"Your portrait has been delivered. It is in the dining room, ready for hanging. He is refusing to take any money for it. A note came with it."

He pulled a piece of paper from his pocket and read it aloud.

"Dear Mr. Cunninghame, here is the portrait. I cannot accept any fee for this. It is not for sale, but I am prepared to make a gift of it to Mrs. Cunninghame. Sincerely, Torquil MacRae."

He handed her the paper and pulled at his lower lip.

"It's damned impertinence. Who does he think he is, patronizing me?"

"Is it a bad portrait?" she asked.

"It's a simply splendid one, that's what's so odd, that's why I wondered . . . Oh, well, I didn't mean to put it the way I did. I was going to ask him to do me, too, help him along you know. Stirling says he is the coming man in the entire country. And now the idiot is refusing the largest fee he's ever likely to get."

"What will you do?" she asked. The note did not entirely surprise her, although she had not taken him seriously.

"I don't know. I won't part with the portrait. I know, I'll send him a check for five pounds. That will teach him a lesson."

"I wouldn't do that," she warned.

"Why not?"

"Because he says it is not for sale. He'll return the check and come and take the portrait away. He's an unusual man, Andrew. Why not just send the portrait back? Better still, I will."

"No," he disagreed vehemently. "I'm keeping it. I commissioned it and it is morally mine. I'll keep it and I'll spread the word around that his fee was too high and I didn't pay it. And it's true. I'm not going to pay. People will misunderstand and it will lower his price in the market. Stupid nobody!"

"Don't do that, Andrew. Either send it back, or keep it and drop the whole subject."

"You don't suppose this is his way of trying to force me to offer more, do you?" he asked.

She suppressed a smile. She knew exactly why Torquil was refusing a fee. It was all part of this ridiculous idea that only he really understood and loved her. And of course he knew she couldn't give him away. How typical of Andrew to seek the answer in terms of cash.

"He's serious, my dear," she reassured him. "He's a very independent young man making a gesture for reasons which we don't know. If you offer him more money, he may very likely snub you."

"Then he is some sort of fool. All right, my dear, I'll take your advice, but I will tell Stirling this in confidence. He deserves to be told, since he's going about recommending MacRae."

They went to admire the portrait, and when she saw it, she caught her breath. Now that it was completed, varnished, and framed, it was a thing of beauty. Flattering or not, it had life in it so that one half expected the golden woman with the laughing eyes and the divine smile to step out from the frame and speak. She shivered and tucked her arm through his.

"God, it's good, isn't it?" Andrew remarked. "He's clever even if he is a fool who doesn't know on which side his bread is buttered. Now you see why I won't return it to him."

"When we hang the picture, dear, I insist on sitting with my back to it."

"Why?"

"One doesn't sit and admire oneself. The portrait is not really for *me* to stare at."

"You have such good taste," he exclaimed and kissed her forehead. "I hadn't thought of that. And of course if you sit with your back to it one can compare it with the original. Splendid idea."

He had no idea that she did not want to be reminded of Torquil MacRae any more often than she could help. He was altogether too disturbing an influence.

"And to think it's free," Andrew added without warning, a note of amusement in his voice.

She felt a strange pity for him. He knew nothing of the undercurrents. He saw only the surface of things and judged by what was to his advantage and what was not.

"We must talk about Christmas," she said, pulling him away. "I want you to help me persuade Papa to come here and leave his wretched parish for a day or two."

"All right," he agreed readily. "Do you want any help over that girl's death?"

The feeling of pity turned to one of affection, prodded by unrecognized pangs of conscience over Torquil MacRae. Andrew did try. It wasn't his fault that he sometimes failed miserably.

"You are kind, Andrew. Kinder than I deserve."

"Thank you." He looked at her, and she saw an unusual sadness in his eyes. He was reflecting that she was his and yet not his. Anyone seeing her portrait would envy him, but he recalled his lonely bedroom. "I wish you were stronger," he added quietly.

She knew what was in his mind and dealt with it intuitively.

"We must wait and see," she said wisely. "There is lots of time yet."

She knew that it is never good to destroy hope in a man.

Lots of time indeed, he thought. She was only twenty-one and he six years older—but how much more of it was to be squandered in lonely nights?

EIGHT

THE year 1877 was an eventful one in the saga of the Tay Bridge. By now Andrew was obsessed by the bridge. Janet felt quietly scornful about it, not because she knew anything about bridges, but because she heard so much about it at mealtimes that she was tired of what seemed to have been a staple topic for years.

She wished that they would soon start to run trains across the Tay, so that Andrew might find something new to discuss. He had been completely uninterested in Livingstone's death in 1873, cared nothing about the indefatigable work that Miss Nightingale carried on in London, was indifferent to the Court news reported in *The Lady's Newspaper*. Indeed the only thing that had diverted his attention from trains and bridges had been Mr. Lipton's decision to make his own jams. Lipton still sold Rowan's Royal Marmalade, which he could not afford to ignore, but the loss of the jam business to Lipton's shops rankled with Andrew who had seen the Lipton connection as one full of promise for the future.

Martin was now able to walk and talk, and Janet adored him. He had a chubby face, bright blue eyes, and hair as golden as her own. Andrew, surprisingly, found it difficult to interest himself in his son. He was impatient for the boy to grow up, to become recognizable as a male human being. This prattling, gurgling infant might as easily be girl as boy. It was nice to *have* a son, but until that son grew up, he was best left to the women to look after. His own turn would come later.

On Friday, February 2, 1877, Dundee lay snug under gusts of wind and driving rain. It was a typically unpleasant winter's day. At times the wind dropped off, but the sky was threatening and there was no sign of any letup. Toward dusk the wind began to rise again, and as darkness fell, there was a full gale funneling along the firth. Andrew and Janet, warmly ensconced at home, paid little heed to the raging elements outside.

In the morning, however, when Andrew came down punctually to breakfast, Shaw the footman was full of the news.

"We've just heard, sir. Two of the high girders are down."

The center portion of the longest bridge in the world consisted of what were called the high girders, designed to provide a clear channel for ships' masts below.

"Rubbish," Andrew retorted confidently. "That's impossible."

"No, sir," Shaw persisted. "They're down."

"How do you know?" Andrew's confidence was slightly dented.

"The milkman, sir. All Dundee knows. There are crowds out to see it. The milkman saw it himself, sir, and they say someone is dead."

"Very well. I'll have breakfast quickly and be off into the city."

He chewed tasteless food rapidly and hurried off only to find out that Shaw had told no less than the truth. Later, however, when he talked to John Stirling, that older and less easily dismayed businessman laughed it off.

"An accident. Accidents are inevitable."

"But if the bridge was *blown down* . . ." Andrew protested.

"Who says it was blown down?" Stirling demanded. "Andrew, my young friend, you must not repeat stories of that sort. People might believe it, coming from you."

"Then what *did* happen?"

"Who can say? Mr. Groethe will let us know soon."

Groethe was the resident manager of the foundry at Wormit that was casting the girders.

"In fact we have had very few difficulties with the bridge," Stirling added complacently.

Andrew, however, recalled uncomfortable questions that Janet had a habit of asking, and was still uneasy.

"What about that accident in 1873?"

In August of 1873 there had been an explosion when one of the piers was being sunk. Six men had died.

"My dear Andrew, that was nothing to do with the *bridge*. It was some constructional difficulty. It didn't affect the bridge itself. These things happen, you know. Great undertakings are always hazardous. It is the price of progress, and a very low price at that. Now stop worrying."

On the following Thursday, Mr. Groethe, addressing the Glasgow Athenaeum, was able to assure them that the girders were not blown down. The wind had set up vibrations in the uncompleted bridge—he stressed the word "uncompleted" so that there would be no doubt in anyone's mind that, when the bridge was complete, there could be no vibrations. He wrapped it all up cleverly in technical jargon, spoke of loss of equilibrium, of the unusual circumstances, and left everyone absolutely convinced that the bridge was the strongest and most marvelous in the world. He also mentioned in passing, to the relief of everyone, that the cost of the damage was about one percent of the total cost.

When Andrew smugly repeated this last fact to Janet, she stared at him.

"Is that all you think about, Andrew? Money?"

"I merely quote Mr. Groethe. Some people describe this as a disaster. It is nothing of the sort."

"And the dead man? Is he worth nothing? Doesn't he count?"

"The wife will receive help, naturally."

"How nice for her." Janet was rarely openly sarcastic and Andrew glowered at her.

Thereafter the work went ahead quickly, and by September the wonder bridge, two miles long, spanned the mile-wide estuary, a great curving tracery that was at once beautiful and awe-inspiring.

It was decided that the directors of the company should make the first official crossing of the bridge, accompanied by their ladies. Andrew by this time had a seat on the board of the North British, thanks to the influence of his friend Stirling of Kippendavie, popularly known to the lower classes as Old Kippen Davie.

On a bright day, Wednesday, September 26, 1877, the prosperous officials in top hats and fine broadcloth suits, many of them with flowing beards, their ladies' dresses adding a bright touch of color to the scene, congregated to board the special that would take them to Dundee in triumph. On both banks crowds assembled to witness the great occasion.

Janet was perhaps the least impressed of anyone. At Andrew's express command she had brought Martin with her, for Andrew was adamant that his son would be among the first to cross the new bridge. One day Martin Cunninghame would also be a director of the North British, as well as the owner of Rowan's, and he should imbibe his heritage from as early an age as possible.

Janet had not argued, but she held Martin tightly and compressed her lips. The train clacked onto the bridge, and the noise from the rails and sleepers changed, became more menacing. Janet resolutely refused to look down, but Andrew had his head out of the carriage window and laughed when he lost his hat.

"What an achievement," he exulted, turning to Janet and

their friends. "Look down there at the river! Who would have believed that such a thing was possible? Janet, give me Martin."

"No, Andrew! He's a baby. He'll struggle."

"Rubbish." Andrew was insistent and took Martin from her. Martin at once let out a howl of outraged fury. "Quiet," Andrew said absently, and held the child up to the open window. "Look out, Martin. Look out and see what we have done."

Alas, Martin was a disappointment. He struggled and screamed. He let fall no pearls of childish wisdom to be cherished and remembered in later years. Instead he kicked his father in the stomach. Disgusted, Andrew handed him back to his mother.

"Silly child," he muttered, and then forgot wife and son and began to grin to himself as the wind whipped his face and hair.

And so at last they came to the opposite bank in safety.

This journey made up in part for the fact that Andrew had missed the treat at the start of the month when General Ulysses Grant came to visit Scotland, and inspected the bridge. Andrew was away on one of his journeys to the south, to London in fact, and had not been able to return in time.

The former President of the United States of America had not crossed the bridge, of course, but he had crossed the river by ferry, inspecting the bridge from below. Later, after the official luncheon, he had walked out a little way onto the bridge.

It was a great day for Dundee and for the directors of the North British Railway, and of the Tay Bridge Undertaking. Whether it was a great day for General Grant was another matter, for apparently he had had little to say about the bridge, taking refuge in taciturnity.

Andrew hated missing important events, for he felt that it was his duty to be seen at them, among the most important men in the country, in the company where he belonged both by birth and ability. Now he was mollified. He, his wife, and his infant son had taken part in the official crossing.

For Janet the day acquired an unexpected flavor. As they had left their railway carriage, watched by a closely packed throng of people, she spotted one tall figure standing apart, a mocking look in his eyes. There was no mistaking him. It was Torquil MacRae, handsomer than ever. She flushed as he gave her an amused grin, and averted her eyes.

She clutched Martin's little hand firmly and ushered him across the platform. When next she looked back, surreptitiously, MacRae had vanished from sight. Had he ever been there? she wondered fleetingly. Had she imagined him?

She spent the rest of the day wondering about him.

During those years when the bridge was nearing completion, and Janet was preoccupied with Martin, young Davie Robertson and Lawrence Darling had become fast friends. Lawrence had taken an instant liking to the boy, and quickly discovered that he had an alert mind. Davie was no genius, but he would be easy to teach, and he was intelligent. There was much lost ground to make up, and Lawrence set about it methodically and competently. The important thing was to acquire an intimate knowledge of Latin and Greek, which were the basis of all sound education. In addition he taught the boy history, geography, made him read a good deal of carefully chosen English literature, and revealed the hidden mysteries of mathematics. In addition he soon persuaded Davie that the Christian religion, as revealed to the Scottish Episcopal Church, was indeed the true Word of God. Davie abandoned his nominal Presbyterianism without a qualm and in due course became a server in Lawrence's church.

Regularly every second month, Lawrence and his charge would make the long and uncomfortable journey from

St. Andrews to Dundee, crossing by ferry. They would spend one night in Dundee, Lawrence at Aberneist House, Davie with his mother, and return to St. Andrews the following afternoon.

Davie was sixteen now and had grown tall. He remained thin and pale, but Lawrence assured Janet that he was physically strong, ate well, and got plenty of sleep. It was early in the new year of 1878 that Lawrence took up the question of Davie's final education.

"In two years now, no more, Davie will be ready for university. There's no doubt about it. He works hard and well. It would be a waste not to send him. What is Andrew's position in this nowadays?"

"Andrew has no position, Papa. He tolerates Davie, of course, but he has no interest in him. Andrew regards Davie as an eccentricity of mine."

"I'm sorry it's still like that. Such a pity. So it's up to us, is it?"

"It is," Janet smiled. "What do you suggest?"

"Let me take him over completely. I'll prepare him for university and pay the cost. I'll get him into St. Andrews without any difficulty. This will be my contribution. How are the rest of his family?"

"How can they ever be, Papa? I give Mrs. Robertson a pound a week. Incidentally, Andrew knows nothing about that. Three other brothers are working now. One is a railway fireman. They all help Mrs. Robertson, and I've persuaded her to stop working and to stay at home. It was quite a battle, believe me. She misses Davie, of course, though she never complains."

"How do his brothers take it? I've often wondered how they feel about Davie being singled out for attention."

"They're very good," Janet replied. "They accept the fact that he is the clever one of the family, which he is. They aren't especially envious."

When Davie returned from his visit to his mother and brothers, Janet welcomed him warmly. He was gangling, his wrists and ankles too long for his clothing. His hair was jet black, his cheekbones high, and he looked well enough. He smiled shyly at her.

"Well, Davie," she greeted him. "How are they all at home?"

"Fine, thank you, Mrs. Cunninghame. My mother looks just fine."

"My father tells me you are doing well with your studies."

Davie flushed. "I try hard," he answered quietly. "I'll never be really clever, not like Mr. Darling."

Lawrence chuckled appreciatively.

"See how I have him trained?" he joked. "You're a good lad, Davie. Now, let's have a cup of tea, shall we?"

In May of 1878 the first passenger train service across the Tay, over the new Tay Bridge, was inaugurated. It was yet another gala day, and once again Janet and Martin were dragged out to witness the splendid event. This time, Lawrence Darling and Davie Robertson made the crossing, having boarded the train at Leuchars. John Stirling was also on the train, and when it eventually arrived at the Tay Bridge station in Dundee, there was tumultuous applause.

A banquet had been arranged for the more important guests, among them Lawrence and a bewildered Davie. All those with invitations formed themselves into a procession, led by Stirling of Kippendavie. Janet and Martin walked in the body of the procession, beside her father and Davie. Andrew, on the other hand, was up in front, walking beside the chairman of the Tay Bridge Undertaking—a man he did not greatly admire, knowing as he did that without John Stirling and the North British, there would have *been* no Tay Bridge Undertaking. His dislike did not mar the occasion for him. People were not there to be liked, but to be weighed with a view to ascertaining their usefulness to him. He was more interested in the pleasurable fact that he was just behind the only man he truly admired, Stirling of Kippendavie.

Among those watching this procession of privilege was a faded woman who was the wife of a railway fireman. Her name was Kirk, and she was pregnant, but she struggled to maintain her place in the forefront of the crowd. She loved pageantry, and she gazed admiringly at all the gentry.

Suddenly she found herself looking into a pair of gentle blue eyes, and her mouth dropped open as she stared at Janet. Never, she thought, had she seen a lady so truly lovely. She nudged a neighbor.

"Who's yon?" she asked. "The bonny young one. Do you know her?"

"Aye." Her neighbor stared at Janet and sniffed. "Yon's Rowan's Jam. Mistress Cunninghame, if you please." Her voice dropped, conspiratorially. "That'll be her father beside her. One o' they English ministers."

Margaret Kirk ignored the disapproval. She had no theological partisanship. So this was the young leddy of Rowan's. All Dundee knew of Rowan's jam. She studied Davie and Martin.

"They're not both her bairns, are they?" she asked.

"No," the other woman scoffed. "She's only the one. That'll be the wee yin. I've nae idea who the stooky big laddie is. Some friend maybe."

They had passed now. Margaret Kirk resumed her study of the rest of the procession, but when she went back to her own humble home, to await the return of her husband, she kept seeing the bonny young leddy.

There was not one jot of envy in her: just admiration.

NINE

BY the time young Martin was five, in the mid-summer of 1879, Davie Robertson had become a bit of a problem to the perplexed Lawrence. Davie was quite happy to go to university, and indeed seemed eager to get there, but he had absolutely no idea about his own future.

"The only thing for it," Lawrence confessed to Janet, "is to send him there, let him read the classics, which is the best training in the world for almost anything, and hope that, by the time he has taken his degree, he will have decided."

"He's a solitary, lonely boy," Janet said thoughtfully. "At university he will at least mix with others his own age, and it will be good for him. You'll see, Papa, it will turn out all right."

"I hope so." Lawrence sighed. "I hope so. It's strange how one becomes so wrapped up in other people. That boy means so much to me now."

Janet gave him an understanding smile. It simply did not occur to her father that he, too, was lonely, his wife long since dead, his daughter married and living in Dundee, and that Davie had filled a real gap in his life.

"I'm very grateful to you, Papa. You know that."

"No need to be, Janet. It was pure self-indulgence. Tell me, how is that husband of yours?"

Andrew, as usual, was absent at business.

"Very well. I expect you've heard that the Queen is

going to return to Windsor from Balmoral via the new
bridge, instead of going through Perth? Andrew is over his
head with joy. I think he expects to be presented to her."
"He's an ambitious young man. He'll go far, you'll see."
"He already has," Janet remarked. "Sometimes he fright-
ens me a little. He's always talking about John Stirling; oh,
yes, and that man Lipton. Lipton is a hero to him. I've never
even met the man."
"They say he is a business genius."
"No doubt that's why Andrew is so taken with him," she
agreed wryly.
"Andrew is no fool. I've been offered a hundred and
thirty pounds for every hundred pounds I invested. Of
course I'm not selling. The North British is far too good
an investment and only an idiot would sell railway stock
at a time like this—at least N.B. railway stock," he concluded with a rueful smile. "You see? Andrew has con-
verted me. I now worship Mammon in my spare time,
and study company reports, although I confess I rarely
understand anything in them."
"As long as you're happy," Janet replied, squeezing his
hand.
They walked in the garden until teatime, when Davie
came back from a visit to his mother, and Martin was
dressed and brought down for his birthday tea. Andrew had
promised to be home in time for it, so they waited.
Eventually they could wait no longer, and they had the
tea without him.
By Martin's bedtime, Janet was feeling distinctly
annoyed. She tucked Martin into his bed and kissed him.
"Mama, where is Papa?" he asked sleepily, for it had
been an exciting day for him, with special treats at lunchtime and teatime, and lots of expensive presents. "Why
hasn't he come?"
"He has to work for us, darling, to pay for everything.
You know that."
"But it's my biffday," Martin pouted. "You told me he
would come."

"Shush. He'll make up for it when he sees you in the morning."

Martin looked into her eyes for a moment, and then smiled happily.

"I don't mind. I like you better," he said.

Janet shook her head, kissed him again, and left the room quietly. Still Andrew did not come home, and finally a messenger arrived with a note saying that he would not be back in time for dinner. They dined without him, and Lawrence and Davie went to their rooms. After ten o'clock, Andrew arrived, a little flushed and pleased with himself. He kissed Janet's cheek and headed for the decanter.

"What made you so late?" she demanded.

"Sorry, my dear. I had a meeting with John Stirling, about Her Majesty's visit. She is going to stop briefly in Dundee on the way south from Balmoral. I'm to be on the platform with Stirling. Just think, I may be presented to her."

"Oh, Andrew," she complained, "can't John Stirling arrange these things without your help? It was Martin's birthday."

"Sorry, but he's only five. I don't suppose he minded much. He'd be more interested in his new toys."

"That's not the point. You promised. You should never break a promise, especially to a child."

"I didn't know then that I was going to meet Stirling. We had a lot to discuss."

"More important than your son?" she insisted.

"Look here," he countered irritably, "you're the boy's mother. You're supposed to look after him while I'm working. You don't expect me to retire just because we've got a son, do you?"

"No, I don't, but what work are you talking about? So far as I can see, all you did was to persuade your fine friend Mr. Stirling to have you on the platform when the Queen comes. That's not work, Andrew."

"It is. Don't forget that I have the royal warrant."

She shook her head. Hundreds of other people had it, too,

but Andrew regarded it as a personal matter between himself and the Queen. She supposed he was now angling for a knighthood, although on what grounds he hoped to get one, she could not imagine. For services to marmalade, she thought with a flash of humor.

"You'll have to make your peace with Martin in the morning then. He was upset. And Papa and Davie were hoping to see you this evening. I suppose you'll be going to work early as usual."

" 'Fraid so. Busy day tomorrow."

The incident was soon forgotten, and when the inevitable happened, and the Queen *did* stop on the platform at Dundee for several minutes, and Andrew *was* among those presented, he came home so full of boyish glee that she felt a sudden softening toward him. He did try so hard, she reflected, and she was not really very sympathetic. Poor Andrew. Martin was too young to interest him, and she had resolutely kept him out of her bedroom and refused to take an interest in his factory—what else was there for him but work and ambition?

After dinner she came and sat on the arm of his chair, and stroked his head in an unfamiliar gesture. He looked up at her, surprised.

"Something wrong?" he asked.

"No. I was thinking about you; about us. I'm not a particularly satisfactory wife."

He took her hand and squeezed it gently. "What nonsense. If you're talking about sleeping apart, Dr. Neish explained it all to me."

"You're a patient man, and a good husband, and I do nothing for you."

"You run the house and you bring up Martin. What's wrong with that?" He was intrigued by this new behavior.

"I could hardly do less. Andrew . . ." She swallowed bravely and her voice did not falter. "Do you really want to come back to my room?"

"You know I do, but it's out of the question."

"Not anymore, it isn't. I've seen Dr. Neish again, and he says it's all right now."

"*What?*" He sat up with a jerk, his hand tightening on hers. "You told me nothing about this."

"I wanted to surprise you."

She did not understand why she was making this sudden, compulsive gesture, except that she knew she had held him at arm's length for too long, and she wanted to make amends because the faults lay with her, not with him. Other wives treated their husbands better.

"Janet, my dear." He got to his feet and drew her to him and kissed her. "I really am the most fortunate of men. I don't understand it at all."

Dr. Neish had been wonderfully vague and Andrew had been rigidly polite, so that the whole conversation had been as obscure as Neish intended it to be.

"I think Martin should have a brother," she said softly.

It was only as she spoke the words that she formulated the desire that had been growing in her subconscious. A psychologist might have ventured the opinion that she knew deep down that Martin would be taken from her in a few years' time, and that she hungered for another child to take his place. The psychologist would probably have been right. Janet merely knew that it *would* be nice to have another baby. This, in conjunction with her feelings of guilt about Andrew, made her steel herself to the ordeals of the marriage bed once more.

Andrew kissed her even harder, his moustache prickling. "How lucky I am," he repeated. "First Her Majesty, and now this. I scarcely know what to say."

"Why say anything?" she asked, taking his hand. "Shall we go up?"

The next six months saw their relationship enter into a new and happier phase. Surprisingly, she did not find his presence in bed as repugnant as she had done before. He failed to inspire her, of course, but he no longer distressed her. She accepted the situation stoically and he, realizing

that there was an undefinable change for the better,
became more happy and content than he had been since
their wedding day.

Christmas that fateful year passed quietly. Davie spent it
with his mother and Lawrence spent it in bed with a nasty
cold. Martin also had a cold, so they were unable to visit
Lawrence at the rectory.

Andrew had to go to Edinburgh on the twenty-seventh,
but only for one night. It was arranged that Lawrence
would join the train on the Sunday evening, and travel to
Aberneist House with his son-in-law. Accordingly, on Sunday, December 28, Lawrence Darling, still nursing his
cold and still worrying about his flock, left to the tender
mercies of a young curate borrowed from another parish,
waited on the platform at Leuchars.

The train steamed into the station, a squat engine pulling five coaches behind it, and a brake van. One of the
coaches was first class. Locked into a compartment by himself, Andrew sat in solitary state, as befitted a director of
the railway company. Lawrence found him and the door
was unlocked by a porter who saluted them respectfully.
They all knew Mr. Cunninghame on this line, for he took
considerable interest in the railway.

It was a wild and stormy night, but locked inside their
first-class compartment, the two men were snug and comfortable. Up front, on the footplate, was Daniel Kirk, a
fireman who had joined the train at Burntisland, on his
way home after a Sunday duty. He chatted to his two
friends, the driver and the regular fireman.

"What a night to be out in," Kirk grumbled as a gust of
wind hurled itself across the platform.

"A good night to be home," the driver agreed. "And
that's where we'll all be soon, Dan. We're running to time,
storm or no storm."

"I'm starving," Kirk remarked. "I'll be glad o' my supper. I wonder what she'll have ready for me."

A moment or two later the driver opened the regulator.
and the train drew out slowly, gathering speed. They

clickety-clacked on through the darkness, seventy-five men, women, and children, all looking forward to reaching Dundee and getting home out of the storm.

In their compartment Lawrence and Andrew were chatting.

"How is Martin's cold?" Lawrence inquired.

"It's all right now. Janet fusses over him—like the good mother she is. Can you believe it, sir? Martin is five and a half. Yet when I look at Janet it seems like only yesterday I met her at that birthday party at Whinbriggs."

"Are you both happy?"

"Yes." Andrew's sincerity was patent. "Very happy."

"I'm glad about that. I'm looking forward to this visit. A whole week. It makes up for not being able to take the Christmas services this year."

Sometime about quarter-past seven, the little train passed the signal cabin on the south bank of the Tay, traveling at a walking pace, and then entered on the two-mile-long bridge, standing high over the river which was hidden from view by the darkness. The wind howled and tore at it, and in the engine Daniel Kirk shouted to the driver, "This one beats all. If that wind were behind us, we'd be in Dundee ten minutes early."

The driver turned and grinned, his face reflected in the glow from the firebox. As he did so, the wind lifted the train clear off the rails and threw it against the high girders. Sparks flew from the wheels, there was a screeching of tortured metal, the gale gusted; and between the wind and the momentum of the train, the high girders suddenly began to collapse.

One moment the sturdy little engine was pulling its coaches across the waiting cold waters below, next moment the whole thing was collapsing into the storm—girders, train, coaches, everything. The time was approximately seven twenty in the evening.

With a triumphant howl, the gale hurled itself through the gap where the spidery high girders had been.

Where now there was nothing.

TEN

A T Aberneist House, Janet Cunninghame waited patiently for Andrew and her father to arrive. The train was due at Tay Bridge Station in Dundee at seven thirty. They should be home before eight. Eight came and went but there was no sign of them.

At eight thirty, Janet sent Shaw the footman to the station to find out if the train was canceled or running late. At nine, Shaw returned as white as a sheet.

"Well?" Janet asked without premonition. "No train?"

"No, ma'am. No." He spoke in a whisper.

"What's wrong, Shaw?"

"It's the train," the miserable footman blurted. "They say it's gone down. The bridge has gone. There's a great crowd at the station."

"The bridge has collapsed?"

He nodded. "And the train on it."

"But nobody can be sure of that, Shaw."

"It's what they say, ma'am. There's crowds of people there."

She clutched at his arm nervously. "Shaw, please go back and find out all you can. Find out for certain."

"Yes, ma'am. Can I take Mr. White with me?"

The butler would be a wiser head, Janet thought. "Do that, please, Shaw. Hurry now."

The confirmation came quite soon. The train had entered

the bridge, the bridge was down, and the train had not emerged from it. The broken stumps of bridge had been clearly sighted, and the only place the train could be was on the bed of the river.

When Janet heard, she fainted. The cook was summoned, a motherly soul who gathered up her mistress and sent the others scurrying for hot toddy, smelling salts, and blankets.

"My God," White muttered, standing by, helpless for once, "her father was on the train, too, along with the master."

The cook glared at him. "Mr. White, if you don't mind, go and see that that stupid girl is making tea as well as boiling water for the toddy. Off with you."

White nodded and left the room miserably. As he crossed the hall he was startled by the sound of the doorbell. He answered it and saw Davie Robertson and his mother on the step.

"Has Mrs. Cunninghame heard about the disaster?" Davie asked anxiously.

"Yes, sir. Come in, please." He held the door and Davie and his mother entered and began to take off coats and hats.

"I came as soon as we heard," Davie remarked. "My mother will be able to help. Where is Mrs. Cunninghame?"

"In the drawing room, sir, with cook. She took a turn."

"Come along, Mother."

They found the cook trying to persuade a dazed Janet to lie down. Davie ran to her and seized her hand.

"It's me, Davie."

"Davie?" She blinked stupidly. "Where's the train, Davie?"

Davie's eyes filled with tears and Janet, seeing them, remembered it all too clearly.

"Oh, God, Davie," she whispered. "Is it true, then?"

He could not reply. He was sobbing like a child. They

clung together, weeping shamelessly, until the hot toddies arrived. After a little time Janet's sobs ceased, and she stroked the youth's head absently and even smiled wanly at Mrs. Robertson.

"You shouldn't be out on a night like this," she said.

Mrs. Robertson could only shake her head silently.

"Thank you, cook," Janet said, turning to the elderly woman. "Will you please get tea and something to eat for Davie and Mrs. Robertson? Have it sent in here, please."

"Yes, ma'am. The kettle's on for the tea. Ma'am, the servants are awful sorry."

"Thank you, and thank all of them for their help, please. Oh, and see that Shaw gets a hot drink and anything he wants to eat. He'll be cold, poor boy."

When they were alone, she got up and clung to Mrs. Robertson for a few seconds. The older woman was shattered. To Mrs. Robertson, Janet Cunninghame was an angel. She worshiped her, prayed for her nightly, would have died for her. Now she was powerless to help. What sort of fate was it that took a husband and a father, both, on the same night?

In the end she persuaded Janet to go to bed. It had been arranged that she and Davie would spend the night, and rooms were got ready for them. At last silence fell on a stunned household.

The following morning they were astonished at the change in Janet. Somehow or other, during the long agony of the night, she had conquered the fierceness of her sorrow, and found strength to face the world. She was white, dark smudges under her eyes, and subdued; but she was able to supervise Martin's breakfast.

"Where is Papa?" Martin demanded. "Where is Gampa?"

"They couldn't come last night," Janet told him with icy calm. "They'll come later, I expect."

Martin digested this news in silence and then gave a bright smile. "Will Davie read me a story?"

"I expect so. Will you, Davie?"

"Yes," Davie agreed, hoping he sounded normal. "I'd like to."

"Goody."

Martin's day was made for him. If he wondered why Mrs. Robertson was at table with them, he did not say so. He tended to accept things without too many questions.

After breakfast, Janet took Mrs. Robertson on one side. "There's something I'd like you to do for me."

"Anything at all, Mrs. Cunninghame."

"I want to go and find out exactly what happened last night. Could you and Davie take Martin home with you, and keep him today? He'd love it. Only, try not to say anything in front of him."

"We'd be delighted."

"Thank you. There is a lot to attend to. I don't know all what, but there will be funerals to arrange, and I must see our solicitor and visit the factory. There are a lot of things."

"Don't try to do too much."

"I must. I'm in charge now—till Martin is a man."

In the event, she did not have to trouble herself about funeral arrangements. Some twenty-nine bodies were never recovered, and indeed it was a very long time before many of the others were found. Among those who simply disappeared that awful night, lost in the relentless maw of the River Tay, were the Reverend Lawrence Darling, Andrew Cunninghame, Esquire, and Daniel Kirk, a railway fireman.

By March, Janet had brought some semblance of order to the family's affairs. She had had no trouble with Martin, who had taken the news of his father's death very quietly, not fully comprehending it, but reassured by the fact that he was at home in familiar surroundings with his mother.

Andrew had made a will in which he left his personal fortune outright to Janet. This consisted mainly of shares in the North British Railway, plus Aberneist House. The family business had been left to her in trust for Martin, with a number of safeguards to prevent her from selling it. If anything happened to Martin, she would become the outright owner. When Martin was twenty-one, control was to pass to him. It was an unusual will, for not only had he left Rowan's in trust to her, but he had made her sole executor, which gave her a tremendously free hand, provided she did not try to sell the firm or try to change its nature.

Janet, of course, knew she would need all the help she could get, and had no intention of throwing her weight about. Her main concern, at first, was that everyone should carry on with their jobs, exactly as before, and she saw the general manager, the works manager, and the accounts manager and told them so. For the moment they were to report to her regularly, and that was all.

In addition to Andrew's stock, she also inherited her father's North British shares. She supervised the removal of all his effects from the rectory, said good-bye to his friends, and sat down with her solicitor. The result of that particular meeting was that she sold all her shares. This was not because she had any reason to suspect that they might be a bad investment. Certainly the bridge disaster had done them no good, but they were expected to recover quickly. The solicitor would sell at the most propitious moment. Her motive for selling was simply that she had had enough of North British.

She decided to shut up Aberneist House, and found a house to rent just south of St. Andrews. She had one or two personal friends left there, and she had happy memories of her youth. She saw the Dundee staff settled in other jobs, taking a lot of trouble to see that they found what she considered suitable places.

Janet was now a wealthy woman. Her shares were nominally worth some fifty thousand pounds, and when they were sold were expected to realize more than this. The income from Rowan's was now close on a thousand pounds a year, and the firm was flourishing.

The money did not mean much to her. She had never known what it meant to go without, but by the same token she was utterly devoid of any love of money for its own sake. She took hardly any interest in it, except when she was pursuing one of her many small charities.

Before she left Dundee for St. Andrews, she had a talk with Davie who was staying with his mother for the time being.

"Davie, what do you really want to do when you finish at the university?" she asked.

"I really want to go back to Rowan's," he said diffidently.

"You *do?*" She was pleased. "But that's wonderful. I'd like you to come back. First of all, however, I want you to get your degree. Then I'll find a place for you in the factory. You will be my eyes and ears inside the company until Martin is old enough to come and work there himself, and learn all about how to run it. I really am pleased, Davie."

"I always did want to go back."

"Then that's settled. First you have got to work hard at home. You've got all your books there now. I'll make you an allowance of fifty pounds a year, and of course I'll pay your university fees once you're admitted."

"Fifty pounds?" Davie's jaw dropped at this munificence.

"Yes, and I think perhaps I'd better give your mother an extra half sovereign a week, too. I can afford it easily enough. So you will stay here in Dundee until the next university session starts. We'll meet often when you come to St. Andrews, and you must come to me at weekends when you can."

"I don't know how to thank you, Mrs. Cunninghame."

"I think you'd better call me Aunt Janet, don't you? Of course, I'm not your aunt, but we've been friends too long for you to go on calling me Mrs. Cunninghame."

"Er . . . yes, Aunt Janet."

"That's better. Off with you now."

There was so much to do these days, she thought. Time

seemed to fly past. A few days before she was due to
make the move to St. Andrews, she had a caller. The
name meant nothing but she asked for the woman to be
shown in. A careworn youngish person was her first impression, and she noted that, although she belonged to the
poorer sort, she was clean, neat, and tidy.

"Mrs. Kirk, is it?" she asked pleasantly. "I don't think
we've met before, have we?"

"No, ma'am. I saw you once."

"Really? What was it you wanted to speak to me about?"

Margaret Kirk, overawed by her surroundings and this
serene, clear-eyed girl, began to wish she had not come.
It had been an impulse inspired by the memory of a face
in a procession, the face of someone who might understand and who might help. She fidgeted and Janet, watching
her, recollected with startling vividness how Davie's
mother had sat in that very chair many years ago, under
what seemed to be identical circumstances. What now?
she wondered. What did this woman want of her? Nothing
to do with the factory this time, she hoped, for she did
not wish to interfere in its affairs so quickly.

"My husband was on that train. He was coming home
from Burntisland. He worked on the railway, you see."

"I'm so sorry, Mrs. Kirk."

"I've got the one bairn, a wee girl. There's no money."

"Have you had nothing from the fund they raised?"

"A little, but I don't want charity, ma'am. I want work."
She paused. "I wondered if I could do anything in your
house." Margaret Kirk's accent was fairly broad, although
she was trying hard to "speak properly" as she put it to
herself.

"Here?" Janet asked, raising her eyebrows.

"Housework's all I know."

"I'm sorry, Mrs. Kirk, but you see I'm closing up this
house and moving to St. Andrews."

The woman's face fell.

"I just thought," she said miserably.

Janet frowned. She had a good idea of what life had to

offer to the widow of a railwayman, with one child to bring up. Charwoman, washerwoman, long grueling hours for a pitiful reward.

"What is your daughter's name?" she asked, mainly to give herself time to think.

"Helen. She's not two yet."

"Helen Kirk. That's a nice name. Have you no kinsfolk in Dundee, Mrs. Kirk?"

"Only my husband's brother, and he's out of work."

Janet was silent. All her sympathy was aroused. She *did* have some responsibility, she thought. After all, Andrew had been one of those behind the bridge, as well as a director of the railway for which Margaret Kirk's husband had been working when killed. No doubt the bridge would have been built and fallen down, whether Andrew had existed or not. That, however, was not the point.

"I don't know what to say," she remarked. "I don't even know you."

"I can get a character from the minister, ma'am," the woman said eagerly. "I never miss church when I'm fit to go."

Janet smiled involuntarily. She was being trapped. Was she herself not the daughter of a "minister"?

"I tell you what then. If you are prepared to come to St. Andrews with me, I'll give you a trial. I need a housekeeper. You could bring Helen along, and she would stay with us. It isn't a big house I've taken, only about half the size of this. Would you come? I can offer board and lodgings, working clothes, and thirty pounds a year. Of course Helen would be fed free in the servants' hall."

"Och, Mrs. Cunninghame, do ye really mean it?"

"You bring me that character and the job is yours. We move in three days."

"Oh, please, ma'am, thank you."

The woman's agitated gratitude surprised even Janet, who knew very well that she had offered Margaret Kirk a plum job for anyone in her plight.

"Bring Helen to see me when you come back with the line from the minister."

"I can get it tonight. Will tomorrow morning do?"

"Yes," Janet laughed. "After nine o'clock, if you don't mind. Can you settle all your affairs in three days?"

"I could settle them in three hours," was the reply.

What a stupid question that had been, Janet thought. There would be little enough to settle, even less to pack.

"Good. Now I'm going to send for tea, and we can have a nice talk together and I'll explain what I want you to do, and you can tell me about your husband and your family. I don't know anything about you yet."

As she got up to ring the bell, she realized that she enjoyed playing the god in the machine. There was something dangerously satisfying about being able to transform other people's lives. She stood with her back to Margaret Kirk, her eyes tightly shut.

"I must be very careful," she said to herself sternly. "This costs me nothing, and I must *not* begin to feel virtuous about it. This *is* *nothing*, Janet Darling, do you hear? Nothing. You needed a housekeeper anyway. You've just saved yourself a job."

She let out a gentle sigh, and when she turned to the waiting woman her smile was serene.

She had put the devil behind her.

PART II

The LOVER

1880–1918

When even lovers find their peace at last,
And Earth is but a star . . .

J. E. Flecker,
"The Golden Journey
to Samarkand"

ELEVEN

THE house that Janet had rented stood in isolation about three miles southwest of St. Andrews, a plain building but comfortable to live in, easy to manage, and with nice, tree-lined grounds where Martin could play in summer. It was called Braefoot and, true to its name, stood at the foot of a small, tree-covered hill.

Life was dull, predictable, stultifying, but it was also soothing and peaceful. Time seemed to stand still, and she was happy in the company of Martin, who adored his mother. She missed Andrew dreadfully and suffered agonies of guilt when she thought back over her years with him, but as the weeks and months passed, she thought less and less of the past.

It had been her intention to rule Rowan's by remote control, and for the first six months she received regular visits from Neil Skimming, the general manager, and from Hugh Stevenson, the accounts manager. They found her difficult to satisfy, because she had an inquiring mind. Eventually Neil Skimming put the case to her bluntly.

"Mrs. Cunninghame," he said in his heavy, ponderous voice, "I think it's time somebody told you that you've got to come back to Dundee for a few weeks. You don't even know what the factory looks like! Either leave the running of the business to me, or come and sit behind your husband's desk for a bit and see what goes on."

Janet bit her lip and before she could say anything he went on: "Stevenson and I appreciate what you're trying to do. You're trying to keep control without interfering. But don't you see, if you're going to do that, you have to know all about how we operate?"

"I hadn't realized," she apologized contritely. "I must have made things very difficult for you."

"Not for us so much as for yourself. For instance, although I think you trust me, you don't really see what I mean when I say I can't get away from my office to do the sort of sales promotions Mr. Cunninghame used to do."

Janet flushed. This was true, but she had hoped it was not obvious.

"Very well," she agreed. "Please book Martin and myself into a hotel, and arrange for a temporary nanny to look after Martin while I'm at the factory. We'll travel next Monday."

"Thank you," Skimming said with sincerity.

The day after her arrival back in Dundee, Janet walked into the sprawling factory and was shown upstairs to Skimming's office.

"Welcome to Rowan's," he grinned delightedly. "I've had Mr. Cunninghame's office dusted and tidied. I've made a diagram of the factory layout and had some notes prepared. I thought you could study them this morning, and when you're ready we can do a preliminary tour."

"That's very kind of you," she told him. "Shall we get started?"

He left her in Andrew's office and she stood by the heavy desk and looked all around. This had been the center of his life.

On the desk blotter was a diagram and a folder which presumably contained all the notes. She turned the chair to look out of the window and noticed a heavy framed document with a coat of arms on it, hanging on the wall. She got up to inspect it.

The arms were the royal arms and under them were the words "Lord Chamberlain's Office."

She recalled Andrew showing it to her years ago in St. Andrews. This had been the crowning achievement of his life.

It was an eerie sensation to stand there looking at Andrew's prized possession and to think that he would never see it again. With a little sigh she turned to the diagram and notes.

In the days that followed she was astonished at how much there was to learn, and how little she knew of Andrew and his family. She had not known for instance that his grandfather, Dugald Cunninghame, had been quite a wealthy man before getting into the jam business. Apparently the family had owned a quarry in Perth, and had prospered, but the quarry was about worked out and Dugald had been looking for a new outlet for his capital when he had heard of James Rowan who was selling marmalade from his grocer's shop to help increase his turnover.

It was Peter Proudfoot, the works manager, a fierce Old Testament figure with a white spade beard, who told her all about it.

"Aye," he said in his broad Dundee accent, "auld Jimmy Rowan was the genius. Mrs. Rowan made the stuff in jeelly pans, but it was auld Jimmy who knew exactly what quantities to use and how to make it set best. Rowan's was the first real jam factory in the world, you know. Jimmy Rowan was called the jam master, and that's what the works manager has been called ever since."

"What happened to the Rowans?" Janet asked.

"He died. They had no children, and they had to get another jam master. They engaged my father, and when he retired I took over."

"And will your son take over from you one day?"

"Not a bit of it," he said proudly. "He's studying to be a doctor."

She had wanted to know where the marmalade was being made.

Proudfoot shook his head. "Not at this time of year,

Mrs. Cunninghame. This is the jam season. The whole
thing is seasonal. As one fruit goes out, another comes in.
This is no the marmalade season—except of course for
lemon and ginger marmalade which we make all year
round, to fill the gaps, ye ken, but they're no big sellers,
no like our Rowan's Royal."

This, she discovered, was made out of bitter oranges
from Seville and Malaga. She decided that when the marmalade season started, she would come to see the process.
Apparently in a three-to-four-month period they had to
make their whole year's supply, and judging the quantity
had been one of Andrew's strong points, for he knew
with uncanny accuracy how much he could sell. There was
no one to take his place at the moment, and it was
expected that they would run out, but that was preferable
to overproducing.

Proudfoot was a mine of stories. He told her that when
Dugald Cunninghame had opened his first small factory he
had built it next to a cloth factory so that he could pipe
off the used steam to heat the copper preserving pans.

He also told her how marmalade got its name, when in
1561 Mary Queen of Scots sailed to Scotland. Her doctor
made her a mixture for seasickness, made mainly from
oranges, and it had been named the *mer-malade* mixture.

"What an interesting story," Janet said, delighted.

"Aye. Pity it's no' true."

"It's not?"

"It's just one of those stories. They say it really gets its
name from the Portuguese marmelo. That's a quince."

"I prefer Mary Queen of Scots," Janet said firmly.

"Nobody can prove it's wrong, I'll say that much," the
jam master chuckled.

During those weeks of learning, she came to know
every part of the process. When the fruit was unloaded
from the drays, it went for sorting and preparing. The
difficulty of this varied with the fruit, blackberries in particular being fiendish things because they arrived on
branches, and all the little stalks had to be removed by

hand until only the berries remained. Raspberries were far easier. Then the fruit was cleaned and went into the big building where the fruit was weighed meticulously and tipped into the copper pans.

Here Peter Proudfoot's expertise came into full play. He not only supervised the quantities of fruit and sugar being used, and watched the cooking time to make sure that the fruit was cooked exactly as he wanted, but he had another mysterious function. It was Skimming who explained it to her, not Proudfoot.

"The man's a genius," he told her as they sat in the office drinking tea. "This business of setting. Every fruit has its own setting properties. It's a thing called pectin in marmalade, and if the pectin content is low you can put in lemon juice to help it set better. Now if you put in too much, you get the taste of the lemon juice. Peter Proudfoot knows exactly how little he can get away with so that he gets the best setting without spoiling the taste. It's an art, believe me."

"He's an important man, then," she said lightly.

Neil Skimming took the remark seriously. "The most important man in the business. A good jam master is worth his weight in gold, and there aren't many of them about."

The factory was highly labor-intensive and employed mostly women and girls. Later generations would have called it sweated labor but in fact Rowan's paid better than most people, and took an interest in the staff. Janet realized just how lucky Davie Robertson had been to be given the job of tea boy. Apart from clerical staff, the only men were employed in unloading the drays, or in stores and dispatch where they had to manhandle the wooden crates of jam. It was strength that was needed. She began to perceive, dimly, why Andrew had been so furious about the petty theft.

Her favorite pastime was to stand and watch the women capping the bottles when they had been filled. A round, greaseproof disk was placed on top of the jam, and then a circle of parchment was put over the mouth of the jar, pulled down and tied with string, and the edges of the parchment trimmed. The women's fingers seemed to fly as they deftly capped bottle after bottle at a remarkable rate. Janet found it a fascinating sight, for some unknown reason, and the bottling and labeling sections were where they usually found her if they were looking for her.

Stevenson assured her that Rowan's was prospering of its own volition. No doubt the rate of progress could be forced, but times were good, turnover was increasing, and so were profits. They employed over three hundred people, but they had virtually no labor problems.

When Janet finally returned to St. Andrews with Martin, she felt she understood the business at last. There was a lot to learn, but now she understood, and in doing so, she began to understand Andrew—too late.

After that summer Martin was sent to a select little private school in the town. Janet had done a good deal of investigating before deciding that he would come to no harm in Dr. Craig's establishment. It was not quite what Andrew had intended, but it was a good compromise.

Martin loved it because now he met other small boys and made lots of friends. Every morning he set off in the pony and trap, returning at midday with his books and some homework, for Dr. Craig believed that even the smallest and youngest boys should get what he called "the homework habit." It was good for their character. Work, after all, was what life was about.

Margaret Kirk had proved an excellent housekeeper and took almost all the load from Janet's shoulders. She controlled the other servants without difficulty or fuss and anticipated Janet's every need.

Davie Robertson became a regular visitor to Braefoot, during term. In vacationtime he went to Dundee to his mother, but during term he would arrive at weekends, and he and Janet attended church together. He had begun to fill out now and was no longer the skinny, gangling youth he had been such a short time ago. He had good color, laughed a lot, and there was an air of competence about him which Janet appreciated.

One warm summer day, in 1882, two and a half years after the awful Tay Bridge disaster, she sat out in the garden, under a large tree, reading *The Lady's Newspaper*. Martin was visiting a small friend in the town and would not return home till after tea.

Her glorious golden hair was piled high on her head, and she wore a new-style dress with no bustle, cut on the cross to fit smoothly over her hips. Her picture hat and parasol lay on the grass by her feet, and she was totally absorbed in reading an account of a visit to Miss Florence Nightingale, now in her early sixties and still leading a frantically busy life, though reputedly a sick woman and a recluse, who never stirred from her home in South Street in London.

She looked up as the maid crossed the lawn toward her. "You've a caller, ma'am. A gentleman."

"Who is it, do you know?"

"A Mr. MacRae."

"*MacRae?*" She stared. "Well, send him out to me, Elsie."

She felt a flutter of excitement. After all this time Torquil MacRae had turned up again. She had not seen him since . . . when? She remembered. It was the inauguration of that wretched bridge, and she had glimpsed him standing a little apart from the crowd. Four years ago!

Her lips were parted and her eyes bright as she waited, and when he came out of the side door and began to walk toward her, she stood up, smiling. She missed no detail. He was smart in a gray frock coat with silk lapels, a flower in his button hole. He was tanned and his hair was still thickly luxurious.

He approached her with an easy stride, returning her smile, and took her hand and raised it to his lips.

"I hope you don't mind my calling."

"Goodness, no. Do sit down. You have hardly changed. Browner, that's all."

"I've been holidaying. What of you? I can't say you haven't changed, for you have."

"Oh?"

"Yes, you're even lovelier. I didn't think it possible."

"Now I hope we are going to have no more of that nonsense, Mr. MacRae."

"Torquil, please. You forget that beauty is my business. Besides how can the truth be nonsense?"

"Where have you been. I haven't heard of you at all."

"That's a blessing. You'd hear nothing to my credit."

"What do you mean?" she asked anxiously.

"I've been in Paris. Learning to paint."

"Learning to . . . *what?*"

"Learning to paint at last. I've been with Claude Monet, Pierre Renoir, and Alfred Sisley. Especially Alfred Sisley who taught me how to paint landscapes and seascapes. Then I spent a little time with an American artist called Whistler. I tell you, I've lived at last. And then to Scotland where I am regarded as a charlatan."

"But why? I don't understand a word."

"I'm an Impressionist," he said excitedly. "All those years painting *maps* instead of pictures. How can I explain, Janet?"

His enthusiasm was infectious and she leaned forward.

"Listen," he said. "When you look at someone, you get an *impression*. You see form, color, beauty, or ugliness as the case may be. That's all you see. When you get up close and examine them, you notice lines, wrinkles, details, folds in clothing, and so on. That comes on examination. It's not what you normally see. Do you follow me?"

"I think so," she said doubtfully.

"I wish I could show you Renoir's *La Loge*. You'd understand then. It's beautiful. It's real. It's *art*. It's not a blasted map of people."

"I still don't understand what the trouble is."

"Because here in Scotland nobody wants to know about it. They want every detail in a painting and you are judged by the amount you can cram in."

"Is that bad, then?"

He stared at her. "Yes, because you lose the impression in getting the detail."

"Isn't it possible to do both?" she asked innocently.

He stared and then laughed. "I can see I shall have to educate you."

"What are you doing, then?"

"Painting for myself. Nobody will touch my paintings."

"No more portraits?"

"Nobody wants an impression. They want their . . ."

". . . Maps," she said simultaneously, and they both laughed.

"Yes," he agreed. "Luckily I am independent. My sister and her husband sold up and went to Australia, taking my mother with them. My share was quite substantial and I had a lot saved. I manage very well, thank you."

She considered him. He was changed in one way. There was a fire in him now that had not been there before. It was concealed behind that rather bantering manner, but it was unmistakable.

"This new sort of painting, it's important, isn't it?"

"My God, Janet, I wish I could find words."

"I'd like to see your work."

"You shall. That's a promise. I think you are the one person who might understand."

She did not pursue the topic. She was satisfied. Something of tremendous significance had happened to him, and it was something good, whatever the critics might say.

"What brought you here today?" she asked, turning to something she could understand.

"I wondered if you'd ask that. I always wanted to come, once I heard about your husband's death, but something stopped me."

"What was it?"

"I wanted to forget you. At least, I *hoped* I would *learn* to forget you. You never encouraged me, and there was no reason to believe you would want to see me. You see, Janet, I've loved you all the time. I love you more than ever."

"Oh, dear," she sighed.

"Am I so repugnant to you?"

"Torquil, I'm a widow with an eight-year-old son."

"Granted, but what has that to do with anything? If I remember correctly, you're a year younger than I am. You're still in your twenties. Life isn't over yet. Is one not permitted to love a young man just because she was married before and has a child? Is there some Scottish tribal taboo against it?"

"It isn't seemly," she said hesitantly, knowing that the words were idiotic.

"It wouldn't be seemly for us to fall into one another's arms on the strength of meeting today," he agreed, laughing. "However, I can wait. I'm rather good at waiting."

"How did you find me?" she asked, trying to think of some way to turn the conversation.

"I went to Dundee, discovered the house shut up, and dropped in on the royal marmalade manufactory. A man called Skimming gave me your address."

"Where are you staying?"

"Nowhere. My luggage is at the railway station at Leuchars. I'm on my way back to my Glasgow studio, but I was hoping you'd invite me to spend the night."

"Well . . . yes, if you wish." She hesitated only momentarily. "I'll send someone to collect your things and bring them here."

"Thank you, Janet."

She wondered if she was being wise.

TWELVE

HE was very patient with her, for he realized
that she was not the sort of person who could be pushed
into anything. All that warm, sunny summer he kept coming back to St. Andrews, usually to stay for one or even
two nights, and gradually she began to feel that she knew
him properly.

Martin adored him. He was acutely aware of the fact
that, unlike other boys of his acquaintance, he did not have
a father, although he knew that once he did have one, and
sometimes even thought he could remember him. Torquil
spent a lot of time with the child, taking him to the sea-
shore, walking on the moors with him, playing childish
games, and showing him innumerable tricks with bits of
string.

Early in September they went to Lower Largo together,
Janet and Martin staying at a boardinghouse while Torquil
rented a nearby cottage. Martin was provided with a pail
and spade, a magnificent model yacht, and he and Torquil
went along the beach looking for crabs which they collected in the pail, and then turned loose later on. Martin
was in heaven. Soon he found two or three friends his
own age, and Torquil encouraged him to play with them.
He and Janet went for walks around the bay, or sat quietly
on Kincraig Point, looking out to sea. The weather obligingly held good and Janet had a flush on her cheeks.

They were sitting on the point one balmy afternoon when she tried to express her thanks.

"You're so good to us, Torquil, especially to Martin. I wish I knew how to show you how grateful I am."

"No need for that, my dear." He smiled, his teeth gleaming whitely against his deeply tanned face. It struck her, not for the first time, how handsome he really was.

"Martin's at an age when he needs an older man," Torquil went on. "Boys do, you know, even if it's only to show them how to open up a mussel, bait a hook, pick up a crab without getting nipped, and little things like that. Most of them learn from their fathers, of course."

"Did you?" she asked.

"No. My father didn't believe in holidays." He laughed. "That's probably why I have so much sympathy for Martin. I used to go away with a school friend and his family, and every year, for a fortnight, his father became my father, too. God, how I loved that."

"Poor Torquil," she murmured.

"What about you and me?" he asked. "We go back to St. Andrews in two days, and then I had better go back to Glasgow and put in some working hours in the studio. I have a number of things to finish—although as nobody ever buys my paintings now, I don't suppose it matters very much."

"I don't believe you care about work," she chided.

"I don't. *But* . . . painting isn't work and I do care about it. If we painters only painted when we had customers, there would be precious few works of art. I paint because I must, and sometimes I love it and sometimes I hate it, but always I care about it. Janet, why won't you marry me?"

"I don't know. I really don't know, Torquil. I'm not sure if I love you."

"You mean, you didn't take one look and gasp for breath like a silly schoolgirl? Like I did when I first saw you on your twenty-first birthday? That isn't necessary. Love comes in many forms."

"It's not like it was with Andrew," she said reluctantly. She rarely mentioned Andrew's name to him.

"But of course not. He turned your head. You were young. And it didn't turn out like you thought it would, did it?"

"No." They had discussed this once before.

"Now you are confused, and a little frightened, because you don't want another disappointment. You *were* in love with Andrew, and the marriage wasn't a success. You don't feel the same way about me, so how can it possibly be any better? Don't you realize I'm not Andrew, that I'm not married to a marmalade factory, that I live only for you?"

"Where *would* we live?" she asked, her resolve weakening.

"Anywhere you like. I'd like to have a house with a decent studio. There's rather a nice one by Maxwell Park in Glasgow, which I've had my eye on for some time. It's expensive but worth it. Of course if you prefer to stay here, that's all right by me."

"I wouldn't want that," she contradicted quickly. "I wouldn't want to stay in St. Andrews or to go back to Dundee. I'd want to make a new start."

"You are being wise. We can go anywhere in the whole wide world."

"I'd rather like to live in Glasgow, for a time at least. After all, it's where you come from."

"It's not a bad spot. Pollokshields is almost like the country. Sometimes in winter the pond in the park freezes over and there's skating. Why don't we give it a try? You've nothing to lose, really—not like other women."

"Why do you say that?"

"Because if it didn't work well, I'd go away and leave you in peace. You've got far more money than I have. You are independent. Even as my wife, you would be free."

The concept of free wives was a strange one. She turned his words over in her mind. She liked him enormously.

She missed him when he went away. This holiday had been heaven . . . and there was Martin.

"You'd really go away if I said I wanted you to?"

"Naturally." He sounded surprised. "What good would it do me to insist on staying on where I wasn't wanted? None at all. I'm not a bully, Janet, just someone who loves you more than anything in the world."

"How can I keep refusing?" she asked softly, blushing.

"Ah." He put his arms around her and drew her toward him. His kiss was light, sexless, and curiously comforting. She made no movement to resist. "Darling Janet," he whispered. "You won't regret this, I promise you that."

She pulled back and gave a shaky laugh. "I was getting tired of living alone. It isn't very amusing being a widow."

They kissed again, more passionately this time, and sat silently in the warm sun, arms around each other, and she waited for the turmoil of her emotions to subside. When it did, she became aware, with wonderment, that she was happy—so happy that she felt it physically, as one feels pain or hunger.

Martin, who had grown tired of playing with his young friends, and who guessed where they would most likely be, came upon them unexpectedly.

"Hullo," he greeted them, his eyes curious.

"Hullo, Martin," Torquil answered conversationally. "Guess what! I'm going to be your father."

"That's good," Martin said calmly. "Can we catch some crabs and play with them, please?"

Torquil let out a happy shout of laughter. "That's what I call encouragement. Yes, my boy, we'll catch some crabs. Come along, Janet darling. First things first. Let's fill Martin's pail with lovely big crabs."

The three of them walked back to the shore together, hand in hand.

They were married very quietly in Glasgow. Once the decision had been made, they wasted little time. He quickly purchased the house he had spoken about, a fine, red-sandstone mansion with a splendid, big, glass-topped roof studio which caught all the light. The servants from St. Andrews were sent to get it ready for them.

Janet was discovering things about him almost daily —some small, some more important. For instance, he changed the name of the house to Conchra House. When she asked him why, he explained, "Because my name is MacRae."

"What is the connection?"

"You Lowlanders. There are two lots of MacRaes, the MacRaes of Inverinate and the MacRaes of Conchra. I'm from the latter tribe."

"Where is Conchra?"

"Up in the northwest, by Kintail, not far from Eilean Donan Castle. Very picturesque country up there. I must show you a few paintings I did when I belonged to the map-making school of art. My grandfather was born in Kintail, but he moved south where the money was, poor deluded man."

"Why deluded?"

"Chasing after money. He'd probably have been far happier crofting. So far as I know, he never actually went hungry. He didn't have to move south, like some of them who were dispossessed during the clearances. Anyway that's why my house is Conchra House."

Some of the gaps in her knowledge of him were far more significant. The question of where they would marry inevitably arose, and she asked him which church he attended.

"I don't go to any. That sort of thing is not for me. You choose one."

"You've been to church with me in St. Andrews," she protested.

"That's different. On my own I never go. I gave it up years ago. But I don't in the least mind getting married in one and if you want to go on Sundays, naturally I'll escort you."

"What are you officially?" she asked.

"I was baptized into the Scottish Kirk, but I have never

regarded myself as belonging to any special brand of religion. I rather like the Episcopal service, as it happens, but don't ask me to believe in it. I mean, if God has nothing better to do than to listen in to millions of church services, it must be very boring up there in Heaven among all the angels."

"Do you believe in God?" She felt it was important to find this out.

"Oh, yes. I see him everywhere around me when I'm painting sea- and landscapes. I'm afraid I just don't paint churches."

"I wonder if I will ever understand you, Torquil."

"Dearest, there is undoubtedly a god, but I have no idea of what he is like. I don't believe that any one religion, or any one sect of any religion, has exclusive knowledge of God."

She was a little disturbed for, although she frequently harbored doubts about the things she had once taken for granted, doubts she did not like to admit to, she remained staunchly true to the faith of her fathers. Torquil put an arm around her and hugged her.

"You mustn't mind me, my dear. I can't tell you a lie about my beliefs. The religion I see around me was made by men, and they squabble over it endlessly, turning God from a great universal being into some sort of petty tyrant, in whose name they commit endless crimes. That's no good to me, though it seems to satisfy most people. I have to follow my own road, wherever it leads. I promise to come to church with you as often as you like. I really don't mind at all."

"You mustn't come if you don't want to," she said quickly.

"When you love someone, you want to share with them. Loving is sharing and understanding, and a few other nice things. I'll keep you company and who knows? One day some of it may rub off on me."

She knew with certainty that it would not, that he had thought out his position carefully, and she sensed that he might very well know far more about religion in the general sense than either she or her father. She did not mind. Something startling was happening to her. She was falling rapidly in love with him, and it was a deeper, happier love than she had felt toward Andrew at the time of her first marriage. And so they were married in an Episcopal church, with only a handful of people present, and Davie Robertson was Torquil's groomsman.

They did not go away for a honeymoon but moved directly into Conchra House after the wedding. After their few guests had gone, they had an early supper and then sat in the drawing room before the blazing fire, while the cold October rain pattered on the windowpanes.

Janet was silent. The moment she dreaded was approaching, all too quickly, and she was honest enough with herself to admit that one of the reasons she had held him at arm's length for so long that summer was the knowledge that marriage would lead to this. She shivered as she imagined his body bumping up and down on top of hers in the joyless, rather ridiculous, act of mating. How many children would he want? she wondered. Pray God not many and that she would conceive quickly.

Torquil, who had an almost feminine instinct in many ways, had a very shrewd idea of her feelings.

"How about a game?" he said brightly. "Dominoes. Do you play?"

"I used to."

"On a night like this, before the fire, there's nothing like a game to amuse one. I'll get them."

They began to play and soon he had her laughing and relaxed. The time flew by and she was astonished when he suddenly said, "Midnight. Time we went to bed. Fine way to behave on a honeymoon. Come along, darling. You must be as sleepy as I am."

He was so normal about it that she forgot to be afraid. They went upstairs arm in arm, and he talked aimlessly about the garden, which needed attention, and about a summerhouse, which it seemed was something he had always wanted.

Inside the bedroom he kissed her warmly yet tenderly, and went off to his dressing room. She took a deep breath and went into hers. It took her a long time to undress and put on her nightgown, and to brush that wonderfully thick, lustrous, blazing gold hair. This time no one came to see what was delaying her, and reluctantly she went back into the bedroom.

He was sitting up in bed, reading. He smiled and put down his book.

"The bed is lovely and warm, and comfortable, too. Hop in. Plenty of room for two."

Somehow he knew the words to reassure her, and she climbed in shyly. He put an arm around her and kissed her, dropped a hand to her breast and felt her go rigid.

"A lovely wedding day, darling," he murmured, ignoring her response to his caress. "I'm so happy. In fact I'm willing to state that I am the happiest man in the world."

He kissed her again, a longer kiss, and then turned and put out the light. She slid down in the bed, and he followed suit. He lay by her side, gently cuddling her to him. After a few minutes she gave a happy little sigh and snuggled closer to him. This was something she *did* enjoy.

She fell asleep almost at once.

THIRTEEN

WHEN he was just nineteen, Torquil MacRae had had his first real introduction to sex. He had been befriended by a thirty-five-year-old artist, Bernard Bull. Bull, wiry, bearded, with dark eyes and an effervescent spirit, was a man at war with his times. He had not yet discovered Impressionism, but he was intensely dissatisfied with the schools of art that flourished in Britain at that time, particularly the Scottish school. His art was consequently inarticulate, but it had an originality of its own that other artists belittled, as they belittled anything that did not conform to their own homemade rules.

Bull waged a friendly war with his fellow artists, mocking them, receiving their nasty remarks calmly, and continuing his search for a new form that would give freedom to the expression that was bottled up inside of him.

He sensed a kindred spirit in the young Torquil and took him under his wing. Torquil began to spend a lot of time at Bull's studio, and it was there he met Jennie Miller. Jennie was a professional model, one of very few in Glasgow. She was thirty and had been modeling for fourteen years. She had a magnificent, generous body—indeed it was her principal stock in trade, that and the ability to remain still for long periods.

Jennie was an easygoing woman, happy to associate with artists whom, for some mysterious, unknown reason, she admired as she admired no other men, and she was usually kept by some artist or another. At the moment she was between artists and had been wondering how to get some response from the businesslike Bernard. She had spent a few months with him a few years previously, but he had gone off painting nudes then, and she had moved on. Now, perversely, he did not seem to be interested in her other than as a subject. The introduction of Torquil, young, tall, good-looking, with thick dark hair, a good mouth, and a ready smile, took her breath away. When she learned that he was a painter, too, she took a deep breath and prepared to go into action.

If Torquil was taken aback at the sight of this lush nude sprawled invitingly on Bernard's couch, he hid the fact well. He said "hullo" to her when introduced and then inspected the canvas. It shocked him. Although in its early stages, the form of the nude was clear. It was grossly exaggerated in all its sexual attributes.

"Bernard, you can't do that. It's indecent. They'll throw you in jail."

"In this town, I don't doubt it. Don't you see what I'm after?"

"No, and neither will anyone else. What are you doing anyway?"

"When we paint nudes, we lie about them. We shade off the top of their thighs, we drape them, or we give them pale nipples, or shadowy breasts, and the faces of angels. Don't you see, our nudes are so damned dull you can show them to children!"

"Yes." Torquil nodded. He had often thought that nudes were about as uninteresting as any painting could be. They never had character.

"So I am trying something different. I'm exaggerating, I'm painting in detail, and I'm turning that pert, come-hither face of Jennie's into something that's saying, 'Don't just stand there and look at me. Get on to the couch.' "

There was a silence. At length, "Well, if you go to jail

for indecency, don't say I didn't warn you. Originality is one thing, but nobody will stand for this."

"Hey, Jennie, he says you're indecent. Come and look," Bernard called.

The model hopped off the couch and stood between them. She slipped one hand around Torquil's waist, without looking at him, and studied the canvas.

"Christ, I look like a whore."

Up to that moment, Torquil had never heard a woman swear, nor ever expected to. He felt bewildered and even more so when her hand dropped a little and squeezed his buttock.

"He's a bloody awful painter," Jennie went on lightly. "I'm not indecent, am I, Torquil?"

She stepped back and he turned and studied her frankly. He saw the bright eyes, the amused expression on the pleasant face, and the glorious body that had, in truth, been disguised in a hundred paintings, watered down to socially acceptable anonymity.

"No," he said seriously. "Not at all."

"How would you like to paint me?" she invited, and Bernard chuckled.

"I don't paint figures. I've been trying my hand on portraits and a few landscapes and seascapes."

"Time you learned. Have you a studio?"

"I share one."

"Then why don't you wait till Bernard has finished, and you can take me to your studio and show me your work."

"All right," he agreed, fascinated by her. "I'd like that."

It was there, in an empty studio, that they made love that afternoon, on the couch. He was inexperienced—she infinitely experienced. She let him romp over her like an eager puppy, and when he had exhausted himself, she drew his head down on to her breast and told him, "Whether or not you paint nudes, you know nothing about love, Torquil."

"Did I do something wrong?" he asked, surprised.

"Just about everything, and I'm going to teach you. And the first thing I'm going to teach you is that I am a woman, a person, I have feelings and emotions, and I'm not just here to please you. You have to learn to please me, too. That's lesson number one. I'm not a crotch and a pair of tits. I'm me, Jennie Miller. Now you just lie there and I'll bring you on again and then I'll show you one or two things about how to enjoy your loving."

They made love four times, for he was young and his strength untapped, and he went home late, dazed, incredibly at peace with the world, and determined to get a studio of his own as quickly as possible. Meantime she would arrange to use Bernard's couch when he was not working.

The affair lasted seven months. He did try painting nudes, but not even Jennie, whose body he worshiped, could inspire him in that direction. Nudes as paintings gave him no artistic satisfaction. Because he was young, ignorant, intelligent, and always ready to learn, she taught him not only how to make love to a woman in every mood, but how to understand women. Perhaps there was a feminine streak in him, perhaps it was aptitude pure and simple, but he was a good pupil.

He was sorry when she moved on, and he missed her terribly for a long time, so much so that he had had few encounters with other women, and nobody had been able to arouse the innate tenderness and understanding in him till Janet came into his life.

It cost him a real effort of will to let Janet go to sleep on their wedding night, but he knew that Jennie would have approved. After all, he was going to be married to Janet for a long time, so it was worth a little trouble at the outset to get on the right footing.

Janet did not know—indeed never learned—anything of Jennie Miller, and next morning she was oddly disturbed after a restful night's sleep. He was out of bed when she awoke, and when he came out of the dressing room and saw her sitting up, he greeted her cheerfully.

"Good morning, darling. Sleep well?"

"Yes," she said, and he bent over and kissed her.

"Good. I expect you were tired after the wedding. I know I was. I'm just going down to attend to one or two things. I'll see you at breakfast when you're ready."

He kissed her again and went out, leaving her to get up alone, and wash and dress. She ought to have been delighted at her good fortune in being married to such an understanding man, but instead she was uneasy.

Didn't he want her? Did he find her unattractive? He had put his hand over her cloth-covered breast, but that was all. Nothing else. Perhaps he didn't want any children—but didn't he even want her? It wasn't flattering.

She was confused all day, and when they went to bed earlier, she was rather relieved when he showed more interest than on the first night. He kissed her passionately and ran his hands over her body, under her nightgown. She shivered but did not flinch. For a long time—it seemed a lifetime—he kissed and stroked her, murmuring endearments in her ear, telling her how beautiful she was. She relaxed at length and ran her hands over his face and cuddled up to him, and began to return his kisses.

It was with a start that she realized that he had parted her thighs and was stroking her between her legs. Andrew had never done that, not ever. She controlled herself with an effort. It was his *right*; and she had to admit that nobody could be more gentle. It was to be a night of surprises for her. She felt him under the sheets, pulling up her nightgown, and then his lips on her breasts. She stared into the darkness, totally unprepared for these new experiences. Once more, after a time she found she was enjoying this peculiarly intimate form of caressing, so gentle, so pleasurable.

Until . . . A strange new sensation fired her loins. She had never known this before. She began to struggle, but he had her firmly pinned and his lips and hands continued their soft, cunning exploration, and she reached her first climax without knowing what on earth was happening to her. All she knew was that she wanted it to go on forever, and she flung her arms around him and began to make passionate little sounds. She was almost relieved when he mounted her and ever so gently entered her. The whole act was a long, reassuring experience. There was no fierce, animal thrusting—just a steady rhythm that kept her at a peak of desire until with a great shudder they climaxed together and lay, perspiring and happy, until he was unable to remain inside her, and dropped to her side.

She had no coherent thought at all, just a wonderful feeling of peace. She felt him put his arms around her, and turned readily to face him. His mouth found hers, and she put a hand on his face again and stroked his cheek lovingly.

"What happened?" she asked dreamily.

"We made love."

"I didn't know . . ." Her voice trailed away, and he knew that his suspicions of Andrew Cunninghame were well founded.

"Why didn't we do that last night?" she murmured.

"You were tired," he prevaricated. "I thought it would be nicer to wait."

"You're considerate."

"And you're beautiful. That was the most wonderful thing in the world," he lied, hoping Jennie would forgive him. One day the words would be true, but what he had just gone through had shattered him. On the other hand he had succeeded in doing what he guessed had to be done.

Sex had been something to be endured, and he had had to change that so that it was something she welcomed, wanted as much as he did. He had been a good pupil. He knew how to make a woman wild for him. He had been prepared to take a lot longer, but he was lucky. It had worked on the second night.

"You know," he murmured in her ear, casually, "these dreadful nightgowns are a nuisance when we're making love. Why don't we leave them off in future—until we want to go to sleep anyway?"

She blushed in the darkness, remembering things she'd rather forget. This was different. After a silence she whispered, "Anything you say, darling."

He kissed her, and there was a look of triumph on his face, masked by the dark. He had won the battle, and he knew it. It would be all right. It would take time to teach her all that Jennie had taught him, but time was plentiful. The main thing was that he had got through to her.

His last thought, before he fell asleep, was that Andrew Cunninghame must have been the biggest fool on God's earth where women were concerned. So it was that in the twenty-eighth year of her life she took her first lover, who happened to be her second husband. The thought was to amuse her frequently in later life.

One of their first joint problems was Martin's schooling. Torquil had positive ideas on the subject, and she was a little apprehensive about them. He wanted to send the boy to Hutchesons' School, where he himself had received his primary education. The school, which in recent years had been housed in Crown Street, had been a secondary school since 1876, following the introduction of free state primary education in Scotland.

"It's one of Glasgow's best-loved institutions," Torquil told her quietly. "My father was a patron incidentally. Now Martin can stay at Hutchie right up to the end, without having to leave and go to the Grammar School, as I had to do. He can get his complete education in the one school."

"I'd like to visit it," she said.

"And so you shall. I'll arrange it."

He did so, and they walked over what was at the time considered one of the best school buildings in a city where education was in itself a religion. There was an imposing, ornate front entrance, leading to a towering hall, with a broad staircase leading upstairs. At the foot of the staircase was a board with the names of all the school duxes on it. Janet wanted to know what a dux was.

"The top boy. The cleverest one. It's quite an honor, you know. The dux used to be enthroned after the annual procession. I'm afraid you won't find my name there, darling, but Martin's may be one day. Not that that matters, as long as he turns out intelligent."

They were interviewed by the forbidding rector in his study, and when they left Janet was reassured. Martin, it seemed, would not be torn limb from limb, corrupted, bullied, or subjected to any of the horrors that still ran right through the English public-school system, and of which she had heard quite a lot.

The rector, a brilliant classical scholar in his own right, came as close to making a joke as he ever did.

"Any bullying and tearing limb from limb that takes place here, Mrs. MacRae, is done by me. As for corruption, there is none."

One could not imagine it daring to rear its head in *his* school.

It was arranged that Martin would be admitted at once—mainly because of Torquil and his father. The name MacRae was not without some honor in Hutchesons'. Martin was duly kitted out and sent off to school.

Before long she came to love Conchra House. It was an easy house to manage and run, spacious, even a little gracious, and it stood in charming surroundings. Maxwell Park also fascinated her, with its trees, its large pond, and its peace and tranquillity.

Most important, however, was the fact that she was in love, not as a girl but as a mature woman. Torquil continued to exercise self-control and skill in order to draw her out until, after a few months, she was eager for their physical encounters, remarkably well-versed in the varieties of sex, considering her social class and the period in which she lived, and far more responsive to him than even Jennie Miller had been.

One evening, when they were relaxed in each other's arms,

lying naked on the bed with the light on, enjoying one of those delicious moments of contentedness that follow the physical expression of a love that is real and enduring, she whispered, "Darling, I can't think why you haven't beaten me. Lots of husbands beat their wives, don't they?"

He chuckled. "I really don't know. Why? What have you done?"

"Well, you have loved me for so long, and I kept you waiting, and frankly I was dreading this bit of our marriage. You knew that, didn't you?"

"I guessed. So, you really are in love with me, aren't you? It shows in so many ways."

"What ways?" she instantly wanted to know.

"It's hard to explain. It just shows. I don't just mean in bed at night, but the way you look at me, sometimes, the way we touch hands. It just shows, Janet. It was worth waiting for you."

"Suppose I'd refused you, what would you have done?" she teased.

"Painted and pined, I daresay. Of course I'd have stayed in love with you. I don't think I'd have considered marrying anyone else. It happens like that sometimes. You fall in love with someone you can't marry, and you simply have to endure the situation."

"How horrible."

"I daresay I'd have had a few mistresses, but they would have meant nothing."

"*What?*"

"I am a man, after all," he pointed out.

"Have you ever had a mistress?" she asked. She felt alarm at the idea of him behaving like this with another woman.

He had anticipated this question and knew how he intended to deal with it. It was one case in which a lie was far kinder even than an evasion. The truth would serve no good.

"No," he replied easily.

"Would you really have taken one if I'd refused you?"

"Why not? It's like, um, like taking a bath. You have to do it sometimes."

"I believe you mean that," she exclaimed.

He hugged her. "Let's stop worrying about mistresses. Only remember, my love, that men who for any reason cannot marry, or whose wives are invalids or something else is wrong, do have to do something about it. They say that in France mistresses are all the rage."

"We are not in France, Torquil MacRae," she said firmly.

"No, my dear, and the question of a mistress does not arise, does it?"

He lay still, holding her to him, until she dropped off to sleep. Gently he disengaged himself, pulled up the bed-clothes, and turned off the light. In the dark he smiled to himself. She was a delightful person, and he loved her a little more with each passing day. Then a less pleasant thought crossed his mind.

What if he ever *did* take a mistress? How would she react? There was a tough streak in her character that rarely showed openly, and which was at variance with her serene tranquillity, her air of gentleness.

He put the thought firmly from his mind.

Shortly after this, Martin got into serious trouble for the first time in his life. He had never given Janet a moment's uneasiness. It was not that he was goody-goody or namby-pamby; rather that his misdemeanors could generally be dealt with by a warning. He had his mother's happy disposition and liked to please people.

He had settled happily into school life, and he had one or two friends of his own age who lived around the Maxwell Park area.

Janet was crossing the hall one afternoon when the doorbell rang. She answered it herself to see a scowling, well-dressed man and two boys, one of whom was Martin.

"Excuse me, madam, but are you this child's mother?" the man asked, pushing Martin toward her.

"I am, and please don't push him."

"If he were mine I'd do more than push him. I'd thrash

him so that he'd never forget it," the man replied calmly.
Janet frowned. "Please tell me what has happened," she
asked.

"He's been tearing branches off the trees in the park,
that's what. I happened to pass nearby and I saw the
branches on the ground and the scars on the trees. These
two boys were arguing. This other child saw him do it and
was trying to stop him."

"That's right," the other boy said quickly. "He did it.
He broke them off."

Martin looked sullen, his lower lip thrust out, and Janet's
frown deepened.

"I see. Thank you very much. My husband and I will
deal with this."

"Good afternoon," the man answered, and turned and
walked off, the other boy following him jauntily.

Janet took Martin into the drawing room, and sat down
while he stood in front of her examining the toe caps of
his boots.

"Well?" she asked.

Martin shrugged. Janet's eyebrows went up. This was certainly not a typical reaction.

"*Did* you break the branches off some of the trees in
the park?" she demanded.

Once more, an infuriating shrug.

"Have you no tongue in your head?" she asked him
sharply.

When he kept staring silently at his feet, she became
angry. "Do you realize how wrong it is to treat a tree like
that? You're almost nine years old now. Do you think
that God made beautiful things like trees so that stupid
little boys could go about tearing the branches off them?"

She got up after a moment. Torquil was in the city shopping for some artists' materials, and she was not going to
dodge her responsibilities by letting this wait Torquil's
return.

"Stay where you are," she said in an angry voice, and
went into the kitchen. She returned with a cane carpet

beater. "Bend over that chair," she told him, and Martin did so silently.

She set about thrashing his backside with the beater, using considerable strength. After a couple of minutes she had to stop. Martin was white-faced with pain, and biting his lip hard. Janet stepped back, breast heaving.

"That was not just for wanton destruction. It was for your insolence in refusing to answer me. I will not tolerate insolence from you. You will go straight to your room and stay there. You will have nothing to eat or drink until you apologize to me."

"I'm sorry," he cried. "I didn't want to be insolent, Mama."

There was a surprisingly genuine ring to his wail, and she studied him. "I hope you mean that, Martin. I really do. I can't imagine what has got into you. Go to your room until it's your teatime."

"Yes, Mama," he said quietly, and went out.

She sighed and took the beater back to the kitchen, and sat down and puzzled over the odd incident. When Torquil came home, she told him all that had happened.

"You seem to have dealt with it very well," he remarked thoughtfully, "but how unlike him. Shall I speak to him?"

"I don't want him to think he's being punished twice," Janet warned. "Be careful what you say, darling."

"His tea is almost ready, isn't it? I'll go up and chat with him for a few minutes and bring him down."

He climbed up to Martin's bedroom and found the boy lying on his bed with a ferocious scowl on his face. Torquil sat on the big easy chair near the bed and cocked his head on one side.

"Look, Martin," he said gently, "it's all over now. I only want to know if there is something troubling you. We all do silly things at times, but dumb insolence to your mother is something I'd never have expected of you. Is anything wrong?"

"No, Papa."

"Are you sure?"

"Yes, Papa."

There was something odd in his tone of voice, something Torquil could not quite place.

"Very well, then," he said cheerfully, and stood up. "Let's go down together. Your tea is almost ready. The matter is closed."

Janet and Torquil discussed it again at dinner that evening, after Martin had gone to bed, both still mystified by some of the aspects of the incident.

The following morning was a Saturday. Torquil was working in his studio and Martin had gone out to play. Janet decided to walk in the park by herself. She had reached a far corner when she heard scuffling behind some bushes and left the path to investigate.

She stopped in her tracks when she came upon Martin and the other boy of yesterday's incident locked together on the ground. They had not heard her approach. Martin was on top and he was thumping the other boy with a will. The child's nose was bleeding and his face bruised and grazed. Janet's impulse was to grab Martin and pull them apart, when he began to speak fiercely.

"You dirty rotten little liar, Willie Nisbet. You told that man I broke those branches and I never broke a single one. It was you, you dirty little pig."

He thumped Willie Nisbet's head on the grass again and the boy began to cry. Martin sat up, straddling his victim.

"That's right," he said with evident satisfaction. "Have a good snivel to yourself, crybaby. You should have seen the walloping I got last night, for what you did. Next time I'll knock your teeth out. And if you tell on me," he added grimly, "I'll tell them what really happened yesterday, and after that I'll bash you silly."

"I'm sorry," Willie sobbed. "That man lives next door to me. If he had told my father it was me, he'd have killed me. You don't know my father."

"You don't know my mother," Martin retorted, and Janet

smiled to herself. "I could hardly sit down last night. You'd better wash your face before you go home, and I'm not playing with you again—ever—so there."

Janet was still out of their line of vision and slipped away quickly before they could get up and see her. She hurried home excitedly. So *that* was what had happened. Why hadn't Martin told the truth? Why had he taken the other boy's blame and beating? She returned to the house and went up to the studio.

"Hullo, darling," Torquil remarked, turning away from his easel. "A timely interruption. I could do with a cup of tea."

"Before you have your tea, I've a story to tell you," she remarked, and sitting on a chair proceeded to let him have a full account of what she had seen and heard in the park.

"So that was it." Torquil surprised her by laughing. "Of course, he'd never clipe. The boys' code."

"What do you mean?"

"You know what a clipe is, don't you? It's someone who tells on someone else."

"I've heard the word."

"Well, unless Hutchie Grammar has changed since I was a schoolboy, there's only one thing as bad as telling a lie, and that's giving someone else away. The school is very strong on telling the truth, and the boys themselves are equally severe on one another if anyone clipes. Notice that Martin didn't tell a lie. That's why he wouldn't answer you! He wouldn't tell a lie and he couldn't give his friend away. He had to deal with it his own way, so he said nothing and he got a beating. He wasn't being insolent, not deliberately anyway."

"Oh, how silly."

"No," Torquil contradicted. "Martin's a man. You can take pleasure in that fact. You've often talked of tutors, Janet, but that's one thing a tutor can never give a boy, the training in living that association with other boys gives him. Oh, Martin's no saint, I'm sure. But he's learning something at school besides reading, writing, and arithmetic."

"I expect you're right," she agreed. "Now let's have that tea."

The incident was soon forgotten and that summer Davie Robertson graduated from university and came through to Glasgow before going home to Dundee. Janet was delighted with him.

"You'll have a holiday now, Davie," she told him. "Take your mother away to the seaside for a month. I'll pay for you both. Don't spare any expense."

He was a tall, dark, slim young man, with a pointed face, solemn in repose. When he was with Janet, he became animated.

"You don't need to do that, Aunt Janet," he protested. "I've saved a lot of money from the allowance you've been giving me."

"You keep your savings, Davie. I'll pay for your holiday. As soon as you come back, your job is waiting at the factory."

"I'm looking forward to that," he said with deep satisfaction. "What exactly will I be doing?"

"I'm going to start you off as sales manager, but that's just a title. I've worked out a syllabus for you with Mr. Skimming, the general manager. You are going to spend your first month on the factory floor with Peter Proudfoot, the jam master. I want you to have a clear picture in your mind of all that goes on on the factory floor. And not just for a month. Any time when you have nothing to do, get down there and see what's going on. You're starting in the jam season. You won't see the Rowan's Royal until after Christmas. That's something to watch, and our reputation rests more on that than all the rest put together."

He nodded interestedly.

"Then you are going to spend a month with Mr. Stevenson, in the accounts department, and finally a month in Neil

Skimming's office. After that you'll get Mr. Cunninghame's old office. The one thing we are not doing well is finding new markets for our jams and marmalade. Mr. Cunninghame handled that part of the business himself. I want you to take it up."

"I'd like that," he answered. "I don't know anything about it though."

She smiled sunnily. "You'll learn, Davie, but most important you'll bring new ideas into the business. Mr. Cunninghame was interested in exporting jam and marmalade to the United States. You might look into that when you have time. But first, get to know the factory and the people, then find out what our travelers are doing and what can be done to help them to do better; look at the home markets and think about outside markets. It's a big job."

"It sounds it," he agreed. "Are things going well with the factory?"

"Surprisingly well, considering everything. It's the future I'm interested in. When Martin grows up, the factory will be his. I want to hand it over in the best possible order. By the way, Mr. Skimming comes here once a month with various reports for me to see, and we discuss problems. When you start, you'll come with him."

"Thank you. In fact, Aunt Janet, thank you for so much. When I think of all you've done for me and my mother, and for my sister all those years ago—you didn't have to do any of it."

"You owe me no thanks, Davie. If I've helped you, then you're repaying me now by working for me."

He shook his head, choked by emotion. At last he told her, "You're kind. First Mr. Cunninghame, then you and your father. I don't think I knew what happiness was, real happiness I mean, till I went to the rectory. Those were great years."

He couldn't have said anything better calculated to please her.

FOURTEEN

NANCY MACRAE was born on a sunny May day in 1884. Torquil, who had been in a fever of excitement ever since he had learned that Janet was pregnant, was delighted at the birth of his first child. It was he who chose her name, and it had been a daughter he wanted. He explained it to Janet.

"I want another you, my dear. Now, a boy who looked like you would be a bit of a sissy, wouldn't he? But a girl, almost as beautiful as you? That's different. I want another Janet but we'll call her Nancy."

"Why Nancy?"

"I just like it, that's all."

When the baby was born he opened champagne, and could be heard singing to himself for the next twenty-four hours much to Janet's amusement. His interest in Nancy was a matter of wonder to her. He insisted on learning how to change diapers, to bathe the baby, and when Nancy graduated to a feeding bottle, how to feed her, too.

It was a few months before it suddenly occurred to Janet that he never went near the studio nowadays. She tackled him about it one evening.

"Are you giving up painting?" she asked.

She was not concerned financially. He had a moderately good income from investments and she herself was a wealthy woman now. It would not matter if Torquil never earned another penny.

"No," he replied after a moment's thought. "I'm going through a bad phase. I'm discontented with what I'm doing. I want to go to London for a bit, to the Slade. Perhaps I'll get some idea of where I'm going, there. I'm just not happy with my work."

"Then you must go."

"I don't want to leave you and Nancy," he smiled.

"That's not like you, Torquil. You're not tied to my apron strings."

"No," he agreed. "I suppose I'm using you as an excuse. It isn't easy being an artist. Not when you are at war within yourself anyway."

She had been startled by his new style of painting when she first saw it, but by now she had come to recognize its merit, to appreciate what he meant by painting maps instead of painting the truth. It was not a deep understanding, but it served to bring her closer to him.

"Go then, Torquil. You must get your ideas sorted out."

Early in the new year he set off for a month or two in London, and she missed his presence in the house, and, even more, in her bed. The first week or two were quite miserable. Then her mind switched to business, when Neil Skimming and Davie came to Glasgow on one of their regular visits. Davie had been taking an interest in the process of making marmalade, and he discussed marmalade sales at some length. Soon however he introduced a new subject.

"I had an interesting talk with a man about fruit farming," he said. "There's money in it. One of our biggest products is raspberry jam, and we buy most of our raspberries locally, from farms in the Carse of Gowrie. Why don't we buy up one or two fruit farms and supply ourselves?"

Janet looked at Skimming, who nodded.

"It makes sense," the older man said. "I don't know why

nobody thought of it before. It's the sort of thing Lipton does."

"Lipton is supplying his own retail shops," Janet pointed out. "He's not supplying a single factory. Still, it's an idea."

"I've looked into this carefully," Davie went on, speaking with slow deliberation. "There are two of our suppliers who would sell if the price was right, and perhaps a third later on."

"If there is money in fruit growing, why do they want to sell?" Janet asked quickly.

"I knew you'd ask that," Davie laughed. "One because of ill health, one is too old for it, and the third may be emigrating to Canada next summer, and he wants capital."

"Ask Hugh Stevenson to let me have a report on the financial side of it. I want to know where this leaves us financially. No, ask him to get the report ready. I'll come up to Dundee for a few days. Can I stay with you and your mother, Davie? Your mother could look after Nancy for me during the day."

"Yes, of course," Davie said readily. "We'd like that."

"All right then, that's settled."

Davie talked a bit more about expanding sales in England and a projected trip to Canada and the United States for the following year. Janet was pleased with the way things were going, particularly with the reports she received privately from Neil Skimming on Davie's progress. He was intelligent, enthusiastic, and eager to learn.

When Torquil returned, he was much happier and more relaxed.

"I think I know what I want to do now," he told her. "It's funny how a change of surroundings can focus your attention on essentials."

"I'm glad. What did you learn?"

"My painting lacks direction. Seascapes are very anonymous, you know. What I want to do is to paint rural scenes as I see them, only they must be Scottish. I want to get out into the countryside. I'm going to start with the Highlands, because I've always loved them and nobody has ever done them justice. The only person who ever tried was Landseer and that sort of stuff is out of date." Torquil rarely attacked fellow artists, however much he disliked their work. It was a matter of principle. He personally loathed the work of Landseer, and even more loathed the false impression it gave of ordinary life in the Highlands of Scotland. "First and foremost I have to be a Scottish painter," he concluded. "I've got to have identity."

"Yes, dear," she remarked placidly. She was pleased to see him animated once more.

"When we come back from our summer holiday this year, I'll go off on my own, probably up the west coast somewhere. Perhaps I'll be able to rent a cottage where I can go and paint from time to time."

"That's a good idea. Meantime you haven't asked about Nancy."

"Yes, let's go and see her," he agreed, and they went up to the nursery together.

That night, in bed, she was more eager and responsive than he had ever known her, her need for him arousing him to new heights of passion. Later as they lay together, their damp bodies pressed close, he told her, "You still have the power to surprise me."

"Of course," she replied drowsily. "You surprise me, too. That's how it should be. Sometimes I feel I know you, and then you say or do something and almost immediately I realize that however close we are, we must always remain a little apart. I don't believe anyone ever can understand anyone else."

"That doesn't sound encouraging," he told her.

"No, think. I remember a bit of Shakespeare my father was fond of. I think it came from *As You Like It*. Anyway it says 'I do desire we may be better strangers.' My father was always interested in that remark. Perhaps that's all we can expect—to become better strangers."

"I know," he admitted. "I've sometimes had a sudden

horrible thought that you don't really know me and I don't know you."

"I know you enough to say I love you, Torquil MacRae." She turned and kissed him.

"And I love you, Janet Darling MacRae," he replied and they began their lovemaking again.

That summer of 1885 Rowan's acquired three large fruit farms, all of which had hitherto supplied them with fruit on contract, and after the summer holiday, Torquil went off to Oban. He returned delighted, for he had found a cottage to rent at a village called Connel, quite near to Oban.

"It's ideal," he told her enthusiastically. "I can find all sorts of different scenery without having to go far. I shall hire a pony and ride the countryside. I really am going to do something that's never been done before, Janet. I'm going to put the Highlands of Scotland on canvas as they really are, not as a series of stylized deceptions."

"Shall we be allowed to visit you?" she asked.

"Well, yes," he agreed a little less vehemently. "You could come up for a holiday, but I shall want to be there alone at times. You know I can't work and have a holiday at the same time. Besides, the seaside is better for Martin. He'd find it dull. Come up for a day or two next summer."

"Isn't Connel near the sea?" she asked, curious.

"Well, yes, but it isn't exactly what Martin would call 'seaside.' He'd enjoy it better at Girvan or some place like that."

"I know you," she accused. "You don't want intruders. Is there any furniture in this cottage? Or is it just a glorified studio?"

"There's not much in it. I planned to move up one or two things, plus painting equipment. There isn't a bed at the moment."

She laughed. "I might have known. You keep your cottage to yourself, then."

"I don't mind, if you really want to come," he protested.

"No, my dear. It was only curiosity, and besides it's

almost worth getting rid of you for a week or two, just for the sake of the first night together again."

"You have a point there," he agreed, kissing her.

In the winter of 1887, when he was thirteen, Martin had his first serious illness. Nobody knew quite what was wrong with him, and the doctor was puzzled as was the second doctor whom he called in. Martin had a high temperature, his breath was shallow, he slept most of the time, and it was difficult to diagnose exactly what was wrong. There was no need to move him to a hospital when he was so well looked after at home, and Janet spent long hours by his bedside, which reminded her poignantly of the last years of Andrew's mother.

Suddenly, in the third week, he turned the corner. The fever went, and his breathing became normal. The day after the fever went, when she was visiting Martin in his room, he asked, "Where is Papa?"

"He's upstairs painting. Why? Do you want to see him?"

"Yes please. I want to ask him something."

"Is it something I can help with?"

"It's not that sort of something," he answered, managing a weak smile.

"Something between men, is that it? All right, I'll let him know."

She smiled and kissed him. About an hour later Torquil walked in and found Martin buried in one of his many books.

"Hullo, old chum," Torquil said, hugging him. "How are we today?"

"Oh, much better, Papa. I feel quite well now. And hungry, too."

"That's a change for the better. You wanted to see me about something special, is that right?"

"I did, rather," Martin admitted hesitantly.

"What is it?"

"Someone at school said you aren't a gentleman, because you're a painter. What did they mean by that?"

"Who on earth told you that?" Torquil demanded, shaken.

"My form master. What he really said was that he'd make a gentleman of me yet, even if my father is only a painter—which is the same thing, isn't it?"

"Um." Torquil nodded. "What a stupid individual he sounds. What had you been doing anyway?"

"He said I was rude to him, but I didn't mean to be. I just didn't hear him speaking to me, that was all. Oh, and I forgot to say sorry, I was so surprised at being called rude."

"What is this gentleman's name?" Torquil asked.

"Mr. Carliston. He's my Latin teacher, and form master."

"I shouldn't let him worry you, Martin." Torquil ruffled his hair. "He's not worth troubling about."

"Yes, but . . . what did he mean? What *is* a gentleman? *Aren't* you one?"

"I hope I am." Torquil took thought for a moment. "It's difficult to explain, but I'll try. There are some stupid people, snobs you'd call them, who think that if you are in trade you can't be a gentleman. That means that if you own a great big business or factories or a coal mine or anything, you aren't a real gentleman, but if you are a rotten bad landowner, you can be. It's all ridiculous, but then people do make themselves ridiculous. You'll find that out when you grow up. You have to learn to understand people and to forgive them. God knows it's hard enough sometimes," he added quietly.

"Are you in trade, then?"

"No," he laughed. "Some people don't think it is very respectable to be an artist, that it's worse than being in trade. I'm surprised to learn that one of your masters at Hutchesons' talks that sort of rubbish. And it is rubbish. For instance, army officers consider that they are gentlemen, but they don't think lawyers are. Then again, the cavalry officers think that only they are real gentlemen, and that the infantry officers are terribly inferior. It's idiotic, I know. I warned you it was. One has to ignore such things."

Martin considered these revelations seriously, more than a little baffled by them.

"What *is* a gentleman, then?" he wanted to know.

"I was afraid you'd ask that. It isn't easy to answer you. I'd say a gentleman was a person of courtesy, consideration, and self-deprecation. That's about as good a definition as you'll get, and it doesn't have anything to do with whether you work in a shop, or own a lot of farmland, or are an officer in the army, or have a coat of arms, or anything. It's not important to be a gentleman."

"What?" Martin looked at him wide-eyed.

"Anyone can be courteous, self-deprecating, and considerate. Indeed everyone ought to be, and not just men either. These are nice qualities, and I hope you'll show them, but they aren't remarkable. The important thing is to be a man. At least that's what I think."

"What's the difference?"

"A real man would automatically be a gentleman, but he is more. He is someone who accepts full responsibility for himself. He doesn't start to whine when things go wrong. He doesn't try to blame other people or bad luck for his own mistakes. If you think about it, you will find as you grow older that not many people are like that. Some seem to be like it, but when there is real trouble their true colors show. They find excuses and they shift the blame away from themselves, and they feel sorry for themselves."

"I know," Martin nodded sagely, remembering a certain incident in Maxwell Park involving his friend Willie, now his very best friend.

"Real men are the salt of the earth, old chum, whether they are in a palace or in a prison cell. Remember that. Try to be one yourself, but at your age you shouldn't concern yourself too much about these things. You're turning out well, and if I see anything going wrong, I'll let you know. As for Mr. What's-his-name, just ignore what he said."

Martin gave him a shy smile. He always felt better after

talking to Torquil, even when it was difficult to understand him. He had no thought nowadays for his real father. Torquil was all the father he needed.

Torquil paused by the door and gave the boy an encouraging grin. But as he went downstairs he was boiling inwardly, and he told Janet so at the first opportunity.

"I've a damned good mind to go to the school and have a few words with this form master of Martin's. What a cruel thing to do, to try to make a boy feel inferior, and in front of others. It doesn't matter a tuppenny damn to *me* who thinks I'm a gentleman and who thinks I'm not, but I do object to anyone embarrassing Martin like that."

Janet had rarely heard him so heated. He was always quiet and controlled.

"Don't do that," she warned.

"Why not?"

"You're forgetting that that man probably had a crowd of boys to contend with all day. He was probably tired and irritated, and spoke thoughtlessly."

Torquil glanced at her. "How like you to think of that," he said. "I'll admit that I'd hate to be a teacher. I suppose he could have been in a temper. It was still an irresponsible thing to say. I never came across any snobbery at Hutchie when I was there."

Suddenly his normal good humor asserted itself, and he laughed.

"The fellow is probably right, when one thinks of it. I imagine that there are a lot of people in high places who would agree that an artist is by definition not a gentleman. On the other hand, considering how they would define the word, I don't want to be one. To paint well is enough for me."

"You're a very perfect gentleman," Janet reproved him and kissed him.

"I'd rather be told I'm a very perfect husband and lover."

"It's no good fishing for compliments. You'll get no more today. What did you say to Martin? You haven't told me."

"Oh, that it was a stupid remark and he should ignore it."

"I suspect you said a lot more than that."

He kissed her, and she watched him closely as he left the room, noting his erect figure, the way he held his head, and she smiled.

Dear Torquil, she thought. How happy they were together, bringing up their family.

FIFTEEN

IN the late spring of 1888, a grim-faced Davie arrived
at Conchra House to confer with Janet. When he had taken
his overnight bag up to one of the spare bedrooms, and
washed after his journey, they closeted themselves together
in her drawing room.

"It's bad news," he told her bluntly. "I'm sorry, because
I feel responsible."

"The farms? *Again?*"

For two years running their farms had proved disastrous
investments. The first year there was an unusually hard
frost and fruit farming in the area was very hard hit. In
the second year a blight had destroyed more than half
their crops. What now, she wondered fearfully?

"Yes, Aunt Janet. We've had a sudden late frost. Not
everywhere, but on our farms. It's something to do with
the lie of the land, and the wind, and I don't know all
what. Farms a matter of yards away are fine, and all
three of ours are blackened."

"Don't look so upset, Davie. We'll survive. I know the
financial position."

"It isn't that. We paid out a lot of capital for those
farms. We employ people and farm managers to work
them for us. The only justification for us doing this was
the fact that we would get a lot of our fruit very much
cheaper than we've had it before. In fact we get no fruit

from them. Instead we have to make late contracts for the fruit, and pay *more* for it than we would have done if we'd never had farms, and made the usual contracts. The only people making money out of these farms are the managers and the farm workers."

"That's true, but it's been an unprecedented run of bad luck."

"Yes, but I know more about fruit farming now than I did when we went into this. The truth is that individual farms do have bad years, and even bad periods. That's never troubled us before, because we contract out to lots of farm owners, and if one of them has a bad year, we simply go elsewhere to someone with a surplus. It isn't our worry. Now it is. Three farms—three years. It's like one farm with a nine-year blight."

"What's the best thing to do, Davie?" she asked.

"I think I've done it. I've found someone who will buy all three. They are practically adjoining, as you know."

"Someone who thinks the run of bad luck is over?" she asked lightly.

"No, someone who isn't interested in fruit. He intends to grow other things. No fruit. In fact, he approached me only yesterday. He'd heard about our bad luck and correctly assumed that we might be considering selling. He's offering a fair price. I think we ought to take it."

They talked over the offer till dinnertime, not even stopping for tea which Janet had sent in to them. At last they were agreed about what must be done, including the placing of late contracts for a considerable part of their jam fruit.

"I can't think why you were so upset when you arrived, Davie," Janet remarked at the end of it all. "You knew about the offer to buy. We'll get the bulk of our capital back. We've learned a valuable lesson. *Don't* get into the fruit-growing business if your object is to run a jam factory."

"I feel I've failed you," he said miserably. "You spent so much on me, and all I've done is to involve you in further losses. We've had no interest on that capital, we've paid far more than we need have done for quite a lot of fruit, and it was all for nothing."

"You mustn't talk like that. You've done a lot for the factory and you know it. Everyone makes mistakes. This one at least hasn't been too serious. And remember, someone would have thought of it sometime in the future. You've probably saved Martin from burning his fingers."

"You're just trying to cheer me up. I'll have to work hard to make up for this."

She put an arm around his shoulders. "Our sales are improving all the time, and you know it. You're doing splendidly."

"I'd feel better if I could think of something like your new method of labeling," he told her with a smile.

This was something Janet was ridiculously proud about. She had been watching the girls hand-labeling the jam jars one day, with their piles of gaily printed labels, their pots.of paste and their brushes. The cumbersomeness of it offended her sense of efficiency.

She had come away thoughtfully, and that night she sat down and did some rough drawings. Next morning she had shown them to an amazed Peter Proudfoot. Her idea was devastatingly simple. The jars were propped on a ledge so that they lay at an angle, and on a shelf above were the piles of labels, one in front of each girl. Between the shelf and the top of the jars was a strip of thick felt impregnated with gum. All the girl had to do was to slide a label down over the felt and straight onto the side of the jar below it, and then she put the jar onto a bench behind where someone else collected them up for packing.

It had taken a little bit of working out in detail, but in the end it proved successful and speeded up the labeling. It improved Janet's already high standing with her staff, for the girls preferred the new system.

"The factory still fascinates me," Davie added quietly.

"I know. It has the same effect on me and always has," she agreed. "Some of them think I'm daft, standing watching the girls at work," she said, laughing. "Well, come along, Davie. Work's over for the day. It's dinnertime."

Her smile made up for all the self-recrimination that had tortured him ever since he had learned that the frost was lying, not melting.

While Davie slept peacefully that night, Janet lay awake thinking of the factory. It occupied far more of her thoughts than anyone properly realized, because of her regard for it as Martin's heritage, and not simply her own source of income. In the early days, unknown to anyone in the factory, she had gone to her solicitor who had put her in touch with a firm of chartered accountants, the junior partner of which, for a handsome consideration, taught her how to read and interpret accounts. Her knowledge of accounts was both deep and sound, and she watched like a hawk for any significant variation in figures.

As it happened, the loyalty of people like Skimming and Proudfoot was in itself a guarantee against her being swindled by her employees, but neither of them knew just how difficult it would have been had the attempt ever been made. Also, her interest in watching the women at work was not quite the idle amusement some of the office staff imagined it was. The women appreciated her spending so much time on the factory floor—there was a normal amount of mild rivalry between factory workers and office staff—and she enjoyed talking to them when it did not mean holding up their work. She knew most of them by name, and was ahead of her time in the interest she showed in their lives outside the factory. They thought highly of her, and it was on their efforts that the factory mainly existed.

But all this she regarded as normal and minimal—she could not do less. Her aim was to do much more. The experiment with the fruit farms had meant more than she had let Davie see, because it represented an expansion of business interests. It went against the grain to admit defeat, to withdraw back into the old boundaries of the firm's activities. And it was early in the morning, shortly before exhaustion sent her into her slumbers, that illumination came.

She went into session with Davie again immediately after breakfast.

"I was thinking in bed last night, Davie. Fruit farming is obviously not worth it, but the idea behind it is good. I want you to go to Spain."

"What?"

"I want you to go to Spain. I want you to visit Malaga and Seville. There are two objectives. First of all, find out if we are getting the very finest bitter oranges that there are. If not, then negotiate contracts for next year. But more important, Davie, I want to buy into Spain. We'll forget about fruit for jam and concentrate on oranges and lemons. If we import our *own*, we'll save money hand over fist—and if we can grow more than we need, we can sell to other people."

He stared at her.

"I hadn't thought of that. It will take a lot of money—if it can be done."

"I'm relying on you to see that it *is* done, Davie. As for money, I can lend the firm money until it's in a position to repay me. And the money we get back from the fruit farms can go into this."

"I don't speak Spanish," he mused. "I'll have to be very careful what I get into."

"We'll need a good local man. You must take your time. Don't hurry it. We have one or two people known to us— you can start by sounding them out. But don't give too much away." She paused and snapped her fingers. "I have it. You won't say anything about Rowan's at all. Let them think you are a young man looking for a business interest on your own account. If the word gets out that Rowan's want to buy orange and lemon groves, the price will go up sharply and they may refuse to sell anyway."

They discussed the project for two hours, examining it from all angles, making their plans as they went along.

Davie became infected with her enthusiasm. Not only was it the biggest challenge he had yet faced, but he could see all the advantages. There was none of the risk they had faced with fruit farming in Scotland.

"You see the principle?" she asked. "We supply ourselves wherever we can. If this works, we can start thinking about making our own barrels to ship the oranges and lemons in. Every time we cut costs, we can trim our prices and increase our sales and our profits, and we may even have sidelines that are profitable on their own account, if we can supply other people."

He nodded happily. "Yes, it's a grand idea," he agreed enthusiastically. "When shall I go?"

"Now, of course. It's the end of the season, which isn't a bad time when one thinks about it."

"It's funny," he said half to himself. "I had a similar idea this morning."

"About Spain?" She was surprised.

"No, not that, but when I was dressing, I thought about the failure of the fruit farms, and I suddenly thought about sugar beet. I don't know anything about it, but if it's a hardier crop we could supply a lot of our own sugar. Either that or get into sugar in the West Indies, but sugar beet is local and more easily controlled. I was going to find out about it before mentioning it."

"Now you're really thinking the way I want you to," she smiled. "Spain first and then, once that's settled, you can find out about sugar and we'll see what can be done. One thing at a time. It all costs money."

"It will be ships next," he laughed.

"I don't think so," she answered quite seriously. "Shipping is a risky business. I'm not keen on it. But sugar is another matter. It's something to think about."

She was well satisfied with the morning's discussion. By the time Martin was old enough to take over the running of the factory, it would be a far bigger and more profitable business than it had ever been before. They had a long way to go yet, but she had no doubts about Davie's ability to implement and augment all her own ideas. They were a very good team indeed.

Davie Robertson's visit to Spain had been very successful and they now owned quite a lot of land, which was in her maiden name, J. Darling. So far the connection with Rowan's was secret. He had handled the negotiations well and driven good bargains. He had also made a brief sales trip to the United States, and things looked hopeful on the other side of the Atlantic. Now he was eager to investigate the sugar industry even though it would be a little time before there would be any capital available for further diversification. He was also interested in developing the domestic market, south of the border. They could do a lot better in England than they had done so far. He became quite enthusiastic as he talked. Yet again it occurred to her how very fortunate she had been in him. A simple act of kindness had been repaid a thousandfold.

"Things will be easier soon," Davie said casually. "When the Forth Bridge is opened."

Janet's face clouded over. The bridge over the River Forth was now no longer something to discuss, but a solid structure nearing completion. It would open early in the following year, all being well.

The mere mention of river bridges disturbed her. The Tay Bridge had cost so much in human life. In the building of it, twenty-five men had died, sacrifices on the altar of progress; in its destruction a further seventy-five men, women, and children had perished. A hundred lives. Those involved in its planning had been disgraced and its designer had gone mad and finally died along with the bridge's other victims.

"Yes," she said in a subdued voice, "it will make a difference, Davie. It will make it easier and cheaper to supply the markets in the south. Tell me, how do our workers compare with others? I mean the lowest paid ones. You know more about these things than I do."

Davie nodded. He certainly did.

"Very well," he said without hesitation.

"Are you sure, Davie? Do they have enough to eat and keep warm?"

"Yes, they're about the best paid in Dundee. Most people don't pay women and girls very much. Of course we employ hardly anyone under fifteen. It's against our policy. Our people come from ordinary working-class homes, and they are well paid, and they know it. Catch them leaving for other jobs!"

"All right, Davie. I know we're said to pay a fair wage, but I wasn't sure if it was fair to them, or just to me."

He felt uneasy when she spoke like this. It was radical talk, and Davie, product of the lower working class, who owed everything to this clergyman's daughter, was no radical. He was extremely satisfied with the status quo. Things were constantly improving at the factory, and nobody at Rowan's would ever again have to steal a few pennies to get food for a dying sister. There was the Rowan's Provident Society and there was a system for helping out in cases of real distress, a sort of emergency fund.

"It's fair to them, Aunt Janet. More than fair."

"Please see that it stays that way, Davie."

"Yes, but how could it be anything else?" he asked. She after all was the one who dictated company policy.

"We can't see into the future, Davie. I just want to know that you'll look after that side of things too, in case anything happens to me."

SIXTEEN

IN the spring of 1890 Torquil went to the cottage at Connel to paint, for the month of May. It was one of his favorite months because of the contrasts of weather in the Highlands. He warned Janet that he would probably be away from the cottage quite a lot, and might visit a loch in Skye, Loch Coruisk, which was said to be a frightening sight as it sat cold and brooding amid its dark ring of mountains. He wanted to see it for himself, perhaps to sketch or paint it.

Janet hugged him.

"That's all right. You go where you please and return when you feel like it. Just send me a telegram saying when you are returning. If I have to get in touch with you, I won't expect an early reply."

"You know how it is," he apologized.

"It's all right, darling," she laughed. She was serenely happy these days. "We play this scene every year. Only don't be too long. I miss you as much as ever."

He kissed her passionately and she responded. Their love continued to grow stronger and her need for him was boundless. She hated that empty place in the big bed, beside her, but he had to have his few weeks' solitude.

She had some of the rooms redecorated while he was away and this kept her occupied. One morning she was surprised when Martin came home when he should have been at school. One look at his face told her that something was wrong.

"What has happened, darling?" she asked anxiously.

"I've been sent home, Mama."

"I can see that. Why?"

"There's a letter from the rector."

He took a crumpled envelope from his jacket pocket and handed it to her. It was short and ominously uninformative.

> *Dear Mr. MacRae,*
>
> *I would be glad if you could call to see me at your earliest convenience during school hours to discuss your son's behavior. I deeply regret having to deal so severely with the son of one of our former pupils, and the grandson of a patron of the school, but there are some things that I cannot overlook. I have also the rest of the school to consider, to say nothing of the standards that it is my duty to enforce.*
>
> *Yours faithfully,*
> *W. Ritchie Hepburn,*
>
> *Rector.*

"What exactly has happened?" Janet asked Martin, who was staring hard at the carpet.

"I've been expelled."

"Expelled?" she repeated, disbelieving.

"I can't go back. I got a beating, and then expelled."

"What did you do, Martin?"

"Punched a teacher." For the first time the hint of a smile played at the corner of his mouth.

Janet swallowed. "Very well. Sit down and tell me all about it. Take your time."

"There's nothing to tell. I hit him. It's true."

"There is plenty to tell. Who was this person you hit?"

"Mr. Carliston." The name sounded familiar and she gave him an inquiring look. "My form master," he explained.

"Ah, yes. You hit your form master?"

"I punched his nose. Hard. It bled." There was no mistaking his satisfaction.

Janet wondered if she were dreaming. "You must have had some reason," she said.

"He was pulling me along by the ear."

"Will you please begin at the beginning, Martin?" she demanded, feeling exasperated.

He shrugged. "I got a beating for breaking a window. Carly reported me to the beak, and when I came out of Old Heppy's study after the beating, he grabbed me by the ear, so I turned and punched him. Old Heppy came out and grabbed me, beat me again, wrote that letter and told me I was expelled."

"I see." She glanced at the grandfather clock in the corner. "We will go back at once and see Mr. Hepburn."

"I don't want to go back," he objected.

"You will do as you are told, young man."

"It's no good," he said desperately. "It's finished. I don't care anyway. I don't like being in Carliston's form."

"I thought you were happy at Hutchesons'."

"The school is all right, but I don't like Carly and you can't change form, you know."

"Nevertheless we will see Mr. Hepburn and I want you to be with me. I'll be ready in ten minutes."

Despite his protests, they went to the school where Janet demanded to see the rector. She was admitted to his study almost at once, and Hepburn, a small grizzled man with a lined face but with understanding eyes, stood up to greet her.

"My dear Mrs. MacRae," he said, "it would have been better if Mr. MacRae had come."

"My husband is away from home," she told him, sitting down. "I wish to have a fuller explanation of what has happened than I have been able to get from Martin."

The little rector's mouth drew down at the corners, and he placed the tips of his fingers against one another and stared at his hands for a few moments. Then he sighed.

"I am most sorry about this. It is not a pleasant story. It began when Martin broke a window in his form room. His form master was out of the room, but he returned at that moment, and had just opened the door. The boys did not see him."

"Go on, please."

"You probably know our school motto is *veritas*. It means 'truth.' We do our utmost to inculcate truthfulness into our pupils. No matter what they do, they must own up to it. After all, most of them go out of here to become respected Glasgow merchants or professional men, or even to become noted scholars. They have to learn the need for honesty in their lives."

Janet was puzzled. "What has this to do with Martin?"

"Mr. Carliston, following a general principle that I have laid down for my staff, did not hurry into the room and accuse your son. Instead he went into the room, restored order, and demanded to know who had broken the window. It was Martin's opportunity to own up. He did not."

He paused for a moment and stared at Martin with distaste.

"Mr. Carliston gave Martin another chance. He asked him had he broken the window. Martin denied it. You must remember that, although Martin did not know it, Mr. Carliston had seen him do it."

Janet tried to imagine the tense scene in the form room, but never having been to school, could not. Boy versus man, she thought grimly. Why had Martin been so stupid?

"To cut a long story short, Martin persisted in denying what he had done, and was brought to me. He would not even own up to me. He persisted in his lying."

"But Martin doesn't tell lies!" Janet exploded angrily.

"I agree that he is not normally a troublesome boy. Highspirited, perhaps, and careless sometimes, but there have been few complaints about him. That was why I did not expel him on the spot. I decided to give him a second chance. I warned him that from now on he would have to be on his best behavior, I warned him of the consequences of going through life telling lies, and I gave him a beating that he richly deserved."

He held out his hands. "Mrs. MacRae, I do not punish boys for the pleasure it gives me, but in order to impress on them the need for living in a decent, orderly, upright way. We have stupid boys and we have clever boys, but we cannot tolerate liars and ruffians."

Janet turned to Martin who was staring out of the window, woodenly, as though he were not with them.

"You didn't tell me all this, Martin," she said sadly.

"I knew *he* would," Martin answered carelessly.

"Do not call Mr. Hepburn 'he' in that insolent manner," she snapped. "Is he telling me the truth?"

Hepburn's bushy eyebrows shot up. His own veracity had never before been called in doubt, and for a parent to inquire about it from a newly expelled schoolboy was a new experience. Martin however did not hesitate.

"Everything Mr. Hepburn says is true," he answered quietly.

"Good heavens," Janet said faintly. "What happened next, Mr. Hepburn?"

Hepburn tore his gaze away from Martin. "Where were we? Oh, yes, after that I dismissed him. He apparently encountered his form master outside my study, and Mr. Carliston may have exceeded himself a little in taking Martin by the ear, but he had been greatly provoked. Besides I do it myself sometimes."

"He nearly twisted it off," Martin interrupted, showing animation for the first time. "He was enjoying himself. He called me a dirty little liar and tried to pull me along by the ear, so I hit him. What's more, I'm not sorry."

Mr. Hepburn could not have been more pleased had the patrons of the school voted him an increase in his stipend.

"There you are, Mrs. MacRae. Out of his own mouth he condemns himself. He is one of our senior boys, almost sixteen now. What sort of example is this to set to the younger boys? I assure you, the incident was witnessed. What distresses me most is his lying and his attitude when caught out. It is the exact reverse of what we try to instill into our boys. Breaking windows is a small matter. But the rest . . ." He threw up his hands again.

Janet sat, stunned. Martin's apparent indifference, and his delight in having punched Mr. Carliston, were beyond her understanding.

"Can you please send for Mr. Carliston?" she asked suddenly. "I should like to meet him."

"What good can that do?" Hepburn asked, reluctant to have a scene on his hands.

"Surely I have the right? It is his testimony after all that got Martin into this trouble. I wish to see him and to ask him one question."

"May I correct you? You yourself have heard Martin admit to the truth. It is not just Mr. Carliston's testimony. Had Martin admitted the truth at the beginning we should not be in this present predicament. However . . ."

Reluctantly he sent for the form master who arrived quickly. He was small, rapidly balding, with a pendulous lower lip and tufts of hair sprouting from his ears. Janet disliked him on sight. He stared at the trio in the study before closing the door.

"You sent for me, Rector?"

"Yes. Mrs. MacRae, may I present Mr. Carliston, Martin's form master. This is Martin's mother, Mr. Carliston. I have been explaining this morning's events to her. She wished to see you herself."

"Mrs. MacRae," he acknowledged with a curt nod, giving Martin a cold, hostile look.

"Mr. Carliston, is it true that you tried to drag my son along, forcibly, by pulling his ear?"

"Certainly not." The reply was immediate, bland, confident. "I held him by the ear, I admit. It is painful, of course, but it does no harm and is a lot less painful than a beating. Martin had put us all to a great deal of trouble with his lies, and was lucky not to have been expelled. As for dragging him along, I told him to return to his form room. I myself was waiting to see Mr. Hepburn."

"Martin claims that you almost twisted his ear off and that you were pulling him by it, and even that you were enjoying it."

"Martin's word is hardly currency here, Mrs. MacRae," Carliston told her pompously.

Janet looked at Martin, who was staring at Joshua Carliston as though he would like to punch him on the nose again.

"Martin?" she asked.

He turned to her and slumped in his seat. "I want to go home," he muttered.

"So you shall," Janet promised.

Then the thing nagging at the back of her mind crystallized. She remembered the name Carliston clearly now. The time Martin had been ill, and had told Torquil about a remark made in school.

"Mr. Carliston," she said briskly, "was it not you who told my son some time ago that you would make a gentleman out of him, even if his father was only a painter? I forget your exact words, but Martin came home very distressed and asked us what was wrong with his father."

Carliston flushed, and Hepburn looked up sharply, his eyes wide. Carliston took a deep breath.

"I don't recall any such incident," he said, "but I doubt if Martin's account of it was accurate. I may have said I'd make a gentleman out of him, if he had been misbehaving. We do try to make gentlemen out of our pupils. I could never have said that your husband was only a painter. I understand he is a successful artist. Martin must have mistaken my meaning."

"You're lying again," Martin yelled, jumping to his feet furiously, astonishing them all.

"Don't you dare," Carliston snarled and raised his hand.

At once Janet pulled Martin to her. "Don't *you* dare, Mr. Carliston," she said coolly. "My son has been expelled. He is no longer a pupil here. If you touch him, you will have my husband to answer to."

Hepburn was on his feet, eyes bulging, and Carliston dropped his hand and stepped back. Janet got up and took Martin by the shoulder.

"Good-bye, Mr. Hepburn," she said coldly. "We shall not trouble you again. Come along, Martin."

Exercising full control of herself, she walked out of the room, passing Carliston without so much as a glance, and remained silent until they had reached home. She was shattered and needed a pot of tea. When it had been served, she stared at Martin, shaking her head slowly.

"You amaze me. You don't like that man, do you, Martin?"

"I hate him," Martin agreed.

"Because he implied your father is no gentleman?"

"I don't know. He's always picking on me."

"He isn't even your father," Janet smiled. "He's your stepfather. But that isn't the point. I can understand your punching him. It's very wrong of you, but it makes sense. But why did you refuse to own up about the window? It's so unlike you. I wouldn't have thought breaking a window was the end of the world."

"I'm sorry." He was fighting back the tears that were gathering under his eyelids. "I really am sorry."

"Did you apologize to Mr. Hepburn or Mr. Carliston?" she asked, her mind going off at a tangent.

"No."

"You ought to have done. Where are your manners?"

"I don't owe anybody an apology," he said stubbornly. "Only you and Papa for making all this trouble. Can I go to Dundee now and start work?"

"We will discuss your future later," she said firmly. "I don't know what I'm going to do with you. I just don't understand you anymore. I'm bitterly disappointed in you."

At that, he burst into tears and ran from the room, leaving her exhausted. She wished Torquil were here, to talk it over, but she would not see Torquil for another ten days or a fortnight. She would have to cope herself. After all, she reminded herself, he was her son, not Torquil's.

For the next three nights Janet slept badly. She kept dreaming about Martin. Unlike Mr. Hepburn, she did expect children to tell lies, although Martin was not exactly a child any longer. But he had never been a liar. She distrusted Carliston on sight, yet Hepburn, the rector, was a man she would trust anywhere, and he was no fool. She did not know what to think.

It was on the fourth night, half awake and half asleep, that a great truth dawned on her.

Martin had never admitted breaking the window. What exactly had he said? He had said he'd got a beating for breaking a window. She remembered that. But when the full story came out, it transpired that he had been accused and had denied the accusation, and had then been beaten. And he had said that Hepburn was telling the truth, but Hepburn had *not* directly accused Martin of breaking the window. He had repeated that Martin had been accused, told he had been seen, and had denied it. And that much patently was true.

But had he broken the window? The more she lay and thought about it the more certain she was that he had always denied it throughout. Hepburn had said something about Martin condemning himself, but had he not been jumping to a conclusion?

There was something naggingly familiar in this pattern, something that she almost grasped but that yet eluded her. She slept badly that night, and was silent and withdrawn next morning, surprising Mrs. Kirk who had been accustomed to her recent sunny cheerfulness.

It was when she was arranging some flowers that it all came back clearly.

A small boy nearly nine, accused of vandalism in the park, a man accusing him, and another boy as witness, *and he had said nothing.* Just as he had said nothing at school. No; correction, she thought. At school he had gone further. He *had* denied the charge.

There was something else. What was it? The man in the park had come across two boys and the other boy,

Willie Nisbet, now Martin's friend, had lied about Martin. She knew she was standing on the brink of a truth. The three things were linked—the trees in the park, the business about Torquil being a gentleman, and the broken window.

Martin had taken Helen to the pond in the park that morning, to sail one of his old model boats which he had given to her, and Janet had to wait for him to return. When he came in, she led him into the privacy of her drawing room, took his shoulders in her hands, and looked down into his eyes.

"Martin, did you break that window? Just tell me yes or no."

"No, Mama," he replied without hesitation.

"Then, you must know who did."

"Yes, I do."

"Is he a friend of yours?"

"No, I hate him."

In a perverse sort of way she began to understand this child of hers.

"Why didn't the other boy own up?" she asked.

"I 'spect he might have if he'd got a chance, Mama. Carly asked who did it, and then practically at once turned on me and asked me if I had. I could see he was after me and so could everybody else. I 'spect the other boy got scared. I couldn't think why Carly took me before the beak. I mean, I thought he'd beat me. He always does if he gets the chance. Then he said he'd seen me." Martin shrugged eloquently.

"Martin dear, I want to get this quite clear. If Mr. Carliston saw what happened, he must have known it wasn't you, that it was someone else. Isn't that right?"

"Well, yes, Mama."

"Then why did he do what he did to you?"

"He doesn't like me much."

"Oh, Martin." She kissed him. "Don't you realize what you are telling me? You didn't tell a lie. Mr. Carliston did. That's what happened, isn't it?"

"Yes," he said quietly, nodding.

"Then why didn't you stand up for yourself?"

"I did. I punched his rotten nose."

She suppressed an insane desire to giggle.

"Why didn't you tell the rector?"

"It's hard to explain, Mama," he said awkwardly. "I mean they tell you the biggest sin in the world is to tell a lie. They're always on about it, about being truthful, owning up and all that rot. Then one of the masters lies, and he knows he's doing it, and he knows *I* know, too. I mean, why bother, Mama? Papa said I must be a man and not whine. Well I'm not whining."

"Oh, Martin, Martin. Darling, being a man is one thing, but you gave in. You admitted defeat. You've got to stand up for yourself, too. It's not like the trees in the park, darling."

"What trees?" he asked cautiously.

"The branches you didn't break off. The branches Willie Nisbet broke off, and you fought him about it, didn't you? Well, you're not fighting Mr. Carliston, are you?"

"You knew about the trees?"

"I found out, darling. I don't give you up as easily as other people do. God forgive me, I almost did this time, until I thought it over properly and realized that you had never admitted breaking that window. Who did it, Martin?"

"Jack Carliston—Carly's son. He's in the form. Carly was a Hutchie bug, too. What could I do?"

The enormity of his problem was borne in on her and she hugged him fiercely.

"I'll never distrust you again, Martin. Not ever. But please, Martin, when you go to Dundee, never run away from a fight. Being a man doesn't mean letting people walk over you."

"How did you know about the trees?" he asked, returning to the subject that most interested him.

"I found out afterward. I didn't say anything. It was your affair and you dealt with it yourself."

"Oh, Mama." He flung his arms around her neck and hugged her. "When you said I was being cheeky for not answering you, I felt awful."

She pushed him to arm's length and smiled dazzlingly at him.

"All right, darling. It won't happen again, but do be fair to those who love you. Not being a telltale is one thing, but think of your old mother, too."

"You're not old. You're young and pretty. Nobody else has a mother like you, nobody. They're all old and horrible."

She gave a shaky laugh. "That's enough flattery, young man. Well, I wouldn't send you back to school anyway, but I can't help feeling Mr. Hepburn ought to know the truth."

"It doesn't matter, Mama."

"Why did none of the other boys say anything?" she demanded.

"It was my business, Mama. If anyone was going to tell, it had to be me, and I wouldn't. Besides, " he added grimly, "young Carly will be beaten black and blue every day for ages. They all know I got the sack because of him." He gave a sinister chuckle. "Poor Carly. I'd rather be me."

"Go and leave me," she laughed. "Your man's world doesn't make sense to a mere woman."

She was eager to tell Torquil all about it, but on the same day that his telegram arrived announcing his return, she had an unexpected caller in the form of Mr. Hepburn. He arrived at teatime.

"I took the liberty . . . I hope you don't mind, Mrs. MacRae. It was important," he began, in the hall.

"Please come in, Mr. Hepburn. You'll have tea?"

"Er, yes, thank you. Very kind. I had to speak to you."

She would not let him get a word out till tea was served and she had poured and then, "Well, Mr. Hepburn, this is an unexpected visit."

"I scarcely know how to begin. I had a most distressing
interview this morning with one of my pupils, a boy in
Martin's form. It seems the other boys have been victimiz-
ing him. He's been beaten at least twice a day, every day,
until the boy is a nervous wreck. I have rarely seen anyone in such a state. In the end he had to come to me."
She gave a faint smile and inclined her head.
"It seems—well, to put it bluntly . . ."
"His name is Jack Carliston, he broke the window, and
his father is an out-and-out liar. Mr. Hepburn, you have
my sympathy."
The rector sat, mouth agape, and stared at her.
"*You knew this?*"
"Certainly. I don't dismiss Martin as easily as you may
do. He is my son and I know him. It took time, but I got
the story in the end. I'm sorry the other boy has been so
badly treated."
"Jack Carliston will not be returning to the school, and
I have just accepted his father's resignation." The rector
seemed to shrink as he spoke. "I have to be able to trust
my staff. If I can't trust them, there is nothing left. The
worst thing of all is that Mr. Carliston is a former pupil
of the school."
"I know all this, Mr. Hepburn. I sympathize with you."
"I came to apologize and to explain. Tell me, why did
Martin not tell me his form master was lying? Am I a
figure of fear to him?"
"I don't think so. I suspect the bottom was knocked out
of his world. I think he felt a kind of hopelessness. It's
difficult to put into words. I'm sure it wasn't fear of you."
"Martin is free to return, of course."
"I'm sorry," Janet said flatly. "There is no question of
that now. As you know, Martin will automatically take
over the family business when he is old enough. I've
decided that the best education for him now is on the
factory floor."
"Perhaps you're right. Then I need not take up any

more of your time. I shan't forget this, Mrs. MacRae, not for as long as I live. I blame myself for failing to get the truth from Martin."

"When Martin decides to keep quiet, Mr. Hepburn, he keeps quiet. He has done this before. He doesn't like telling tales."

The rector raised his eyebrows.

"That is very commendable, but surely there is a limit? It would have been better if he had defended himself."

"So I have told him."

Poor little man, she thought when he had gone. *His* world had been turned upside down.

When Torquil came home, she told him the entire story after dinner, the first evening. He listened silently and then rubbed his hand across his mouth once or twice.

"I think you coped remarkably well, darling. I'm bothered about Martin though. He knew who broke that window and he didn't say. He put it on a basis of his word against a master's, and that's rather stupid. The rector had to take Carliston's word."

"It probably won't ever happen again," she told him. "I think he sees that it was a mistake. It was a shock to him, Torquil, to catch a master out in a blatant lie."

"Of course." He laughed. "I couldn't have managed half so well. I think I must buy a kilt. How would I look in one?"

"What's all this about a kilt?" she asked, baffled.

"Just a clumsy joke, darling. I was thinking you could wear my trousers, as befits the real head of the family."

"We'll see about that upstairs," she answered daringly. "You might change your mind about me in trousers."

"I've missed you, too," he said in a low voice and got up and came around to kiss her. "Very much. Let's have coffee quickly and then go to bed."

"Whatever you say, darling," she agreed demurely, a gleam in her eye.

SEVENTEEN

AT the end of the summer, Martin went to Dundee. As he was only sixteen, he was to lodge with Mr. and Mrs. Skimming and their family. Janet would have preferred him to be with Davie Robertson, but there were other considerations, one of them being that Mrs. Robertson did not enjoy good health nowadays and another being Skimming's seniority plus his long experience in the factory. Martin could learn a lot from Mr. Skimming. Later he would learn other things from Davie.

Before he left, she gave him some advice.

"People know that you are Andrew Cunninghame's son," she warned him, and indeed he needed to be reminded, for he had been known as Martin MacRae for years. "You'll have to use your proper name in Dundee."

"Must I?" he pleaded.

"Yes. Your father left his business to you. I'm only looking after it till you're of age. Don't you think his name should continue?"

"If you put it like that, Mama, I suppose so."

"To continue. People know whose son you are, and that one day you will own Rowan's. Watch out for people who flatter you. Your common sense will tell you that they know little or nothing about you. Don't let flattery or attention go to your head."

"I shan't," he promised.

"One other thing. No more of that quixotic nonsense that got you expelled from school. If Rowan's comes under attack, you will defend it. This is business, not the schoolroom. Never let an attack go unchallenged."

"I'll remember."

"Good. Finally, trust Davie Robertson in everything. Listen to him. He is full of good sense and good ideas. He has been a tower of strength to us since he finished at university. His loyalty to our family is something you can always count on."

"I know."

She regarded him with some pride. He had grown tall, and his figure was rapidly filling out. His hair was thick and was now tow-colored, and he had good brows and a square jaw.

"I'll work hard, Mama," he assured her. "I'll try to make you proud of me."

"I'm sure you will. Remember though that fame and fortune are poor playthings, which bring no comfort to anyone. Do your best, do it honestly, and look after the people who depend on you for their living. If you can do that, you will be a success."

Armed with such good advice, he left the comfortable house overlooking the park, but before he went he had a private good-bye to make. Over the years he and Helen Kirk had grown close, not spectacularly but steadily and slowly. He walked in the garden with her, and they were both a little sad. They would miss each other.

"When do you leave?" she asked in a subdued voice.

"First thing in the morning. It will be a great adventure," he added eagerly. He was much more boyish with her than he was in front of Janet and Torquil.

"I wish I could come with you," she said wistfully. "I'd like to see Dundee and Rowan's factory. Perhaps I can get a job there one day, instead of going into service."

"Go into service!" He turned and stared. "No, you can't do that, Helen. You go to a good school. Mama would never let you go into service. *I* won't let you do it."

"My mother is in service."

"That's different. I mean, she's our friend, isn't she?"

He was stuck for words. He had never thought of Margaret Kirk as a servant. She was Helen's mother.

"What else can I do? I suppose I might get a job as a governess, but I'd far rather work for you. Couldn't I look after your office and keep it tidy?"

"What a good idea," he laughed. "I don't think it's allowed though. I think secretaries are always men."

"Then I'll be your charwoman," she giggled.

"I'll miss you, Helen."

At once her face fell. "It will be terrible without you," she agreed mournfully.

He put an arm around her shoulders and hugged her close.

"You'll have Nancy for company."

"She's an infant." Helen sniffed back a tear.

Martin looked at her with confused feelings. She was only a child, four years younger than himself, and he was off to the man's world outside the sanctuary of Conchra House. Yet he took no pleasure now in his departure. Instead he remembered how he had taught her to catch bees in cupped hands so that they didn't sting, and how to sail his boats in the pond, and how to play conkers with chestnuts threaded on string. They had done all sorts of things together.

Without thinking, he turned her to him, put his arms around her, and kissed her soft cheek. They stood like that for a split second, frozen into immobility, and he was aware of her soft hair, which hung to her waist, and the sweet fragrance of her body. They looked into one another's eyes, and immediately both turned scarlet. Martin had never kissed a girl before, except his much younger sister, and he considered even that to be unmanly.

"I . . . I . . . I . . ." He tried to extricate himself awkwardly. "We must go in, Helen. I've a lot to do today. It will be all right, honestly it will."

She was paying no attention to his frantic attempt to

sound cool. He had *kissed* her. He was sixteen, a *man*, and he had kissed her on the cheek. Not just a peck, but a real kiss. She could still feel his cool lips on her cheek. She put up a hand, unconsciously, to touch the spot. Quietly they walked toward the house, close but not touching. At the door he gave her his familiar grin.

"I'll see you before I go, Helen."

"Yes."

She went to her bedroom while he went upstairs. When Margaret Kirk discovered her, she was crying and would not say why. Her mother, who was preoccupied with other matters, thought that growing girls could be a real problem and was glad that Helen did not often behave like this.

When Martin had gone, the big house seemed strangely empty to Janet as well as to Helen. Nancy, aged six, was a quiet child who gave no trouble and, perhaps because of her withdrawn nature, she was no substitute for her brother. Torquil was going through one of his periods of agony again, spending long hours in the studio staring at canvases and brooding. Janet had learned to leave him alone during these moods when he turned savagely against his own work. She had known for some time that he was deeply dissatisfied with what he was doing, and he had destroyed a huge pile of canvases in a fit of tightly controlled temper. At such moments she could do nothing but wait for him to come to her for comfort which somehow, without knowing how, she always managed to give him.

It distressed her that she could never understand him, but she knew that he needed her and that was sufficient.

And then Davie Robertson and Walter Duffy, the new chief accountant, came to discuss the year's accounts and trial balance. Their faces were unsmiling, and Janet took them into the library which she used as an office on occasion.

"Your rooms are ready," she said as they sat down. "You'll stay the night, of course. You have brought the accounts?"

Duffy nodded. "Yes, Mrs. MacRae. These are the draft figures."

He handed a folder to her, and she glanced through it quickly and expertly, picking out all the salient points of interest. Later on she would study the detail, but meantime she rapidly grasped the company's financial position. "Um, a little better than last year. That's not too bad. Profit is being maintained. There should be a big improvement next year, I think."

Davie glanced encouragingly at Duffy, who was new and still a little afraid of Janet. Duffy was tongue-tied, so Davie spoke up.

"The figures aren't really good enough, Aunt Janet. We should have done a lot better than that. You see, we have been picking up a lot of new business, and it doesn't show in the accounts. The reason for that is that we are losing local sales, hand over fist."

"What is happening?" Janet demanded.

"Thomas Lipton has taken a hand in the game. I suppose it was inevitable. He has opened his own jam factory, as you know, and at the same time his shops are expanding. He was one of our big customers, but now he only comes to us for Rowan's Royal Marmalade. He now supplies his own fruit, and until we can get into sugar, we can't do much to offset his competition, not when he controls his sales points."

"Lipton has bought fruit farms?" she asked incredulously.

"Yes," Davie nodded. "On a large scale, too, and he has had a very good year. We buy from him incidentally. His prices are competitive."

"He's a clever man," Janet admitted grudgingly. "They say he has an artist working for him here in Glasgow who does paintings for him that cover the whole back of his shop windows. The police have had to be called out to control the crowds blocking the streets."

"That will be Charlie Love. We've heard about him in Dundee," Davie nodded. "If Lipton weren't making his own jam now, Love's work would be helping to sell our products in Lipton's shops. It's a great pity."

"So what do we do?" she asked.

"We can't undercut Lipton," Davie said firmly. "Our prices are as low as we can make them. What we have to do is to sell as we have never sold before, in places where Lipton has no shops. In England. In the United States. In Canada."

She nodded. "But you've been looking into that for some time now, Davie."

"I want to do more. I want to go on a long overseas trip and appoint agents in the principal cities where we can expect good sales—agents who will get a good commission on all new business. Manchester, Birmingham, Liverpool, London, New York, Boston, Pittsburgh, anywhere. It isn't enough for me to make periodic visits, not anymore. We need representation. It will cost a little bit to start with. I was thinking of paying a small retainer, and making the possible commission the real bait. But I will have to select these people, Aunt Janet. It is going to be a long and expensive trip for me."

"Never mind that. Make it." She spoke without hesitation.

"I want to take Martin."

"*What?*" She stared. "He's only a boy."

"This will be something for him to remember all his life. He will be with me when our first agents are appointed. One day he will be controlling all this. I don't want to take him every time I go away—just this one special long trip."

"I suppose so," she agreed reluctantly. "When will this be?"

"I have quite a lot to clear up here. I think I ought to leave it till next spring. We will be away for six months at the very least, possibly eight."

Janet nodded.

"Meantime," Davie pointed out, "Martin has been

spending all his time with Peter Proudfoot. He retires in two months. Mr. Skimming felt that Martin should learn as much from Peter as he could. Then he'll go into Mr. Duffy's office until our big sales trip."

Janet smiled at the silent Duffy.

"We've been ignoring you, Mr. Duffy. I think perhaps I'll send for some tea and then you can discuss the accounts with me. I expect there are special points to raise. There always are."

"Yes," he agreed, relaxing. "There were a few minor matters. I also wanted to talk about our provident fund."

"Good. I can see we are in for a busy evening one way and another."

Later that night as she lay in bed, Torquil breathing gently at her side, she wondered if she were wise to allow Martin to go away for so long. At least he could come to no harm if Davie were looking after him.

She wondered if she had been right to intrude into a man's world, to take upon herself the decision-making in the business. She had prided herself on keeping Rowan's in trust for her son, but ought she not perhaps to have left it to men, whose business it was?

Pride, she reflected, was certainly her besetting sin. She had felt proud about the missionary fund long years ago in St. Andrews, and in giving a helping hand to Mrs. Robertson and Margaret and Helen Kirk. She even felt pride in being what Torquil jokingly called "the real head of the house."

Where did she get it from? she wondered. Her father had been a humble and gentle man. Perhaps it was from her mother's family. Her grandfather had been a bishop and that probably took a lot of pride and ambition. She could never imagine her father in mitered splendor!

She made a silent promise to be more humble and grateful in the future. How could she possibly have managed anything at the factory without the help of people like Neil Skimming, Peter Proudfoot, Hugh Stevenson, and now, in recent years, Davie Robertson?

Satisfactorily chastened she fell asleep at last, full of good resolutions.

In the midsummer of 1893, Davie Robertson returned from what was now one of his regular visits to the United States. Ever since the appointment of the first agents in the spring and summer of 1891, things had been improving steadily at Rowan's.

This year Martin had accompanied him, Martin's first sales trip since the big one of 1891, and they were coming directly to Glasgow before going on to Dundee. When they arrived, Janet was astonished to receive three people, the third a dark-haired, shy-looking young woman with big eyes.

"Mama, guess what," Martin greeted her exuberantly before anybody had a chance to say anything. "Davie's brought home a surprise. His wife."

"Why, Davie!" Janet exclaimed.

"It happened very quickly, Aunt Janet," Davie apologized, advancing with the girl on his arm. "It was all a last-minute rush. I wrote to my mother, but Martin insisted that we surprise you. Aunt Janet, may I present Mrs. Amanda Robertson?"

Janet embraced the girl warmly.

"Sit down. Tell me all about it. How did it happen?"

It transpired that Davie had known Amanda since the previous year. He had been on a sales trip in Pennsylvania, at the time of the Homestead Massacre at the Carnegie Steel Works, in which seven workers were killed by Carnegie's hired detectives, and one of his prospective buyers was a Pittsburgh man called Robert Palmer. Like Davie, Robert Palmer had a low opinion of the celebrated Andrew Carnegie, and the two men had struck up a friendship that resulted in Davie's being invited to stay at the Palmer house for a few days. There he had met the daughter, Amanda, and had fallen in love.

This year, naturally enough, he had returned to the

Palmer home and there, on a spur of the moment decision, they had married.

"I hope you don't mind," Davie apologized to Janet again. "I mean, mixing business with pleasure. I must admit I made an extra trip to Pittsburgh to get married."

"Don't be daft, Davie," she chided, amused.

"Anyway, Martin covered for me, didn't you, Martin? He did a nice bit of business in Baltimore. Anyway, here we are."

"Davie, I'm so glad for you." She turned to the girl. "Davie has been like a son to me. So far as I am concerned, he is one of the family."

"He has told me all about you," Amanda answered softly.

"I hope not," Janet chuckled. "Well, we must take you up to your room, and allow you to get your breath back. Come along."

While Janet took them upstairs, Martin seized the chance to slip away into the kitchen. He discovered Mrs. Kirk in her parlor, with Helen who was bent over some schoolbooks.

"Boo," he said loudly.

They looked up and exclaimed with pleasure.

"I can't stay long just now," he apologized. "I must go and unpack and then I expect Mama will want to know all about the trip. I only came to say hullo."

His eyes were on Helen, now fifteen and on the brink of womanhood. "I'll come back later, if I may," he added.

"I expect I'll be busy," Mrs. Kirk laughed, as the bell rang.

"You will," Martin agreed. "Davie got married and has brought his wife with him. I'll tell Helen all the news if she'll be in."

"I'll be in," Helen agreed, coloring.

"That's a promise," Martin said, grinning. "I'll be back as soon as I can."

He winked at her and followed Mrs. Kirk out of the

room, leaving Helen with a thumping heart. He was brown from the sun, broad-shouldered, handsome, a real man now with a thick, fair moustache. She tried to settle to her books but couldn't, and so gave up and hoped she wouldn't be asked any awkward questions in class next morning.

It seemed hours but was in fact only about half an hour before he returned. She was alone in the little parlor, and he knocked, came in, and sat down facing her.

"Hello, Helen."

"Hello, Martin."

"They're all busy, and dinner won't be for ages, so here I am. You look so much older."

"So do you."

"How's school?" he asked.

"All right." She was tongue-tied now that they were face to face. "How did you enjoy America?"

"Very much. Things seem to happen over there. It's not like Scotland. People seem to be on the go all the time. It's exciting." He laughed. "Despite which, I'm thankful to be home again."

"What's Davie's wife like?"

"Amanda is her name. She's very pretty. A bit shy, but you can't blame her for that. It all happened quickly. You'll like her."

"I probably won't even meet her." Helen began to relax.

"Of course you will."

"Mum says they're leaving in the morning. Are you going, too?"

"No, I've got a few days off. I'll stay till Sunday. I must be back in the office on Monday morning."

"That's nice."

"Isn't it? We'll be able to talk," he agreed cheerfully, but he was not really paying much attention to their conversation. Instead he was noticing that at fifteen she had a woman's figure, and a full, soft, red mouth.

How pretty she was. Incredible to think that this was the

little child he used to take into the park years ago, not always willingly either. His mother would say, "Martin, take Helen out to the park for an hour or two," and they'd set off, her hand in his. Sometimes he had to withstand the smirks of his chums as he walked past with a small girl skipping at his side.

He wouldn't mind taking her into the park right now.

"What will you do when you leave school?" he asked.

"I'm to be your mother's companion," she said, with evident pleasure.

"When was this decided?" he asked, taken aback.

"A week or two ago. Your mother says my education mustn't be wasted, so I'm to be her companion till someone wants to marry me. She's going to pay me for it, too," Helen added in a tone of voice that suggested that miracles had not yet ceased.

"Oh, but . . ." He was about to say that his mother was the last person in the world to need a companion. He bit back the words. What else could they do with her? Her schooling was far superior to that of anyone else in her social class. She was neither one thing nor another—neither servant nor mistress. At least he could read the real happiness in her eyes.

"I'm glad," he amended. "Yes, I really am. When will all this happen?"

"When I'm seventeen. I'm going to a finishing school next year, quite near here."

"Going to learn to be a lady?" he said in a nancy voice, and they looked at one another and burst out laughing together. "Anyway, you are one already," he chuckled. "Why you're practically my sister."

She sobered a little. "I wish I *were* your sister, Martin."

"You're much better than my sister," he scoffed. "She's a little brat."

"Better not say so to her," Helen warned. "She's nine now, and quite the young madam."

"Where is she anyway?"

"Your father took her out, hours ago. You know how he is sometimes. He forgets time."

"Yes. Have you been swotting for exams? I saw you at your books earlier."

"Next week. End-of-year exams. Ugh."

"Poor you. Will they have exams at the finishing school? What's it called anyway?"

"Miss Lumsden's Academy for Young Ladies."

"Help," he exclaimed, making a face. "I bet the girls have a nickname for it. What a mouthful."

"They do music and dancing and painting, and arranging flowers and things like that," she said vaguely.

"How dull."

"To you, perhaps, but not to me. You're an important man now, aren't you?"

"Far from it, but it's fun in Dundee. I like it."

She felt a little pang. This was something she could not share, a strange world of his own. She felt sad.

When he left her, there was still a vestigial awkwardness between them. They did not consciously realize it, but the happiness of innocence had gone forever. They were man and woman now, and from now on they would fence with words where once they had spoken naturally and guilelessly.

Torquil and Nancy arrived home a few minutes later, Torquil full of apologies. He had taken Nancy to visit Charlie Love, the painter who was doing such extraordinary work for Thomas Lipton, and he and Love had got into an involved discussion about painting. Love had a son about Nancy's age, so she had not lacked company.

"Dinner is almost ready," Janet said reprovingly. "Come along and talk to Amanda and Davie. Martin, take Nancy into the kitchen for her supper."

"I want dinner," Nancy said petulantly.

"Not tonight, darling. It is far too late, we have guests, and you ought to be in bed. Martin?"

"Yes, Mama. Come along, Nancy."

Ungraciously, she allowed herself to be led from the room. Martin glanced down at her. Helen had been right about one thing, she was growing up fast. Funny, she didn't look like any of the family. Right now, of course, her brows were drawn down and her lower lip was thrust out. She was in a temper.

"How's school?" he asked, falling back on the overworked opening gambit.

"Awful." She said it theatrically, drawing out the word. "Just awful. I wish I were Helen's age."

"You will be one day."

"You talk like a tummy."

"A whatty-what?"

"A tummy. A grown-up. I suppose you think you're a man."

"Why a tummy?" he asked, stopping in the passage outside the kitchen.

"Because all grown-ups have big tummies. Haven't you noticed?" She stuck her stomach out ludicrously.

He laughed. "Mama doesn't."

"She is different," Nancy agreed. "Everyone else does."

"Neither does Papa."

"He does so. A round fat one. It looks quite funny."

"How do you know that?" Martin demanded.

She began to giggle. "He forgot to close the bedroom door one Sunday and I saw him *with nothing on.*" Her eyes gleamed. "He doesn't know. I'm glad I don't look like that when I've nothing on."

"Yes. Um." Martin was at a loss. "Come along. Bread and milk for you."

"That's all you know, Tummy." She put out her tongue at him. "I get a proper supper *and* I put myself to bed. You can go away now. Tell Mama I'm having my supper." She dismissed him airily.

"I'll stand here till you go through that door. And be polite to Mrs. Kirk."

With a toss of her head she opened the door and went

into the kitchen. He stared after her. Ten years difference in their ages. He always thought of her as a baby, but not any longer.

One thing puzzled him. She had suddenly become a spoiled brat, and he could not understand it, because his mother and father were not given to spoiling children. He wondered what had happened.

EIGHTEEN

I F Martin was puzzled by the fact that his sister was spoiled, Janet was not. It was the source of a great deal of trouble to her recently.

It was entirely Torquil's doing, but when she had tried to discuss it sensibly with him, on one or two occasions, he simply scoffed and laughed and then jollied her out of it, usually with a lot of kissing and cuddling which she was unable to resist. In short, Torquil was not prepared to discuss Nancy with her, and it was a difficult situation, because Nancy was really his only flesh and blood. His mother had died in Australia some years past, and he and his sister no longer corresponded.

Nancy was all he had, and Nancy capitalized on it. She escaped many a well-deserved beating because Janet was unwilling to upset Torquil. Even the mildest criticism of Nancy distressed him.

A growing daughter, who was not fully subject to her control, was the sort of problem Janet felt she could well do without. As a natural reaction, she grew even fonder of Helen Kirk. She had always been very close both to Helen and her mother, and she was determined that, if she could not mold Nancy's life, she would do everything she could for Helen, make sure she married well, that she would live a secure, comfortable, happy life.

She followed Helen's progress at her finishing school with

keen interest, and was satisfied with her handiwork. It was a two-year course, costing twenty pounds a year, which was extremely expensive for a day school, even a private one; but as Helen grew and blossomed into womanhood, Janet was sure she had done the right thing.

One Thursday morning in October 1894, she was awakened by Torquil who was kissing her. She blinked at him sleepily as he grinned down at her.

"Happy birthday, darling," he said. "Welcome to the club."

"Thank you. Is it really the twenty-fifth?"

"It is. You're twenty-one again, sweetheart."

He swung out of bed and came back to her with a little pile of gift-wrapped boxes. She sat up excitedly; her face flushed, her hair over her shoulders, for all the world like a schoolgirl, and opened them. There was a beautiful fur muff, a gold locket on a bracelet, a large box of sugared fruits and another box of expensive embroidered handkerchiefs with her initials on them.

"Why did you have J.D. put on them?" she asked.

"Because you are my darling, and it does happen to be your maiden name."

"What a nice husband you are."

They kissed and he held her off and admired her. "You know, I think you must have discovered the secret of eternal youth. I swear you grow younger every year."

"And I swear there's Irish blood in you somewhere," she laughed. "You could charm a bird off a bush. What lovely presents. What was that you said about joining the club, dear?"

"Just my clumsy little joke. You've now joined the over-forties. I suppose it's a sort of milestone. As a matter of fact, you put the rest of us to shame. Do you realize you're three years older than Vicky Shawburn?"

Janet stared at him. The Shawburns were a pleasant family who lived in one of the neighboring big houses, who had a daughter about Nancy's age, and with whom they had dinner perhaps six or seven times a year. Vicky

Shawburn was plump and middle-aged, and Janet had never thought of her as being younger than herself. She cast a quick mental eye over their other contemporaries, and felt depressed.

Torquil gave an embarrassed laugh at her silence and kissed her cheek. "Why so pensive? You've not changed. Look at me!"

And that was true, too, she thought miserably. Torquil had put on weight—not a great deal but it was unmistakable, and his hair was graying. He was still a fine-looking man, especially when dressed up, but he was uncompromisingly middle-aged, although he didn't seem to mind. The morning had fallen flat. She looked at the little pile of presents and derived no further joy from them.

She watched while Torquil dressed and let him go on downstairs ahead of her before getting up and sitting at her dressing table. She brushed that richly gleaming head of golden hair, and brooded miserably.

Forty! Where had the years gone? What had happened to life? She wasn't merely middle-aged, she was well past the halfway mark. Sixty was considered old. In no time at all now she'd be old and spent, waiting for the yawning grave. She shivered uncontrollably.

I don't want to die, she thought desperately. Not ever. Why do I have to be forty? I don't feel forty—but I am.

Her sense of desolation became so acute that she began to wish that she really were dead, now, for only in death would she get relief from this awful misery. It took her fully five minutes to pull herself together and start dressing. She would have to look cheerful when she went down. There would be a gift from Nancy, and gifts from Margaret Kirk and the other servants, who always produced some little thing on her birthday.

She managed to get through the morning with a fixed smile on her face, but it did not reflect in her eyes. In the afternoon she was able to escape alone to her drawing room, with her embroidery, and there she tried to grapple with the mystery of life and death.

This was the first time that the prospect of death scared her. Her father, that saintly man, had always spoken of death as a release, as the end of an inferior existence and the beginning of eternal glory. The memory of that merely added to her burden.

Her fear was not a physical one, but rather a reluctance to surrender the world that she loved. She really did love life. She was not interested in the possible joys of Heaven. Conchra House was heaven enough for her. Yet the sands of time were running out quickly.

Why, she thought, lots of people died at forty. If they died at fifty, people shrugged and implied that they had had a good run. If they hung on to sixty they were envied their long lives.

Why had Torquil to ruin her birthday by drawing her attention to her age? Unreasonably, she blamed him, for all the world as though she herself would not have known her age. She resented him and began also to resent his apparent zest for life when he must know it was nearing an end.

She could not shake off these feelings, but she had enough sense to know that she must conceal them if life was to have any semblance of pleasure left in it. She tried reading her Bible daily, in the manner she had been brought up to do, but she found no solace in it. She turned to her prayer book, reading the Collects, Epistle, and Gospel for the day, but soon stopped. She didn't want to be saved. She wanted to be left alone, in peace.

For the first time Torquil was unable to arouse her passions. She submitted to him, much as she had latterly submitted to Andrew, finding neither pleasure nor displeasure in the act of sex. Her sexual appetite had been lost, and when, after two or three months, menstruation ceased, she felt a deep relief. No more sex. It was a well-known fact that women did not sleep with their husbands after the menopause. She had no one to tell her that this was the sheerest nonsense. She had been told it, she believed it implicitly, and therefore it was so.

With a delicacy that would have filled Lawrence Darling with admiration, she broke the news to Torquil that she had passed the age for sex and that it would be appreciated if he could keep to his own side of the bed. Torquil himself believed that the vast majority of women turned against sex in middle age, and he felt obliged to make the best of it. The difficulty was that she was as slim, as smooth-skinned, as breathtakingly lovely as he had ever known her, and what was true for women was definitely not true for men. He felt more vigorous than ever.

After two tortured nights he decided to move into the bedroom across the hall, which was the main guest bedroom and had its own dressing room. Janet was secretly relieved. Right now she found Torquil something of an unpleasant distraction.

Torquil in turn grew moody as frustration mounted, and he spent time in the roof studio glaring at his work. Even it was frustrating, and once again he cleared out a lot of it and burned it in the garden. The only painting in which he took any pride was his portrait of Janet and that, he reminded himself savagely, had been done in his ignorant youth when he painted maps of people.

One Sunday morning Janet found Nancy sobbing on her bed. It was midmorning, and outside the weather was bright and clear. She sat on the bed, beside the weeping girl, and tried to comfort her. Nancy shook her off petulantly.

"What's *wrong*?" Janet asked. "Please tell me, darling."

"You wouldn't understand," Nancy informed her between deep sobs.

"You'd be surprised at what I understand. Now do tell me. We're both women."

The flattery failed. "That's not it," Nancy gasped. "*Your* father is dead!"

Janet tried to make sense out of this. "Yes, dear, I know. What of it?"

"Papa has gone to walk in the park. He didn't want me.

He . . . he said he was thinking about a painting and wanted to be alone."

Oh, dear, thought Janet. This was the price of spoiling her. But how unlike Torquil to spurn the child. She pulled Nancy close to her and tried to explain that Torquil really did have to get away by himself, to think. Nancy was not even listening.

Her father's rejection that morning had hit her far harder than Janet could ever know. Janet had never experienced this rejection. Nancy had been right when she had said her mother would not understand. As she heard Janet's voice, became aware of the words, a resentment crept over her. It was all right for *her*. She could see Papa whenever she wanted. She was his wife! It was so unfair. Daughters ought to have rights, too.

She pulled away from Janet and ran into the bathroom and locked the door behind her.

When Janet told Torquil about it later in the day, he was immediately contrite, but in the days that followed he tended to avoid Nancy. At times when he would normally have taken her into the city, or to visit one of his few cronies, he slipped away alone. And in the summer he went off to Connel again, and wrote after ten days to say he would be away longer than usual, and that he was sure Janet would understand.

Janet did, of course, and was not altogether sorry to have the house to herself. She was no longer acutely depressed, but life had changed and she was not eagerly awaiting Torquil's return. The change was so subtle that she herself was not conscious of it. She merely felt rather more cheerful than she had done for months, and this was reinforced when Helen left the finishing school and became her companion officially.

Janet, Nancy, and Helen went off together to a quiet sea-side resort on the Clyde coast, for a summer holiday in August, leaving Mrs. Kirk in charge of the house. It was a warm, sunny month, and they spent their days walking by the shore, or sitting in deck chairs on the sandy beach.

It was part of Helen's job to take Nancy bathing and to keep an eye on her in the water.

Everything went well at first until one day Helen had a little trouble getting Nancy to come ashore, and called to her in a sharp voice, reminding her that her mother was waiting.

Eleven-year-old Nancy came ashore, glaring. "You act as though *you* were my mother," she said crossly. "You're nothing but a servant."

Helen could hardly believe her ears. Never before had anyone reminded her or her mother that they were employees in the MacRae household. It had not only been unnecessary, but to the MacRaes it would be unthinkable.

"Your mother asked me to get you to come out of the water," Helen said firmly, biting back her anger. "In future do as you are told. I am your mother's companion, which means I do things for her to save her having to do them herself. If she heard you talking to me like that, you wouldn't be able to sit down for a week."

"Huh," Nancy scoffed. "I'm not afraid of you. I'd tell Papa, and *then* you'd see."

She walked off, nose in air, and Helen followed, baffled. There was something here that she did not understand. What had been going on in Conchra House that neither she nor the rest of the staff had noticed? Nancy had never been the likable child that Martin had been, but she had not been aggressively objectionable like this.

As she and Janet sat together that evening, Helen broached the subject cautiously.

"Is something troubling Nancy, Mrs. MacRae?"

"Why do you ask?"

"Her manner this morning was rather sullen and impertinent. I wondered if something were upsetting her."

"What did she say?" Janet demanded.

"Oh, I forget exactly," Helen lied loyally. "It was something out of character, and it made me wonder."

Janet studied the girl. She was young but she was mature enough to be her companion, and a companion was supposed to be someone in whom you could confide. She decided to test Helen with a confidence.

"Nancy is going through a bad patch," she said slowly. "Her father doesn't make as much fuss of her as he used to do, and it distresses her. Unfortunately, she has always been her father's daughter, rather than mine, and I have never been able to get close to her. I'd like to help her, but she won't let me."

"I see." Helen was thoughtful. "Perhaps I could try. I'm not very many years older than she is."

"Go ahead," Janet smiled, "but be prepared for a disappointment. If only she would make friends with other girls her own age, but she has never liked other children. It's probably my fault for not having brought her up differently."

"I'm sure it isn't your fault," Helen cut in quickly, and Janet smiled at the vehemence with which she spoke.

Helen thought about it and decided to make a real effort to become friendly with Nancy. She became very considerate, spoke gently, tried to find ways to please her. She received nothing in exchange except rude rebuffs, some of which merited a good whipping.

One morning when they were walking along the beach, some distance from Janet, Helen turned on the child angrily.

"What's wrong with you, Nancy MacRae? You're having a lovely holiday, your mother and I do all we can to make you happy, and you can't even keep a civil tongue in your head. If you were mine, I'd shake some sense into you."

"You try," Nancy invited, her eyes filled with hate. "You just try."

"Don't worry. I wouldn't soil my hands on a brat like you."

"Soil your hands on a brat like me?" Nancy was delighted. The enemy had delivered herself into her hands. "Wait till I tell Mama."

"I hope you will," Helen replied coolly. "Of course you know what will happen. She'll want to know why I said it. Will you tell her—or shall I?"

"You're as bad as all of them," Nancy cried in quick frustration. "Pretend you're a friend, try to suck up, and you don't really care. You don't *care!*"

She burst into tears, forlorn because Torquil was not there to take her hand, chuck her under the chin, and tell her one of his daft, funny stories.

"We do," Helen protested, her anger instantly gone. "We really do, my dear."

Impulsively she pulled Nancy to her, to comfort her. In a flash Nancy turned and spat straight in her face and then, frightened by what she had done, ran on ahead as fast as she could.

Helen, kneeling in the sand, put her hand up to her face in utter disbelief. She found her handkerchief and wiped off the spittle. That was that, she thought coldly. She would say nothing, and Nancy could stew for a while in the uncertainty of whether or not she would be reported. So far as Helen was concerned, Nancy MacRae was reduced to the status of employer's daughter and nothing more. She would never again waste time on her.

As she got up and followed slowly, she was heavyhearted. Something had gone terribly wrong and nobody seemed to know what. How did it happen that a child with a lovely, happy home, a wonderful family, devoted servants, and with every advantage that a girl could possibly ask for in this world could behave like a guttersnipe?

To spit in a servant's face? It was incredible. If Margaret Kirk ever discovered that, there would be ructions that none of them would ever forget. Not that Margaret would, nor Janet.

Your secret is safe with me, Nancy, my girl, she thought grimly. I'd be ashamed for anyone to know that I stayed on after being treated like that. And then, irrationally, she thought of Martin and tears gathered in her eyes.

* * *

Despite her worries about Nancy, and despite Torquil's more frequent absences, Janet had settled down to a contented life in the big stone house overlooking the lovely little park. Her depression faded away on its own accord. The fear of impending death receded. After all, she reasoned, there was a lot of life left in her and she enjoyed it. She had come to accept the role of middle-aged matron, and found that it had advantages, among them the fact that she worried less about almost everything.

When Torquil came home late in September 1895, brown as a berry and more cheerful than she had seen him for some time, he had news for her.

"I've got rid of the place at Connel," he announced.

"Have you, dear? What will you do instead?"

"I've rented another one on the other side of the country. It's near Perth, on the road to Dunkeld."

"How nice. Perhaps Martin could visit you? It can't be very far from Dundee."

"We'll have to see about that later," he remarked, suddenly becoming vague. "Of course it isn't ready yet. Anyway I should have thought Martin saw enough of my studio here to not want to see another."

"What is it? A house or a cottage?"

"A sort of cottage. Not very big."

"Why Perth?" she asked suddenly. "I thought you liked to be near the sea."

"No, darling, you're out of date. I do like to be near water, which is different. Perthshire is full of rivers and lochs. Remember what Scott said in *The Fair Maid of Perth*? He said Perth is the most beautiful county in Scotland and that even if you place your native county first, you would always place Perth second."

She studied him. He was jauntier, bouncier. Something had happened.

"Did you have a successful time at Connel?"

"Yes. I suddenly discovered what I've been doing wrong. It's color. It's all color. You know, you have to exaggerate color. There's impressionism of color just as there is of form. I've been too slavish to real color instead of concentrating on the impression of color." He grinned. "I expect I sound mad, but I think I've found my feet at last."

"Did you bring anything home with you?"

"No. I scrapped the lot. I'll experiment a bit in the studio.here and then when I go to Perth I'll be ready to begin."

She gave up in despair. When she had first met him, he was supposed to be on the brink of a brilliant career. Seemingly he had thrown it away, and all these years he had been experimenting. It was a good job he was financially independent and that she was wealthy. Despite the depth of his feeling for his work, he was not the type to starve in a garret.

"When do you go to Perth?" she asked.

"I don't know. Soon perhaps. I want to get everything straight there. How have things been at home?"

"Everything is very well. It generally is. Nancy's school report wasn't very good, but it never has been."

"Not the clever type," Torquil agreed, "but it hardly matters, does it? It's not as though she will have to go out to work. Is Martin all right?"

"He's doing very well. He'll be away for his twenty-first birthday."

"Too bad. Why's that?"

"He'll be in the United States—on his own this time."

"I thought that was Davie's job."

"Technically, I suppose it is, but Martin will be taking over control of the factory soon and he wants to make the trip. He's immersed in business these days."

Talk of the Dundee factory always left Torquil bemused and he preferred to talk about other things.

"I must go out shortly," he remarked, "but I'll be back in time for dinner."

"Must you? Nancy will be home in an hour."

"I'll see her when I get back."

"Darling," she protested, "you've no idea how she *waits* for your return. She'll be bitterly disappointed."

"Because she won't see me till dinnertime?" He laughed.
"She's still only eleven. She isn't allowed to stay up late."
"Make an exception tonight, then. Anyway I'll be at
home all day tomorrow. I'll take her for a walk."
It was no use going on discussing it. If Torquil had
decided he was going out, out he would go. He hated
anyone trying to mess about with his plans.

When he did come home, full of apologies at being late
for dinner, Nancy flung herself at him. He whirled her
around in his arms, knocking over a small table in the
process.

"Hullo, young lady. You're getting too heavy for this."

"Where have you been?" she demanded.

"Visiting a friend. I hear you went to the seaside for a
holiday."

"What did they say?" she asked suspiciously.

"What did who say, my love?"

"Mama and Helen?"

"Nothing," he chuckled. "Mama just said you'd been for
a holiday. Did you have a nice time?"

"No," she replied scornfully.

"Why not?" He led her to a seat and perched her on his
knee. She clung to his arm fiercely.

"Because you weren't there. It was horrible."

"Oh, dear." He hugged her. "Look, you're a big girl now.
I can't always be here. I have my work."

"Why can't I come away with you?" she wanted to know.

"That wouldn't do at all. *I* can't look after a young
woman, and besides I'm out a lot of the time. Who'd look
after you?"

"I could look after myself."

"You'd be bored to tears in no time at all, if you were
allowed to come, which you won't be. It just won't do.
Anyway, I'm home now."

"You go away so much," she complained.

"Not really. Anyway it's a matter of mood. If I'm in a
working mood, I must work."

"You never used to have these moods."

"That's your opinion," he chuckled. "Your mama would tell you differently. You were too young to notice before."

"I hate your paintings," she told him in a low, vibrant voice.

"What? That's a fine thing to say about your old father's work."

"I'd rather you stayed at home with me."

"That's what you say now, but one day you'll marry some handsome young man and go away and leave us."

"Never. Never, never, never. I won't leave you."

"Thank you." He kissed her. "You'll feel differently when you're older."

"I'll never marry anyone." She snarled the words, and he recoiled a little in the face of such vehemence.

"Good," he said in a jolly voice, trying to get her out of her mood. "I'd just as soon you stayed at home anyway."

She said nothing, and he saw that she was staring toward the window, her face set in an unbecoming scowl. He squeezed her waist and swung her to the floor. She was so like her mother in some ways, and so completely unlike her in others. Where did she get her moody temper from?

Two days later he saw another side to her moodiness. He had been working on a canvas, experimenting with new ways of expressing light values, working from some sketches in his sketchbook. He was quite pleased with the result and knew that at long last he had completed the discovery that began with his visit to the Impressionists in Paris years earlier.

He went into the studio and his glance automatically went to his easel as he closed the door behind him. Then he stood stock-still, eyebrows drawn down. He walked closer, disbelief in his eyes. There were great blobs of color smeared all over the canvas. Someone had daubed it heavily. It would take weary hours to clean it off, if indeed it was worth trying to salvage it.

"I hate your paintings." He could hear Nancy's voice

again. He did not want to believe it, but who else? Not
Janet or the servants. He slumped into his old armchair and
stared vacantly at the mess, trying to think.

In the end he decided to do what he always did—to consult Janet. She was writing a letter and looked up and
smiled, and then raised her eyebrows questioningly when
she saw his evident distress. He told her what had happened and asked her what he ought to do about it.

She was silent for two or three minutes.

"I'm sorry this has happened, Torquil," she said gently.
"You have spoiled her outrageously for years, and now
she can't understand why you have less time for her."

"Hang it all, she's no longer a baby."

"Perhaps so, but she is young and she can only see that
you ignore her where once you would have made a fuss of
her. Couldn't you take her to Perth when you go to
straighten things out there?"

"Out of the question." His reply was abrupt and force-
ful, taking her aback.

"All right. Then I don't see what you can do. Obviously
she is the culprit. If you accuse her, you'll only make matters worse. The kindest thing would be to pretend nothing
has happened. It was just the one painting she damaged?"

"There isn't anything much to damage except this one.
The rest is rubbish. But now that I know what I'm really
trying to do . . . well, she'd better not try this again."

"Then ignore it, and try to show her more attention. Not
too much. Don't swing the other way, only to go away and
leave her high and dry once more. You used to treat Martin so well. Why can't you be as natural with Nancy?
You've babied her for years. Treat her as a companion, an
adult."

"I'll try, my dear." He kissed the back of her neck,
noticing as he did so how smooth and young her skin was.
"You're right. You always are. You're a remarkable
woman, and I don't deserve you."

"What nonsense," she protested, but she was smiling

with pleasure. "I blame myself a good deal for not being firmer with Nancy when she was young."

He pulled her face around and kissed her full on the lips. "Wise and beautiful. They should preserve you forever, in a glass case, to show to the world. The perfect woman."

"You needn't try out your blarney on me. I'm not Nancy."

But her sinful pride in his flattery was not troubling her at the moment. Instead she felt an unreasonable chill. She was a woman, not a thing to be put in a glass case, a specimen to display. His compliment had failed miserably, for once.

Nancy cried herself to sleep that night, lost in a sea of young, heart-rending desolation. She had done what she did on impulse, and had been dreading the awful consequences. She knew he had been to the studio and in an odd way she looked forward to the angry scene that must ensue. Instead, nothing happened. Nothing at all. He was friendly and pleasant. He wasn't even *angry!*

Her bid for attention had been a failure.

NINETEEN

THE following summer, while Torquil was away in Perth, Mrs. Robertson died, aged sixty. Janet went to Dundee for the funeral, leaving Nancy in the care of Helen and her mother. After the funeral she went to Martin's home. For the past two years he had rented a place of his own on the first floor of a big terrace house.

His housekeeper made tea for them, and Janet examined her surroundings with approval. He kept a nice place, and it had a comfortable, lived-in atmosphere. Her sharp eyes searched diligently for dirt and found traces of none.

"Well," she asked, "how are things at Rowan's now that you're in full control? Are you enjoying it?"

"Yes," he chuckled. "I was lucky in being so well-trained for the job, but everyone misses you."

"I'm sure you all get on much better without me. Do you rely much on Davie?"

"Quite a lot. He has so much energy. Sugar is our main concern now, making a success of it. I don't know where we'd be without your interest-free loan to help us with all this expansion."

"You know you're welcome. What good is money if you can't use it? Besides, I'll make a profit out of sugar in the long run."

When Davie and Martin had been buying West Indian sugar plantations to augment their own beet supply, Davie had bought a very profitable business for Janet. It was in her own name—J. Darling & Company—and was managed for her by a bright young planter. One of Davie's more valuable traits was his ability to find good local people to run things. He had done it in Spain and again in the Caribbean. J. Darling was strictly a private venture and did not supply Rowan's, much to Martin's surprise, but that was how Janet wanted it.

So far as Janet was concerned, she had put Rowan's onto a sound footing for Martin. The money she had lent the company, firstly for oranges and lemons and latterly for sugar beet and then sugarcane, was all being repaid over a period of years, and she was confident that the loss of interest on her capital would be made up by the profit from her prosperous little sugar plantation. There was the added bonus that Rowan's kept an eye on her interests in the West Indies free of charge, which was an important consideration for her.

"Davie is quite extraordinary," Martin said slowly. "He has an ability to grasp things quickly. His knowledge of oranges and lemons and sugar is quite amazing. I don't know what I'd do without him. I was thinking of giving him an interest in the firm—not a big one, but enough to ensure that he stays with us."

"That's a wise decision."

"It isn't that I don't trust him, or that I think he wants to leave us. Only, when you have someone who is important to you, it pays to look after them."

"That's certainly right," she agreed. "I would have done something myself a long time ago, only I felt it was wrong for me to do it. The decision had to be yours."

"You're funny," he smiled. "You've never said anything."

"It's better this way. You're in control. If you want my advice at any time, you can always have it for the asking. You know that."

"The more I find out about it," he said quietly, "the more impressed I am with all you've accomplished. I'm forever coming across little refinements which I find you introduced. You certainly surprised Dundee, you know. The story is that most of the leading businessmen of the city gave you five years before running the firm into the ground. They all said a woman couldn't run a factory."

"I couldn't have done it without a lot of very valuable help," she pointed out. "Never underrate your staff, Martin."

"I don't, believe me. Talking of which, when Neil Skimming retires next year I'm making Davie Robertson a director. I'll give him a part of Skimming's job to look after, and a couple of very senior assistants, one of them on the sales side and one on the administrative side. It means virtually three jobs where there were two. I'm also going to put Duffy on the board, and Dan Knox, the new jam master. The thing is, I'd like you to come onto it as well. You have a lot of experience and so much to contribute."

She shook her head. "No. I made up my mind that once you had passed twenty-one I would hand over to you completely—unless you weren't interested or capable. You are both, and I'm not going to interfere in any way. I'm always glad to talk about the factory, and I'd like to visit it informally while I'm here. But it is all yours now, Martin."

"I was afraid you'd say that. Pity. I think we need you."

"And I know you need to manage without me. I'd better go to my room and change."

They were to have dinner with Davie and Amanda.

"Before you do . . . how's Helen?"

"Very well. She is an absolute treasure. I have been trying to get her to go out more, but curiously enough she prefers to stay at home with me."

"She's eighteen now, isn't she?"

"That's right. It's high time she found herself a nice young man to pay court to her. I'm considering holding a small dance for her. I want her to marry well, and that means meeting people."

"Isn't that really her own business?" Martin asked, a little stiff.

"Perhaps, but I feel I owe it to Margaret Kirk. She's been such a wonderful housekeeper and a good friend. If Helen makes a good marriage, Margaret Kirk will be very happy. So shall I, come to that."

"What about making Helen happy?" he demanded, flushing.

"You silly boy, of course Helen will be happy. That's the whole point."

"Is it right to try to arrange her life for her?"

"I'm only trying to ensure that she gets into decent society where she will meet the sort of young man who *can* make her happy. After that it is up to her, isn't it?" She was gazing at him curiously.

"I suppose so. She is looking after Nancy, is she?"

"Yes, and they don't get along well together. Nancy is downright unpleasant sometimes. I've had to speak to her about it. She is only a child, but she behaves as though she were mistress of the house. It's an awkward age, of course."

"Remind me not to have girls when I'm married," he laughed.

"Is there some prospect of that?" Janet asked.

"Not really. I hardly know any girls. I was merely theorizing."

"You're young. There's plenty of time. You should get out, too—like Helen."

He did not answer, and with a smile she kissed his cheek and went to her room to change.

After this he became a more frequent visitor to Conchra House, and a year later he took a month's holiday and spent it with them. Janet was delighted, for she had missed him in his early years at Dundee. In the past twelvemonth Nancy had quieted down a lot, a tall, solemn girl who did not say much. She was attractive, and Janet was pleased at the change.

Torquil was away, of course, but she was so accustomed to Torquil's trips that she did not trouble about them. He was still the same pleasant, kind bantering man she had once loved so deeply and passionately, and since he had moved to Perth, he had been working hard and getting obvious satisfaction from it. She loved him still, in a different and, she imagined, a deeper way. Privately she considered herself the luckiest woman in the world.

"What are your plans?" she asked Martin on the day after his arrival, a Sunday.

The three of them were sitting under an awning in the garden. Nancy was visiting a school friend and would not return till teatime.

"Laze about, enjoy the sunshine and good food, and allow you to spoil me." He turned to glance at Helen. "I was wondering if I could borrow Helen."

"Borrow her?" Janet laughed. "Why do you want to do that?"

"I thought of taking a trip up the Clyde on a pleasure steamer tomorrow. It would be nice to have company."

"What a lovely idea. Of course she can go along, if that is what she wishes."

"Yes, please," Helen said quickly, and then blushed.

"Good, that's settled," Martin said smugly. "Thank you, Mama. I promise to return her to you in perfect working order."

They laughed at his joke.

Next morning he and Helen set off early for the Broomielaw, where they would board a paddle steamer that would take them on a day's pleasure excursion round the Kyles of Bute and the two Cumbraes. It was gloriously warm and sunny, and Martin bought two first-class tickets and assisted Helen up the gangplank. They stood leaning over the upper deck rail and watched other trippers clambering aboard.

He glanced at her and she looked at him sideways, and then they smiled. Boldly he took her hand and put it through his arm. She offered no resistance.

"Lovely day," he said awkwardly.

"Isn't it."

"There will be a German band, once we sail, and the food is very good. It will be great fun."

"I know, I've been before, but not first class."

"It's the only way to travel," he said grandly, and almost at once realized his ineptitude. "You . . . er . . . you look very nice in that hat."

"Do I? It's one of your mother's. She gave it to me."

"She always did have good taste." He grinned boyishly. "Shall we go and watch the view from the stern as we sail?"

"If you like."

"Thank goodness we aren't crowded. Look, there's another boat sailing now."

They watched the other paddle steamer set off ahead of them, and waved back at the people who lined its side. Martin tucked Helen's hand more securely into his arm, and his chest swelled. What a great idea this had been.

Before very long they were clear of the shipyards, and heading out into the open firth, the sun sparkling on the wavelets. It was a long trip among beautiful scenery. Helen was fascinated by glimpses of big mansions standing among trees near the water's edge.

"Wouldn't it be nice to live in a house like that?" she asked Martin.

He nodded. It would be very nice indeed to live in a big house on the Clyde coast, but it was not for him.

"Unfortunately, it would be too far for me to get to the office. Maybe one day when I retire I'll buy a house near here."

"I suppose you've got to live in Dundee."

"Near it anyway. There are some nice big houses along the Firth of Tay, not far from Dundee. Rather like these, you know, except that the weather is a bit colder in winter over on the east coast."

"Are there really houses like these?"

"Certainly. It's a pity you can't come up to see them.

I've a friend who has a yacht, and who could take us for a sail on the river."

"How lovely."

"When I marry and buy my own house, it will be somewhere near the river, in a house like that. Of course, first I have to find a girl who will have me."

He put his hand over hers, where it lay on his arm, as he spoke.

"I may not have very far to look," he ventured uncertainly.

"Really?" She avoided his gaze.

"How old are you now, Helen? Nineteen, isn't it?"

"Yes."

"You're grown up. People get married at nineteen."

"Some do," she agreed.

"I'll soon be twenty-three." He plucked up his courage. It was easier here, in semipublic. Somehow he was less tongue-tied. "I've always wanted to marry you, Helen. I hate being away from you."

She said nothing.

"I love you," he told her in a low voice.

"I wish you hadn't said that," she whispered so that he had to bend toward her to hear her.

"Why, don't you like me?"

"I love you, too." Her voice was muffled.

"Then what's wrong?" he exclaimed.

"Have you forgotten who I am, Martin? After all your mother has done for me and mine, do you think I could repay her by ruining all her hopes for you?"

"What hopes? Mama doesn't run my life. She's never even talked to me about marriage, not seriously. I'll tell her, and that will be that."

"Are you actually proposing to me?" she asked, curiosity overcoming embarrassment. After all, if this was her first proposal, she wanted to get the most out of it.

"Yes. Yes I am. Will you marry me—please?"

Her chin went up bravely. "You know I can't, Martin. But I'll never forget the fact that you asked me. I shall never marry anyone else. I'll be your mother's companion for the rest of her life."

"And then what?" he asked, practical if unromantic.

"I can get another job."

"No you cannot. I want you. I've known it for a long time, really. If we weren't standing here in full view of everyone, I'd kiss you."

It was amazingly easy to be bold when you didn't have to make good your words!

"That would be nice," she giggled, "but seriously, you know we can't get married. It would be cruel to your mother, and she has been so kind to me."

"Oh, rubbish," he said impatiently.

"It isn't, and you know it."

Someone came and stood near them, thus terminating the conversation. Martin, however, had finally reached his decision and he was not going to be put off. Would his mother really become heartbroken because he was happy? He didn't believe it. It was true, of course, that he was marrying beneath himself—at least most people would say so. Almost everyone, in fact, including the servants. Especially the servants.

But it didn't really matter, not when it was the man who was superior. Besides she had gone to the same school as his sister, and she was a lady's companion. It wasn't at all the same thing as wanting to marry the scullery maid.

They were quiet, listening to the band. When they finally returned to the city, they took a horse tram part of the way, and then walked the rest. It was a mild, still evening. Suddenly he pulled her into a little lane running alongside the walled garden of a house, concealed by trees. He took her in his arms and kissed her. For a long time they stood there, holding tight, kissing wildly. When he released her, her lips were parted and her eyes shone.

"I'm not sorry," he blurted out.

She smiled. "Nor am I."

They kissed again.

"I do love you, Helen," he whispered.

"I know, and I love you, too."

"Then it *is* all right. It must be."

"Don't let's talk about it. Let's just do this," she whispered back.

"Not here. Someone may come along. Listen, they'll be indoors by now. We can go home through the side gate, and go to that seat behind the rhododendrons without them seeing us. It will be all right there. We could sit there for a little while, and nobody will ever know."

She gave him a conspiratorial smile and a quick kiss, and they set off hurriedly for Conchra House.

Janet smiled as Martin came into the room. It was the last day of his holiday. The time had flown past, and he was to leave next morning. It had been a happy visit, and she was delighted to see that his friendship with Helen had survived the changes of time. Many another young man would have tended to ignore his mother's companion, despite a childhood friendship, but Martin had taken her for walks in Kelvingrove Park, and to Glasgow Green to listen to the bands. Indeed he seemed to spend all his time either with Helen or with them both.

"Where have you been, my dear?" she asked.

"In the garden, walking with Helen. She's gone up to change for dinner."

"Good. I wanted to talk to you alone. I've made a fresh will recently. I'm leaving Nancy ten percent in Rowan's, out of my forty percent. The rest will revert to you. I hope she will marry well, but she ought to have some money of her own. It is enough to make her independent—just."

"I don't mind," he smiled, "but you really ought not to be thinking of wills at your age."

"It is because of my age that I am," she retorted. "I've also got money of my own, Martin, money left by my father and by yours, too. There's rather a lot of it. It's been invested for years. Nancy will get one-third and you will get two-thirds. There's over seventy thousand pounds."

He had had no idea that she had so much. She had had

the whole shareholding in Rowan's until he was twenty-one, and she retained forty percent of it even now, but he had never thought about his father's and grandfather's private money.

"There's just one thing. You haven't had time to save any capital. One day soon you will want to marry and buy a house. When you marry I shall give you five thousand pounds as a wedding present."

"I don't know what to say."

"Don't say anything," she laughed. "It's time you knew where you stood. You're the real head of the family now, Martin. The money is ours, and its disposal concerns you as much as it does me."

"But, Papa . . ."

"Papa is all right. This house and its contents are all in his name and he does have an income of his own, sufficient for himself."

"Anyway he'll never want while I'm alive," Martin remarked.

"I'm well aware of that fact. You see, I know you well."

They smiled at one another, and he thought that she was really far too pretty to be the mother of a man his age. It dawned on him that his stepfather was a lucky man indeed.

Helen left them after coffee, and about twenty minutes later Martin got up.

"I think I'll turn in early, Mama. See you in the morning at breakfast."

They kissed and he went upstairs. In his room he changed into his nightshirt and dressing gown, and sat trying to concentrate on a book. About an hour later, when he was certain Janet was in bed, and only the night light burned in the hall, he heard the now-familiar tap at his door. Helen slipped in quietly.

He jumped up and went to her and they embraced silently, then removed their clothes and slid into his bed. There was a sweet poignancy about their loving tonight, for it might be weeks before they had the chance again.

Afterward, sated and happy, they lay back together, and he put his light on and they talked in low whispers.

"Helen, you really must marry me after this," he insisted.

When she had first allowed him to make love to her, he had exulted, assuming that she would naturally wish him to make an honest woman of her. To his utter amazement she had flatly refused, saying that she did not mind being his mistress, because she loved him so much, but that she would not make trouble in the family by marrying him.

"We've talked about it before, darling," she whispered back. "I'm happy. Can't we just leave things as they are?"

"But I'm not happy . . ."

"Shhhh," she warned.

"Well, I'm not. I'm miserable. I want you. Good Lord, we can't go on like this forever."

"Why not—if we're careful?"

They had been particularly careful. She would not let him come to her room, for she knew better than he how to get in and out of the servants' wing without risking getting caught. Also, if she were found in the main house, she could always plead some excuse about not being sure if anyone had remembered to close the downstairs hall window. She *was* the mistress's companion, after all.

"I'm sorry, Helen, but I never wanted just to have an affair."

She laughed softly. "I know. I know exactly what you were thinking. You thought that if you compromised me, I'd be certain to jump at the chance of marrying you. Well, I love you far too much for that."

"Suppose you have a baby."

"Let's hope I don't. Anyway, nobody would ever suspect you."

"I want one," he protested. "Oh, dash it, Helen, I want to do this all the time."

"I had noticed that," she teased.

"I love you so much."

"And I adore you," she told him. "Which is why I won't let you ruin your life. You must make a really brilliant match. I'll be all right, my dear. Nobody can ever take this away from me."

His arms went around her and they kissed passionately, writhing in one another's arms, their naked bodies intertwined.

Neither of them heard the door open, only the sudden, sharp gasp which seemed to shatter the silence. They fell apart and turned to stare, horror-struck, at Janet who stood in the doorway, her mouth open, her eyes wide.

Then Martin grabbed at the sheets and pulled them up.

TWENTY

JANET swallowed hard as she tried to take command of the situation. Her mind was still reeling under the impact of what she had seen.

"Helen, you had better go directly to your room. Martin, I shall return in five minutes. I wish to speak to you."

She did not wait for a reply, but hurried off to everyone's relief. Martin turned to Helen.

"That's done it," he said. "Don't worry, I'll make sure you don't get into trouble."

Helen looked at him steadily. "There's no need to worry about me. The damage is done. Did you see your mother's face?"

"Yes. You'd better go, and I'll put on my nightshirt and dressing gown before Mama comes back. I'll see you in the morning—whatever happens."

"Perhaps you won't be able to. Good-bye, Martin."

"Only for a little while." He kissed her, dressed hurriedly, and sat down to wait his mother's return.

In exactly five minutes she came in and closed the door behind her. She sat on the edge of his bed and regarded him gravely.

"Have you any idea what you've done to that girl?"

"I want to marry her, Mama."

"Marry Helen?"

"Yes, let me explain."

"I think you'd better. Try to start at the beginning."

She was unsmiling and he took a deep breath and told her the whole story, starting with the trip down the Clyde on the paddle steamer. As the story unfolded, she realized that it was slightly better than it might have been. At least they were in love with one another, and he plainly did want to marry Helen.

What was more it seemed that Helen was refusing to marry him because she did not wish to spoil the family relationship, which was quixotic if she really loved him. There was, however, one point he was avoiding, and when he had done, she led him back to it.

"Thank you for telling me all this. I wish you'd done so before. I could have talked to Helen. You *don't* think I'd discourage you if you really are in love with one another, do you? She's a very nice girl. I certainly don't regard your marriage to her as the social catastrophe she believes I would. Other people might, of course, but then in Dundee who would know anyway? But that's not the real point, Martin. Did you have to . . . to behave like this? I won't use the proper word for it. It's vulgar. Apart from any moral argument, hasn't it occurred to you that she will probably have a baby?"

"I was hoping she would."

"You hoped she would! She would, perhaps will, find out in say three months from now, and no matter how quickly you got married after that, five or six months between the wedding and the birth of the baby tells the whole world your story. You foolish boy. You really are."

"I didn't think of that—only that she'd be sure to marry me." He brightened. "Anyway, I don't mind. I don't care what they say."

"Your firstborn child might mind," Janet flashed fiercely. "What a nice pickle you've got yourself into now. She may be going to have a baby, already, though we don't know it yet. You are going to have to get engaged and married all at once, and soon. We can't afford to take chances. When was the first time?"

"Nearly a month ago. The day of the Clyde trip."

"Oh, dear. Well it's going to look odd. We'll have to let it be known that you've been secretly engaged for months. I've got my mother's engagement ring. She will have to wear it and say you gave it to her months ago. We must get the engraving changed." She sighed. "I can't understand you, Martin. I didn't think you'd seduce the girl you loved."

"*Seduce* her?" he protested.

"Well, you know what I mean. It's your father who should be talking to you."

"Mama, I want to say something. I'm not trying to excuse myself, but it takes two people, you know. This was Helen's idea in the first place. She said she wanted to be my mistress until I found someone else, and that she intended never to marry. I'm not telling tales, but I thought she was just being noble and that if I fell in with her idea, she'd change her mind pretty soon. I couldn't believe it tonight when she still said no. I didn't set out to do it this way. It's . . ." He was floundering.

It had *not* been a planned seduction, and he did not want her to think Helen was the sort of girl one could seduce. It was so hard to put it all into words without appearing to be blaming Helen.

"All right," Janet interrupted, to his profound relief. "I know what you are saying. I'm glad it was like that, though you are a proper pair of ninnies. You'd better get some sleep. Of course, you won't go to Dundee tomorrow."

"Oh."

"No, we have things to arrange. They can manage without you for a few days. I'll let Davie know you're staying on a little longer. Please do *not* leave the house tomorrow without my permission, and don't speak to Helen till I've seen her first, and her mother."

"You're not going to tell her mother!"

"Of course I'm going to tell her mother. Your engagement will be announced tomorrow. What sort of fool do

you think Margaret Kirk is? Now go to bed and sleep."
They got up, and she held him in her arms for a
moment.

"How quickly you grow up, you children. At least you
haven't made excuses and I'm glad about that."

She went to the door and looked back. He was standing
where she had left him, an overgrown little boy who had
been caught in the jam cupboard. She gave him a fleeting
smile, and went to her room where she lay awake.

Tomorrow morning was likely to be a busy one.

When the maid brought her her early cup of tea the
following morning, she was outwardly her usual serene
self.

"Is Mrs. Kirk in the kitchen?" she asked.

"Yes, ma'am."

"Would you please ask her to come up? Now?"

"Yes, ma'am."

A few minutes later Mrs. Kirk tapped on the door and
went inside. She was now a stout, graying, ruddy-faced
woman, and there was affection in her expression when she
smiled and said good morning. Janet invited her to sit by
the bed.

"I don't know how to tell you about this, Margaret," she
began.

"About Helen? You don't have to tell me. Helen came and
told me all about it herself."

The smile had gone and there was a curious look of
pride on her face.

"Did she? That was courageous of her. I wonder if she
told you everything. For instance that they are in love
with one another?"

"She told me that."

"And Martin is eager to marry her—always has been."

"She told me that, too. Of course she realized that it
just wouldn't do."

Margaret Kirk's Dundee accent was stronger than usual
this morning.

"I don't think so," Janet contradicted calmly. "My hus-

band and I wouldn't have stood in their way. I don't disapprove of their marrying. You know how fond I am of
Helen. I really ought to have foreseen this possibility, but
I've always tended to think of Helen as a daughter. I
forgot that Martin might not see her as a sister, but as an
attractive woman."

"Thank you very much," Mrs. Kirk said stiffly. "I'll leave,
of course, and take Helen with me. If I could have a day
or two to arrange matters . . ."

"What sort of nonsense is this?" Janet demanded, smiling
and stretching out a hand. "You will do nothing of the
sort. They are going to marry one another. Today we will
announce the engagement. They can get married next
week, at a private ceremony with no fuss. Before anybody
realizes what is going on, they will be in Dundee together,
man and wife."

"You can't be serious," Mrs. Kirk exclaimed.

"Of course I am, Margaret."

"You took us in when I was penniless. We owe everything
to you. I won't allow you to be repaid like this."

Janet laughed softly. "Repayment has nothing to do
with Martin's and Helen's feelings about one another. Of
course they've been incredibly silly, but I don't blame them
too much. This is 1897, not 1798! It is up to you and me
to push forward the marriage, just in case there is a baby.
Surely you didn't think I'd let you both leave me?"

Mrs. Kirk could find no words. Like a lot of people in her
social class, she mistrusted liberalism in any form. Liberalism was the affectation of the middle classes and eccen-
trics. Where Mrs. Kirk came from, you accepted the world
as it was, or you rebelled against it and became an agitator
and probably ended in the gutter. Mrs. Kirk liked radical
agitators no more than she liked liberals. And in her
philosophy the Kirks of this world did not marry the
MacRaes. At least they didn't used to. No good ever came
of such a thing.

Janet understood the struggle going on inside the other
woman and spoke softly.

"Helen is a credit to us all. Helen is a lady. I couldn't ask for a finer wife for my son, and I doubt if he could ever find one. So, no more arguments, Margaret. I'm going to have enough trouble persuading Helen that she doesn't need to renounce Martin. I'll see her in my drawing room after breakfast, and please tell her that there is nothing to worry about."

"I think you're an angel," Margaret Kirk blurted out, overwhelmed.

"Far from it. Oh, and I do want to apologize for what my son did to your daughter. Love or no love, it was unforgivable. That it happened under my roof makes me ashamed."

"*You* apologize to *me?*"

Mrs. Kirk slid down from her chair onto her plump knees, and kissed Janet's hand. Janet pulled it away quickly, equally embarrassed, and helped the housekeeper to her feet.

"Don't you ever do that again," she chided gently. "Let's stop thinking about ourselves and think about those two children. Between us we will get them to the altar, won't we?"

"Yes," Mrs. Kirk agreed, mastering her emotions.

"Now, I'm going to be busy. I shall probably be out a lot. There is the announcement to see to, and the wedding to arrange, and lots of things. Don't try to stop them being together." She paused as a thought struck her, and her face was illuminated by one of her sunniest smiles. "Do you know, I can't possibly allow my son's mother-in-law to be my housekeeper. You'd better take over as my companion."

"I think I should leave after the wedding. I have a little money put by."

"Perhaps you're right, but I wish you wouldn't. The house wouldn't be the same without you. I'm losing Helen. Won't you please stay?"

"For a little while, then," Margaret Kirk conceded. "It may be awkward for the other servants."

"I doubt it, but we can discuss that later. I have to get dressed and start the day. Remember, from now on you and I must stand together."

Margaret Kirk nodded and Janet embraced her. "Thank you," she said.

Later, when she went down to breakfast, she found Martin waiting for her. He stood up politely and put down the morning newspaper.

"Hullo, darling. Did you sleep well?" she asked, as though nothing had happened.

"Not very."

"Nor did I," she agreed lightly. "Too much to plan. After breakfast I want you to write out the engagement notice. I'll be going into the city and I'll take it to the *Herald* office. I'll take the ring in, too, once Helen has tried it on, and get the engraving changed. Your wedding will be in about a week. That's another thing I have to attend to. Just a quiet affair. In one of the side chapels, I expect."

"Has Helen agreed to this?" he asked, astonished.

"Not yet, but you may be sure she will."

"I don't know what to say. You're wonderful."

"Don't you start on that nonsense, please. I've had enough flattery for one day already. I'm being sensible, that's all. It's a good job somebody in this house is. Mrs. Kirk wanted to carry Helen off."

"She knows already?" Martin asked, his jaw dropping.

"Helen went to her and told her everything, which was a very brave thing to do, and Mrs. Kirk and I have discussed our plans. If only you'd come to me at the beginning of your holiday and said you wanted to marry Helen, we wouldn't have had to rush like this. You could have married at leisure, a proper wedding— Oh well, no use thinking about that now."

"I don't know how I can look Mrs. Kirk in the eye."

"Think of Helen looking me in the eye, and perhaps that will help you. Just grit your teeth. After all, you're getting away with this very lightly."

"Getting away with it?" He laughed at that. "I'm getting a prize for it."

They were laughing when Nancy came into the room.

"What's funny?" she asked, sitting down.

"Oh, just a little joke." This was the only part Janet had really been dreading. She said in a matter-of-fact voice, "Martin and Helen have decided to marry. Next week, probably."

Nancy opened her mouth, thought again, and shut it. Her face was a study. Janet suppressed a smile.

"Toast?" she asked, holding out the toast rack.

It took Janet quite a long time to persuade Helen that the marriage was necessary, desirable, and the only sensible ending to the story. Helen's feelings were so tumultuous and confused, such a mixture of pride and guilt, that she was unable to think clearly. She continued to insist that the marriage would be unfair to Martin and Janet, and it was clear that her sense of having betrayed Janet was very strong. In the end Janet wore her down, and she was forced to admit that her objections had no real validity, and to agree that she did not really want to break Martin's heart.

She cried a little and Janet comforted her. Then she produced a small velvet box lined with silk, and opened it to reveal a lovely old engagement ring.

"Let's see if this fits you," she said, taking Helen's hand. She slipped it over the girl's finger.

"Just a little loose, but it will do. When you are in Dundee you can have it altered if you think you ought to. It was my mother's. I'm taking it to have it reengraved, and after that it is yours. Now listen carefully, Helen. Officially, you have been secretly engaged since Martin's last visit, and only I and your mother knew. You didn't tell anyone earlier because at the time you were my companion. Now that I've made new arrangements, you and Martin don't want to wait any longer. I'm arranging for you to get married next week, and I'm afraid it will have to be a very quiet, private affair. I'm sorry about that, but I think you understand."

"Yes, I do," Helen agreed.

"Good. I know you are going to make a fine wife for Martin. Martin will have to go back to Dundee for two or three days before the wedding, but you can leave all the details to me." She smiled and patted Helen's hand. "You'll be in Dundee yourself, setting up house, before you know what is happening."

"I don't know how to thank you."

"By looking after Martin. Now, as from this minute you are no longer my companion. You will move your things into the bedroom next to mine. You are a guest here now. I think you and Martin should spend as much time together as you can. You have a lot to talk about, you know. During the day, that is," she added with a friendly smile.

She sent Helen to move her things, and took a deep breath. She felt exhausted and the day had hardly begun. She considered the hurdles ahead, and bustled out of the room, grateful that Nancy would be out all morning.

Somehow she managed to arrange everything before evening. The ring would be ready next morning, the announcement would be in the morning paper, the license had been taken care of, and the date and time of the wedding fixed.

Tomorrow Martin and Helen could go and collect the ring, and buy a wedding band while they were at it.

She had sent a telegram to Torquil in Perth. He arrived home two days later, just missing Martin by a matter of hours. When he heard the entire story from her, his shoulders began to heave.

"What is the joke?" she demanded a little coldly. She felt as though she had been put through a wringer. Torquil had had an easy time of it, messing about with his paints.

"Sorry, my dear. I was picturing you, standing in the doorway, watching the two of them in bed. I know it isn't really funny, but I'd love to sketch it."

"Don't you dare. I'm surprised at you."

"Well, my dear, before you, er, before we stopped, we both found bed a very pleasant affair. I'm sure Martin and Helen do, too."

"I'm glad it amuses you."

"Oh, heavens, Janet, they're getting married. That makes it all nice and respectable. They aren't the first young couple who have leaped into bed when they thought nobody was looking."

"You didn't used to be vulgar," she commented, and he stared at her.

"You didn't used to be a prude, my sweet. Besides I can't think what we are arguing about. You were absolutely magnificent. I don't know how it is, but you can always rise to any occasion. But one thing remains to be answered."

"What?"

"What on earth were you doing, visiting Martin's bedroom in the middle of the night?"

"I couldn't sleep and I got up to go to the bathroom. There was a thin line of light under his door, and I thought he'd fallen asleep with his light on. That's all."

"What a lucky coincidence. If you hadn't been sleepless, there's no saying what a knot those two would have tied themselves into. Especially if Helen *is* starting a pregnancy."

"I hope she isn't. But you are right," she admitted. "If I hadn't found them, he'd have gone to Dundee and who knows how things would have turned out? How was Perth?"

"Fine." He brightened. "I've done it, Janet. I've discovered how to paint at last. For the first time I'm really happy with what I'm doing."

"That's something, then."

"Wait till those passionless idiots who call themselves the Scottish School see my new work. It will shake all their ideas out of their stupid fat heads. Not that they have any ideas of their own. They get them all from Reynolds' *Discourses*. Peasants."

He spoke without great heat. She had noticed before that

he was impatient with himself rather than with others, no matter how much scorn they poured on his work.

"One day they will recognize you, dear," she said placidly.

"It doesn't really matter. As long as I know I'm doing good work."

The wedding took place six days later in the Lady Chapel of the Episcopal church nearby. Davie Robertson and Amanda were the only outsiders present and Davie acted as groomsman. The rector wondered a little about the secrecy which apparently surrounded the affair, but a glance at Helen's trim figure reassured him a little. It didn't *look* like a shotgun wedding.

The following day Helen and Martin left for Dundee, and Torquil took Nancy out for the day, and Janet was able to sit back and recover her composure. These hectic occurrences took more out of her than they used to do. Or was that right? she wondered. After all, she had not had to arrange a wedding before!

One thing kept nagging in the back of her mind. Torquil had called her a prude, and it hurt. She used to be almost totally abandoned with him, in the privacy of their room. She considered she had been very broad-minded in the matter of Martin and Helen.

Was she really a prude? Even if she hadn't always acted like one, did she perhaps think like one?

Slowly it occurred to her that she and Torquil were drawing apart. He spent more and more time away from home now, and she wondered if it was entirely due to his dedication to his art, or if he found her dull and uninteresting.

The thought troubled her a good deal in the weeks that followed.

TWENTY-ONE

PERHAPS because he sensed a loneliness in her, or perhaps his conscience troubled him because of the time he was away from home, Torquil began to take Janet out more. They held little dinner parties and were invited out by his friends, most of whom, up to that time, had been names to her. Some of them were people he habitually jeered at, yet when she met them they were pleasant, interesting and they seemed to get along famously with Torquil. Most of them mirrored Torquil's own mild eccentricities, and although they all habitually disagreed, there seemed to be no malice.

She suddenly found herself enjoying life. She liked dressing for dinner, and was proud of the fact that she looked so much younger than she really was.

It was not till September 1898, however, that she came face to face with two men whose names were almost as familiar as her own. They had been invited to a soiree at a big house on the north side of the city where, to her surprise, most people were strangers. These were business people, rather than artistic ones, reminiscent of Andrew's friends in Dundee so many years ago. Suddenly Torquil spotted someone.

"Hello, Charlie," he exclaimed. "Come along and meet my wife."

A small, broad-shouldered man turned to look at them.

He had dark, curly hair and merry eyes, and she guessed that he would be about her own age. He came up to them, beaming.

"Janet, this is Charlie Love. You've heard of him."

"I certainly have," she exclaimed. "How do you do, Mr. Love."

"I'm speechless," the commercial artist said pleasantly. "Torquil, you villain, why have you kept her hidden all these years?"

Torquil looked pleased. "Can I leave you two together for a moment?" he asked. "I want to have a word with the lord provost."

"Goodness," said Janet. "Is the lord provost here, too?"

"Oh yes," Love assured her. "This is a very high-class soiree indeed. Didn't Torquil warn you?"

"Not specially. Let me see, now. You're the man who stops all the traffic in the Trongate with your paintings, aren't you?"

"It has been known to happen. I'm really a landscape painter at heart, but not a very good one. One has to live and I'm branded forever as the traffic-stopping advertising fellow."

From the way he spoke, she did not think this bothered him in the least.

"You're Rowan's Jams, aren't you?" he asked.

"My first husband was. My son runs the business now."

"Then you must know my friend over there—Tom Lipton."

"Lipton! No, I've never met him. Of course I know his name very well."

"Then we must remedy that at once. I know he'll be interested."

He took her across to a small group and attracted the attention of a man standing with his back to them. When he turned, Janet was conscious only of the alertness in his eyes. He vibrated personality in an almost physical sense.

"Mrs. MacRae, may I present Sir Thomas Lipton? Tom,

this is Torquil MacRae's wife, and also Rowan's Jams and Marmalade. She tells me you have never met."

"No, indeed, we have not." Lipton took her hand and studied her closely. "I met your Mr. Robertson a year or two ago. You have a good man there. I offered to double his salary if he would come to me, but he refused."

"He didn't tell me," Janet answered, amused. "But then he wouldn't, just in case I thought he was trying to get *me* to double his salary."

"I was quite certain he wouldn't, which is why I mentioned it. He deserves credit for his loyalty."

He interested her. Only that year he had been knighted and, coincidentally, formed a limited liability company. She knew that he had been born in Glasgow's Gorbals, that his parents were Irish and had owned a small grocer's shop. His was one of the outstanding stories of the era, and now he controlled a vast business empire which included tea, coffee, and cocoa plantations, his own hog-packing house in Chicago, his own fruit farms and jam factories, his own bacon-curing factories, all in addition to the growing chain of grocery and provisions shops.

Nobody knew how rich he was, merely that he was so wealthy that the degree of wealth was irrelevant.

"Is Robertson still with you?" he asked.

"Yes. My son made him a director."

"A wise move, I'd say. You know, Mrs. MacRae, I admired the way you looked after that business. Hardly a woman's job, yet you had the foresight to invest in Spain and to supply your own sugar."

"I was fortunate in the people who worked for me," she disclaimed. "My main triumph of course has been selling sugar to you."

"To me? I don't buy from Rowan's."

"No." She smiled demurely. "But last year you signed a five-year contract with a small firm called J. Darling and Company, to supplement your sugar supplies. I am J. Darling. Darling was my maiden name."

He stared and then laughed. "I'm blessed," he said. "So you are in sugar on your own account?"

"Why not, Sir Thomas? If it's good business for Rowan's, then it should be good business for me."

They talked together for several minutes, until at last he had to take his leave of her. Shortly after that Torquil returned to her side, and Love also made his excuses.

Later when they returned to Conchra House, she asked Torquil about the strange little artist.

"Is he English?" she wanted to know.

"Nobody really knows," Torquil replied lazily from the depths of his favorite armchair. "He's a bit of a mystery man, is our Charlie. He's supposed to have run away from home in England, but he's also rumored to have been born in Inverness. I suspect he tells a good story."

"He seems friendly with Sir Thomas."

"They've been friends for years. Of course Lipton is too grand for him now. He doesn't have the same time at his disposal as he used to have. Funny, your never meeting him."

"There was never any real reason why we should meet." She sighed and stretched contentedly.

"Janet, are you happy?" he asked, out of the blue.

"Why, yes," she laughed. "Don't I look it?"

"You never have complained about anything, and I found myself wondering."

"I love this house," she assured him. "Naturally I miss Martin and Helen now that they've gone, and I suppose in a way I miss being involved in Rowan's. One gets used to things, and there's always you and Nancy."

"I'm away such a lot."

"True. Perhaps I could come with you, now that Nancy is older."

"No, that wouldn't do at all. I'll have to give up these trips of mine. I'm getting a little tired of them anyway. I've got enough work now to keep me occupied for years."

"Are you serious about staying at home?"

"Yes. I'm going to Perth in November. I'll make that the last trip."

"I'm glad about that."

She got up and went over to him, and kissed his brow.

"I'm tired. I'm going to bed. I'll see you at breakfast. Sleep well."

"And you," he replied, and watched broodingly as she left the room. With a sigh he poured himself a nightcap.

When he left on his last Perth visit, the following month, she saw him off cheerfully, knowing that he would soon be home to stay. She was looking forward to that. He would fill the gap left by Martin. She planned to get a lot of odd jobs done to the house, to make it as nice as possible for him, and she urged the servants into increased activity.

Shortly before he was due to return, two of his friends called on her unexpectedly, a Mr. and Mrs. Dickie. Janet did not like them overmuch, but they were friendly and pleasant and it was difficult to be short with them. The purpose of their visit was to invite her to their house that evening, and they refused to take no for an answer. There would be drinks and a buffet, and a piano recital.

Janet eventually capitulated, and set off for the Dickie residence that evening after Nancy had had supper. She was not altogether sorry to get a break after a tiring few weeks.

There were about twenty-five people assembled in the Dickies' house, and Janet recognized many of them and began to enjoy her evening. Toward the end of her stay she left the room for several minutes. On her return she glanced around quickly for someone to talk to.

By her side, concealed by a heavy drape, was a small group of men, talking and laughing. Suddenly and with great clarity she heard one of them say, "What about that crafty fox, MacRae, then? There's a card for you. He's got that ravishing wife of his here in Glasgow, and Meg Seton tucked away in a little love nest in Perth. That's

what I call free enterprise." The speaker gave a bibulous
laugh. "Two lovelies, not one. And he can't even paint a
decent picture."

Janet felt faint and hardly heard another voice hissing
fiercely, "Quiet, you fool. Shut up."

After what seemed a very long time indeed, she drew
herself up and walked into the room and joined two
women talking on the far side. She had no idea how she
got through that night. It was with relief that she went
home and was able to fling herself on the bed.

In her bones she knew that what she heard was true. The
men had been talking among themselves, not spreading
gossip. It explained several things. She sobbed herself to
sleep, lying on top of the bed, fully dressed.

The following morning she made certain arrangements,
early, and left for the railway station carrying a valise.

Meg Seton, naked under an open robe, kissed Torquil full
on the mouth, a lingering clinging of the lips.

"Do you have to go tomorrow?" she asked sadly.

"Yes I do, and what's more we'd better get up, darling.
Look at the time."

"We're not going anywhere. Only one more day and one
more night. Who wants to get up? Torquil, come and stay
here."

"I can't, Meg. I'm sorry, but if you remember I never
made any promises anyway. We both agreed that this
would last only as long as we both wanted it. It's been
wonderful, but I can't stand the strain of a double life."

"Why do you have to go back to her?" Meg demanded.
"She hasn't slept with you for years, you said."

"I know, but she's my wife, and I still love her."

"You said you love me."

"So I do. There's nothing difficult about that. I love you
both in different ways. It's no good, Meg. Don't spoil everything by trying to argue. I must go back to my wife and
my daughter."

She sat on the edge of the bed, her arm around his waist,

and made a face. She was a well-built woman in her mid-
thirties with raven black hair, dark fathomless eyes, and a
bold, ready mouth. Torquil once told her she had been
specially designed for loving, and indeed there was much
truth in it. Her husband had been dead for several years
and she had no children. She was lonely, bored, and afraid
of approaching middle age.

"God, it's been good," she remarked. "There will never
be another like you."

"Nonsense, you've got several admirers in Perth. Give
them a chance and you'll be surprised."

"I'd rather have you."

He turned and smiled, and pushed her back on the bed
and began to make love to her again. Their copulatory
gymnastics had ceased and she was lying, sated, her face
buried in his chest, when the doorbell rang stridently.

Torquil gave a start and sat up.

"Who the devil is that?" he complained. "Are you expecting anyone?"

"No. Get rid of them and come back."

"We'd better get up. There are things to do."

He put on his dressing gown and slippers and padded
to the attic window of the little bedroom above the studio
and living room. There was a cab in the road, but the
roof of the porch concealed the identity of his caller.

"Someone in a cab," he said over his shoulder. "Get
dressed, Meg, there's a dear."

He went down the narrow staircase and unbolted the
door and opened it. When he saw Janet his face froze.

"Good morning, darling," she greeted him calmly. "I
thought I'd come and visit you on your last day. After all,
I've never seen either of your country retreats."

He gibbered incoherently.

"I brought a few things in a valise. Shall I send the
cabby away?"

"No, no, don't do that," he said excitedly. "You can't stay.
It's a mess."

"Very well." She turned and called to the cabdriver.

"Please wait for me." Then she turned back. "Won't you even ask me in?"

He stood aside silently, and she stepped into the hall and went through the open living-room door facing her. She glanced about her, noting dirty dishes on the table and a fireplace choked with ashes.

"It's a mess," Torquil gabbled. "I was up late last night. I've only just got up. There's nothing to see."

"I don't know. It's tiny, but rather nice—or would be if it were looked after. It needs a woman's touch."

She left him speechless while she poked her head into the small kitchen, and then looked into the studio.

"Where do you sleep?"

"The . . . the . . . the bedroom's in the attic upstairs."

"Oh, I must see that."

"*No!* I mean, the bed isn't made or anything. It's a mess. Sit down while I make some tea. You sit."

She sat in a comfortable chair and her steady blue eyes held his.

"Why did you do it, Torquil?" she asked.

He could find no words. Suddenly a voice called down from above.

"Who is it, darling? Have they gone?"

"Aren't you going to introduce me to Meg?" Janet suggested quietly. "I'm sure she must be as curious as I am."

He wished the floor would open and swallow him up.

"Come down," he called, and they waited.

The door opened and Meg walked in, her robe loosely tied, revealing the curve of her full breasts. Her hair was awry and she was in slippers. She saw Janet and her eyes narrowed.

"What are *you* doing here?" Meg asked harshly. "You're his wife, aren't you?"

"I'm inspecting the love nest. It's seedy. I didn't know you liked black-haired women, Torquil."

"He likes *real* women," Meg sneered. "The sort who can look after a man in bed."

Janet was on her feet in an instant, and there was the sound of a slap and another and another. She back- and forehanded Meg Seton's face four times before Meg realized what was happening to her.

"Why you bitch," Meg screamed.

Torquil reacted instantly. He coiled his arms around Meg and held her before she could rake Janet's face with her nails. Janet stood her ground and her eyes blazed at the other woman. Suddenly Meg quailed and went limp in Torquil's arms.

"For God's sake, stop it, both of you," Torquil said harshly.

"Don't quote God at me, you libertine." Janet's voice was steely. Her eyes were still blazing and Torquil was amazed at the change in her. He had never seen this side of her personality. "Get that slut out of here before I give her the shaking she deserves."

He pushed the silent Meg to the door and she went upstairs meekly without a word, another fact that shook him, for Meg had a temper of her own. Janet sat down and adjusted her skirt as though nothing had happened.

"I had to come, you know," she remarked conversationally. "Once I knew about her, I had to see her for myself. You disappoint me? I thought you had better taste. I don't think I'll bother about tea. The cab can take me to the Station Hotel. I shall wait there for you. Don't keep me waiting. We have a lot to talk about."

"I was coming home tomorrow," he said foolishly. "Honestly. It was all over, Janet. I wasn't lying when I said I was coming home for good. I may have done foolish things, but I haven't lied to you."

"I'm sure you're a model of the virtues," she sneered. She was far more upset than she would ever let him know. "Be at the hotel in an hour's time. Don't force me to come looking for you. That's a warning."

"I won't," he said hastily, and saw her to the door.

When she had driven off, he shut his eyes and exhaled

slowly. He stood in the doorway for a minute or two, getting his breath back, and then closed the door and went wearily upstairs.

"That's the end of it, Meg," he said dully. "Sorry, but I had no idea. I can't imagine how she found out." He sighed. "You deserved better, my dear. Pack your things, sweetheart, and I'll drive you into Perth. Then I must go and see Janet."

"Where is she?"

"She has gone to the Station Hotel to wait for me. It ain't going to be much fun, I'll tell you that."

She felt the hopelessness of it all. She was the "other" woman, and as such would receive nobody's sympathy. She supposed she would have to accept Freddie Murray's offer after all. It would be an anticlimax after Torquil. She had always hoped that Torquil's wife would die or do something equally convenient, leaving Torquil free to marry her. Yet she was honest enough, even at this moment, to admit to herself that Torquil had taken her as a mistress and had been insistent that he would never marry her.

He went downstairs and put on the kettle, and they had a final cup of tea together before leaving. At the door she clung to him for a minute, her lips seeking his frantically as tears gathered in her eyes. Then they went out together for the last time.

He waited for Janet in the hotel lounge, pacing about nervously. He had the place to himself and was not sure that this was what he wanted. When she came in, she was red-eyed but her chin was up.

"Well," she said, sitting down, "I suppose you have some sort of excuse. I'm curious to know what it is."

"No excuses, only a reason. How did you find out?" he demanded.

"The Dickies invited me to a little party, and I overheard some of your friends discussing your prowess. They didn't

know I was behind a curtain. They even talked of her by
name."

"*What?*" He was astonished.

"Oh, yes, your friends apparently know all about you. No
doubt their wives do, too. I expect they have all been pity-
ing me behind my back. Poor little woman, sort of thing.
Did you really think it was a secret?"

"Of course I did," he said heatedly. "Do you think I'd
parade you in front of people who were sniggering at you
behind your back? They have minds like cockroaches.
Damn them all."

"Swearing at them won't help. How long has this been
going on, Torquil?"

"I met her in Oban. She was on holiday and we met at
a ball."

"At a ball? I imagined you slaving over your easel till all
hours."

"I have to have a break sometimes," he protested. "Anyway, she was the one who pointed out to me that my colors
were all wrong. Strange business that." For a moment his
mind was distracted, and then he returned to what he had
been saying. "She was lonely. She needed a man and I
needed a woman, so I took the cottage here to be near
her."

"Just like that. She was lonely!"

"She's a widow. That's not much fun for a vibrant
woman."

"Apparently not. And you say you were giving her up?"

"Yes. It was settled." He paced about nervously. "You
see, at the outset it was fine. She was a mistress, nothing
more. Of course we were great friends. We liked one
another. Then I realized that she was beginning to get
ideas about me." He hesitated and then said bravely, "I
believe she fell in love. That meant I was being forced to
make a choice, so I told her that this was the last time."

Janet, listening, recognized the truth when she heard it. It
was small comfort, but it helped a little.

"Torquil, I know perfectly well that other men have . . . affairs. I don't mean I know which men, but most women know that men are naturally unfaithful. I thought you were different, far, far better than other men. You said 'no excuses, only a reason.' What did that mean?"

He was silent. "It's so difficult now," he complained. "I feel awkward when I'm talking to you about making love."

"Hardly surprising," she murmured.

"Please, Janet, no more sarcasm. Look, when you were forty you went through the change of life. We stopped sleeping together. We lived together, but at night we went our separate ways. Don't you see, Janet, that nothing like that has happened to me? I need you and want you as much as ever I did! What makes it worse is that you're so damned young and attractive. You'd drive any man mad with desire, never mind your husband. It was more than flesh and blood could stand."

She stared at him silently, taken aback by the force with which he spoke.

"That's why I began to enjoy my trips away. I wasn't being permanently teased by your presence. Then Meg just happened. I suppose I was desperate for a woman, and she was pretty desperate for a man. But she's a nice person," he added. "She's no slut. She could have remarried, but she preferred me, and God knows I found solace with her. Do you really think I wouldn't have preferred it to be with you? My lawful wedded wife?"

She was effectively silenced. This was the last sort of defense she had expected to hear. Why, he virtually blamed *her!* Could he be serious in saying that the sight of her inflamed his passions still, after all the years? Men must indeed be different from women.

"I'm not defending my conduct," he concluded wearily. "I'm just telling you what happened and why. I had hoped it was a secret and then when I came home tomorrow the secret would be buried forever. I wish I knew how it got out."

"I can tell you that. I got it out of Doris Dickie before

leaving her house. She didn't want to discuss it, but I made her." Janet's lips compressed at the recollection. "Your Meg Seton has a brother who visits Glasgow regularly on business. He drinks a lot and he talks a lot and he knows at least some of your friends. Word soon gets around. You aren't exactly unknown in Glasgow, Torquil."

"Friends indeed," he snorted. "Well, what are you going to do, Janet?"

"I shall go home this afternoon, I think."

"Will you be leaving me?"

"Why should I leave my home?" she asked, raising her eyebrows. "There's Nancy to consider, too. If anyone leaves, you will."

"Are you telling me to get out?"

"No." She shook her head. "No you can come home. Just leave me alone for a time. I have to try to learn to live with this knowledge. One thing. Is she the only one? Tell me the truth."

"Of course she is. What on earth do you take me for?"

"We're discussing quantity, not quality," she retorted in a moment of rare spite.

"What sort of remark is that?" he protested. "There was no one else, and there never will be."

"So, we just pretend nothing has happened, is that it?" she asked.

"Why not?" His reply took her unawares. "You didn't want me, not my body anyway. She did, and I needed to be wanted. That's all. You haven't lost anything you want. I never considered leaving you. If you must know, I love you."

"What a funny time to tell me," she said with a shaky laugh.

"But it's true, Janet. That's what's so damnable about it. She's hurt, make no mistake about that. And you are, too. Each in your different way. I've hurt two women I care for. I love you both, in some funny fashion, and I've only succeeded in hurting you both." He flung up his arms in despair.

"How can you love us both?" Janet demanded quickly.

"I don't know. I only know I can. The French understand it better. When a man takes a mistress, he doesn't stop loving his wife, but at the same time he has to have real feeling for his mistress. To treat her just as a body would strike him as immoral."

"Don't you start tying me in knots again," Janet warned.

"I'm sorry. You used to be able to understand things that other, prudish people didn't."

"And now you think I'm a prude?"

"No, no, but I thought you might glimpse the truth in what I'm trying to say. You've every right to leave me. You're a wealthy woman. You don't need me."

"Nancy needs a mother and father. Please never speak to me about this again, Torquil. I've thought about it while I was waiting for you. A lot depended on what you had to say. I don't understand you, not one little bit, but I do recognize sincerity. Just don't ever talk about it," her voice rose. "And don't ever touch me. Leave me alone. We'll manage somehow, for the family's sake."

"I'd better go. I have quite a lot to bring back to Glasgow. The carriers are coming this afternoon and I'm behind."

"Will you be seeing her again?" Janet could not resist the question.

"No, my dear. Not ever."

She sat silent, head down, and after a moment he turned and left the room. She remained in her seat for several minutes, going over it all in her mind. She was still a little numb, but two strange facts kept bobbing up in her thoughts. He loved her! And he needed and wanted her as much as ever—in the physical sense! It was quite incredible.

She ate a solitary luncheon before returning to Glasgow, and as she did so she formed two resolves. One was that never ever would she let Torquil see how deeply he had hurt her. Her pride would not let her do that.

The other was that somehow in some way she would pay him back for his betrayal. She had no idea how.

Indeed it was not easy for a woman to pay back her husband for infidelity, and she was not thinking in terms of taking a lover. But he had hurt her more than anyone ever had, and although common sense told her that she would learn to live with the hurt, it could never quite be eradicated.

Meantime there was nothing to do but hang on. That was always the woman's role—to hang on grimly.

TWENTY-TWO

INEVITABLY, if slowly, they adjusted to the new situation. Outwardly nothing appeared to have happened. Margaret Kirk, always quick to sense any real trouble in the house, suspected nothing. They stopped going out, of course, for neither of them wanted to meet their erstwhile friends for the moment, and they had less to say to one another at mealtimes. Torquil was hard at work in his studio for much of the time.

As the peaceful influence of the big old house exerted its influence on them, the sharp edge was worn off their exacerbated feelings, and bitterness began to recede.

In the following year Helen gave birth to a girl, whom she and Martin named Marion, and Janet spent two weeks in Dundee with them. Torquil only came for three days. Shortly after this exciting event, Mrs. Kirk left Glasgow finally. She had never been really at ease in her role of companion, and Janet understood this. So Mrs. Kirk was given a small pension and Janet bought her a cottage on the outskirts of Dundee.

It was only when she had left that Janet realized how much Margaret Kirk had come to mean to her. First Helen, now Margaret. There was no housekeeper now, and no companion, and Janet was kept busier, which was her intention.

At the beginning of 1901, a few days after Queen Vic-

toria died with her son's name on her lips, but in the arms
of her German nephew, the Kaiser, Helen had her second
baby, another girl. This time they chose the name Ailsa
for the baby.

It was the birth of this second grandchild that, strangely
enough, did much to heal the breach between Janet and
Torquil. For more than two years they had done nothing
more than exchange pleasantries, but when they returned
from the christening in Dundee, and were having breakfast together the next morning, Janet remarked out of the
blue, "I don't know why it is, but somehow having a
second grandchild makes me much more aware of my age
than just having one did. Does it have that effect on you?"

Torquil looked up and gave a shy smile. "Not really.
Age never enters my mind. I know I've got gray hair, a
double chin, wrinkles, and a paunch, but I just never give
it a thought. Yet you, with the complexion of a child and
the figure of a young bride, worry about age. I suppose
that may be it," he added thoughtfully. "When you look in
the mirror daily at a young girl, it must come as a shock
to know you're growing older like the rest of us."

"Forty-seven on my next birthday," she confessed.

"It's months away yet. You're so young inside that your
age doesn't mean anything."

"That's a nice thing to say."

"It's the truth, my dear," he said.

She hesitated, reluctant to go too deeply into the past.
Then she asked, "Do you remember my fortieth birthday?"

"Vaguely, yes. You mean the day itself?"

"That's right. That morning you welcomed me to the
club. That was your word. I remember it. And do you
know, starting then I became really afraid, frightened. I
was terrified at the thought of death and it lasted for
months before it began to wear off. The worst of it was
that I couldn't do anything about it. Even now, although
it doesn't bother me anymore, I don't want to die."

He realized that for the first time in a long time she

was opening her heart to him, and he was careful not to shatter the mood.

"No one does, my dear. I'm sure I don't. Your feelings are natural."

"You don't understand," she insisted. "I don't really believe there's a beautiful big world up in the sky, where I'm going to be happy ever after. It may be true. My father believed something like that. Lots of people do, clever people. We're taught that we're put into this world simply in order to prepare ourselves for a better one, and that if we don't pass the test, we're going to a far worse one. I can't imagine a God with a mind warped enough to play a trick like that. I like it here. I don't want a better place or a worse one."

"Yes, but you see they have to teach us things like that."

"Why *have* to?"

"It's necessary to give the not-so-lucky people some sort of hope. Your world is a nice world, and to make sure you behave, you're told that if you do wrong, you'll go to a very nasty one when you die. Other people have nothing to live for, so they're told that if only they are good and obedient, they'll go to a heavenly paradise when they die." He laughed. "It's the perfect way of keeping the population in order. You see, dear, if all the poor people were to turn on the rich people and kill them and take their money away, there would be chaos."

"How could that happen?" she exclaimed with amusement.

"Because they outnumber us ten, twenty, a hundred to one. Maybe more."

Her smile died. "You mean they *could?*" she asked disbelievingly.

"In theory, yes. In practice, probably not. Yet there have been peasants' revolts in history, when they found a leader. Sometimes they gave a lot of trouble before they were put down."

"Torquil, are you saying religion is some sort of government trick?"

He shook his head. "I wouldn't go that far. What I am saying is that governments are quick to see its value. The secular government and the Church have played the same game for centuries. It suits both their books. I'm afraid, you see, that I'm very cynical about it all. I don't want to be cynical, but it all seems such an obvious ruse."

"Don't you believe in life after death?" She leaned across the table toward him as she spoke.

"I don't know what to believe. I've long since given up trying to work it all out. I simply take life as it comes, and like you I'm in no hurry to move on. I suppose if I had to give an answer right now, I'd say I don't believe there is anything after we die."

"Yet you aren't afraid to die?"

"No. I don't want life to end, but we all die, all life on this earth dies. Death is one of the facts of life. There's nothing to be afraid of. Everybody does it," he concluded with a crooked smile.

"It still bothers me," she said gloomily.

"I tell you what," he assured her in that confident tone she liked so much. "Wait another forty years, and you'll find that you aren't bothered about anything. You'll just take life and love it and not give a thought about the future."

She burst out laughing. "I'd like to take that advice."

"Why not?"

Afterward, when she went up to her room, she stood before the tall pier glass and studied herself thoughtfully.

"Who are you?" she asked her reflection. "Where have you come from, and where are you going, and why?"

Then she saw the ridiculous aspect of her behavior.

"So much for you, Grannie MacRae," she jeered at the reflection, and stuck out her tongue in a girlish gesture of defiance. She twirled away from the mirror, unaccountably lighthearted all of a sudden, and went to Nancy's room and knocked. Nancy called to her to come in.

Nancy was at home now. She had left school, did not

want to go to a finishing school, and spent her time incessantly reading plays, which she got from the library. All her allowance was spent on going to the theater with a friend.

She was rising seventeen, now, taller than her mother, and good-looking in a striking sort of way. Sometimes Janet felt she was talking to a stranger when she was with Nancy, yet she had to admit that Nancy had given them no trouble in the past few years.

"Aren't you going down for breakfast?" Janet asked.

Nancy put down her book. "Sorry, I didn't notice the time. May I speak to you for a minute?"

"You don't have to ask. What is it?"

"I've been asked out this evening. By a man."

"Do we know him?"

"No. I met him at May's house. He's very nice. His name is Jim Baxter."

"I'd rather have met him."

"Yes, I know, so I asked him to come around this morning to see you. Is it all right?"

Janet was taken aback. "I suppose so. Tell me about him."

According to Nancy, Jim Baxter was twenty, he was very nice—she mentioned this four times in four sentences —his father was a Church of Scotland minister, and Jim was at the university studying to become a doctor.

"Where is he taking you?"

"To the theater."

"Yes," Janet chuckled, "that was a silly question. Why isn't he at university this morning?"

"He'll cut a lecture. He says it isn't an important one and he knows what it's all about. He's terribly clever."

"Then I shall be glad to meet him."

"And I may go out with him?"

"I should think so, unless he does something outrageous while he's here."

When young Mr. Baxter arrived an hour later, Janet and Torquil were waiting for him. They were filled with pardonable curiosity, for he was the first young man in whom Nancy had ever shown any interest. He was pleasant, well-dressed, well-spoken, and very, very respectful. Within a minute or two he had passed the unspoken test, and when he eventually made a formal request to take Nancy out, it was freely granted and he was told to call at Conchra House to see her whenever he wished.

He left after about forty minutes, shown out by Nancy who looked better pleased with life than she had done for a long time.

"That's the other one growing up," Torquil remarked, going to the window.

"Umm. How odd of her to pick on a minister's son. It seems out of character."

"They say they're the wildest ones of all," Torquil laughed. "What's worse, he's a medical student. Still, Jim Baxter seems quiet and good-mannered. That's another milestone, my dear. Nancy's first young man. Next thing we know, she'll be married and showering more grandchildren on us. Never a dull moment."

"She's much too young."

"Not very much. At her age you had Andrew calling on you, remember?"

"I'd forgotten," she admitted.

"About what we were discussing at breakfast," he went on slowly. "I wonder if you realize what an unusual person you are."

"I'm nothing of the sort," she denied with total sincerity.

"Yes, you are. You were raised in that absolute bastion of conservatism, a parsonage. Your father was a man of deep religious faith, he accepted the existing order, he accepted the standards that had been handed down to him by fairly affluent parents. Yet ever since I've known you, you've challenged everything you ought to believe in."

"I'm sure that's not true," she protested. He was exaggerating.

"It is. You take nothing for granted. You question

everything, you try to weigh things up for yourself. It's one of the things that have always attracted me to you, for I'm the same."

"Oh, I know *you* are," she laughed.

"I'm being serious. There isn't a woman in the whole of our acquaintance, and probably not a man, certainly not in this prosperous little district of Glasgow, who would talk as you did at breakfast. Or, who would permit their husbands to indulge in my sort of heresy. It would outrage their entire upbringing. Yet your upbringing was the same as theirs, only more so."

"I hadn't thought of that. I don't want to be unusual."

"It's part of your charm, my dear. More important, you have nothing to fear. It's the others who ought to be afraid, not you."

"Thank you," she said a little uncertainly.

"I suppose you'll never forgive me, and I don't blame you, but I honestly never did stop loving you. And I love you more as each year goes by, and I always will. There's nothing you can do about it."

It was the first reference to his affair with Meg Seton, and she bit her lip.

"Have you ever heard anything more about . . . about her?" she asked, and immediately wished she hadn't.

"There's no harm in telling you. There was a letter, about a week after I came back from Perth." He paused at some recollection, and then went on. "I was amazed. I thought she had too much pride, too much self-respect."

Janet felt miserable at having raised the matter.

"Did you answer?"

"No, I tore it up. There was no answer. Then I heard about a year later, from one of those malicious gossips, that she'd married. So I suppose she's all right. That's all I know. I'm no longer interested."

"I said we would never talk about it again. I'm sorry I brought it up," she apologized. "It's in the past now."

"The trouble with the past is that you can't change it," he said ruefully.

"Well, we don't have to think about it anyway," she said firmly. "There are more cheerful topics."

"Amen to that," he agreed.

That year they had agreed to spend Christmas with Martin and Helen and the children in Dundee. Shortly before they were due to travel, Nancy came looking for Janet, her young face set in a serious expression.

"Mama, I want to go to acting school after the New Year," she said without preamble.

Janet blinked at this bolt from the blue. "But why?"

"I've been interested in the theater for a long time. Now I'd like to learn how they do it—the actors I mean. You can understand a play so much better if you know something about acting and what goes on behind the scenes."

"Oh. For a moment I thought you wanted to go on the stage."

"Would that be very wrong?" Nancy asked, stiffening.

"I don't know. I wouldn't have thought it was your sort of life. They aren't terribly respectable, are they?"

"How can you say that? Do you know anyone on the stage? I don't mean the music halls, I mean the proper theater."

"No, I don't. I'm sorry, it just seems so unlike you."

"Drama is an art. It has nothing to do with social class. My father is a painter. He is doing exactly the same thing, but in a different way."

Janet paused at this. It was true that painters were regarded by many as a harum-scarum, dissolute lot, and so indeed some of them were. Torquil was different. He was unorthodox and so were his friends, but hardly dissolute.

"Well," she temporized, "if you just want to learn about acting, I expect it's all right. I'll have to ask your father."

"I've already done that. He said he would talk to you."

"Hmm. When is all this going to take place, and where?"

"In the city, near the Athenaeum. There's a place called the Glasgow Theatre School. It is said to be one of the finest in the entire country. It is run by a couple called Wilson, and the fees are only twenty pounds a term."

"*Only?* That's a lot of money."

"Not for a really good drama school, Mama."

"All right, I'll talk it over with your father and if he is agreeable you can go, but first I want to see the place and meet these Wilsons for myself."

She was surprised when Nancy impulsively kissed her.

"Thank you. Thank you. I knew you would understand. You always do, in the end."

The compliment was so unexpected that it left Janet speechless. Nancy skipped out of the room and Janet followed slowly. It was good that Nancy would have an outside interest, but she could not help wishing that it had taken another form. Of course, there were some very famous actors in London. Even she had heard their names although she rarely went to the theater.

Yet they were unconventional. Against that, weren't she and Torquil unconventional in their thinking, and, if so, was it surprising that Nancy would turn out the same? Martin had Andrew Cunninghame's cautious blood in his veins. Nancy did not.

At the foot of the stairs she paused and smiled to herself. According to the irrepressible and irreverent Torquil, King Edward VII was a fat lecher, notorious for gluttony, gambling, and tumbling into bed with any female handy, particularly other men's wives. If that were true, and it was common gossip throughout the kingdom, then standing in front of an audience spouting Shakespeare did not seem too terrible. As Nancy had said, it wasn't music hall. Anyway she had not actually expressed any desire to go on the stage, only to study acting.

As always, one would have to wait and see how things turned out.

It was a full family gathering at Dundee that Christmas, including Margaret Kirk, and on Christmas Day and Boxing Day, Davie and Amanda would be staying with them. Janet immediately felt at home among these members of her little clan, and she was delighted with her two grand-daughters. On the second evening she and Martin slipped away for a long talk in his study.

"You've got a lovely home here, Martin," she complimented, not for the first time.

"I've told you before, it's all Helen's doing. She's a wonder."

"You're both happy, aren't you?"

"Yes, very much so."

"How are things at the factory?" She always asked about it, and he knew that before she returned to Glasgow she would visit it and look for her old acquaintances among the women. She was very good that way.

"Quite well."

"Only quite?" she asked, raising her eyebrows.

"This hasn't been one of our best years, but I don't think there's anything seriously wrong. It's just an ordinary fluctuation."

"How bad is it?"

"It isn't bad," he laughed. "Ask Davie when he comes. It's just that we've been making great strides recently, and this year it has fallen off a little. We're still up on the previous year, you know."

"That's not so bad then."

"No. I'm starting something new. We can afford it."

"What's that?"

"I'm giving an extra week's pay to everyone in the factory on New Year's Eve. You know that they're all Presbyterian, and New Year is their celebration, not Christmas."

She nodded.

"Those who have been with us less than a year will only get half a week's money, but the rest will get a week. Salaried staff will get a month's salary. Including me," he laughed.

"It sounds like a lot of money to give away."

"I know, and Walter Duffy thinks I've lost my reason, but we keep our staff, you know. They're very loyal to us, and when they have to, they work like slaves. We owe them something. It won't hurt. I'll go over to the States for a week or two and frighten the life out of our agents, and they'll recover the cost of it. Or else." He laughed again.

"Perhaps it's a good thing," she said thoughtfully.

"I think it will prove to be. We rely on them so much, you see. Changing the subject, Nancy is going around looking like the cat who got the cream. What's all this about taking acting lessons?"

"It's true."

"It will be a good thing when she marries and settles down. She was always a strange child."

"All children are strange. You'll discover that for yourself as Marion and Ailsa grow up."

"Was I?" he asked.

"You once surprised me almost out of my wits."

"Oh." He colored and she reached out a hand to him.

"I'm sorry, Martin. Don't look so upset. The main thing is that it all turns out well."

"Did I turn out well? Is that what you are saying?" he asked.

"It is. It's strange how it is children who dominate your life. Tell me, my dear, does it trouble you that you have no son?"

"Not in the least. I don't share the fashionable male preoccupation over having sons. I'm quite content with my girls."

"But you do want a son, don't you?"

"No, I don't. I don't want any more children."

"Why not?" she asked.

"Just an idea I have that you can't share your love too much. I think a wife and two children are about all a man can fairly manage. If you have a large family, you can't give them all the love and attention you want. Well, that's how it strikes me anyway. Helen agrees."

"But Rowan's," she protested. "Who is going to take over from you?"

"Marion or Ailsa may marry someone who can carry on after me. I don't think it's important. We can hire management. Rowan's will provide them with an income all their lives, and that's the main thing."

"Your father wouldn't like to hear that sort of talk."

"No, I don't suppose he would, from all I've heard of him. Nor do I much care. This is my own life. The business is my servant, not my master. I intend to retire young and enjoy my declining years in the bosom of my family—or at least with Helen. I'm lucky enough to have money and I'm going to enjoy it."

"You sound more like your stepfather than your father."

"My stepfather has been my father in every important way. I daresay I get some of my ideas from him, although I've never discussed Rowan's with him. He isn't interested, and I don't blame him."

He hesitated and chose his next words with care.

"There was a story about him, some time back. You know how gossip gets around. I never liked to ask before, but is everything all right?"

"You mean you heard a story here about your father and another woman?"

"It was just one of those vague rumors, but yes."

"There was someone else," she said slowly. "I'd be grateful if you'd keep this to yourself. By the time I found out, it was all over anyway. There was a bit of awkwardness which I'd rather forget. None of it matters now. Everything is all right."

"I can't understand it. You're such an attractive woman, and Papa never seemed the sort of man who'd play about. Some men do, but not him."

"There's one thing you have to learn, Martin, as I had to learn it. If you can't give people what they want or need, the chances are that they will find it somewhere else. Men do funny things in middle age, and I let him drift into it."

"Aren't you being excessively forgiving?" He was a little hurt to know that the rumor had been true.

"It's far too easy to blame other people. The fact is that we ought not to sit in judgment on one another. It makes hypocrites of us. I don't mean that we should pretend that nobody ever does anything wrong—but instead of blaming people, we ought to try to understand them. That way we learn to understand ourselves. It's probably the most important lesson in life. There's usually a reason for what people do, Martin."

He put an arm around her shoulders and hugged her.

"You're a splendid person. You are far too good for all of us. Ncne of us deserves you one little bit."

"That's a very nice Christmas present." She kissed his cheek. "It's also enough of this soul-searching. I came here to have a good time. I must go and talk to Helen. Look after her, Martin."

"I will. She's really all that matters, when you come right down to it."

They walked to the door, and there she paused for a final word.

"You'll do," she said in a satisfied voice.

TWENTY-THREE

THAT was the first of a series of Christmas holidays at The Rowans, as Martin had humorously named the house overlooking the River Tay—the river that had claimed the lives of his father and grandfather in its majestic anger.

Janet loved them. They all insisted that she take the head of the table, and Torquil had teasingly christened her The Matriarch, a title with which no one took issue. And as she would sit there, the table laden with food, silver and crystal gleaming against the dark wood, candles throwing a soft glow on the company, she knew a deep satisfaction such as she had never known before. The Christmas visits became for a time the high pinnacle in a pleasant and generally carefree life.

Nancy began to change. Once she began her acting lessons, it was obvious that some deep need in her was at last being met. She was brighter and more considerate at home. She continued to see a lot of Jim Baxter, but, to Janet's mild disappointment, nothing seemed to come of the friendship.

At the end of three years at the Glasgow Theatre School, Nancy had exhausted what it had to offer her. Janet assumed that when this happened Nancy would come home and "settle down," half hoping that she would make up her mind to marry the newly qualified Jim Baxter.

She was unprepared when Mrs. Wilson called on her one afternoon.

As usual, Janet arranged for tea to be served in the drawing room, and then they got down to business.

"I've come to talk to you about Nancy," said Mrs. Wilson, stating what was fairly obvious.

"I hope she isn't in trouble," Janet replied apprehensively.

"On the contrary, Nancy is our star pupil. I suppose you are aware that she could have an excellent career on the stage?"

"What exactly would you call a good career on the stage, Mrs. Wilson?" Janet asked coldly. If Nancy was hoping that she could go off to join some théatrical company, she had better think again.

"She might turn out to be another Sarah Bernhardt. She is that good."

"I've heard the name—from Nancy, I daresay. She is an actress, I assume."

"Only the greatest in the world."

"And Nancy is going to be another greatest?" Janet laughed without humor. "Mrs. Wilson, Nancy is not going on the stage. It was clearly understood, when I allowed her to enroll at your school, that the purpose of the tuition was to enable her to get a deeper satisfaction out of her theatergoing."

"Nancy has explained all that to me. I think it is my duty, however, to tell you plainly that in my opinion there is a great actress in her. My husband and I can only do so much. She should be in London, Mrs. MacRae. That is where she will learn what she now needs to know. London and Paris."

"Out of the question," Janet snapped. She felt sudden anger. "I object very strongly to this whole conversation."

"Nancy said you would," Mrs. Wilson remarked, and Janet's lips tightened. How *dare* Nancy discuss her with this vulgar woman. What monumental impertinence.

"I had to say what I did," Mrs. Wilson went on, ignoring the danger signals. "It was my duty. Had I been able to persuade you, it would have been worth any effort. I see now that I cannot. Which brings me to something else."

"What?"

"Nancy's future. She is deeply in love with acting and I think she knows that you will never consent to her being a professional actress. However, would you consider allowing her to join my husband and me in teaching? I know it is unusual, but she has unusual talent."

"Nancy does not need a job."

"I know that, too," the infuriating woman remarked. "Don't you think, though, that it would make her happy? And it is useful work, work she would really find satisfaction in doing. I know she would work for nothing, but I wouldn't allow that. Young people ought to earn money."

"She's only a child. Would she really be of help to you?" This was unexpected news. Janet had never taken the school seriously.

"Oh, yes. We aren't doing her a favor."

"I'll have to think it over. I'll talk to Nancy about it, and to my husband, and we'll let you know our decision as soon as possible."

They finished their tea in an awkward silence, and Mrs. Wilson was glad to get away. Janet, when she had dug in her heels, was a formidable opponent. Janet mulled it all over in her mind until Nancy herself arrived home.

"Did Mrs. Wilson come to see you?" she asked brightly.

"She did." Janet did not mean to snap, but she did, and Nancy's face fell.

"What happened?"

"Nothing. I'm still thinking about what she said. You can take note, however, that you are definitely not going on the stage. I won't have it. Nor are you going off to London or Paris, a girl of your age. You're much too young and you'd get into bad company."

Nancy had never been one to shirk a fight, and she picked on this remark at once.

"Why would I be bound to?" she asked indignantly. "Are you saying that there are no nice people in Paris and London? Is Glasgow such a superior place?"

"Stop arguing. You are not going on the stage and that is final."

"I never expected to," Nancy sneered. "What about the job they have offered me? What's wrong with that?"

"Probably nothing," Janet admitted, regretting her peremptory manner. "I just don't know why you want a job. Aren't you going to marry Jim?"

"What makes you think that?"

"He's been calling on us for long enough. Anyone can see he's in love with you. Has he never proposed?"

"Often," Nancy retorted, affecting indifference. "Too often."

"You didn't tell me."

"Why should I? I haven't accepted him. He's beginning to bore me."

Janet was thunderstruck. "*Bore* you? What sort of man do you want to marry? A circus clown?"

"That mightn't be such a bad idea. Not a dull doctor anyway. Jim hasn't a single original thought in his head. At first I thought he was clever, but in fact he merely repeats what he reads and hears."

"You're free with your opinion about a man who is now a qualified doctor."

"I'm almost twenty. I'm grown up."

"I still think you're too critical."

"The question is, can I work at the Theatre School or not?"

"I'm thinking about it."

"What is there to *think* about?" Nancy cried.

"Quite a lot. I expected you to leave that place and come home and settle down and live a normal life with us. I know you love the theater and you've always been given money for tickets, and allowed to do more or less as you please. Now there's talk about your having a career on the stage, or failing that, teaching at that wretched school. This is all unexpected. I'm not sure I like the influence the Wilsons have on you."

"They don't have any influence. I am what I am. I was made like this."

"Not by your father or me, you weren't. I just don't like the idea of you mixing with theatrical people."

"It's a school, Mama. A theater *school*. You've seen it for yourself."

Janet did not reply, and Nancy gave a theatrical sigh. "All right." Nancy threw up her hands. "Perhaps you will let us all know your decision soon." She flounced out of the room, thoroughly annoyed.

Torquil arrived back about half an hour later. He had been out for one of the long, solitary walks which he seemed to enjoy nowadays. He had dropped most of his old friends after the Meg Seton affair. Just recently he had not been painting much, but was recovering from a long spell of frenzied activity, getting his breath back.

Janet sat him down by the fire, which had been lit to keep out the chill spring evening air, and told him about Mrs. Wilson's visit while he warmed his fingers.

"Well," he said when he had heard it all, "she might as well have an occupation of some sort. It's quite a respectable place, isn't it? It's not an undignified job. It will make her happy for the moment. Someone else will take Jim Baxter's place and then she'll talk of nothing but her wedding."

"I distrust the theatrical influence. I can't explain it, but I really do."

"I know and you may be right, but she has always been daft about the stage. If you hold her back now, you will simply fan the flames. Let her play at teaching and work it out of her system. Nothing in this world is more discouraging than teaching. You really do have to be dedicated to do it. She'll soon have had enough of it."

"Then you're in favor?"

"I'm not saying that this is what I'd have chosen had it been left to me, but under the circumstances, yes, I am. Let her go ahead. There's nothing to lose."

"Very well, then. I feel uneasy about her, but perhaps I'm just being silly and old-fashioned. A prude," she added with a rueful smile.

"You worry too much about us all, that's the trouble," he grinned.

"No, I don't. I don't really worry about anyone except Nancy. We'll tell her at dinner."

"Watch her face," Torquil advised. "You'll get your reward."

"You deserve the credit. On my own I'd probably have refused."

"I don't think you would. I wonder, though . . ."

"What do you wonder?"

"What sort of actress she'd have been, given the chance. Suppose the Wilsons are right, and she has great promise. We'll never know now, will we?"

Nancy took to teaching at the Theatre School as a duck takes to water. She was happier than ever before. There were no references to going on the stage, but all her conversation was about her pupils and her work. It was scarcely noticed when Jim Baxter stopped calling at the house facing the park.

Her twenty-first birthday fell in May of 1905, and Janet and Torquil planned a celebration well in advance. The family were discreetly told that there would be junketings at Conchra House to which they were commanded, Davie and Amanda were invited, too, and they decided that about a week beforehand they would tell Nancy they were giving a party and allow her to invite her friends from the Theatre School. They knew she would appreciate that. Meantime they bought her a pearl necklace, a gold watch, a set of illustrated books on the stage, and made arrangements for an enormous cake. Janet spent hours planning a special birthday dinner.

The birthday was on a Saturday, and on the Friday but one before the great day, Janet was excitedly waiting for Nancy to come home, for now they could tell her all about the celebrations they were arranging and get her to invite her own friends.

Torquil, watching her, wondered how she would get through dinner that night, she was so excited.

They were rather surprised when, at four o'clock, Mrs. Wilson arrived, again without warning. Janet's greeting was more friendly now, and Mrs. Wilson, who bore no grudges, and had long since become used to parental opposition to her pupils' ambitions, was pleasant.

"I can't stay," she remarked, taking off her gloves. "I only looked in to ask how Nancy is."

"Nancy? What do you mean?"

"Her migraine."

"But Nancy is at the school," Janet said, puzzled.

"No, she left at nine thirty this morning. The poor child looked quite pale."

"But she hasn't been home."

Torquil felt a sudden stab of premonition. "I'll look in her room in case she slipped in, darling," he said, and went upstairs in a great hurry. Janet and Mrs. Wilson sat down and stared at each other.

"She came at the usual time this morning," Mrs. Wilson said. "She was complaining of a headache and about half an hour later it was so bad that she asked to be excused. One could see she was unwell. Of course we told her to come home and rest and not to come back till she was well again."

"Where can she be?" Janet asked. "I'm certain she didn't come home. I've been here all day."

Torquil came into the room slowly, holding a letter in his hand. He paused near the door and Janet, seeing the expression on his face, rose in alarm.

"What is it?" she asked.

"She has run away. She left a note beside her bed."

"Why didn't the maid find it?" Janet asked automatically.

"I don't know," Torquil answered irritably. "She probably told her not to touch it. She has gone. She says that by the time we find her she will probably be twenty-one, and anyway she won't come back."

He held out the note, but Janet was rooted to the spot.

"Gone *where?*"

"To London. To go on the stage. I'm afraid she's gone with a man. Someone called Fell."

"Herbert Fell?" This was Mrs. Wilson, whom they had both forgotten.

"Do you know him?" Torquil asked quickly.

"Yes. He's an actor in Fairford's Company. He came up here to look over our pupils. They do that sometimes."

"Well, they've gone off together. Just like that."

Janet, who had finally gotten around to reading the note, turned angrily to Mrs. Wilson.

"Did you know anything about this?" she demanded aggressively.

"Certainly not. In fact . . ."

"In fact what?" Janet pressed.

"I can't understand it. Herbert was interested in her, naturally. Anyone so young and inexperienced who can teach competently is an unusual person. But he didn't agree with us about her." She paused to gather her thoughts. "He said that she had a facile gift for picking up stagecraft, and that she was a natural teacher, but that he didn't think there was any depth to her acting. He told me she'd never get by on the stage, that the school was her limit. I disagreed with him violently, of course. That's why I don't understand . . ."

"Perhaps you are looking for the wrong explanation," Janet said in a tight voice. "How old is this Mr. Fell?"

"He's about forty."

"Married?"

"I believe he has a wife, but that they haven't lived together for years."

"Then it is entirely possible that his interest in Nancy has nothing to do with acting."

There was a silence and then, "I think I had best go to London," Torquil said slowly, "and try to find Mr. Fell. It shouldn't be too difficult. Where do you think I might find him, Mrs. Wilson?"

"Fairford is at the Court Theatre in Sloane Square. Fell was free to come to Scotland because he hasn't been in their current play. He had a bad cold. However he's bound to gravitate back to his company soon."

"Thank you. That will do to start off with. I'll trace him, and through him I'll find Nancy. I'll go first thing in the morning."

He turned to Janet.

"You mustn't blame Mrs. Wilson for this, my dear. She is plainly as distressed and stunned by it as we are."

Janet looked guilty for a moment. "I'm sorry. I really blame myself." Her mouth tightened into an uncharacteristic thin line. "Yes, I ought never to have allowed this situation to arise. I was against all this acting from the beginning. I should have trusted my own instinct, no matter how much unpleasantness it meant."

Torquil cocked his head on the side. Janet would take a long time to get over this, and he was uncomfortably aware of his own part in persuading her to allow Nancy to teach at the school.

It was likely to be a very awkward and unpleasant evening, to put it mildly.

TWENTY-FOUR

TORQUIL was away for a week, returning on the ruined twenty-first birthday. Of course he was on the telephone every evening. They had finally decided that they must have one, although Torquil strangely enough had been against it, saying that it would ruin all their privacy. Now they were both glad of it.

Janet suffered and fretted and fumed for several days. She had the unpleasant task of telling the family why the party was off, and their sympathy only served to turn a knife in her wound. During these days she grew to hate the acting profession with a deep, burning hatred. She irrationally, but perhaps understandably, blamed "the stage" for all her present trouble.

Torquil had found Fell easily enough after three days in London, but Fell had made him wait a further two days before agreeing to take him to see Nancy, an attitude that shook Torquil's usual calm. However Fell said flatly that Nancy did not want to see her father, and all Torquil's threats were in vain. Eventually Torquil was taken to a small flat in Baker Street where a pale Nancy faced him steadily. Not entirely to his surprise she was Fell's mistress, rented the flat under the name of Mrs. Fell, and although he kept his own apartment, he spent several nights a week with his "wife."

Nancy took the initiative, after Fell had served drinks
—including a sherry for Nancy, Torquil noticed.

"I'm practically twenty-one," she told him. "The day
after tomorrow is my birthday. You can't do anything. It's
too late now."

"Oddly enough," Torquil said, forcing himself to be
calm and relaxed, "I didn't come to London to drag you
back, screaming. I came to see you, to talk to you, and to
find out how you are. You did give us a shock," he added
mildly.

"What else could I do?"

"Not much, I suppose," he reflected aloud. "Not after
you'd made up your mind to take up acting. I suppose you
know Mr. Fell is married?"

"Of course I do," she answered, scorn in her voice.

"You don't mind?"

"What's good enough for Ellen Terry is good enough for
me," Nancy replied, not very logically.

Torquil glanced at the silent, sardonic Fell, and prodded
again.

"There is one difference. You're no Ellen Terry. I suppose Mr. Fell also told you that? He told Mrs. Wilson
you'd never get far on the stage."

"That isn't exactly what I said," Fell objected.

"Anyway I know what he said," Nancy interrupted trium-
phantly. "I can get satisfaction from acting without being
the leading lady. I would have thought an artist could
understand that."

The trouble was, Torquil thought, that he could.

"Has anyone given you a part yet?" he asked, still mild.

"She was engaged this morning," Fell told him blandly.
"At the Lyceum. She has a small but satisfactory part. It
is a good start."

"In that case, there is nothing for me to say, is there?"
Torquil asked Nancy.

"Nothing that will change anything," she agreed, softening a little. "I'm sorry, Papa. I expect Mama is livid,

but I love Herbert, and I am determined to be an actress."

"It won't be easy to explain to your mother, and you may as well know that I disapprove strongly of the way you went about things. I don't like underhanded behavior."

"You agreed that I had no option."

He let that pass. "Are you happy?" he asked.

"Very, very happy."

Looking at her, he could believe her. She was plainly infatuated with Fell and he did not think it would last, but that was not something he could do anything about. She would have to work it out for herself. The main thing was that she was achieving what she had set out to achieve. She had her lover, she had her small part on the professional stage, and he knew almost exactly how she felt about both.

"More whisky?" Fell suggested, and Torquil looked down at his empty glass.

"I suppose so, thanks. It's a special occasion, isn't it? Will I have a chance to see you on the stage before I return, Nancy?"

"I start rehearsing with the company tomorrow. Could you come to that?"

"I ought to get back to your mother, but yes, I'll spend another day in London if it means seeing you."

She lost her composure, and flung herself at him and kissed him.

"Thank you, Papa. At least you try to understand."

"Your mother does, too," he reminded her gently. "You must believe that."

"I always did until the idea of my going on the stage was mentioned. That's one thing she will never understand —and it happens to be the most important thing to me."

He let her words lie unchallenged. He did not want to get drawn into an argument on the subject. He suspected that Nancy was right, and that this would be Janet's blind spot. It was sad, very sad, but there it was.

Next morning he watched with unexpected pride as she

played her small part in the rehearsals. It was nothing much, but as Fell had pointed out, it was a start and with a good company in a good theater. When they said good-bye, they both had lumps in their throats.

Back in Glasgow, however, it was beyond his ability to convey anything of all this to Janet. He had to confine himself to statements of fact and, on the surface, they were pretty unpalatable. She had gone on the stage. She was living in sin with a married man almost twice her age. She was unrepentant. He tried to find some way of sugaring the pill.

"It could be much worse," he remarked. "She'll be acting with Sir Henry Irving. He was knighted ten years ago. It's a great beginning for her."

"One swallow doesn't make a summer," Janet retorted tritely. "*Sir* Henry Irving may not object to employing girls who live with married actors, but I would."

Torquil kissed her forehead gently.

"It's so difficult to understand and to forgive," he said gently.

Janet's heart gave a guilty start. What had she once told Martin about learning to understand instead of trying to apportion blame? The trouble was that she could not help herself in this instance.

"Where did I go wrong?" she asked plaintively. "I tried to give her a good home, to bring her up well. Perhaps she was spoiled when she was younger, but she's been good these past few years."

She just wouldn't understand, he thought, that Nancy's decision had nothing whatever to do with Janet or her home.

"You mustn't blame yourself," he said soothingly.

"I'm her mother, aren't I?" Janet was determined to scourge herself.

"Yes, but not her keeper. Nancy has always been independent. You'll feel better in a day or two, when you've got used to the situation."

"It was awful, telephoning Martin. But the worst part was telling Davie. He sounded sorry for me. Davie—sorry for *me!*"

"Their sympathy is natural. You're upset, darling."

She broke away from him and sat down.

"Well." She tried to be brisk. "There's no one left except you and me. I hope you aren't going to run away."

"You know I'm not," he smiled. "However we ought to visit Nancy in a month or two, for a few days, to see how she is."

"Never!"

"She's not likely to come here, not for a long time. We ought to keep an eye on her. I'll have to go, even if you don't come. I wish you'd think about it."

Janet did not reply. With a little thrill of horror, she realized that she grudged Nancy even this small concession.

After that dreadful summer of 1905, Janet felt that the magic of the family circle had diminished beyond repair. They still spent Christmas with Martin and Helen in Dundee, and she loved her grandchildren. Yet it was not the same. The shadow of Nancy lay over everything. It wore off gradually, as time passed, but it never went away completely.

Torquil never lost an opportunity to try to soften Janet's attitude. One morning at breakfast, near the end of 1905, he read her the newspaper account of Henry Irving's burial in Westminster Abbey, and how Queen Victoria had sent a floral cross.

Such attempts to dignify the profession, which Janet believed had seduced her daughter, were doomed to failure, and eventually he gave up. Twice a year he traveled to London to see her. Fell had been right. She was competent in minor roles, and astonishingly attractive when seen from the other side of the footlights, but big parts eluded her.

After two years, Nancy and Herbert Fell drifted apart,

a fact that secretly delighted Janet when she heard of it. Nancy however remained dedicated to the stage.

In 1908 Torquil made a winter visit to Nancy's little flat in London, a longer one than usual, for while he was down south he hopped over to Paris for three weeks to renew old friendships and compare notes, to meet new artists and to study their work. He also spent some time at the Slade, in London, and talked with men who had learned their craft from the great Whistler. By now he was acquiring a small reputation as the rebel Scottish artist, though very few people had seen any of his work at this time. There was one important exception.

When he came back to Glasgow, he was in high spirits.

"You sound as though you've come into a fortune," Janet commented, coming into his bedroom where he was unpacking after an overnight journey on the train.

"I had a great time. Very invigorating. I wish you'd been with me."

"How is Nancy?"

"Fine. She has that flat of hers looking beautiful. Also I have news. She has a young man, a highly respectable one."

"Really?" Janet could not hide her interest.

"Yes." He stopped what he was doing, straightened up, and smiled at her. She was fifty-four now, he realized, yet she had not a single gray hair. Her skin was smooth, her eyes clear. If one put her beside Nancy, he realized with a shock, they might be taken for sisters.

"Yes," he repeated. "She has a beau paying court to her as though his life depended on it. I met him. His name is Farquhar Skene, and his family live in some Gothic castle near Aboyne. That's up in Aberdeenshire somewhere."

"What does he do? Why is he in London?"

"Wait for a surprise. Young Mr. Skene—he is the same age as Nancy by the way—is the baby of the House of Commons. In other words he's an M.P."

"And he's serious about Nancy?" Janet sounded incredulous.

"It certainly seems that way."

She considered. "That's a change," she reflected.

"Janet, I do wish you'd relent and come to see Nancy. She doesn't talk much about it, but I know she is hurt by your refusal to visit her or write to her or have anything to do with her."

"She could visit me, couldn't she? If she really wanted to see me."

"She has her work, my dear. It isn't like you to be so unyielding. Couldn't you make just one visit?"

"We'll talk about it another time."

This was her stock reply when he tried to get her to commit herself to any course of action involving Nancy. Avoiding the issue, he thought. Another uncharacteristic piece of behavior. Why was it that Nancy and her acting career had such a profound effect on Janet? He wished he knew.

"I have a bit of news for you," he said, changing the subject. "A surprise of sorts."

"What is it?"

"Let's go downstairs. I could do with a drink."

On their way down she asked tentatively, "Is this something else about Nancy?"

"About me," he corrected. "Something quite unexpected."

He would say no more till he had poured himself a warming brandy, and she had ordered a pot of tea for herself.

"Last time I was in London I met an American. I didn't mention it at the time because I wasn't sure if I'd see him again. His name is Mack Bradford. He's a very important man in the art world. We met quite by chance at Sickert's, and got talking, and the upshot was that he wanted to see some of my work. I sent a few canvases down to London, you may remember. They were for him."

"I remember. Did he like them?"

"Apparently he did. He took them back to the United States anyway and put them on show at his gallery."

"His gallery?"

"Yes, dear. I'd better explain about him. He's a very wealthy and very important man. So far as I can make out, he's a very powerful person behind the scenes—in the U.S.A., that is. He owns the Bradford Gallery in Boston, and another one in New York where he exhibits work by new painters. He also owns a Bradford Gallery in Paris, and he's an art dealer as well."

"He must be very rich indeed," she murmured.

"He is. Rich, important, and powerful."

"I'd like to meet him," she said curiously. "What's he like?"

"To look at? Tall, distinguished, good-looking. He has quite a way with women, they say. It wouldn't surprise me if it's true. Anyway you'll have a chance to meet him all right. He's putting on an exhibition of my work in New York next spring. About May, I think. He wants me to go across and he has invited you, too. We're to be his guests."

"Torquil, how wonderful for you."

"Yes, it is. It's the chance of recognition at last. I was lucky in meeting him, because he doesn't spend much time in London. For reasons of his own he's never been much interested in British artists. He spends far more time in Paris than he does in London. Anyway he seems to think I have a future, which is more than anyone else has ever done."

"I'd love to see America, and your Mr. Bradford sounds interesting. Torquil, wouldn't it be nice if he made you famous?"

"I don't know if I want to be famous, but I'd like to see my work exhibited."

"How old is Mr. Bradford?"

"The same age as you are—he was born on the same memorable day."

"Oh. So we'd be going in May?"

"About then. We'd sail from Liverpool. If we left a few days early there would be time to visit London briefly . . ."

"No, you don't," she said abruptly. "I'm not going to be pushed so blatantly."

"I just thought . . . After all, we're going to be in England anyway. Oh, well, it was an idea."

His voice trailed away and he grinned at her for a moment.

"Well," he said lightly, "I suppose the news of Dr. Bradford is excitement enough for one day."

"Dr. Bradford?"

"He's not a medical man. He got a Ph.D. degree from his university."

"More and more interesting. You must tell me all you can remember about him. And Torquil . . . don't try to force me into things, please," she said less vehemently.

"No, dear," he said, meekly. "It was only a suggestion."

They sailed for New York at the end of April 1909. For Janet it was a great adventure. She had never been out of Scotland and everything was new and exciting, even the journey to Liverpool. The size of the ship startled her, and she was sure she would get lost in its seemingly endless corridors and passages. They had a first-class stateroom, and she was impressed with its comfort. When they sailed, another of her fears vanished. Far from being seasick, she acquired a healthy appetite and did justice to the elaborate menu even on the one rough day of the voyage when a great many ladies kept to their cabins.

One thing that surprised her was that she saw Torquil in a new light. She thought she knew all the facets of his character, but where she was confused and bewildered, he was full of self-confidence. One would have thought he popped back and forth between England and the United States every week. She was impressed, despite herself, and arrived in New York in a happy frame of mind.

There was a note for them from Mack Bradford, apologizing for not being there to meet them. He was detained at a meeting somewhere in Manhattan, but would call on them at their hotel that evening, early. His car and driver were at their disposal.

Janet was thrilled to be driven to their hotel. Cars were

something new to her. Once in their room she sank onto the bed gratefully, and flung her hat and gloves down beside her.

"What fun!" she exclaimed. "What an exciting time we're having. I'm quite breathless."

"I think we should have a rest now," Torquil replied, smiling at her, impressed by her enthusiasm. "I expect Mack will be taking us out to dinner."

It was five thirty when Mack Bradford called at the hotel. He was admitted to their suite by Torquil and then he turned to face Janet. They were both motionless as they stared at one another, and Torquil, who was closing the door, turned and looked from one to the other, faintly puzzled.

His first impression of her was one of youth and loveliness, but Mack Bradford knew her age to the day, and he was disbelieving. He had an impression of thick, glistening, pale-gold hair, an oval face, a soft mouth, smooth neck and arms, a young figure.

Janet had been similarly unprepared for what she saw, a tall, slim man, gray-haired certainly, but with an unlined face and a tanned skin and eyes almost as clear as her own. He was expensively and elegantly dressed, and she thought he was the most attractive man she had ever laid eyes on.

"Janet, this is Mack Bradford," Torquil said, interrupting their bemused silence.

"How do you do, Dr. Bradford."

"Mrs. MacRae." He snapped out of it and walked over to her, took her hand, bowed over it, and touched it fleetingly with his lips. "This is an unexpected pleasure. I have heard a lot about you from Torquil, but I had no idea you were so lovely."

He straightened up.

"Torquil, you're a lucky fellow."

He sat down and admired Janet openly. "Your husband's paintings have begun to arouse a little interest here, Mrs. MacRae."

"Please call me Janet."

"I'd be honored, and you must call me Mack. I know from Torquil that we were both born on the day of the Charge of the Light Brigade, so we have something in common already. However I shan't mention it again. Men aren't supposed to know ladies' ages."

"Don't worry about that," Janet replied. "I've long since passed the stage of caring."

"But you should care," he corrected. "You must maintain your mystery. Beautiful women must always be shrouded in mystery."

He was smooth, she thought—smooth and full of charm and she could believe that women would readily fall into his arms. There was something about him, an air of purpose, a powerful presence. She was fascinated, but she turned the compliment nonetheless.

"Grandmothers are beyond flattery," she remarked. "We don't bother pretending about our ages."

He smiled at that. "Did you have a good crossing?" he asked.

"Oh, yes. We're going back on the same ship, too. The *Lusitania.*"

"A fine ship. I sailed to England in her in '07, on her return maiden voyage. Now, before we do anything else, I have something to ask you both. The exhibition begins next week, and I think you ought to be on hand for a few days after the private viewing, but when that's over I'd like you both to come to my home for a holiday. Can you manage that?"

"Very kind of you," Torquil said, glancing at Janet for confirmation.

She nodded. "That would be nice," she agreed. "Where do you live?"

"A place called Meadowford, in New Hampshire. It's in a district called the White Mountain region. It's very beautiful with its mountains and lakes and forests."

"It sounds lovely," she commented.

"I rather think it is," he smiled. "So if I can take that as settled, I'll send word to my housekeeper."

She knew he was a bachelor, from Torquil.

"Have you always lived in Meadowford?" she asked.

"Not quite. I was born in Rockville, which is about five miles away—quite a thriving township. After my parents died I moved out to Meadowford. I prefer country life. Nothing wrong with Rockville, mark you. A fine place, a fine place."

There was a note of self-satisfaction in his voice which she did not understand. Later she would learn that the Bradfords virtually owned Rockville, and had done so for generations.

Torquil was content to listen to them, pleased that Janet liked his patron so much. During dinner Mack opened up about his past, mentioning that he had been a diplomat among other things.

"Not a career man, of course," he said easily. "I went to Turkey as ambassador during McKinley's Presidency, and before that I was in Vienna for Benjamin Harrison— shortly after the Mayerling affair."

"I don't understand," Janet said, puzzled.

"Well," Mack explained, "sometimes Presidents have reasons for making private appointments. You see I was personally known by both Harrison and McKinley, and I was able to represent them better than a career diplomat who didn't know them. *Sometimes* there are tricky situations, and it's thought better to appoint someone who enjoys the President's personal confidence. You'll have gathered, of course, that I'm a dedicated Republican."

"Aren't all Americans republicans?" Janet asked, bewildered. After all, she knew it was a republic.

"By no means." Mack laughed delightedly. "By no means. Some of our more misguided citizens are Democrats."

"Oh, dear, I didn't know there was a difference."

"How refreshing to hear someone say so. I suspect a lot of American citizens could say the same, if they were strictly truthful."

"How did you become involved in the world of art?" she asked.

"By accident, mostly. I would probably have been an amateur, a mere collector, if it hadn't been for my uncle. He was a dealer and he left me his business. He also educated me in art. I decided to found my own gallery—I have three now, you know."

"Torquil told me."

"I have two main interests, really, apart from running my business, of course, which takes up quite a lot of my time. One is to encourage American artists. I founded an art school in Boston, and there have been one or two promising young artists come out of it. The other thing is to encourage good artists anywhere—which is where my galleries come into it, because I can put on exhibitions and arouse interest in the work of my protégés. I like to think that, although I myself can't paint, I've been able to contribute something to the world of art."

"I don't think you need worry about that," Torquil remarked.

"I hope you're right." He glanced at Janet. "When you're born with a silver spoon in your mouth, as I was, it can be difficult to leave your mark on the world. There would be no real achievement in my going into business when I would be starting off with plenty of money. Politics would have been even easier for me, and besides that, I'm not the sort of person who would get much satisfaction out of political life. I had to look for something different. I was lucky in having an introduction into the art world through my uncle. There's a real feeling of success in being able to spot new talent and seeing your judgment vindicated."

"I hope Torquil's work will vindicate your judgment," she murmured.

"Oh, it will. Don't worry about that."

He said it with unconscious confidence, and she realized dimly that this man's power was far greater than was apparent.

TWENTY-FIVE

THE private viewing of Torquil's paintings, at the Gallerie Moderne on 54th Street, took Janet's breath away. She had never imagined anything like it. It was a full-dress affair, with champagne and other drinks laid on tables groaning with elaborate cocktail snacks, and admission was by private invitation only. Mack had succeeded in getting together a glittering array of important people—critics, collectors, dealers, and the cream of New York society.

She was quickly separated from Torquil, who was quite literally besieged when the guests began to arrive. Mack, too, was forcibly detached, and Janet watched with interest as well-dressed and beautiful women offered him their cheeks to kiss, and made a fuss over him. All Torquil had told her was too plainly true. This man represented power and influence of an unusually high order.

She was quickly rescued by Clarence Withy, the director of the gallery and one of Mack's protégés.

"I've never seen anything like this in my life," she confessed.

"Even by Mr. Bradford's standards it's unusual," Clarence agreed. "There are some high-powered people here tonight. It's going to be a great success—I can tell."

"Will people really like my husband's paintings? Nobody has ever paid much attention to him before. I've come to look upon being a painter as completely unrewarding."

"Oh, yes, they'll buy his paintings. Mr. Bradford can arrange a viewing, but unless the paintings are good, he might as well keep his money in his pocket. You see, your husband has found a new form of Impressionism. It's modern and there are people who can't stand the idea of modern art. There are more reactionaries in the art world than the Republican Party," he added with a quiet smile. "But the discerning can see that this is new, original, and important."

Janet refused another champagne from a white-gloved waiter just as Withy whispered, "Here's Marcus Feldman coming across. He's the most important private collector in America and one of the richest men. I'll introduce you."

Feldman was tall and fleshy and, like so many men that evening, he had that unmistakable air of dynamism and confidence, and to Janet once again the word "power" seemed the only appropriate one.

"Evening, Withy. A good turnout."

"Yes, Mr. Feldman. May I introduce you to Mrs. MacRae? Mrs. MacRae, Mr. Marcus Feldman."

"How do you do, Mr. Feldman."

He stared at her. "The artist's wife?"

"Yes." She smiled.

"Well, this *is* a pleasure."

Withy murmured an excuse and left them, and Feldman beckoned to a waiter. Janet refused a drink and he took a whisky.

"Can't stand champagne," he explained. "It's pretentious. Now I begin to understand."

"To understand what, Mr. Feldman?"

"What Mack is up to. He really has gone to extreme lengths this evening. He's an old friend of mine, and I can tell you that he doesn't take quite so much trouble over his artistic protégés. Of course your husband's work is extremely good. Mack has a real find there. How long have you known him?"

"Only since arriving in New York a few days ago."

"Yes, I'm not surprised. That's why there were a lot of last-minute invitations, and why some of the arrangements were changed."

"I don't understand."

"Mack never could resist a beautiful woman, and if you will permit an older man to be personal, Mrs. MacRae, your husband is the first artist I've heard of who married a raving beauty."

Janet blushed at this heavy compliment. "I'm sure Mr. Bradford is only interested in my husband's work," she said.

Feldman chuckled. "And I'm sure you've done it no harm. Your husband is a far luckier man than I thought ten minutes ago. Come and meet some of my friends."

"Mr. Feldman," she asked anxiously.

"Yes?"

"Is Torquil's work really good? You see, I'm no judge. I like it, but that means nothing. In Scotland they laugh at him, most of them."

"I've always heard it was a barbarous country. Your husband is probably a genius. Does that satisfy you? It's the truth."

"Yes. Thank you."

She did not quite know why she had asked the question, except that for the first time she had an opportunity to ask experts about Torquil, and her curiosity was strong.

She was quickly absorbed into groups of knowledgeable people, none of whose names meant anything to her, and had to answer the same questions over and over again. Most people, she noted, were surprised that nobody had heard of Torquil before, and surprised that his work was not widely recognized in either England or Scotland. It was pleasant to bask in his reflected glory, and to receive the frank compliments of cultured men, and it was only on the way back to their hotel that a new thought occurred to her.

Suppose Marcus Feldman was right? And he was not the

sort of man to make mistakes! Suppose Mack had made a special effort over Torquil just because of her? It was a thought.

Just suppose Torquil's success was partly attributable to her! She knew enough to realize that whether or not an artist received recognition in his lifetime was largely a matter of luck. Torquil had always had luck on his side— luck in being modestly independent when she first met him, luck in marrying a woman with money so that he could experiment with his art, free from nagging poverty and despair, luck in happening to meet Mack Bradford. It gave her a little thrill that part of his luck might be the effect *she* had on Mack Bradford. After all, Mack .had been attentive, and they had become instant friends.

She glanced at Torquil out of the corner of her eye. He was happier tonight than she ever remembered him. She recalled that he had told her, a long time ago, that it was Meg Seton who helped him to find out what dissatisfied him about his work. It would be a nice leveling of the score if it were Janet Darling who put him on the map as a successful painter.

They stayed in New York for a few days before going up to New Hampshire. Mack took her to lunch one day while Torquil was busy elsewhere, and she was able to fish for information.

"The exhibition's a success, isn't it?" she asked.

"Indeed, yes. The most successful I've ever held."

"Lucky for Torquil that he met you."

He glanced at her and smiled. "I suppose so."

"You've done so much to make people come and look at his work. Not many people would take all this trouble. We're very grateful to you."

"Are you? You, too?"

"But, of course."

"You care about his work?" he probed.

"Naturally, Mack."

"But it doesn't matter to you financially. You're a rich woman."

"Not rich," she contradicted. "Not what you would call rich. Independent is a better word."

"It doesn't matter to you if he never earns a penny from his art."

"True," she admitted, "but one likes one's husband to be a success. People say 'What a clever girl she was to marry such a clever artist.' Besides look at all the interesting people I'm meeting. It's nice to see society at first hand."

"You deserve more than this," he said impulsively. "If you were mine . . ."

She glanced at him interestedly.

"I'm sorry. You aren't. You should move among royalty and aristocracy. That's where you belong."

"I'd be totally out of place," she said with common sense. "I'm middle class and very ignorant."

He shook his head. "If I'd had more warning I'd have invited people from all over America to the viewing."

"But you had lots of warning. You arranged this months ago. I recall Torquil telling me all about it."

"Oh." He was momentarily confused for the first time since she had met him, and she knew then that Marcus Feldman had been right. He *had* made some sort of change to his arrangements after meeting her. Her heart swelled a little. It was a heady realization.

He said no more that day. Instead, their talk drifted to some of his experiences as a diplomat. He was a witty, amusing conversationalist.

"Wasn't President McKinley assassinated?" she asked, when he had been telling her of one of his conversations with the President, following his return from Turkey.

"Yes, he was." Mack's face clouded. "At the Pan American Exposition in Buffalo, in September 1901. I was there. He was a particular friend, and a very great President."

"You were there? You saw it happen?" she asked.

"That's right. It was a hot afternoon and I remember people were lining up to shake hands with the President. A lot of people were mopping their faces with handkerchiefs, and a man stepped up to shake hands and fired a gun through a handkerchief in his hand. Two shots. I don't think I've ever been so shaken in my life. I'll tell you something interesting. The guards jumped on the assassin, and began to beat him with rifle butts, and there's no doubt they would have killed him. The President stopped them and told them to go easy on the man."

She stared silently.

"A great man, as I said. It took him eight days to die. We even thought he'd pull through, but it wasn't to be."

"Who did it?"

"Some crazy anarchist with an unpronounceable name —an immigrant, I think."

"What happened to him?"

"They sent him to the electric chair, of course. That too was interesting."

"How?" she asked.

"There was so much bad feeling about the killing that they poured acid into his grave to stop grave robbers from digging up the corpse."

She shivered.

"I stopped taking an active interest in party affairs after that," Mack said, staring across the room. "I lost heart." He was silent for a moment and then he smiled quickly. "Luckily for me I had art to console me. Let's talk of pleasanter things."

She was glad to, but although he still exercised a strong fascination, she was aware of the great gulf that separated him from provincial nobodies like Torquil and herself. It seemed unlikely that he should be so concerned over them.

They stayed with him in New Hampshire for ten wonderful days, ten days of rest, of good food, of long walks in the country and drives along lovely leafy lanes, of splendid, majestic scenery, and the fragrance of wood fires in the chill of the evenings.

The friendship between Janet and Mack grew and intensified rapidly in the elegant surroundings of his country home. Torquil was delighted by this, for he, more than anyone else, knew just how much he owed to Mack's efforts to promote his work. On their last day at Meadowford, Torquil went out in the afternoon, alone, for a walk, leaving Janet to finish her packing. Mack came up to her room and knocked, and was admitted.

"I thought I'd look in to see how things are going. Is there anything I can do to help?"

"No, thank you. I'm almost finished. Packing's a sad business, isn't it?"

"You find it so?" he asked.

She nodded. "I love it here. If I were you, I'd never leave Meadowford, not even for a day."

He laughed with pleasure.

"I wish you would stay. I wish you would stay forever."

She dropped her eyes and flushed slightly.

"I'm sad, too, Janet," he insisted. "I warn you, I shall pursue you to that terrible place, Scotland."

She laughed shakily. "Perhaps that's what I want."

"Don't make fun of me, please, Janet." He put his hand on her shoulder and squeezed it gently as he spoke.

"I'm not making fun, Mack," she denied quietly.

"It's too bad, isn't it? All these years I've traveled, I've moved in society, and all the time I was looking for, hoping for, and never finding the right woman to share my life. But no one I met was ever quite right. Always something held me back—until now, when it's too late, and I find her married to a friend."

"Please, Mack," she protested, confused. She had not expected an open declaration.

"I can't let you go without saying something," he persisted. "I think you already guessed my feelings, didn't you?"

"Perhaps," she said in a low voice.

"You know what I'm saying, don't you?" he asked.

She nodded. His eyes held hers and for a moment her head seemed to swim. *I love him*, she thought wildly. *I really do.* It was incredible, but it was true. It was ridiculous, mad, impossible. He was a creature from another world. She was hardly conscious of him as he came and lifted her to her feet, and embraced her. They stood together for long, silent seconds, her head resting on his shoulder, their arms around one another.

At last he kissed her on her smooth forehead, and smiled very, very gently.

"I'll be there to see you. Nothing can keep me away, not now. Nothing."

He left the room abruptly, and she sat down and began to weep; but there was no unhappiness in her tears.

Janet was never a hasty person, and therefore she did not immediately rush to visit Nancy after their return from the United States. She did not even mention Nancy at first, and if Torquil thought she was pensive, he put it down to all the exciting new things she had seen and done on their trip. The fact was, however, that she was principally thinking about how to make the first move to heal the breach with Nancy, and her thinking was constantly interrupted by memories of the charming two-story house in Meadowford, in that secluded river valley a few miles to the north of the Twin Mountains. The house, the tree-clad mountains that surrounded it, and above all Mack himself, Mack holding her close. She would shiver as she felt again the pressure of his body against hers, his arms around her, and the gentleness of his lips on her forehead.

She wondered how long it would be till he followed her to Scotland, as he had promised.

One day she asked Torquil about his plans for the future.

"I'm almost fifty-six now," he pointed out. "I've done most of my best work. There's quite a lot up in the studio, enough to meet any likely demand. At the moment I'm thinking about a special project."

"Tell me about it?"

"I want to paint you again, in my new style. It's going to be the best thing I've ever done."

"Paint *me* again! What for?"

"Perhaps to show how little you've changed, how even

the most beautiful girl in the world can grow more beautiful."

"Did you have to wait till I've one foot in the grave?" she joked, secretly pleased.

"You can prop yourself up with my silver-mounted walking stick," he offered.

"Why not do the children, or the grandchildren?"

"I probably will." He had painted Martin and Nancy many years before. "But first I want to do you again. It will be the same size and I'll have an identical frame for it, so that they will make a pair. I shall call them *The Darling Girl* and *The Darling Woman. The Two Darlings*, by Torquil MacRae himself, dabbler in oils, will never be sold. One day they'll be priceless and the National Gallery will try to buy them from our descendants."

"I refuse to comment. I'm not going to feed your vanity, Torquil MacRae."

He kissed her lightly. "I prefer to give compliments anyway," he laughed.

About a fortnight later he began the portrait. It was painted in the dining room against a backdrop of scarlet drapes fringed with gold. He had bought a white and gold chair and a matching table on which were placed a scattered bunch of flowers from the garden. When Janet protested that they should be in a vase, he scoffed.

"This isn't for a chocolate box. Leave them as they are. They're far more effective."

He positioned her to one side of the original portrait, which would dominate the background of the new one. Janet was interested in the amount of care that went into the setting of the scene. She wore her most flattering evening gown and her best jewelry, and privately wondered how it would all turn out. She was fifty-four now. She had been twenty-one when the original portrait was painted.

He refused to let her see the progress of the work. During the next week or two the dining room was uninhabitable, littered with paints, brushes, and charcoal sketches, and they ate in the sitting room. Only when it was completed, and when he had had it framed and had hung it on the wall as a companion piece—only when the dining room had been cleaned and tidied—did he invite her in and uncover the new portrait.

She noticed that there was a silver tray on the polished mahogany table, with crystal glasses and a decanter on it. "Sherry to mark the gala opening," he joked.

"Just a small one," she warned.

"Brace yourself. You may wish to finish the bottle." This was something of a joke. She rarely drank anything stronger than coffee.

He poured two sherries and then pulled the flimsy cloth away from his portrait and joined her at the foot of the table. Janet gasped audibly. It was a striking portrait, done in his own inimitable Impressionist style, the portrait of a lovely, ageless woman. Cunningly, however, he had reproduced behind her the other portrait in exactly the style it had been painted, so that there was a breathtaking contrast of the two styles.

Torquil himself had entertained doubts about how this would work out. He knew now that this was a *tour de force*, a triumph, probably the finest thing he would ever paint.

"I don't know what to say," Janet remarked. "It's strikingly beautiful, but is that really me?"

"Yes, and very good, too," he said in a pleased voice. "That is exactly you."

"Isn't it, well, flattering?"

"No. I took care that it shouldn't be."

"I can hardly take my eyes off it. How clever of you to put the first portrait into the second, and I do see now why you wouldn't let me put those flowers into a vase."

"You are looking at my last word as a painter," Torquil told her. "Oh, I don't mean I've retired as from this minute. I'll have to do the rest of the family, and there are a couple of Glasgow scenes I'd like to get on canvas before I finally quit. However, this is the high spot. From here I can only go downhill. Wait till Mack Bradford sees those."

"Mack? Is he coming?"

"He's threatening to come soon. He's bound to come eventually, because he's heard me talk of that first portrait, and he's very anxious to see it."

They stood, his arm around her waist, sipping their sherries. At the mention of Mack's name she had felt a momentary excitement, but it had died down. Now that she had been at home for a time, and the memories had receded, she felt a little guilty, and even more silly, about Mack. She had decided that in his case it was a combination of age and the fact that he was a bachelor. She knew, and was privately pleased, that she had not aged as other women did. Mack had been carried away and in his enthusiasm had kindled a last spark in her.

It was sweet, of course, but not very adult. She had this surprising husband of hers, who was so clever and so critical of himself, and who had given her all that her first marriage lacked.

She turned her face up to smile at him and allowed him to kiss her. The kiss intensified, and she put down her glass and twined her arms around his neck and kissed him back, like the lover he had once known. They parted and she felt breathless.

"Oh, Torquil." She felt the years falling away. "I do love you."

"Come up to my room for a little while," he begged.

She was mute for a moment, and then unexpectedly she smiled. "All right, dear," she agreed; "I just hope you won't be too disappointed."

Torquil's happiness became complete when, shortly after their return from Dundee in January of 1910, Janet said, "I think it is time I went to see Nancy." She looked at him sharply. "I haven't changed my mind about the stage," she said sternly. "It isn't suitable. But I'd like to see her. Do you think it's all right?"

"All right? I'll telephone her tonight. She'll be wild with joy."

"I wonder. It's you she writes to, not me."

"I'm the one who has visited her so far. Things will be different now. When will we go?"

"Not now in midwinter. About Easter, when it's milder."

"Oh. Well I needn't phone tonight, need I? Still I think she ought to know soon. She'll look forward to it as much as I do. It will be good to be together again."

"I feel awkward about it," Janet admitted. "Frightened, perhaps."

"There's no need to, but I suppose it's to be expected."

"I know what. I'll write to her tonight, and you can telephone her next week and see how she has taken the news."

"A good idea," he nodded.

The relationship between them had gone into yet another phase. Although they retained separate bedrooms, as much from choice as from habit, he came to her room two, sometimes three nights a week, and they indulged in a comfortable, rather relaxed form of lovemaking. Janet had been surprised to find that she could still respond to him. Obviously some of her ideas about sex had been wrong, or else she was the exception.

She was no longer aroused to frenzy by him as she had used to be. She did not expect that, but it was rather pleasant to be so intimate with him again. It was also the final seal of forgiveness for the past. And it brought them close.

She closed her mind to the memory of Mack Bradford. She loved her husband. Was she not now proving it in a most unexpected manner?

Those weeks were perhaps the highlight of a marriage that had given them both so very much pleasure. As they followed one another in succession, life at Conchra House became idyllic.

Janet's letter had been answered by a restrained and cautious note from Nancy, in which pleasure could not be concealed. When Torquil spoke to her on the telephone,

she was less restrained. Thereafter Janet wrote regularly
and Nancy replied promptly. In one of her letters she
referred casually to the fact that some time earlier she had
spent a week in Aboyne, visiting Farquhar Skene's family.

"Do you think they're serious?" Janet asked Torquil.

"You know more about them than I do."

Torquil thought before answering. One of the things
that had been concealed from Janet was that Skene and
Nancy were lovers. They were discreet about it, but Skene
spent many a night at her flat. Nancy was the one who
was opposed to marriage. What Janet would say about
that when she found out—and she must find out, because
Nancy herself would probably make sure she did—was
anybody's guess.

"I'm pretty sure he wants to marry her, but I don't
know if she's ready to settle yet."

"It's time she did. Goodness, she'll be twenty-six next
birthday. I know, let's go to London on her birthday,
shall we?"

"Now you're talking," Torquil grinned.

Consequently they arrived in London on Friday, May
6, a few days before Nancy's birthday. As they were
driven from the station to the flat, Janet stared out of the
window at the bustling London scene. It was her first visit
to the capital. It reminded her a little of New York, but
only a little. The incongruity of it amused her, and she
remarked to Torquil, "Do you realize I've been to America,
but never been to London before?"

"I always knew you had style, my dear," he quipped
back at her.

When they got out at the flat, Janet stood on the pave-
ment and inspected the building before going inside. It was
a first-floor flat, and, as Torquil rang the bell, Janet forced
herself to be calm.

Nancy opened the door, and she and Janet stood for an
interminable second, just drinking in the sight of one
another, and then Janet stepped into her daughter's arms,
and they kissed.

"Oh, darling," Janet exclaimed, a catch in her voice.

"Mama." Nancy was close to tears.

"Come along you two," Torquil told them. "I want to come inside."

They went into the hall and Janet inspected Nancy, noticing the bloom, the brightness and warmth that her daughter had acquired. She was striking rather than pretty in the conventional sense, but Janet thought that most men would find her attractive. There was a calmness in Nancy's gaze that had never been there before.

Goodness, she's grown up so much, Janet thought.

"Come and take your things off, Mama. Oh, Farquhar, help Papa with the suitcases."

Janet turned to the tall, dark, sallow-complexioned man with the thick mop of hair, and returned his smile.

"How do you do, Mrs. MacRae," Farquhar greeted her. "How are you, sir?"

He helped Torquil carry the suitcases into the spare bedroom where Janet was taking off her coat, hat, and gloves. They all went into her sitting room, and Farquhar gave Torquil a drink while Nancy went off to make tea for her mother. At last they were settled.

"You must be tired after the journey," Nancy suggested. "I thought we'd stay at home tonight. You can see what sort of cook I turned out to be."

"You must let me help you," Janet exclaimed.

"No, no. This is my home."

"Tell me about yourself. How are you getting on?"

Nancy described her latest part in her latest play, and then after a time she took Janet off to show her the kitchen and bathroom and the rest of the flat. The tour culminated in her own bedroom, and Janet's quick eye did not fail to notice the man's dressing gown, or the male slippers at one side of the bed.

"Tell me, are you happy, Nancy?"

"Very, Mama. I really am. I love my work, and then there's Farquhar."

"Are you serious about him?"

"He wouldn't be my lover if I weren't," Nancy replied lightly. "He wants to marry me, but I'm not ready for that yet. Perhaps I never will be. It doesn't matter at the moment."

"It's a little unconventional, isn't it?"

"I'm an unconventional person."

"I don't know why, but I suspected this. It's none of my business, Nancy." Nancy, who had been waiting for some sort of remonstrance, was speechless for a moment. "You must live your own life," Janet continued. "Is he living here now?"

"No. He really doesn't live here, Mama. He has his own flat near the House of Commons. He comes here as often as he can. Sometimes I spend the night at his place. It all depends."

"Do his parents know about this?"

"I doubt it. There's never been any reason to tell them. They know we're in love, and I daresay they expect us to get engaged soon, but they've never been to London, so why tell them what doesn't concern them?"

"Darling," Janet said impulsively, "I just want to say one thing now, and then we needn't refer to it again. What's past is past. I'm quite happy to accept the situation. I shouldn't be here otherwise. You're my daughter and I love you. I'm sorry about what happened, but it's over now. I just want your friendship, that's all."

"Oh, Mama." Nancy put her arms round her mother and wept a little until Janet reminded her gently, "This is supposed to be a happy occasion. Dry your eyes."

"It is," Nancy sniffed. She gave a watery smile. "Thank you. Now I really *am* completely happy." Then she burst out, "You really are good!"

This was the last thing Janet had expected, and the least thing she felt she deserved.

"That's not true, my dear."

"Yes it is. I know how you felt about my becoming an actress. I know how you must have curled up inside when you heard I was living with Herbert. Now you come here and find Farquhar's things in my bedroom, and all you say is that you want to be friends. Do you think I don't know what that costs?"

"Oh, tush. I want another cup of tea."

The visit simply had to be a great success after that. Fifteen minutes before midnight that night King Edward VII died, and next morning the nation went into mourning, but there was no evidence of the fact at Nancy's flat. They talked a lot and laughed a lot, and Farquhar Skene and Janet decided they liked one another. Janet was taken to the Tower, to Madame Tussaud's, and to stare at Buckingham Palace and the Horse Guards. They dined out every night, and by the end of their stay Janet had had a surfeit of new and interesting sights, to say nothing of more rich food than she normally ate in an entire year.

In their first-class compartment, on the way back to Glasgow, Torquil held her hand.

"I'm so glad it turned out as it did."

"So am I, darling. I had a lovely time. Life is going to seem very quiet for the next few days, isn't it? I just wish she'd marry Farquhar. He's such a nice man and so much in love with her."

"She probably will," Torquil prophesied. "She isn't really as unconventional as she likes to think she is. She'll give in. You wait and see."

Janet smiled happily, her face lighting up in that special way of hers that he loved so much. For no particular reason that he could identify, he felt tremendously proud of her.

TWENTY-SIX

THERE was a letter from Mack Bradford waiting for them at Conchra House on their return. He would be arriving in London the following week, and proposed to visit them a day or two later if it was convenient. Torquil replied care of Mack's London club, and Janet began to think of meals and menus.

The mounting excitement grew in her daily, and she knew that she had not got him out of her system at all. She had been perfectly serious when she told Torquil that she loved him, yet here was another man who could transform her into a trembling schoolgirl.

When he finally arrived from the station, with Torquil, and they stood face to face again, her senses swam. She closed her eyes for a second or two as he bent over her hand, and tried to make herself relax and be natural. Over drinks they chatted about his trip, and Nancy whom he had visited while in London, and then about Torquil's paintings.

"Everything is going splendidly," Mack said with satisfaction. "There's lots more money to come. More to the point, three young artists at my art school in Boston were so impressed by those Glasgow street scenes of yours that they've started doing the same thing in Boston. The MacRae School has been founded!"

Torquil chuckled.

"Don't laugh," Mack said seriously. "Imitation is by far the greatest tribute that fellow artists can pay you. I hope you have lots more paintings for me to ship back to the States."

"Yes, there's quite a lot."

"Thank goodness for that. I was alarmed when you wrote to say that you had painted yourself to a standstill and were retiring. However, I want to see those portraits of Janet. I've waited a long time for this moment."

The three of them went into the dining room, and Torquil switched on the lights above the pictures, and Mack let out an exclamation.

"My God," he said in an awed voice. "I had no idea, no idea at all. They're . . . they're unbelievable, Torquil. That second one is incredibly good."

"They're not *that* good," Torquil disclaimed, "but I admit I'm more satisfied with the second portrait than I am with anything else I've ever done."

"What do you call these portraits?"

"*The Two Darlings—The Darling Girl* and *The Darling Woman*. Janet's maiden name was Darling, if you remember."

"Very good. Very suitable."

He inspected the pictures for a long time in silence, while Torquil gave Janet a smile and an eloquent shrug. At last Mack turned back to them.

"I'm torn," he said with simplicity. "I feel as though I've had a wonderful experience; yet at the same time I half wish I hadn't seen them."

"Oh, dear," Janet said.

"For the rest of my life it will bother me, knowing that they are locked away here in a private room where nobody can see them. However I do understand why they aren't for sale. It would be a crime to sell them. I'll let you know later whether you've made my trip, or ruined it," he concluded with a laugh.

"I hope I haven't ruined it."

"Torquil, I'm not an artist, but I have spent a lifetime

promoting art and helping artists. I know almost all the great ones of my lifetime, and I think I can honestly claim to know a good painting immediately I see it. Those are outstanding. If they aren't great works of art, then I know nothing at all. I just wish some of my friends could see them. However . . ." Mack paused and stroked his chin thoughtfully. "Those three young artists in Boston I told you about ought to see them. After all, they're the first members of your own school of painting. Would you allow them to visit you here?"

"Well, yes, I suppose so." Torquil glanced at Janet, who nodded. "But are they really going to go to all that trouble just to visit me and see my two portraits?"

"Why not? I'll send them over later on this year."

"I'm flattered. By all means, then. We can put them up here. We've got plenty of room."

"We can settle the details later on," Mack said, clapping him on the shoulder. "The main thing is that they can meet you. You may have retired, Torquil, but you have a lot to pass on to others coming up behind you."

Torquil gave him a grateful glance. He had always maintained that he painted to please himself, but he had known for some time that recognition and acclaim had been needed to put the seal on his life, to make him feel that he had been a serious painter and not just a dilettante dabbler married to a rich woman.

Later on, after dinner, when they were sitting out in the garden enjoying the sunset, Mack remarked, "It is difficult, when one is at peace like this, on such a fine evening and after a lovely meal, to realize that some people are worried about the possibility of a war in Europe. I still have my contacts, and there's a lot of talk about it."

"Surely nobody wants to go to war?" Torquil asked, surprised.

"I don't think that what people want has much to do with it," Mack replied slowly. "Governments can always whip up popular sentiment when they need it, but sometimes there's no real decision to go to war. What I mean by that is that situations get out of hand, and the politicians find themselves in a corner of their own making. At the moment there's too much unrest in the Balkans, and Austria is sitting on a powder keg."

"What does that have to do with us here in Britain?" Torquil wanted to know.

"Perhaps nothing. Let's hope so, but there *will* be trouble in the Balkans. There must be. It's absolutely unavoidable. Then again, some people think Germany is too ambitious."

"What do *you* think, Mack?" Janet asked, leaning forwards.

"I don't know. One never can be certain if people mean what they say, or say what they mean. There was a joke when I was in the Foreign Service, about the difference between a diplomat and a lady. Let's see. Yes. When a diplomat says 'yes,' he means 'perhaps.' When he says 'perhaps,' he means 'no.' And when he says 'no,' he isn't a diplomat."

They all chuckled, and Janet asked, "And what about the lady?"

"I was coming to that. When a lady says 'no,' she means 'perhaps.' When she says 'perhaps,' she means 'yes.' And if she says 'yes,' she isn't a lady. I always enjoyed that little anecdote. Apart from being witty, it enshrines an important truth, which is that we don't always know what people mean. They say words are a means of communication, but often we use them to hide rather than to reveal our true thoughts. Let's just hope all this posturing saber-rattling is a pose."

"Killing people is stupid," Janet said heatedly, surprising them. "It's wicked."

"But occasionally necessary," Torquil suggested.

"That's not true."

"What would you do with a murderer?" Torquil asked. "What about your old friend Jack the Ripper? Suppose you caught him. What then?"

"I don't know, but hanging him wouldn't do any good.

Don't you see that once you've taken a life, you can never replace it? It's the most final act there is."

"Well," Torquil went on, enjoying the argument, "suppose I found some naked savage with a spear, about to kill you, and I had a gun in my hand. I'd shoot him, wouldn't I?"

"You don't have to shoot to kill. What you should be trying to do is to stop him, not take his life. Besides I don't know that I'd want my life at the expense of someone else's."

"A noble sentiment," Mack observed.

Janet flushed. "It isn't meant to be noble. You men see everything in black and white, but life isn't like that at all."

"As an amateur diplomat, I fully agree," Mack smiled. "I've never thought much about murder, but I'm sure wars are a foolish and wasteful way of settling arguments. Look at your Boer War! It accomplished almost nothing and was certainly not worth the sacrifice of a single human life."

"You see?" Janet turned to Torquil. "Mack agrees with me."

"So do I," Torquil laughed, "but I enjoy hearing you argue your point. I'm going in for a drink. Can I get either of you one?"

"No, thanks," Janet said. "I'm going to stroll in the garden."

"I think I'll keep you company, if you don't mind," Mack added.

Janet smiled, took his arm, and they set off for a stroll among the flower beds while Torquil went indoors.

"I've missed you," he told her. "I wonder, did you ever think of me?"

"This is all wrong," she countered, evasively.

"Perhaps it is, Janet, but so far as I am concerned it is real. Sometimes I think it is the only real thing in a very artificial life. I had to come to see you, just as I will contrive to see you again . . . and again. I don't believe I'm unwelcome."

She turned to him. "You know you aren't, Mack."

The smile he gave her was possessive and she trembled a little because she wanted him so much.

The following morning Torquil received a letter from London, and read it twice before looking up and saying, "Listen to this. It's from the Slade in London. They want me to go down there for a few days."

"How interesting," Mack observed. "What do they want you for?"

"To give a couple of lectures. Me! Of all people."

"That's wonderful!" Janet exclaimed. "When is this to be?"

"That's the point. They want me to go now. It will mean being away for three or four days."

"You must go," Janet urged him.

"What about Mack?"

"Don't worry about me," Mack laughed. "I want to explore this sprawling industrial city of yours. If Janet will permit me to stay, that is. I promise not to be a nuisance."

"I don't mind," Janet said readily enough, but she was watching Mack.

"I suppose I'd better telephone and say I'll go down tonight, if you're sure you don't mind, Mack."

"Of course not. It's only for a day or two. We'll have plenty of time together on your return."

Torquil was obviously excited. It was something of an honor, after all these years, after constant rejection, to find himself sought after. They went to the station with him and waited till his train had pulled out before walking to their waiting taxi. The house was dark and silent when Janet let them in. Before she could reach for a light switch, Mack took her in his arms, and she felt his lips on hers.

Instinctively she tried to twist free, but he held her, and after a moment she started to return his kiss. They strained together in the darkness for a time, and at length broke free.

"You knew about this," she accused in a whisper.

"Say, rather, that I arranged it," he replied. "He'll be away for a week. We have a week, Janet."

"Sure of yourself, aren't you?" she asked coolly.

"No," he answered, his voice changing. "If only you knew how unsure of myself I am, you'd be surprised. If the worst comes to the worst, I can visit all the city's museums and galleries."

The hall light went on and she looked at him steadily, her expression somber.

"Shall we go up?" she invited, and he took a very deep breath.

Mack undressed and folded his clothes neatly as always, and slipped on his robe and slippers. He left his room and tapped on her door, opened it, and went in. She was in her nightgown, brushing her hair before the mirror. He came and stood behind her, his hands resting lightly on her shoulders.

"That lovely hair," he murmured.

She ignored the compliment. "You'll have to be very careful," she warned. "The servants have a fixed routine, so it won't be difficult, but if you're careless, I'll never forgive you."

"Don't worry."

"I expect you've had experience," she remarked and wondered why she was being catty. Nerves, perhaps.

"You know how old I am," he murmured. "That's one thing you and I will always know about each other. I haven't spent my life in a monastery. All I can say is that I have never been in love before."

She put down the brush and turned.

"Do you really love me, Mack?"

He took her hands and she rose.

"I swear I've never loved anyone else, that this is real."

"Because I love you, too," she whispered.

"Oh, my darling."

His hands went around her and slid up to her breasts.

He could feel them, remarkably firm under the thin material.

"Bed," she reminded him, kissing the tip of his nose.

At the bedside she turned off the light. As he stripped, he heard the rustle as her nightgown fell to the floor. Then they lay down together and she turned to him.

He was gentle, partly because this was the first time, partly because it was his nature. Janet discovered that she needed no arousing, that she was ready, far more ready than she had realized. After a few moments of his gentle stroking and kissing, she rolled over on top of him. She guided his face to her breast and felt his lips fasten on her nipple. Her hand slid down his belly and she grasped him and she felt him respond.

"Love me, Mack," she whispered fiercely. "Love me. Don't waste time. I want you to love me."

He responded to the urgency in her whispering, threw her off onto her back and began to kiss and fondle her passionately.

"I'm waiting, Mack," her fingers kneading his shoulders.

When he mounted her, she clung to him wildly, urging her hips against him, totally abandoned, and her wildness triggered off a wildness he himself had never experienced before.

Their first mating was tempestuous, and when the climax had passed, they lay panting and perspiring, and she felt as though she had experienced sex for the first time. She was far too happy at that moment to try to analyze her feelings.

"That was . . . unforgettable," he murmured at her side.

"I wanted you," she said simply. "Next time we'll make it last longer."

He marveled. She spoke like a courtesan, yet she was nothing of the sort. He knew that if she had not loved him, she would have slapped his face had he so much as tried to kiss her.

"You know," she said happily, "I usually lie down for an

hour or two in the afternoon, after lunch, when the servants have their rest. Don't you think that's a good idea?"

"Twice a day?" he chuckled. "I'd better see about a tonic."

"I'll be your tonic," Janet suggested, and she leaned over him and guided his face to her breasts, and stroked his head.

After a time she roused him again, and this time, as she had forecast, they made it last longer, but still, when it was finally over, Mack had that uncanny feeling that he had been raped.

It was also very enjoyable.

It was a week during which Janet closed her mind to everything except this slender man whom she loved so much. Her lovemaking continued to be aggressive, and she took the initiative far more often than he did. She had never done this before, in her entire life, and one night when he had gone back to his own room, she lay and thought about it for a time.

Looking back, she could remember that she had loved Andrew, loved him romantically and girlishly but with no sexual feelings. He had been the one who wanted her, poor, crude, clumsy Andrew. He had never once aroused desire in her, and the girlish romance had given way to unprotesting obedience.

Torquil had been the first person to rouse her. Looking back on that, too, she knew that when she had married Torquil, she had loved him, if love was the word, in a placid, matronly sort of way. There was no romantic illusion. Once married, however, Torquil had revolutionized her life by awakening her sexually. All their marriage, however, Torquil had been the one to arouse her. He had taken the initiative, he had cunningly and cleverly kissed and caressed her body until she was desperate for him.

This affair with Mack was like neither of these others. For one thing, she loved Mack wildly, romantically. He was handsome. Her heart beat faster when she saw him.

Most important, he had somehow aroused hidden feelings in her. *She* wanted *him*. She had no shame where he was concerned, no reticence. And, most amazing of all, she had learned almost at once that he was relatively inexperienced, that she could teach him more about the art of love than he could possibly teach her.

She wondered why she felt no guilt. It was not, and of this she was sure, it was not paying Torquil back for Meg Seton. That had nothing to do with it. The complexity of human emotion and feeling intrigued her, and that night she lay awake a long time, not because she could not sleep but because she did not particularly want to.

On the last evening Torquil telephoned to say he was catching the overnight train. He sounded pleased. He had been lecturing on techniques of light and shade—impressionistic light as he liked to call it—and he had been well received.

Mack sat and watched and listened, and marveled at Janet's composure. There was something here that he did not understand, something that he felt he had to find out.

That night, after their second and last coupling, a long-drawn-out affair full of tenderness, he lay exhausted on the bed beside her. It crossed his mind that he was not totally sorry about Torquil's return. He would not have believed that he could have performed such feats, and he doubted how much longer he could keep them up.

He raised the question that had been troubling him.

"Janet, we both love one another. It's so obvious we don't even have to mention it. Why don't you come back to the States with me? Nobody in New Hampshire would know we weren't married. We could say we'd got married in England. I can't stand the thought of leaving you."

"I couldn't do that," she answered gently. "Torquil is my husband."

"Yes, but you love me."

"And Torquil," she pointed out. "In a different way. Mack, I would no more dream of walking out on Torquil than I would of committing suicide."

"That's what I thought you'd say," he muttered. "It doesn't make sense. If you feel like that about Torquil, why ...?"

"Why am I playing fast and loose?" She finished the sentence for him. "I wondered when you'd ask about that. I love you, Mack. I'm *in love with* you. You arouse me as no one has done before, neither Torquil nor my first husband. But I love Torquil, too, and my home and my family. Don't ask me too many questions. Perhaps one day they'll allow women to have two husbands," she chuckled. "Until then, we must meet when we can, discreetly. Besides, my darling, how long can this go on? The fires must burn out some time."

"Not yet awhile. I was serious about asking you to come to the States. I think you know that. It's what I want. But, well if that's how you feel, I suppose I'll have to be content with this. By the way, when those young Boston artists turn up in a few months, you'd probably feel in the way. It would be a good time to visit Nancy. I wouldn't be surprised if I were in London at the time."

"You cunning devil," she complimented him. "I wouldn't be surprised to learn that you'd hired them."

"Not quite. They are genuine enough, and they do want to meet the maestro. Let's just say they're a lucky coincidence that I decided to encourage."

"All right then," she laughed. "Just so long as Torquil never finds out. It isn't myself I'm thinking of, Mack. It's Torquil. I don't think he could withstand the shock. I suppose I'm an immoral woman, but I don't feel it."

"There's nothing immoral about you." He kissed her gently and stroked her face. "Nothing at all."

"They say in Scotland that minister's sons are the wildest. I think it must apply to parson's daughters, too."

As she said it, she thought idiotically, Oh, dear, I do hope he isn't up there looking down. Poor Papa.

TWENTY-SEVEN

AFTER Mack had gone back to London, having arranged to take some more of Torquil's work back to America, Janet and Torquil went off on a short holiday together, which culminated in a shopping expedition in Edinburgh.

He found her more loving than ever, more responsive to his lovemaking, much more like her old self, and his happiness was complete. It seemed to him that the wheel had come full circle, and that he had regained the beautiful bride he had once known and loved so much.

After their holiday they went to Dundee for a few days. Janet always enjoyed seeing Marion and Ailsa, who were rapidly growing up, two vivacious and attractive children, with fair hair and blue eyes. Marion was the plainer of the two, and the more stable. Ailsa showed signs of becoming a beauty, and she was effervescent.

It was Ailsa who managed to corner Janet, alone, soon after their arrival.

"Grandma?" she said eagerly, clambering onto Janet's knee.

"Yes, dear."

"What does Aunt Nancy look like?"

"You've seen her photograph. She's very nice looking."

"Is she beautiful?"

"It depends what you mean by beautiful, doesn't it?" Janet laughed.

Ailsa thought how even the nicest of grown-ups could be obtuse. "But you have to be beautiful to be an actress, don't you?" she asked.

"Oh, I see. No, not beautiful necessarily. Of course, you mustn't be ugly. That would never do."

"Have you seen Aunt Nancy on the stage?"

"Yes, dear."

"I wish I could." Nine-year-old Ailsa sighed dramatically. "I'm going to be an actress when I grow up, and live in London like Aunt Nancy. London's the biggest place in the whole world."

"It's certainly very big," Janet agreed mildly. "Why do you want to be an actress?"

"Because I want to be beautiful and famous. All the men will fall madly in love with me and come to the stage door with bouquets—but I shan't marry any of them. That would put the others off, you see," she explained solemnly, and Janet had to fight back a howl of laughter.

"What it is to be young," she spluttered. "I wish I were your age again."

"Why? I hate being young. Everybody orders you about."

"If only you knew how lucky you are," Janet said half to herself, while Ailsa stared at her. "Youth is so precious, and it lasts such a short time. When it's gone, you never get it back." She turned and gave Ailsa a funny little smile. "I'm afraid you don't understand, and by the time you do, it will be too late already."

The child's face screwed up in concentration. "Too late for what?" she asked.

"Don't mind the haverings of an old woman," Janet said lightly. "Come along, my little actress. Almost lunchtime."

"Don't you *mind* my wanting to be an actress?" Ailsa asked.

"Not particularly," Janet answered, remembering Nancy with a pang.

"Mama says I'm silly. Do you think I'm silly?"

"You won't catch me that way," Janet smiled. "I think it's silly to worry about what you'll do when you're grown up. Wait and see, and have fun while you can."

"What sort of fun," Ailsa snorted.

"I'll tell you a secret, if you like."

"Yes, please!"

"After lunch we're going out together, you and Marion and I. We're going to buy two kittens. One for Marion and one for you."

"A *kitten?* For *me?* All to myself. My very own?"

"Yes. Your mummy says you may have one each."

"Does Marion know?"

"Not yet."

"Can I tell her? I knew first. When I grow up, I shall have lots and lots of kittens. Hundreds of them."

"Who will look after them while you're on the stage all afternoon and evening?"

"Oh, I shan't go on the stage after all. I shall keep a kitten shop, and sell them only to nice little girls, but I'll always keep a lot in the shop for me to play with. I have a friend who has a tortoise. Kittens are more fun. *May* I tell Marion, please?"

"Yes, off you go."

She watched the child scamper out of the room and sighed. How lucky Martin and Helen were in their children. Yet they grew up so quickly. Marion was eleven. In another ten years, if she were spared, she could easily be a great-grandmother.

The incongruity of life struck her forcibly. She had a husband and a lover, and in ten years she might very probably be a great-grandmother.

She began to laugh silently.

In the last two years of peace, Janet contrived to see Mack twice a year in London, ostensibly visiting Nancy, and indeed she did stay with Nancy, but Mack had rented a furnished flat, and, while Nancy was at the theater, Janet spent her time at the flat. Their lovemaking was slightly more sedate now than it had been in its first week, but only slightly, and both of them thrived on it. In some mysterious way it seemed to keep them young and buoyant. Torquil always remarked on how well she looked when she came back from London, and remarked privately to himself how these absences seemed to kindle her ardor.

They were good years, those last years of peace, the end of an old order that was destined to end in any case, one way or another, but which had been so kind to those with the money to enjoy it.

Mack talked to her a lot about the young boy he had made his heir. Apparently one of Mack's many relatives was a cousin, Howard Winthrop, who had during the past year or two moved to Rockville where he had an auto agency. Winthrop was younger than Mack, a thin man, not very robust, a widower with one son.

It was of this son, Kim, that Mack talked a lot. He was a husky thirteen-year-old, with bleached hair and big freckles, an outdoor boy who fished and swam and loved tinkering with cars. It was obvious to Janet that Kim had become the son Mack apparently had wanted, and she encouraged him to talk about the boy. Mack had given up most of his amateur activities, apart from occasional visits to art galleries in Boston and New York. His main interest outside of Meadowford and Kim was Janet herself.

During one of the last of those visits to London, Nancy dropped a bombshell. It was one evening after they had dined quietly together at home.

"Mama, I know it's none of my business, but you come here twice a year, always when I'm busy working, and you moon about the place all day while I'm working. I only see you at nights."

"I don't mind," the unsuspecting Janet replied.

"Yes, but my dear you never come with Papa when he's visiting the Slade."

"He's busy then," Janet cut in quickly.

"Not all that busy. I don't know how to put it. I'm not blind. You are always here when Mack Bradford is in town. Not just once or twice but every time. I know he's a friend, but . . ."

"You think I'm having an affair with Mack? A woman my age?" Janet tried to make light of it.

"I don't think your age has much to do with it. You're a very young woman at heart. Yes, I do. I wish you'd tell me."

Janet began to bridle, and then forced herself to think coolly.

"If it were true, why would you want to know?"

"Because you might as well spend your nights with him," Nancy said bluntly. "I wouldn't tell anyone you weren't here. I don't like to think of you playing hole-and-corner games."

Janet began to laugh. The laughing went on and on and Nancy came and hugged her and tried to calm her.

"Stop it. I'm sorry I spoke. Stop laughing."

After some moments Janet gained control of herself.

"I couldn't help it. I was thinking about you and me. The stage, Herbert Fell, Farquhar—remember you once said I was good because I swallowed all that. I forget your words, but you remember? And now you've caught me out—a wicked old woman. And you're offering to help me be unfaithful to your father. If I don't laugh, I'll go mad or something."

Nancy held her fiercely.

"I don't care what you're up to," she declared. "You're my mother."

Janet sobered up.

"Thank you, darling. I suppose I was foolish to think you wouldn't put two and two together, no matter how careful and discreet we were. Yes, Mack and I have been having an affair for some time. There's no question of my leaving your father and he knows nothing about it. At least I hope he suspects nothing. I don't want to hurt him."

"I understand." She stared at the window. "I don't think I really approve of marriage," she added.

"You're wrong about that," Janet warned, turning to face her squarely. "Marriage is good. I wish you'd marry Farquhar."

"He's persistent anyway, and I wouldn't marry anyone else. Is that enough?"

"If you love him, yes it is."

"I'll think about it. I often do. And do go out at night when you feel like it and come back when you feel like it, at any time at all. You know where the spare key is kept."

"Thank you," Janet whispered.

So for the rest of that visit, and the whole of the next one, Janet spent several nights a week at Mack Bradford's London flat, and afterward she was grateful, for the world was already rushing downhill to destruction. A few weeks after her final visit to London, war was declared.

To Janet and Torquil, as to many others who did not inquire too deeply into foreign affairs, it came as a surprise. Nobody really seemed to know why there was a war. There was a lot of talk, in those early days, of brave little Belgium—talk that did not endure—but they found it difficult to follow just why they had to go to war over Belgium.

In the beginning they did not foresee that the war would affect their lives in any direct way. Martin was forty and had a responsibility toward Rowan's, and was not likely to be needed. No one thought of Farquhar Skene until Nancy telephoned from London to say he'd gone off to war.

"But, darling," Janet protested, "surely Members of Parliament are much too important to go to war."

"You'd think so, wouldn't you," Nancy said gloomily. "I didn't know it, but he had some sort of reserve commission. He's a captain in the Gordon Highlanders, of all things."

"But how old is he?" Janet was thinking of Martin as she spoke.

"Thirty-one. A year older than I am."

"Poor you. What will you do?"

"Carry on, I suppose. Entertaining the boys on leave or something dreary. London is awful without Farquhar."

"Take my advice, Nancy. Marry him."

"I'm going to, Mama."

"How glad I am to hear that," Janet sighed.

"I suppose," Nancy's voice automatically lowered, "you won't see Mack till it's all over, will you?"

"I shouldn't think so, darling."

"Sorry about that."

"It can't be helped, dear. Look after yourself, won't you?"

A little later they found out that Martin had made the gesture of trying to join up. He had thought that he might get some sort of staff job, if they wouldn't take him in the infantry, but he failed his medical. Janet and Helen were profoundly relieved to learn about it.

Farquhar Skene did not get his first leave till May of 1915. He and Nancy had decided that they would announce their engagement on his first leave, and get married on his second one. However as the war settled down, it occurred to Farquhar that only an incurable optimist in the British infantry would make plans on what to do on the leave *after* the next one. And so he wrote and suggested that they had waited long enough and that they get married without bothering about an engagement.

Nancy agreed readily, phoned the news to Conchra House, and waited impatiently for word of his return. One Friday morning in May a long-awaited telegram arrived at the flat, from Farquhar in France.

LEAVE AT LAST. MEET ME ABOYNE TWENTY-THIRD WITH TROUSSEAU. LOVE, FARQUHAR.

She wanted to shout her joy aloud. She swung into action. First of all she telephoned the theater and explained the situation. They had known of course that she was likely to leave at short notice when her fiancé got leave. Her stand-in would take over her part and the whole cast wished her luck.

Next she went to the bank and drew out quite a lot of money and did a good deal of shopping. By teatime she was ready to go. She decided to travel next day, spend the night in Edinburgh, and then go on to Aboyne on the twenty-third. She sent a telegram to Farquhar's home in Aboyne announcing the time of her arrival on the twenty-third, and went out to have dinner alone and a bottle of champagne to celebrate. It was still possible to get a good meal in the West End, if you could afford to pay for it. At ten thirty she returned to the flat, curiously impatient.

Then it occurred to her that she could catch an overnight train to Scotland that night, and arrive in Aboyne a day early. That way, she would be there to meet Farquhar. Why hadn't she thought of that before? She would have to hurry, but it could be done. The Skenes wouldn't mind, she was certain. She would send a telegram from Glasgow next morning, when she had checked on trains to Aboyne.

She packed her last suitcase hurriedly and telephoned for a taxi. When it arrived, she told the driver, "I want to get a train to Scotland tonight. What's the best one, do you know?"

The man consulted his turnip watch. "We've just about got time to catch the midnight express from Euston to Glasgow."

"Good. Please hurry."

He took her luggage down, and she locked up and followed him. They arrived at Euston Station with about ten minutes to spare, no more. She ran to the ticket office and got her ticket. There was no time to go to the sleeper reservation office. Instead she walked along the train till she found a first-class sleeper with an attendant by the door.

"Excuse me, I have no reservation. There was no time. I'm traveling to Glasgow on this train. Is there a vacant first-class sleeper?"

Attendant Dyer looked at this nice-looking woman, and smiled. He liked her on sight.

"Yes, there is, madam. You can pay me and I'll issue you a ticket. This way."

She breathed a sigh of relief, signaled to the porter, and followed him to a vacant compartment. The suitcases, dressing case, and hatbox were piled on the luggage rack, and after the train pulled out, Dyer collected the cost of the sleeper, punched her train ticket, and asked her about morning tea.

"We get into Carlisle about six thirty," he said. "I usually bring tea to passengers then, if they want it."

"That would be very nice, thank you," Nancy said.

He made a note of this on his list, and went off, leaving her to undress, wash, and climb into her bunk.

All through the hours of darkness, the express thundered northward, to arrive in Carlisle, near the Scottish border, at six thirty next morning, Saturday May 22, 1915.

There, in the space of seven minutes, the engine was uncoupled and replaced by two Caledonian McIntosh superheated 4-4-0s, for the final part of the journey which involved a very long uphill climb. At 6:37, just as they were pulling out, the attendant knocked on Nancy's door and brought her tea. When he had gone, she sat on the edge of the bunk and stirred in the sugar.

She thought of Farquhar, who could not be far behind her, and was impatient to get to Glasgow and make the connection for Aboyne, and send the telegram announcing her earlier arrival.

By now they were minutes from destiny. Just past Gretna Green, on the Scottish side of the border, was Quintinshill signal box with its two loop lines. Either there, or converging on it, were a total of five trains.

On one of the loops was the goods train known as the

"Welsh coal empties." On the other was the 4:50 goods. Both loops were thus occupied.

The slow train from Carlisle that normally followed the London express was ahead of it this morning and had been shunted onto the up main line where it stopped to allow the express to pass. Inside the signal box the fireman of the 6:10 slow train was standing chatting to the signalman who, in a moment of incredible carelessness, forgot to put a signal collar on the signal lever. Because of this there occurred the most fearsome railway disaster the world had known. Earlier the signalman had been informed that a special troop train, from Larbert in Stirlingshire, destined for Liverpool, had passed through Lockerbie.

At 6:42 he accepted the up troop train, which was thundering south carrying five hundred men, half of the 7th battalion of the Royal Scots, all bound for Gallipoli. He had completely forgotten the stationary slow train on the up line.

At 6:50 the troop train, hauled by a four-coupled bogie express engine, which was picking up speed on the down gradient, ran headlong into the stationary train on the same line. So great was the collision that the troop train, 213 yards long, was telescoped into only 67 yards, and the wreckage blocked both lines, and fire broke out.

One minute later the midnight express from Euston thundered into sight and ran headlong into the wreckage of the first two trains. In car 5132, which was the third vehicle behind the two great express engines, the attendant was killed outright and fire immediately broke out. Among those mercifully killed in this sleeping coach was Nancy. Mercifully, for the Pintsch oil gas cylinders, which provided the gas lighting on the trains, soon turned the wreckage into a vast funeral pyre in which people were cremated alive.

For hours on that sunny morning in late May, while the sun shone on the rolling green countryside, while larks sang their songs of joy overhead, men labored among sights far worse than those that Gallipoli held in store for the five hundred soldiers on their way to war.

It was a race to free trapped people from the wreckage before the spreading flames claimed them. Doctors hacked away at limbs, without anesthetic, to release people who would otherwise have perished by fire. All around the area, dead, wounded, injured, maimed people littered the scene.

In the final count it was calculated that there were 227 dead and 246 injured, and some of the injured would have been better dead. In the freshness of that glorious summer morning, while the birds trilled in the sweet air, and nature rejoiced, Nancy's dead body was destroyed by fire amid scenes of carnage that defied description. Nobody even knew she was there. There was no record of her having traveled. Attendant Dyer's list had been burned to ashes in the remains of car 5132.

On the day following, Sunday, the regimental dead were sent to the Royal Scots drill hall at Leith. Among the coffins were found two which did not belong to the regiment. One was labeled as an unrecognizable girl, and the other, more gruesomely, as "three trunks," probably belonging to children. They remained unclaimed, and so they were sent on to Glasgow where they were buried on the Wednesday, in the presence of the chairman of the Caledonian Railway, and the lord provost of Glasgow.

Of all this the family remained happily ignorant until, on Monday, Farquhar Skene telephoned to Conchra House from his own home. Janet answered the telephone.

"This is Captain Skene, Mrs. MacRae. Is Nancy with you?"

"Why no. I thought she was in London. Where are you calling from?"

"From home. Perhaps she hadn't told you, but I got some leave and sent her a telegram asking her to meet me up here so that we could get married. She sent a wire to my people saying she would arrive yesterday, Sunday, but there's no sign of her, and I can't get any reply from her flat."

"I don't understand." Janet was puzzled. "I do hope you're all right, by the way. You aren't wounded, are you?"

"Nancy doesn't know it, but I am. I've got a shrapnel wound in my foot and I'll limp for the rest of my life. I'm lucky," he added with a bitter laugh. "No more trenches for me. I suppose they'll give me a desk job at home till the war is over. But it's Nancy I'm worried about. I can't think where she has disappeared to."

"Neither can I. I tell you what, I'll telephone my son in Dundee. Have you tried the theater in London?"

"No. I've sent a telegram to her flat asking her to call me as soon as she receives it. I'll ring the theater and we can call each other back this evening."

"Yes, of course. Earlier, perhaps. Oh, dear, and you're waiting to get married. I wonder what she can be up to."

They rang off, and when they spoke again they had both drawn a blank. Martin had neither heard from nor seen Nancy, and at the theater all they knew was that she was supposed to have gone to Scotland on Saturday. At that point they decided that Farquhar should stay put in case she contacted him, and that Torquil should go to London in the hope of finding out something.

It was on the train that Torquil got his first inkling of what could possibly have happened, when the car attendant, chatting to him, mentioned Saturday's disaster at Quintinshill. It had been kept quiet, and no mention had been made in the national press for reasons of military security.

"What happened?" Torquil asked out of routine curiosity.

"There was a big smash up near Gretna Green, sir. A troop train and a local train, and then the midnight express from London ran smack into the wreckage. Terrible, they say it was. Like a battlefield, only worse. Dead and dying everywhere."

"There was nothing in the papers."

"No, and there won't be. They're keeping it all quiet, but there's hundreds as knows."

"What train would that be?" Torquil asked, more alert now. "The train that left London at midnight on Friday night?"

"That's the one, sir. Euston to Glasgow Central."

Which was a relief, Torquil thought when the man went off to regale others with his grim gossip. Nancy wouldn't have taken a Friday night train to Glasgow if she intended to arrive at Aboyne on Sunday. She'd take the east coast route to Edinburgh on Saturday.

He found Nancy's flat locked, and there was no answer to his persistent ringing. None of the neighbors knew anything, except that she had not been seen for several days. At last Torquil went to the nearest police station and explained the problem carefully to the desk sergeant.

"We'd better come along with you, sir, and break in. Just to make sure all's well inside. If you're agreeable, that is."

"Yes, please, that's what I hoped you'd say. I suppose she could be ill in there."

"Quite. I'll get two constables to go along with you."

Half an hour later they stood in Nancy's bedroom, looking all around.

"No sign anywhere, sir," one of the constables said.

"No, she's not at home. Hang on. I'll check through her things."

He opened cupboards and drawers, watched by the policemen.

"She has obviously gone. Shoes, underwear, and handkerchiefs all gone, not many clothes in the cupboards, and no sign of any suitcases. She must have packed up and gone away."

"Looks like it, sir," the policeman agreed.

They checked the bathroom and the empty cabinet told its own story.

"Thank you very much," Torquil told the men. "What will we do about the door?"

"Don't worry about that, sir. One of us will stay here and we'll get someone to come and put a lock on it, with a note to say that the key is at the station. If she comes back unexpectedly, she'll know what to do. I suppose you'll want to report her as a missing person?"

"I suppose so," Torquil agreed wretchedly. "Then I'd better go home. I'll telephone first, to make sure she hasn't turned up."

He used Nancy's phone, and of course she hadn't. He stood there, defeated.

"I don't know what to do," he muttered to himself. "I just don't know."

TWENTY-EIGHT

NORMAN SWANSON was a seedy man of middle age, untidy in habit, but methodical when it came to work. He was a private inquiry agent in Glasgow, a man whose work was sordid and unenjoyable, but occasionally financially rewarding.

Torquil obtained his name and address from an acquaintance whose wife had once run off with another man. Neither Janet nor Torquil approved of Swanson, which put the detective on his mettle. He decided that he would show them. He rarely worked for people of their class.

On Wednesday, when Nancy's unidentified and unidentifiable trunk was being buried right there in Glasgow, at the Western Necropolis, erroneously identified as that of a girl, Swanson took the train to London.

The following Wednesday he arrived back with his report.

"There is no definite news," he told them without preamble. "She has disappeared into thin air. We have two facts to work on. The first is that she sent a telegram to Aboyne to say that she would arrive on Sunday, and the second is that she definitely packed and left her flat, left it tidy, as though it were a planned departure."

"We know that," Janet interrupted.

"I'm sorry, Mrs. MacRae. I want to set things out in order. On Friday morning she rang the theater and told them she was going to Scotland to get married. Funnily enough, the manager, who spoke to her, thought she was going at once, yet her telegram said she was arriving on Sunday. However she may have traveled on Friday. She may have decided to visit you to tell you the good news. Perhaps it was a last-minute decision."

"Gretna!" Torquil turned pale.

"Yes, sir. I've been making inquiries here as well as in England. It is too important to overlook. On Friday she announces that she is going to Scotland. Not when, nor how, but merely when she expects to arrive at Aboyne. That night's express was in a terrible accident and by no means all the bodies have been identified. For instance I have discovered that two coffins interred here in Glasgow contained unidentified remains. One was said to be the, er, body of a girl, and the other had three people in it, believed to be children. I must tell you that the condition of these, er, remains makes any positive conclusion almost impossible. Was your daughter a tall woman?"

"No," Janet whispered. "We hoped she would be, but she was of medium height. As a matter of fact she had quite a . . . small . . . torso." She spoke with an effort.

"Then Gretna cannot be ruled out. The coincidence is significant."

"Surely they can tell the remains of a child from those of a woman."

"In this case, no, sir. I spoke to the doctor who labeled the coffins. At best, he was expressing an opinion."

"But she might not have been on that train," Janet burst out.

"Correct, Mrs. MacRae. I checked the sleeping-car bookings, for I thought that a young lady like that would be bound to take a sleeper. She was not booked." They brightened, and reluctantly he wiped the relief off their faces. "But people often arrive late and go straight to the sleeping car, and if there is a vacant berth they buy the ticket from the train attendant. It proves nothing. There is one possibility."

"What?" Janet asked fearfully.

"She would be likely to take a taxi to the station, with her luggage, wouldn't you say? Yes? Well I went to Scotland Yard, and the London police are searching for any cabdriver who might have taken her to Euston or anywhere else that night. They are very thorough in these matters. They will get in touch with me when they have news. If that driver exists, they will find him."

"And if not?"

"Well that leaves us up in the air. If she wasn't on that train, where can she be? There is only one thing to do. Wait. The police have her listed as a missing person. But from what you have told me, she had no reason to stage a disappearance. I'd say it was next door to impossible that she would do so. She was about to get married."

"Quite impossible," Torquil snapped.

"Then something must have happened. The police will make inquiries, of course, but every year people disappear and are never heard of again. Nobody knows what happens to them."

"But Nancy wasn't that sort of person," Janet protested.

"I agree most of them are of a lower class, but not all. By no means all."

"How long shall we have to wait?" Torquil asked.

"Not long, sir. A day or two. I'll report all news to you."

When he had gone, they sat silently hand in hand, and Janet saw that Torquil had suddenly turned very old. He had aged almost overnight. She led him upstairs and made him rest.

The following afternoon Swanson arrived back at the house. He had determined to do what he had to do quickly. It was the kindest way. He refused a seat.

"The driver has been found," he said heavily.

"*No!*" Janet put a hand to her mouth.

"Yes, Mrs. MacRae. I'm sorry. He drove your daughter to Euston to catch the midnight express to Glasgow, the one that was in collision at Gretna."

"*No, no, no!*"

He shook his head unhappily and glanced at Torquil, but Torquil's eyes were glazed and lifeless.

"I'm really sorry, but there is no doubt. I came at once. I'll send you my full report and my bill. Believe me, it is foolish to hope. She caught the train with a few minutes to spare."

He turned and walked out, almost as upset as they were. Janet sat in her chair, sobbing quietly until a noise startled her. Torquil had toppled from his chair and lay quiet and still on the carpet.

"*Torquil!*" she shrieked, falling on her knees beside him.

Torquil's stroke left him partially paralyzed and affected his speech. Janet nursed him conscientiously and had the satisfaction of seeing him getting up and about again, but he had to walk with a stick, and the least exertion exhausted him. He had become a permanent semi-invalid.

In a way his stroke helped her, because it wrenched her mind away from the tragedy of Nancy's gruesome death. It kept her busy, and Helen came through from Dundee to help her. It was a miserable year for them all, and the only relief in it for Janet was her correspondence with Mack.

"How I wish I could come to you," he wrote, "but it is impossible at this time. Besides what could I do, Janet? Only clutter up the house. I wish there were words for these occasions. I remember Nancy often, so vital, so wrapped up in her work, such a fulfilled sort of person. I was as pleased as you must have been when you wrote to say she was going to marry young Skene.

"It is you I worry about most, for you are left to shoulder the burden. Torquil—well, you know as well as I do that he will just go on the way he is until the next one. In a sense he is more fortunate than you. He will never know the load you carry.

"I wish this war were all over and I could come back to Britain, back to Glasgow, to see you both again. Wishing will accomplish nothing. We must just see things through. It's no comfort at all, is it? When you most need it, I can do nothing for you. It doesn't say much for me, does it?"

But his letters did a lot. She read and reread them, for much of them was about Meadowford and Rockville, and about his cousin and young Kim, still at school.

For the rest of the war she did not leave Conchra House. Torquil could not travel, and she remained to look after him, to try to make his life easier. He seemed quite happy in her company, but he was frail, and she knew that the doctor worried about him. In mid-November 1918, Torquil caught a chill and had to go to bed. The doctor looked more serious than ever, but refused to be drawn out.

Only a few days earlier, on Armistice Day, Davie Robertson, and his son had come through from Dundee to visit them. John Robertson, already a graduate from the university, had joined Rowan's, working under his father. Janet was pleased to see him, and pleased that he was carrying on his father's tradition. At least there would be a Robertson at Rowan's for a long time to come. It was a pleasant antidote to all the chaotic change in the world.

Torquil lingered on till Christmas, and on Christmas Eve that year, he appeared more cheerful and much better. He sat up in bed and demanded a small glass of brandy, and he ate a good meal. Janet had lit a fire in his bedroom fireplace, and the flickering flames gave the room a warm, comforting air.

Torquil, bright-eyed, looked at her as she sat near the bed. Her face was serene in the light of the fire, and he stretched out a thin, worn hand to her.

"I feel so much better tonight, darling," he told her. "Wouldn't it be nice if I can get up in the morning and spend Christmas Day downstairs with you?"

She squeezed his hand gently. "Yes, my dear."

"You know, in the firelight you look twenty-one again —like the girl I was sent for to paint. Do you remember that first night we met, at your party at Aberneist House?"

"I've never forgotten."

He lay back on the pillows, smiling. "That business with Meg Seton. I was lucky not to get my marching orders. There were so many things you could have done and didn't do, Janet. You could have left me, or you could have been cold and unkind to me afterward, but you didn't do any of those things."

"One can't very well throw out the head of the house," she replied lightly, making a joke of it.

"You were independent enough to walk out anyway. You've been so good to me. Where did you learn all that forgiveness?"

"I didn't," she murmured. "I just learned to love."

"I've only sinned the one time," he replied with a flash of his old humor. "If you can forgive me, perhaps God can."

"Are you worried about God?"

"No, but you never know, all those other people may be right. Wouldn't it be funny if they were? But I don't care. He must have made you, so he can't be a bad chap."

She got up and kissed him.

"Stop your havering. I think it's time you rested. Tomorrow is Christmas."

"I love Christmas," he whispered. "Now that this war is over, perhaps we can go away for a proper holiday next summer."

"That would be nice. You just take care of yourself," she said.

"I'll catch crabs in a pail, and build sand castles, and be young again. It will be like it was with Martin and Nancy. God, just looking at you makes me feel young again. Kiss me, Janet."

"Only one more, then I'll read to you for a little and you must try to go to sleep."

She kissed him tenderly and stroked the thin wisps of hair from his forehead, and sat down in the chair to read. A few seconds later he had drifted off to sleep.

In the morning he was dead.

PART III

1919–

Love all alike, no season knows, nor clime,
Nor hours, days, months, which are the rags of time.

John Donne,
"The Sun Rising"

TWENTY-NINE

MACK BRADFORD had not changed much during the war years. He arrived in May of 1919, a handsome, still slender, courtly man, elegant as always, and the wrinkles at his eyes somehow only served to make him look more mature.

He kissed her hand in the old way, but when he had done that he took her shoulders and kissed her lightly on the mouth.

"How nice to see you again, darling," he said quietly. "It's been a long time. Much, much too long."

"Mack. I missed you."

She took his arm and they walked into her drawing room and sat down side by side on the high-backed settee. There she unburdened herself. She told him about the funeral, a drab affair on a drab, drizzling day, just the family and the Robertsons, how acutely she felt the loss of Torquil, and still did but not so painfully, how much Mack's own letters had helped her.

"I've got over the worst of it now," she told him with a smile. "Sometimes one remembers something a little too clearly, but I try not to live in the past."

"Of course not. There's always the future to plan for. What are you going to do now? Anything special?"

"Yes, I'm going on a motoring holiday when you leave. Martin has arranged to let me have his car and a driver who works at the factory. Things have changed," she chuckled. "Martin is driven to work every morning and home again every evening by a car and driver belonging to the factory. I wonder what Andrew would have thought of that!"

"It sounds like a good idea. Where will you go?"

"Touring the Highlands. I know very little about Scotland other than the small part of it where I've lived, and the places we used to go for holidays. I don't know most of the places where Torquil once liked to paint. While I'm doing this, I shall be looking for a house. I want to get away from here. For one thing it is too big for one old lady living alone, and for another it has too many memories. I don't want to turn myself into a fossil. As you said, my dear, there is the future. There's no future here."

"You have the right idea. I came here with a suggestion, Janet."

"Wait till after dinner," she told him. "I expect you want to freshen up. It's a long and tiring journey."

"A good idea. I feel scruffy."

"How are things in Meadowford?"

"As good as always. It doesn't change much. More cars about nowadays, of course, and more money."

"Your cousin and his son in Rockville? How are they?"

"Young Kim is in the business now. Howard isn't very well. He was never strong, although I don't know why. Our family is notoriously tough. It must be the Winthrop connection. Kim is doing well. I'm proud of that boy."

"How old is he now?"

"Going on nineteen." He stood up and smiled. "I really must get rid of the grime. I'll be down shortly."

During dinner they discussed Torquil's paintings. There were a number of them in the studio, neatly stacked and covered, which she had been keeping for him.

"Torquil was particularly anxious that those two portraits of me should stay in the family, but neither Martin nor I want the others. We all have paintings by Torquil."

"That's good. I'd like to take them, but I can't promise

much. The war interrupted so many things. I've more or less dropped out of circulation these days. Still, if we could exhibit those two portraits of you in New York and Boston, it might snap people out of their morbid preoccupation with war. I'd like to let people see what Torquil was really capable of—I owe it to his memory."

"I was so glad when he became a success in America," Janet nodded. "He'd always made out that it didn't matter, but he was only human like the rest of us. It made a big difference to him."

"I know. Too many artists spend their whole lives struggling. That's why it's important for someone like me, who has a lot of money and lots of important friends, to encourage them. Money imposes its own obligations, you know."

"Torquil never cared about money," Janet mused, "but then he was never down and out. What made him really happy was when those three young men came here from Boston, and the occasional lectures he gave at the Slade and at the Glasgow School of Art. I think it made it all worthwhile, somehow. I never understood him," she added with a little laugh.

"I'm sure you did."

"No. He wasn't a violent man, but there were times when he was savage with his own work. He'd destroy paintings wholesale, dozens of them, saying they were rubbish."

"My God," Mack said weakly.

"Yes. The funny thing was—I never told you about this —he had a love affair years ago. I realize now that I forced him into it, although at the time I was very hurt. Anyway, this woman, who apparently knew very little about art, was the one who criticized his light values, or said something about them. That was when he really began to love his work, without being tortured by it. I never understood it, Mack, that strange world of the artist and his art. Torquil was so restless and dissatisfied at times, yet he kept on looking for whatever it was he was looking for. The wonderful thing was that he never took it out on me."

"You've been privileged," he remarked.

They took their coffee into her drawing room where she spent most of her time nowadays.

"You had some sort of suggestion?" she reminded him.

"Yes. As you yourself remarked, you are alone now. So am I, Janet. You know where I live, what sort of home I have. Why don't you come over and marry me?"

"A proposal, at sixty-five? How sweet of you!" She was delighted.

"We once agreed that what we shared didn't need the sanction of marriage," he went on, "but things were different then. Torquil was alive. So was Nancy. I'm not saying that now, at our age—and incidentally we won't be sixty-five for several months yet—we need marriage, but I think we do need companionship. I can give you a home worthy of you, and I can offer you love. What do you say?"

She stretched out her arms and they kissed. Then she pushed him away and smiled gently.

"Dear Mack. I'd love to, but I won't do it. I have a son and two grown-up granddaughters in Dundee. I can't explain it, because I don't visit them often, but I feel that I ought to be here in Scotland. I'm too set in my ways to start a new life. Your home is beautiful. The place where you live is beautiful. I know what it would mean to be Mrs. Bradford."

Over the years she had come to realize that the Bradfords were real aristocrats, such as the Cunninghames, Darlings, and MacRaes never had been nor would be. Mack was as much a thoroughbred blue blood as any English lordling in his manor house.

"Are you sure? I want you very much, Janet."

"I'm sure, Mack. There's too little time left. I don't know how much, but at our age it is limited. I don't want to be far from home. I have a feeling I might be needed by someone someday. Anyway," she laughed, "I have you to myself for three weeks, and I'll be surprised if you aren't back again to see my new home when I find it."

"Oh, well. It wasn't marriage as such, but it would have been nice to have you by my side always."

"And so I shall be, in spirit anyway."

They kept early hours in Conchra House, and by ten the servants had all retired for the night. Janet and Mack sat chatting till ten thirty, and then she glanced at the gilt clock on the mantelpiece.

"You must be tired. I know I am. Shall we go up?"

"Yes." He rose and offered her his arm, and she took it. They went up the big staircase arm in arm, and he stopped at her door.

"Ten minutes?" he asked.

"Are you sure?" she asked. "I mean, well I'm a lot older now."

"You and your age," he chuckled. "Would you like me to come to you?"

She nodded slowly. "Yes, I would, Mack."

She went into her bedroom and undressed and then washed and powdered herself, cleaned her teeth, and sat naked before the mirror to brush her hair. He found her like that, and caught his breath.

She turned to him and gave him one of those old, special smiles.

"I feel so ridiculous," she said softly. "Hold me, Mack."

He hugged her and led her to the bed. There they lay entwined and still for a time, simply enjoying being together again, until she began to stroke his body and felt him tremble and stiffen, and she knew that she had lost neither her desire nor her skill. Their lovemaking was tame compared with their first mating, but it was deeply satisfying, and they fell asleep in each other's arms until her alarm clock woke them early and he slipped back to his own room.

He visited her every night, although they did not always go to bed. On those nights when the fires of their love burned lower, they would sit and talk for a time, arms

around one another, her head on his shoulder. It was a
lovely time, and she knew that she would miss him terribly when he went. When Torquil had died, it was the
knowledge that Mack would come back that had sometimes given her the strength to keep cheerful.

"When will you come back?" she asked him on his last
night.

"I don't know exactly, I'll try to get away in the fall. I
don't want to leave it till next spring or summer if I can
help it. We do want to make the most of our time, don't
we?"

They chuckled together. Nevertheless there was a haunt-
ing melancholy underlying her happiness which she could
not shake off.

When he had gone off to London, after making arrangements for Torquil's paintings to be crated and shipped to
Meadowford, she telephoned to Martin about the car. A
few days later Michael MacMorran reported for duty to
Conchra House driving a large, upright Daimler.

He was a middle-aged, stern-featured man whose voice
reminded Janet of one of the more fundamentalist type of
Scottish divine. He was a skilled driver and mechanic, and
he showed her over the car and answered all her many
questions. She explained what she wanted to do.

"I want you to take me on a tour of the Highlands,
Mr. MacMorran. I've never been north of Dundee. Each
night we shall stay at a hotel, and you must look for nice
places to stop for luncheon."

"How long do you wish to be away for?" he asked.

"Who knows? I shall take plenty of money, and we will
see how the weather lasts. I leave the route to you. I know
nothing about these things."

"Well, in that case you'll be wanting to see Loch
Lomond, and the road westward up to Fort William, and
then we could go up the Great Glen to Inverness, and
down again into Perthshire and the Trossachs. That would

be a nice journey—unless of course there are particular places you wish to visit."

"No, no. I leave it to you. Not too much driving each day. I want to be able to get out and walk about, if the weather is fine, so don't plan journeys that are too long."

"Very good, ma'am. When shall we be leaving?"

"Tomorrow morning. Immediately after breakfast. Say nine o'clock?"

"Very good."

He had heard of her, of course, in Dundee. Everyone in the company knew that Mr. Cunninghame's mother had run the company for years. Lots of the women actually remembered her. She was something of a legend, although the legend was blurred and badly defined. They said that once she had spent hours in the factory watching the women working and that she never forgot a name or a face. He was glad to have this chance of meeting her. She was a fine-looking woman, and you could see that years ago she must have been a raving beauty. He decided he would probably enjoy this break from his routine work.

They set off next morning, in clear, bright weather, not too warm. Janet sat upright in the back of the Daimler, glancing all around, enjoying the experience. Cars still fascinated her, although she had never felt any particular need to possess one. The Daimler was most comfortable, quite luxurious in fact, and she wondered how much Martin had paid for it.

They made a leisurely progress north and west, then up the Great Glen to Dingwall, and finally back to Inverness. From here their route would run south on the Perth road, through the central Highlands, amid some of Scotland's loveliest scenery.

It was a warm Saturday afternoon when they stopped in the little village of Newtonmore to have lunch. It was a peaceful place, surrounded by the tree-clad finery of the mountains—the Monadliaths on one side, and the Cairngorms and the Grampians on the other. They intended to drive on to Pitlochry to spend the night there. There was something about the village that aroused a response in Janet, and she was sorry when they drove off, for she would have liked to stay, but by now she was growing eager to see what lay around the next bend. There had been so much beauty, surprise piled on surprise, that she was becoming impatient to see what each turn of the road would reveal.

Just outside of Newtonmore she spotted a side road with a particularly nice vista.

"Turn up there, please, Michael," she asked.

"Certainly, ma'am."

He slowed down, took the corner carefully, and drove sedately along a winding road between trees, with a burn chuckling and gurgling alongside. There, a little way along, they came upon a small two-story house standing in a miniature glen of its own. A short private drive led up to it, and beside one of the wooden gateposts was a large "For Sale" sign.

"Stop," Janet said suddenly, and when the car had come to rest, she walked to the gates and inspected the house and grounds. They were only three or four minutes from Newtonmore, she fancied, yet they might be in the middle of some forest, a charming, friendly forest. She decided to take a closer look and walked right up to the house. It seemed to be deserted, and she calculated that it must have some six or seven rooms, and it looked as though it were in good condition.

She knew then that this was what she had been searching for, this house and no other. This would be her Highland home. It had to be this one.

She went back, read the "For Sale" sign. She beckoned to Michael who got out of the car and joined her.

"Can you make a note of the address and telephone number of those solicitors, please, Michael? Today's Saturday, so we can do nothing. On Monday we must see them in Inverness. Perhaps we can spend tonight at Pitlochry and return to Inverness tomorrow? Is that all right?"

"Yes, ma'am."

She was bubbling with excitement all the way to Pit-lochry and could hardly wait to get to Inverness the next day, although she insisted on stopping at Newtonmore again for lunch at the hotel.

Michael MacMorran wondered what all the fuss was about. He was unaware that she was looking for a new home. On Monday she saw the solicitors and arranged to purchase the house. That done she interviewed Michael in her hotel room, and told him that she had just bought the house.

"What I would like to do, Michael, if it can be arranged with my son, is to take over you and this car from the factory. If I'm going to live up here, I shall need a car and a chauffeur. Are you married?"

"Yes, ma'am."

"Are you particularly attached to Dundee? Or would you be prepared to leave?"

"We have no kinsfolk in Dundee, ma'am."

"Then if I could find a cottage in Newtonmore, you wouldn't mind living there? Free, of course. It would be part of your emoluments."

"I think we'd like that. It's a pleasant place."

They drove back to Newtonmore, made inquiries, and discovered that there was a cottage for sale. Back to Inverness, and the cottage was bought. She arranged for painters and decorators to smarten up both house and cottage, and then they drove directly to Glasgow, for there were things to do. Furniture would have to be sent north, things sold, the house disposed of, staff settled in new jobs.

And of course Martin had to be advised that he had just lost his Daimler and its driver.

THIRTY

JANET could produce unexpected and sustained bursts of energy when she had to, and she demonstrated the fact once she had bought the house and cottage. Both were redecorated, furniture was sent north from Dundee and Glasgow, and the MacMorrans moved into a boardinghouse and she into a hotel. Mrs. MacMorran had obligingly agreed to act as cook-housekeeper for Janet in her new home, and they would engage a maid locally. It was not much of an establishment by past standards, but Janet felt it was plenty for one woman living quietly.

The house near Newtonmore had been named Spey Villa, which Janet thought was a hideous name. She searched around for something more appropriate and selected Feolin. The cottage that Torquil had rented at Connel had been named Feolin, and the word had stuck in her memory.

The two portraits of her were dispatched to Dundee, to The Rowan's. All she took of Torquil's work was a self-portrait that he had given her just after they married and which she prized more than anything else she possessed.

She was in residence at the beginning of September, and at the end of that month Martin, Helen, and the two girls came for a short holiday. They were greatly impressed.

Marion especially. "Oh, Grandma," she said ecstatically,

"how I'd love to live here. It's so beautiful, all that scenery and the mountains and everything. Aren't you lucky."

"Then you must come for a holiday next summer, my dear. You're a lady of leisure now. Come for Christmas, too. In fact you can all come for Christmas this year. But come back in the summer."

"I will, oh, yes, I will." She was a tall, attractive twenty-one now.

"What about you, Ailsa?" she asked the younger girl.

"It's very nice," Ailsa conceded, "but I don't think I'd like to live in the country."

"It wouldn't do if we all liked the same things," Janet agreed.

Ailsa did not answer. She had a preoccupied air. Later Janet asked Helen about her.

"She's been moody for quite a long time now," Helen said. "She isn't a difficult person, but one never quite knows what goes on in that mind of hers. As a matter of fact," she laughed, "it may be that John Robertson has given her something to think about. He spends more time at our house than he does at his own."

They had all known for two or three years that John was especially fond of Ailsa.

"Does she encourage him?" Janet wanted to know.

"Again, it's hard to say. She doesn't *dis*courage him, but that's not the same thing. I suspect he has already proposed but Ailsa never talks about him."

"Does she still want to go on the stage? I don't seem to have heard about that for a while now."

"She hasn't talked about it since Nancy's death. Perhaps that turned her against it."

"She'd be better off properly settled. You must be proud of them, Helen. They're fine girls."

"We've been lucky," Helen smiled. "It's strange how different they are."

"Meaning?"

"Marion is a warmer personality. There's always been

something a little strange about Ailsa. She never has anything to say."

Janet wondered. Mack Bradford had once described life as a confidence trick because nothing was ever quite what it seemed to be, and Torquil had said much the same thing when talking about religion. And it was true, she had learned. Things rarely *were* as they seemed to be. Ailsa might be reticent because she was shallow, because she had nothing to say. On the other hand, she might equally well be a very deep and sensitive sort of person, easily hurt. Somehow Janet did not believe she was shallow.

When they had gone, she settled down to writing long letters to Mack, and to looking for little ornaments for her new home, and to engaging the services of a gardener.

Early in the New Year, not long after Martin and Helen and the girls had returned to Dundee after spending Christmas with her at Feolin, she was taken unawares when a taxi drove up to the door and Ailsa got out, carrying a dressing case. The driver followed her with two suitcases.

Janet bit back her curiosity till the man had been paid, and then looked at Ailsa inquiringly.

Ailsa was in a state of excitement. "Gran, you must promise to help me."

"What are you up to?" Janet asked, smiling.

"I've run away from home. They don't know where I've gone." She gave a nervous little laugh. "I'm going to go to London and go on the stage."

Janet was no longer smiling. "Just like that? Has anyone offered you a job? Do you have any experience?"

"I'll learn," Ailsa prophesied confidently. "I know I can do it. John Robertson proposed again when we got home, but I don't want to marry someone so stuffy. His only ambition is to become a managing director like his father."

"You mustn't scoff at John. He is a very fine young man."

"Who wants a fine young man?" Ailsa demanded impatiently. "I'm going to be an actress, and I shall call myself Nancy MacRae, after Aunt Nancy."

"Sit down and listen," Janet began patiently, marshaling her thoughts. "Now, how long do you think it will be till your father telephones me to ask if I have seen you or heard from you? I'm only surprised that he hasn't done so already. When did you leave home?"

"This morning, but they won't know I've left. You see I smuggled my luggage out in the middle of the night when everyone was asleep, and hid it in some bushes at the foot of the drive, just inside the gate. Then I said I was going out shopping this morning, went and got a taxi, and we stopped to pick up my luggage, but nobody could see me from the house. After that we drove to the station and I caught a train to Perth and then the train here."

She sounded rather proud of her organizing ability.

"Well, they're bound to miss you during the day, and I expect they will telephone tonight."

"What will you say?" Ailsa asked apprehensively.

"Before I answer that, why did you come here? Why didn't you just go to London? Do you need money?"

"No. I've got twenty pounds."

"My dear girl, that will go nowhere. You must let me give you more. I'll give you a check, and, when you reach London, you can open a bank account with it. You haven't answered my question."

"Because you're the only one who will understand. I'm under twenty-one, Gran. I want you to stop my father coming to London and taking me home."

Janet shook her head with amazement. "What makes you so sure your mother and father won't understand, Ailsa? And do you really think your father would rush after you like some mid-Victorian parent and drag you back in chains?" She sighed. "I suppose you've really made up your mind to go, have you?"

"Yes," Ailsa said firmly. "If I fail, then I will have to get a job. Women work in offices nowadays. But I must try to act now, soon. I'm nearly nineteen!" She spoke as though life had already passed her by.

"In that case, when they telephone, I shall tell them

that you are here, and that you are spending the night, and that tomorrow you will catch the express to London. They have to be told. You can't leave them to worry, you know. You don't know what it is like, my dear."

She thought of Nancy as she spoke.

"All right, just so long as you tell them, Gran. I know they'd try to talk me out of it."

"Very sensible of them, too," Janet snorted, "but a waste of time, I suspect."

"*You* can explain, can't you, Gran? It's something I have to do. It's been bottled up inside of me for years, and I didn't know how to tell anybody about it."

Janet put an arm around her. "Yes, I'll explain for you, but you must promise me in return that you won't cut yourself off from them. They love you, you see."

"They don't. They love Marion. Marion is quite happy to sit at home until some stuffy man proposes to her. She'd probably have jumped at John, if he had asked her."

Janet was instantly wary. Here were undercurrents she had not expected.

"Don't be so quick to judge people, Ailsa. Appearances can deceive you. Now finish your tea and go to your room, and unpack a few things for tonight."

Ailsa stood up. "You don't think I'm mad, do you?"

"No. Your Aunt Nancy did more or less the same thing. I've been through this before."

"I *knew* you'd be on my side."

Her words caused Janet a sharp pang. She had not been on Nancy's side, not until it was almost too late. That was a bitter memory that would be with her always. She wished Ailsa would give her parents a chance.

An hour later the telephone rang and she heard Martin.

"She's here," she said, cutting short his agitated recital. "She is perfectly well. As a matter of fact I can hear her coming downstairs now."

"What the devil is she doing at Newtonmore, and why didn't she tell us?" Martin asked irritably.

"Calm yourself, Martin. You must try to see her point

of view. She's running away from home, that's what she's doing."

"She's *what?* That old story?"

"It has come true. Luckily she came to me first, for the silly girl has only twenty pounds and seems to think it is a lot of money. I'll see she has sufficient with her when she catches tomorrow's London express."

"But why you?" Martin asked, bewildered.

"You must try to understand her. She has been bottling her feelings up for years, apparently, and she has convinced herself she will get no sympathy from you or Helen."

"Damned right she won't," he interrupted testily. "Of all the stupid things. I suppose she has decided to go on the stage, is that it?"

"Yes, and your sister did the same, remember?"

"Oh, that was different."

"Not really. I made a bad mistake with Nancy, and I want you to avoid making the same mistake with Ailsa. Please let her have her chance. Let her go to London and try. If she fails, she will have no one to blame but herself."

"What else can we do?" he asked, still upset. "Why hadn't she the decency to tell us?"

"I explained to you. She thought there would be a dreadful scene. Martin, I want you and Helen to speak to her on the phone, please. Let her know that you're wishing her luck, that you want her to keep in close touch and tell you if she needs any help—and not one word of disapproval. Sound happy and pleased, if it kills you. Both of you. You'll never regret it."

"You don't want much, do you? She runs away without a word, and I've been running around in circles trying to find out where she has got to and her mother is quite distraught. Now we are to pretend it's all fun and games."

"Exactly," Janet said clearly. "That is exactly what you are to pretend. For your own sakes. I know what I'm talking about."

There was a pause, and then she heard him sighing.

"You're right, as usual. I'll ring off and have a little chat with Helen. We'll call back in half an hour."

"Good," she said with deep satisfaction.

When Ailsa asked her what had happened, she was very casual.

"Your father was relieved to learn you are all right. They've been worried most of the day, ever since lunchtime anyway. I told him what your plans are, and he was a little surprised because you haven't talked about the stage for a long time. He's telling your mother now, and I daresay they'll call back soon, once they have had time to get used to it."

"As long as I don't have to speak to them. He'll be hopping mad. They both will."

"They've had a shock, and not only a worrying one, but a disappointing one. You never really gave them a chance, did you? Anyway I explained it as best I could and I daresay it will be all right."

When the telephone rang again, she glanced at Ailsa.

"Answer it, dear."

"But it might be *them*," Ailsa protested.

"I expect it is. They'll want to talk to you."

"You promised you'd talk to them."

"And I did. Now it's your turn. It will be all right. And if it isn't, you can always hang up."

Ailsa stared and then laughed, kissed her, and ran from the room. She was on the telephone for ten minutes, and Janet could hear what sounded like a pleasantly animated conversation. When she came back into the room, she was a little dazed.

"They wished me luck!" Her voice was disbelieving. "They wished me luck, Gran. They were . . . well, they were just wonderful. I was so sure they'd be blazing. They want to come to see me when I've settled in. Oh, and Daddy said he'd give me a proper allowance till I got started."

Janet smiled sunnily.

"They were wonderful, Gran."

"People so often are, if they are given the chance."
"Hmm." Ailsa gave her a sharp look. "With some help from you. You're a magician, that's what you are."
"One of the good sort, I hope," Janet replied easily, and Ailsa came and kissed her.

The fact that Ailsa got a very small walk-on part in a not-very-important play, within two months of arrival in postwar London, was due entirely to her own persistence and quite a bit of luck. The pay was a pittance, but Janet had given her two hundred pounds to set up in London, and Martin sent her five pounds a week, which was a great deal for a young girl, and she was actually better off than several veteran actors in the cast.

In the spring of that year, 1920, the post brought a blow. Mack, who had been unable to come to England in the fall, and who had been hoping to come soon, wrote to say that his doctor would not allow him to travel.

"It is nothing serious, my darling," he wrote in his careful, upright fist. "Tiredness, mostly. But he has given his mandamus which I have to accept. He is a good doctor and an old family friend.

"However there is a little good news. Young Kim is going to visit Britain. He is a fine man now, and I know you will like him. I have told him that he must come to visit you. It will probably be later next month. He has a few things to attend to in England on the way north.

"He will be writing to advise you of his arrival. I know you will look after him, and give him that impression of Britain which I wish him to receive.

"As for myself, perhaps I can manage to be with you in September. I shall strive to that end, at any rate. I have missed you so much, and I love you so deeply, that this stricture about travel has come as a real blow, but I am sure we have a lot of time left. Keep writing, Janet. Your letters are everything to me."

He went on to tell her that he was writing a book, a history of New Hampshire, more to pass the time than out of any desire to be an author. In fact she gathered the impression that he was not interested in its publication, but in its writing.

She replied in an anxious letter, saying that Kim would be welcome at Feolin for as long as he wished to stay, and demanding more news about his health. About Kim's visit, she said, "He might find it a little bit dull here. Newtonmore is only a small village, but the car and driver are at his disposal, and it is not a long run to Perth or Inverness, where he will find more to do. I am expecting my elder granddaughter, Marion, to visit me soon, so perhaps they will meet and be company for each other."

Kim arrived two days early, driving a hired car. Janet was puzzled when she heard the car arrive and she saw a tall, tow-haired man with a bronzed face and startling blue eyes get out. He grinned at her.

"I'm Kim Winthrop," he said cheerfully. "Sorry, I'm two days early."

"How nice. Do come in."

"Shall I bring in my bags? I can go to a hotel if you aren't ready for me."

"We're always ready here. Come along inside with your things."

He ferried his suitcases into the hall, and then followed her into the big sitting room.

"Let me look at you," she commanded, inspecting him closely. "Not much of the Bradford look about you. Sit down and tell me about yourself. Would you care for a drink?"

"You mean liquour? No thanks, I don't, but if you know anyone who can make coffee . . ."

"I can," she chuckled. "I had to learn. You wait here and I'll attend to it."

Mack had shown her how to make coffee to his taste and she assumed Kim would like it the same way. When she returned with it on a tray, he sipped it and glanced up approvingly.

"This is good. I'm going to like it here."

"I told you, I made it myself. I'll show you the kitchen later, for you may want to make your own sometimes. The maid and the cook have no idea."

He laughed.

"How is your father, Kim?"

He became still, and his eyes clouded.

"I'm afraid he is very ill. He is in a clinic, near Uncle Mack's house at Meadowford. It's a nice enough place, but the fact is that he'll never get out. He doesn't know that."

"My dear boy, I'm so sorry."

"He isn't in pain or anything. He's weak and anemic. It may be a year, or a little longer. He'll just waste away until one day it will all be over. I guess it could be a lot worse."

"What a burden for you to carry. You run the business now, do you?"

"Yes," he said, brightening. "With Uncle Mack's help. He's a clever man. I have my father's power of attorney. Things are really booming."

"It's a car business, isn't it?"

"Yes, I do have the agency and a big garage where we do servicing and sell gasoline. But that is just the basis of things. I'm spreading out into new fields."

"What sort of thing?" she wanted to know. She was interested in him.

"You are looking at the president of the Friski-Fang Toothbrush Company, Incorporated. Not that we have sold any toothbrushes yet, but we will soon."

"Toothbrushes?"

"Yes. Uncle Mack agreed with me. You just take a look at your ordinary toothbrush. It's a dull, functional thing, uninspiring, no style to it. Yet we use it twice a day every day—or we should. I had this idea that if someone marketed a toothbrush that looked interesting, elegant, attractive, it would sweep the market. I decided to give it a proper shape, to use transparent-colored materials, to experiment with colors that people will like, and to get especially long-lasting bristles. I'm even thinking of tinting them to match the handles, package them nicely, and wham, you're in business." His excitement was infectious.

"What a clever young man you are. Will it work?"

"Uncle Mack is certain it will. He has put up a lot of capital. I've been seeing some people in England. There's a man in Manchester who knows quite a lot about bristles. He's coming over to Rockville next month. The handle part is already taken care of. There's just packaging and coloring to wrap up, and we're ready to go."

"I wish you could meet my son. He runs a jam and marmalade business in Dundee. He could use someone like you."

"I know nothing about them, though from what I see at breakfast someone ought to design new-shaped jars, more attractive."

Janet made a mental note to pass that along.

"You see," Kim went on happily, "when Dad got into the auto-agency business, it was new and booming. It was the thing with a future. Now everybody is at it, and I'm looking for more new things. The thing is to fix on something basic. There's so much to do. I've been buying up a lot of real estate around Rockville, very quietly. I'll want to build several factories before I'm through. So will other people, and I'll have the land."

"More factories?"

He nodded. "Uncle Mack remarked one night that if there was one thing even more uninspiring than a toothbrush, it is the average bathing suit. I went over to Paris for three days and talked to a top designer there. He'd never thought about bathing suits, but he's interested. Anyway we registered a trade name and we'll see what he comes up with for me to manufacture. I'm calling it Monaco Beachwear. All our swimsuits will have a fancy letter *M* embroidered on them, under a coronet. That should sell them all right, if we have good designs and attractive colors."

"I think I see."

"People are always going to clean their teeth, and my bet

is that swimming will get more and more popular. I want
to get in now and set the pace. Mind you, I'm going to
produce quality merchandise. I'm not going for the cheap
and shoddy market."

"More coffee?" she asked.

"Yes, please. Sorry for the lecture. I get carried away."
He laughed.

"That's all right."

When she had given him a second cup of coffee, she
asked a little timidly about Mack. For the second time his
face fell.

"I don't know what's wrong with Uncle Mack," he
admitted. "Something is, but he won't talk about it. I
probably don't know much more than you do. He was
disappointed that he couldn't come."

"How long has this been going on?" Janet asked, suddenly suspicious.

"Months. He planned to come here last fall."

"I thought he was detained on business. He has only just
told me that the doctor won't let him travel."

"I see." Kim looked at her steadily. "He's been seeing the
doctor, or rather the other way around, for seven or eight
months. I have a feeling it is a heart condition, but
nobody has said so."

"It sounds like it," Janet agreed sadly.

"He's getting old, of course."

"He's the same age as I am," she protested, and Kim
looked surprised.

"You'd never know that," he assured her. "He has
become frail, and he has started to lose his hair. He
writes a lot of letters, and he potters about the garden,
and he sees me in the evenings and we talk about work,
but it's a pretty quiet life, you know."

"Poor Kim."

"What's that?" he asked.

"I said, poor Kim. Your father and your Uncle Mack
both ill."

"I'm all right. Anyway it may be nothing serious with

Uncle Mack. He isn't an invalid. It's just that he doesn't do much anymore. Oh, he gave me a message for you. He said it would be better than a letter."

"What was the message?"

"There are two portraits of you, I believe. A matched pair, I think. He wants to know if he could have them for a few months, after which he'd return them."

Janet blinked away a tear. "Yes," she said, her voice steady. "Of course he may have them for as long as he wishes. My son has them. I'll see that they are sent, and he can return them to my son when he is ready."

"He's always talking about them. They must be something special. I mean he knows a tremendous amount about paintings. People consult him for his opinion."

"Yes, I know that."

She thought of Mack, unable to travel, sitting alone at home with her two portraits, and her heart was full. Well, if that would bring him solace, he should have his wish. Anyway she, too, was growing old now and was no longer the radiant girl or the attractive mature woman Torquil had painted. One could not hold age at bay forever. She had found two white hairs only a week ago!

"By the way," she remarked absently, "you'd better call me Aunt Janet. I'm the same age as your Uncle Mack."

"Okay," he agreed brightly. "I'd appreciate that."

When he had finished his coffee, she suggested a walk in the garden, which was looking very beautiful. He offered her his arm and she gave him a smile of appreciation as she took it.

They walked out together, the young man and the old woman.

The following day, Michael MacMorran drove them to the railway station in the shiny, old-fashioned Daimler, which Kim openly admired. Janet had told him about Marion, who was arriving for a summer holiday, and about Ailsa who was still struggling hard in London, trying to get a foothold on the precarious ladder of theatrical success.

Kim was interested to see what sort of granddaughters this remarkable old woman had.

The train halted at the little wayside halt, and Kim watched expectantly as three people got out—a man, then a woman, and finally The Girl. His eyes widened fractionally as she looked toward them, smiled, and waved. He might have known it—nothing about Janet MacRae was second rate, not even her granddaughter. He strode toward her, his heart thumping.

"Hullo there," he said awkwardly. "I'm Kim Winthrop. May I carry your bags?"

"Thank you very much. There are just those two there, on the seat."

He saw the suitcases and adroitly hefted them out and shut the compartment door. She was waiting, a little smile on her lips.

"I've heard all about you. I thought you weren't due till tomorrow."

"I got here ahead of schedule and arrived without warning," he laughed.

They went over to Janet who kissed Marion. As they walked out of the entrance, Michael MacMorran hurried up and offered to relieve Kim of the luggage, but Kim refused to surrender it to the old man, and carried it to the car.

On the short drive home Marion asked him, "How do you like it here?"

"Beautiful. Aunt Janet said it might remind me of home, and it does in many ways. Where I come from in New Hampshire, a lot of the scenery is like this. Of course I live in a town, a growing town, but one day I'll move out into the country, over by Meadowford. I have to be near my business."

"What sort of business?"

"Please, darling," Janet laughed, "don't start him on that topic till we are home. It's a long story and worth listening to properly."

Marion glanced at him, thinking that he was very young

to have his own business, as presumably he had. She decided that it was going to be fun getting to know him. She gave him a warm smile and sat back in the seat, and glanced at the passing countryside.

From the outset they were totally wrapped up in one another, much to Janet's delight. She was enormously pleased that they should be good friends, her son's daughter and her lover's heir, the nearest thing to a son Mack would ever have.

They went out almost daily in Kim's car, and Janet firmly refused to accompany them. They tried hard to persuade her, but she always managed to beg off. She wanted them to be together without anyone else to spoil their pleasure. They always came home for dinner, and afterward all three of them would sit outside in the garden.

The days slipped past, unnoticed, until they realized with a start that it was Kim's last day. He arranged to take Marion out to dinner that night, after consulting with Janet.

"We'd just go to a local hotel," he explained, "and we'd be back quite early. I don't want to be out late on my last night. We'd be back before your bedtime. Is it all right?"

She was touched that he should ask for permission.

"You go ahead," she answered happily.

"Would you like to come with us? We'll be home by nine."

"No, no Kim. I don't enjoy going out to dinner anymore. You two go and have fun, and don't hurry home on my account. I've enjoyed your visit."

"I'll be back," he promised. "If you'll have me, that is."

"Silly boy. Come as often as you like and for as long as you wish. I'm glad you get along so well with Marion," she added mischievously.

He flushed. "She's very nice."

"Extremely," Janet agreed gravely.

"She has invited me to visit with her folks in Dundee.

I can't manage it now, because of that man in Manchester who is going out to Rockville."

"It will be something for us all to look forward to next year."

"Yes, yes it will," he agreed with feeling.

While they were out, she dined alone, busy with memories, and hardly noticed the passage of time.

Things were working out in an unexpectedly suitable way, unless she was mistaken. Of course, one could never afford to take young people for granted, but she was certain that he was in love with Marion.

The question was, what did Marion feel about him? Obviously she liked him, but he was a stranger, technically even a foreigner. Marion had led a quiet, sheltered life. She might well have second thoughts about becoming too closely involved with Kim Winthrop of Rockville, New Hampshire.

She heard the car returning while she was crossing the hall, and decided to go out to meet them. It was a glorious evening, and it would be nice to have a final stroll in the garden. As she came out onto the drive, she saw them walking back from the end of the drive where the car was parked, by the garage, which contained the Daimler.

She was about to wave when they stopped, turned toward one another, and kissed. Janet watched for a brief second, Marion on tiptoe, her arms around Kim's neck, and then with a gentle sigh she moved as quickly as she could out of their line of vision. She hurried back into the house.

It would be better to meet them in the hall, she thought, amused. Very much more discreet!

THIRTY-ONE

IT had been arranged that Marion would return the following summer for a holiday, when Kim Winthrop would probably be in Britain. Janet was surprised when, just after Easter, Marion telephoned one evening.

"Gran, darling, may I invite myself up for the weekend?"

"You know you can. Is something wrong?"

"Not wrong, but I'd like your advice about something."

"Then by all means come. If you let me know what train you're traveling on, Michael will meet you at the station."

Janet was curious to learn what it could possibly be that called for her advice rather than, say, Helen's. Marion had always been close to her mother, unlike Ailsa. She had to wait till Marion arrived at lunchtime on Saturday, and she would not allow Marion to discuss it until they were having their coffee in the sitting room. Then she said, "All right, my dear. What's it all about? I've been bursting with curiosity."

"It's about Kim Winthrop."

Janet raised her eyebrows in surprise.

"We write to each other. Every week, matter of fact."

Janet nodded encouragingly.

"You know I invited him to Dundee to meet Mother and Father. He's coming over in June, to Dundee. Gran, he wants to marry me!"

"Don't sound so tragic about it," Janet laughed. "What's wrong with that?"

"He wants to come to meet Mother and Father, then he wants us to come here and get married right here. Less than a month after he arrives! I hardly know him."

"I would have put it a little stronger than that," Janet contradicted. "I think you probably know him quite well. Still, I do see what's troubling you, or I think I do."

"People just don't get married on such short notice."

"You'd be surprised at what people really do do," Janet said dryly. "In this family, quite a number of people have a habit of doing as they please. A lot of people would say that your own father married beneath himself, although you and I know that that's rubbish. Still, that's what they'd say. Your Aunt Nancy and Ailsa both ran off to go on the stage. I don't think we are as conventional as you like to believe."

"Hardly any engagement, and I'd have to go to America."

"New Hampshire is nice. Nicer than Dundee, believe me, and Kim is a dear boy. I'm very fond of him."

"I don't know what to reply."

"I wonder if that's true. All these objections you're making—you could put them in a letter to him. I wonder why you didn't? Indeed I wonder why you're here at all. What's wrong with asking your mother's advice?"

"I know what it would be. She'd say wait a year or two till we know each other better. She is very conservative."

"And I'm not?" Janet laughed. "I don't mind. You're answering your own questions, Marion, my dear. You've come all this way to see me because you *don't* want your mother's advice. Haven't you?" She let this sink in. "And really, all those remarks about what people do and don't do, and about going to America, they aren't serious drawbacks. A lot of people would love the chance to go to America. He loves you. I knew that last summer. It was plain enough. The question is, do you love him?"

"I think I do. I never stop thinking of him, and I dream

of him quite often. It's really the unexpectedness of it all, the suddenness. I never thought he'd be in such a hurry."

"If you do love him, don't hesitate. The girl who gets Kim Winthrop for a husband will be a lucky one indeed. I'm certain of that. Of course, if you have any doubt about loving him, that's different. But if you have no doubts, why wait? Go home and tell your mother and father all about it, and tell them that you've accepted. They'll be surprised, of course, and I daresay they'll raise all the objections you yourself have trotted out today, but when they know you are serious, they'll accept the situation. They only want to see you happy."

Marion smiled at her. "Thanks, Gran. I think I know what to do now. I knew it would help if I talked to you. I'll have to tell them I've talked to you."

"Why not? After all, Kim is related to my closest friend, Mack Bradford. What could be more natural than that you should ask me about him?"

"Yes, that's right." Marion brightened.

"So now we can relax and enjoy the weekend, and I'll try to remember everything Mack has told me about Kim. I think we deserve some more coffee, don't you?"

"Gran, I love you," Marion said impulsively and came and hugged her. "You're the best grandmother in the world."

"Fiddlesticks," Janet denied briskly. "You don't know all the others."

So it was all arranged. Kim would go to Dundee for a week or ten days, and then they would come to Feolin to stay with Janet, and after three weeks they would be married. They would spend their honeymoon in New Hampshire.

Janet wrote delightedly to Mack Bradford.

"The thing that pleases me most," she wrote, "is that Marion is my granddaughter, and Kim is your first cousin once removed, or whatever it is. In other words, in a way they symbolize us, and although we never needed to have

any words mumbled over us to 'legalize' our love, it is
nice that those two young ones will marry.

"I suppose you can't get over for the wedding, can you?
That really would crown the happy occasion. You hardly
ever write about your health, and I worry about you a lot.
Please come if you can, Mack."

She was indeed worried about his health, and wrote
occasionally to Kim about him, but Kim was unable to
tell her much except that his Uncle Mack went out less
and less nowadays. Janet was certain Mack was hiding
something from her.

His reply did not quiet her fears.

"What can I say?" he asked in it. "The only woman I
have ever loved asks me to come to her, and I am forced
to refuse. The truth is, Janet darling, that I have to lead
an ever increasingly inactive life. Please don't be alarmed,
or squander your sympathy on such an unrepentant fraud.
I can go on for many years like this. As you have undoubtedly guessed, it is a heart condition. If I look after it, it will
look after me. If I don't, then I shall be in trouble. So here
I sit, watching the world go by.

"How I would love to be with you in that Highland cave
of yours, and join in the wedding celebrations. It gives me
as much pleasure as it does you to know that we are to
become related by marriage, however tenuously. I shall
be seeing a good deal of the young couple when they
come home, for Kim is a frequent visitor to Meadowford.
I shall make sure he is the most model husband in New
England (they don't have them anywhere else)."

The wedding took place quietly in the little church in
Newtonmore. There were only a handful of people present, some of Marion's friends from Dundee and the family, and the MacMorrans. That was all.

It was a Presbyterian wedding. This was because Martin, just after his marriage to Helen, switched to her
Church. As he said at the time, it was silly to have two
brands of Christianity in the one family and it was up to

him, as the gentleman, to make the change. Marion had therefore been reared as a Presbyterian.

Janet knew very little about Presbyterianism, although it was the established faith in Scotland, sanctioned by law. In fact, she had not been to church at all for a very long time. After the service, she got into conversation with the minister, Malcolm MacSorley. She took an instant liking to him.

"I've often wondered why we never see you here, Mrs. MacRae. Are you by any chance a Catholic?"

"No, no. I'm an Episcopalian, as it happens, but the truth is that I've become lax in the matter of church-going. I suppose I ought to be ashamed of myself," she smiled. "My father was a clergyman."

"Was he, indeed? I didn't know that."

"Yes, I was brought up in the rectory. In St. Andrews that was. There's no earthly reason why I shouldn't support the village church. I really ought to take a greater part in local activities, but the fact is that I've been quite busy since coming here."

"You'll be welcome, I assure you."

"I'll come to church on Sunday. I presume you'll let me in?"

"I think I can stretch a point," he agreed, straight-faced. "We're a broad-minded lot up here."

When Kim and Marion had departed, leaving them to their modest celebrations, she sought out Ailsa, very smart, sophisticated, cleverly made up.

"How are you these days, Ailsa? Happy?"

"Very happy indeed, Gran."

"Doing well?"

"No." Ailsa laughed good-naturedly. "Doing badly, I'd say. I manage to get parts, all right, but never a decent one. I enjoy it, and I keep trying. One day you'll see."

"What about boy friends? Have you met any nice young men in London?"

"Lots of them," Ailsa laughed. "I'm not the marrying type. I shan't surrender my freedom to any man."

"Is that what you think it means?" Janet asked, sincerely interested. "Do you think Marion has just surrendered her freedom?"

"Yes, I do. She has to think of Kim now, hasn't she? She can no longer please herself."

"Perhaps thinking of Kim is what pleases her. Perhaps you can only know real freedom when you surrender it."

"You're much too deep for me, Gran. All I know is that I have no intention of getting married, now or later."

With that Janet had to be content. Yet Ailsa was more at ease, more serene, than Janet remembered her being before.

The following day Martin and she had a talk about Rowan's. Martin was now well into his forties, and looked his age. He had receding hair and a middle-aged paunch.

"I'm planning to retire when I'm fifty five," he told her. "Davie will be gone by then, and there's no one to take over."

She nodded. "Yes," she agreed. "It's a pity, but there it is."

"There are one or two people interested in buying us out. It's worth thinking about. Of course I'd safeguard our present employees as much as I can. I don't think there's any danger of people being laid off. It seems to me that it simply won't work if I try to keep a paternal eye on the thing from retirement. It has to be run properly. It wouldn't do to put in a managing director, and cramp his style."

"I see the point," Janet said slowly.

"You still have a shareholding, so I need to consult you, even though mine is the majority."

"About that," Janet said quickly, "I don't need my Rowan's shares. I think I ought to give them to you. Then you can make your own decisions."

"No, no, I didn't mean that."

"I know you didn't, but you still have Ailsa to worry about. I've got lots of money of my own, far more than I will ever need. It was different when you were a child. Then I had to have control. I haven't had control since you were twenty-one, and there is no justification for me taking a share of the profits after all this time."

"No one deserves it more, Mama."

"*Did* deserve it, perhaps," she agreed. "But not any longer. No, I had decided this already and meant to speak to you about it. I suppose Ailsa might still marry, but it doesn't look like it, and it is even less likely that she'd marry someone who'd want to run Rowan's. More likely an actor, I'd say."

"Quite," he agreed. "There's still time, I suppose. I'm a few years away from fifty-five. We'll see how things turn out."

They both knew, however, that the old order was changing.

THIRTY-TWO

NOW, more than ever, she became a spectator in the affairs of her own family. Mack continued to be cheerful and she had grown accustomed by now to a relationship based on correspondence. After all, she was in her late sixties. The memory of her love affair with Mack was more vivid to her than her memories of Torquil, but with seventy beckoning, a lot of the fever had died down in her blood, and her very real love for him was unselfish and undemanding. She wrote assiduously, the only letters that had any real meaning to her.

Events were reported to her. In 1922 Marion had a daughter and they named her Susan. A few weeks later word came that Howard Winthrop had died at the clinic near Meadowford. According to Kim he had slipped away quietly one night.

Three years later Davie Robertson retired from Rowan's, and he and Amanda bought a cottage on the Fife coast, near Crail, and dropped out of her life apart from Christmas cards and gifts.

The following year, 1926, Marion had another daughter, this time named Alexis and nicknamed Lexa. That was the year when Ailsa got her first good part on the West End stage. It was also the year in which Martin handed over executive power to a young managing director, and turned himself into a figurehead. He still went to the office, but the managing director ran the company for him.

And then, in 1927, in his seventy-third year, Mack Bradford died of a heart attack. It was Kim who wrote, a long letter in which, among many other things, he said, "He died at home, which was something he had always wanted to do. He had a dread of dying in some antiseptic, anonymous hospital ward, and wished to be surrounded by his cherished possessions, and to die in his own bed with the view of the garden, the trees around it, and the mountains beyond.

"I was with him when he went. He had been unconscious for some time, and I was sitting by the bedside. Marion was at home with the children. Without warning he opened his eyes and looked at me, and he said 'Take care of the portraits, Kim,' and he died, just like that.

"The portraits, of course, are those two of you. Am I correct in thinking that they should be sent to Marion's father? Or do you want them? Please let me know, and I'll have them shipped off. He loved them, and I can't say I blame him. I know I've never seen anything like them.

"I believe you already knew that I was his sole heir. Among his papers I found a sealed envelope addressed to you, which I enclose."

Janet was reluctant to open Mack's letter, as though reading it would make his death more positive, give it greater validity. Eventually she slit open the flap and took out the expensive rag notepaper. It was dated a year earlier and began:

My Darling Janet,

This will be the last time I tell you I love you, because you will not get this until after my death. There is no real need of words between us. We have always understood one another perfectly, and our need for each other.

I want you to know that I was never jealous or

resentful of Torquil, although I envied him mightily. Nor was I hurt when you refused to come to me, here in New Hampshire, after Torquil's death. Which would suggest I am a good loser. Strange, because I have never liked losing, and rarely ever lost!

I would like to make one last request. Now that Kim and Marion are married and happy together, and founding their family, do you think that the portraits could be given to them? Or, if not that, could Martin arrange to leave them to Marion when he himself dies? I would like to believe that they will stay here, where I have lived, and give pleasure to those two—who incidentally will inherit this house and no doubt move into it. Kim is a successful man now and doesn't have to room above the store anymore.

I leave it to you to arrange to do what is best. You have a genius for that. Wouldn't it be nice if we were to meet again in some other existence? But if not, then, darling, this is to thank you for giving me the happiest years of my life.

> *Love, my love,*
> *Mack*

She folded the letter carefully and put it in a drawer of her dressing table. Then she telephoned to Martin and asked him about the portraits.

"Let them stay out there," he said readily. "They'd only go to Marion in the long run anyway, since Ailsa has no space for them. After all, the thing was to keep them in the family, and that's what we are doing."

"Thank you, Martin."

"I'm sorry about Mack."

"I think I've known for a long time that it would happen like this, but even so you are never properly prepared. One by one, people drop out of our lives."

They exchanged family gossip for a little longer, and she

asked about his blood pressure, which had been troubling him, and then she hung up and settled down to reply to Kim's letter.

Now that she was not living in close contact with people, the mountain of trivia that made up their daily lives and preoccupied them, meant nothing. She was going to have to *do* something. She would have to make a new life.

One day when the Reverend Malcolm MacSorley was calling on her, she mentioned her predicament to him and told him that she lacked a serious interest. He was an understanding young man, and frowned in concentration.

"There isn't a lot to do in a place like this," he said slowly. "Lots of little things, of course, like the Women's Guild. But not things that will give you a *deep* interest. I'll certainly think about it, Mrs. MacRae."

"I have so much, you see," she explained serenely. "I always have done. Life has been more than just good to me. I feel I should be doing something for other people."

He suddenly looked alert. "Are you really anxious to involve yourself deeply?"

"Yes. I want to be helpful."

He looked around at the graciously furnished room in which he sat. He enjoyed visiting here. Then he considered her. He was not sure how old she was, for she had an ageless look about her. She seemed active enough anyway. It might just work. It would be nice if it did.

"There is a child in the village," he began slowly, picking his words with care. "A little boy. His mother and father died quite recently and he needs a home. There are no relatives, nobody to take care of him. I don't want to see him put into a home—an orphanage. They're very good, of course, but only as a last resort."

"How can I help?"

"You could give him a home here. You have servants. You have room."

"Is that legal?" Janet masked her astonishment. This was

not exactly what she had envisaged when she told him she wanted a serious interest in life.

"It can be made legal. You don't have to adopt him. You can be a foster mother. I'll look into that side of it. As a matter of fact he may be over the age for adoption anyway. The legal side can certainly be taken care of," he added confidently.

"Tell me more about him," she temporized, her thoughts busy.

"He is three, a very nice child, very good. His name is Peter Walker. At present he is staying with my wife and me, but we have two young children of our own, and my stipend is a small one. I'd love to keep Peter, but the truth is that, if I did, it would mean depriving my own children of things. I'm a poor man, from a poor home. I'll keep Peter for as long as I can, but I know that it will only be worse for him if he eventually does have to go into an orphanage."

Janet thought fleetingly and made up her mind at once, her heart thumping as she took what was probably going to be one of the most important decisions in her life.

"I'd love to have him. I ought to tell you that in October I will be seventy-four. Naturally I would engage a nanny while he was young, and as you say, there are servants. I've never been ill in my life. I could do it."

"Think it over," he advised. "Sleep on it. Telephone me when you are sure. Meantime I think you ought to come to tea and see him, while you are deciding."

"Tomorrow?" she asked.

"Why, yes. That would be nice."

When he had gone, she began to think furiously. There was a way out that had just occurred to her. Malcolm MacSorley with his young wife and young children could provide a good home. Money was the difficulty. She could pay for Peter Walker's keep, and pay handsomely, without missing the money.

It was tempting for several moments as she worked out

the implications. Then she grew disgusted with herself. She was trying to buy her way into heaven again. Always it had been money, money and jobs, for the Robertsons, the Kirks, and others. This time she had a chance to do something positive, to become really involved, completely committed.

Next afternoon she had tea with the MacSorleys and met Peter Walker, a thin child with large eyes and a shy smile. Her heart warmed to him. After tea she told Malcolm MacSorley, "I have decided. I'll have him. I really do want to help him. I'll send the car in the morning after breakfast, if I may. Now that I've decided, I want to start. Can I have him tomorrow?"

"Yes. I don't see why not. I'll fix up the legal side of it, if it needs any arranging. What about the nanny?"

"That should be a simple matter. Meantime, I have a maid who has several young brothers. She's had a lot of experience helping her mother with children."

He came the following morning, shortly after eleven, solemn, wide-eyed, very quiet. She did not fuss over him, but treated him gently and kindly. Once his few toys had been put into his bedroom and he had a meal inside him, he relaxed and enjoyed himself in the natural way that children do.

That night, after he had been bathed and put to bed, she went up to his room and looked at him while he slept. What a step she had taken, and she had told no one about it. None of the family.

Goodness, she reflected with amusement, what *will* they think when they hear?

What, indeed?